IN THE TIME OF THE MULBERRY

DESMOND ASTLEY-COOPER

turning**point**

Published by Turning Point Books
14th Floor, Concorde Building, Dunan Street
Verdun, Beirut, Lebanon
PO Box 11-4932
Tel: 00961 1 752 100

www.tpbooksonline.com

First edition: October, 2016

Text copyright © Desmond Astley-Cooper, 2016
Layout and graphic design copyright © Turning Point, 2016

Editing: Dima Nasser
Design and layout: Sinan Hallak
Front cover photograph © Ziad Salloum
Carte de la Syrie Méridionale © Murray Hudson – Antique Books, Maps,
Prints & Globes
Printing: RAIDY | www.raidy.com

ISBN 978-9953-0-3823-0

Hannah

I hope this inspires you to travel ever wider!

Dean 14/3/17.

To the people of Lebanon in all its diversity.

ACKNOWLEDGMENTS

There are many people who have helped me with this project. First, I'd like to thank my publisher, Charlotte Hamaoui, for taking a risk on an unknown author like myself. Secondly, my editor, Dima Nasser, deserves much credit for transforming what was once a dusty old history book into a vibrant novel. Her insights have been a revelation to me.

Then there are those loyal friends of mine - Lebanese, British, French, and Greek - who have read the manuscript at varying stages of its evolution and made significant contributions. Without their help, I doubt it would be half as good as I hope it now is. There is one thing I make no apology for and that is the length of the glossary. There are some expressions in the Lebanese dialect which are untranslatable in English.

And a word of thanks, also, to the Lebanese Mountain Trail Association for taking me to some of the remoter and wilder parts of the country.

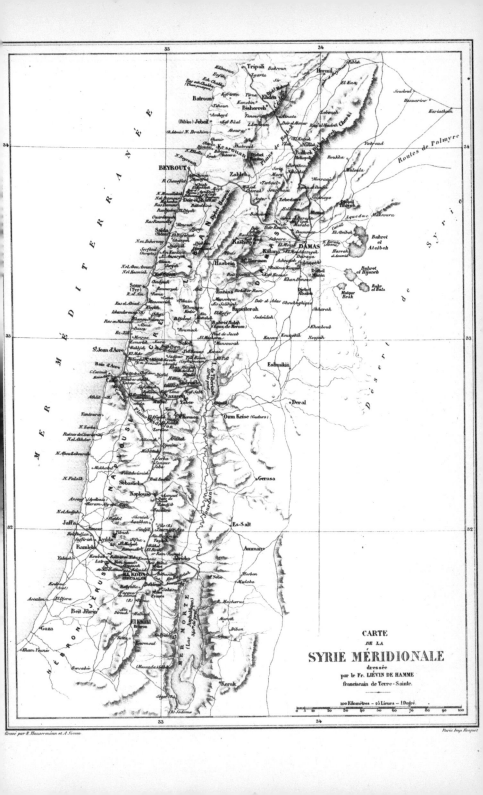

CARTE
DE LA
SYRIE MÉRIDIONALE
dressée
par le Fr. LIÉVIN DE HAMME
franciscain de Terre-Sainte.

100 Kilomètres - 25 Lieues - 1 Degré.

Gravé par R. Hausermann et A. Sosson.

Paris Imp. Becquet.

PREFACE

There was a time when the mulberry tree could have easily surpassed the cedar as a symbol of Lebanon. That was in the 18th and 19th centuries when millions of mulberry trees carpeted its age-old mountains. Today, however, its once vital presence has sadly waned with as little as a few thousand left.

The golden age of the mulberry bred a burgeoning silk industry, which fast became the crux of Mount Lebanon's economic wealth by the late 19th century before witnessing a decline in the early part of the 20th century. The silk and textile industry brought about revolutionary social change. Silk factories, around 180 in operation at the industry's height, came to employ hundreds of local townspeople, predominantly young girls and women who had never before been breadwinners or had any sort of financial independence. What's more, they started mixing with men at work for the first time…

The Silk Museum in Bsous used to be one of those factories. It now houses year-round exhibitions dedicated to the story of the silkworm's life from egg to cocoon to moth as well as the spinning and weaving of the yarn itself. There are also yearly exhibits showcasing silk items ranging from scarves, ties, and dresses to bedspreads from different places around the world. The museum was established in 2001, and it has been our mission since then to show younger generations how important sericulture and silk production have been in the nation's society, economy, and history.

Each year, various schools and educational institutions send their children to visit and learn how silk was first discovered in China, how it developed in the Near East during the Byzantine period, and how factories began to materialize across Mount Lebanon, the first of which were built by French families from Lyon in the mid-19th century. Among other things, the factories' substantial silk exports to merchants in France led to the mobilization of the Beirut Port, the development of the banking sector, and the forging of ties between St. Joseph University and Lyon University.

Under Ottoman rule in the second half of the 19th century, the different communities of Mount Lebanon enjoyed a greater measure of autonomy than elsewhere in Syria. To maintain the right to govern themselves, the inhabitants had to pay taxes to their own leaders who were, in turn, held responsible for their collection by the Ottoman authorities. Inevitably, this state of affairs led to rivalries and, from time to time, outbreaks of violence.

Desmond Astley-Cooper's debut novel, *In the Time of the Mulberry*, traces volatile relationships, both among various communities and within families themselves. Be it a disagreement between father and daughter or a clash among villagers of different faiths, these events all find their way into this vivid story. Though fictional, it nonetheless peers into a part of Lebanese history that is often brushed aside or simply ignored.

Maryam, Layal, and Rose are three women whose lives become intertwined during the course of the narrative. Their experiences speak to countless others like them who were confronted, at that time, with life-altering choices, obligations, and opportunities. Each woman's journey is her own response to the upheaval and transformation that impinged on Mount Lebanon in those days.

George Asseily
The Silk Museum,
Bsous, Lebanon

PART I

Thy plants are an orchard of pomegranates, with pleasant fruits;
camphire with spikenard,
Spikenard and saffron, calamus and cinnamon, with all the trees of
frankincense; myrrh and aloes, with all the chief spices:
A fountain of gardens, a well of living waters,
and streams from Lebanon.

~ Song of Solomon 4:13-15 ~

CHAPTER ONE

The Chouf Mountains
Early May, 1860

Maryam could hear the *clack-clack-clack* of feet on the rough cobblestone steps at the front of the house. The clatter of her mother's wooden clogs was unmistakable, indicating that she was in a hurry. Morning in Ayn el-Louz was the time of the women and children. The men were out on the terraces or in the fields, tilling the stony soil to scratch out a meagre living for themselves and their families. Only the idle and the sick remained behind.

"Hurry up, girl," she heard her mother call out in her husky voice. "Khalo[1] Abdallah is getting sicker by the minute, may God preserve the wretch!"

Maryam was busy propping up mattresses against the south-facing wall of the house that backed onto the valley below. There the sun's rays would warm them all day long, leaving the bedstraw fresh and dry for the night. She ran her hands over each one in turn, carefully examining the folds of the coarse cotton for ticks and fleas.

"*Uuuf!*" Maryam shrieked as a fat cockroach fell out of one of the coverlets and scuttled away. She was particularly horrified by their shiny shells and whispery antennae and always kept a keen eye out for them whenever she cleaned the cupboards or looked behind the big chest where the food was stored.

"I'm coming!" she called out to her mother.

She paused for a moment by the large vine that climbed up the side of the house where she often sat during the long afternoons, playing with the small goat she kept as a pet. From there, she could trace with her eyes the path that led down to the main part of the village and spy on passers-by unseen. In such a crowded house, it was one of the few places where she could be truly alone.

But this particular morning Maryam knew she could not dally. She had barely patted the dust off her skirts before she heard the creak of the wooden door and the sound of brisk footsteps. She turned to see her mother standing in front of her with her hands planted firmly on her hips.

"*Yalla*[2], Maryam," she said, nodding in approval at the bedding laid out neatly on the roof. Her clogs scuffed the ground as she walked away. Unlike many of her neighbours, Sa'adeh kept a clean and orderly house. She made certain that their only room was swept every morning, and if her two older sons came in to eat with dirty hands, she would scold them. More unusual still, she washed her family's undergarments with a piece of smooth basalt against an old board.

Her obsession with cleanliness did not stop there. She took Maryam with her most days to a secluded spot beside the stream in the valley where, hidden from sight by large rocks and poplar trees, they would remove their clothing piece by piece and wash with a homemade bar of olive oil soap. It was one of the few luxuries they enjoyed, obtained from a tradesman who travelled regularly through the mountain villages.

Maryam hurried down the path after her mother, clutching her shawl in her hand. Unlike the Druze[3], who wore white *liffehs*[4] wrapped around their heads, Christian women often went bareheaded in the village. But today they were going to her uncle's sickbed and that kind of visit required a certain formality. With her lustrous black hair tied back in a loose plait which glistened in the sunlight, she followed the track down to the centre of the village. It took Maryam a few minutes to catch up with her mother.

"Slow down, Imme[5]," she called out, but her plea landed on deaf ears as Sa'adeh's wool skirts swished around her ankles with every purposeful step she took.

The sight of a group of Druze women walking in the opposite direction in their distinctive white scarves reminded Maryam that she was still carrying her own in her hand. She draped it loosely over her hair as she walked, knotting it under her plait. In Ayn el-Louz, they wore scarves, but not the old-fashioned conical straw hats with wide brims.

At fourteen, Maryam was already considerably taller than her mother who had the stout body of a village matron. Her large almond-shaped eyes were fringed by dark lashes that fluttered furiously whenever she was upset or alarmed.

"You're the daughter of a gypsy, not one of mine," Sa'adeh would sometimes say when she was annoyed with her.

"Why do you say that, Imme?" Her mother's jibe would cause her to blink nervously.

"It's just a joke," Sa'adeh would chuckle.

On past the spring they went until they came to the ramshackle house of Wadee'ah, Sa'adeh's sister. Outside, a large mule stood tethered in the shade of an ancient walnut tree. Flies swarmed around the animal's eyes and ears, causing its loose skin to twitch like a tattered rug. A leather bag hung down on one side, attached to the saddle by a broad strap. In front of them, a tall stranger was stooping beneath the beam of the doorway. After a moment's hesitation, they followed him in, believing him to be the doctor from a nearby town.

The unmistakable stench of disease assaulted Maryam's nose the moment she stepped into the dimly lit room. She saw the pallid face and sunken eyes of her uncle lying on a mattress and a group of women sitting together on reed mats that lay scattered on the earthen floor. Three men lounged against one wall on a pile of old cushions hastily stacked together to form a makeshift divan. With the exception of a table and two wooden chests pushed into in one corner, the room itself was bare.

A prolonged bout of coughing came from the mattress where her uncle lay. When it had subsided, he spat into a rag held up by his wife who bowed her head and muttered a prayer through tightly drawn lips. There was an ominous silence as the doctor knelt down to examine him, broken only by the rustling of skirts as the women huddled forward for a better view. Maryam's initial disgust gave way to curiosity. It was the first time she had attended the sickbed of a relative and she wanted to see what the doctor would do.

A desperate expression contorted her uncle's wasted face. Perhaps it was the doctor's presence that he feared more than the illness that gripped him. Wadee'ah had only sent for him after her ailing husband's cough had become so persistent that it was obvious to all that he was beyond the help of traditional remedies. Like most people in the village, she preferred the use of teas or tinctures to alleviate fevers and stomach cramps, toothaches and gripes.

"The cloth," the doctor said, pointing to the rag in Wadee'ah's hand.

Taking it by the edge, he clambered to his feet and his knees clicked as he walked over to the door. When he reappeared a few moments later, he was carrying the leather bag. He rummaged through it and took out a number of glass cups that he placed upside down on the table beside the lamp.

One by one, he held them over the flame. At the sight of the heated cups, the sick man squeezed his eyes shut and began to mutter aloud, but his wife ignored his pleas and rolled him over onto his stomach as the doctor ordered. She pulled up his undershirt, revealing a back slick with sweat. The women behind Maryam craned forward as the doctor placed the cups on his back and shoulders. Even the men fell silent and stared with bated breath at the sight of Abdallah writhing in pain as the heated vessels sucked at his pallid skin.

"Hold him down," the doctor barked at two of the stronger looking women. "Don't let him knock them off."

They seized him and pressed him down while the doctor carefully positioned the last of the cups. For a few minutes there was only the sound of Wadee'ah's murmurs as she stroked her husband's hand. Then the silence was broken by a series of loud pops as the doctor removed the cups, replacing them one by one in his bag after a cursory wipe with his sleeve. Two rows of ringlet-shaped blisters appeared on the pale skin.

"Hornet stings," Maryam giggled in her mother's ear. Sa'adeh frowned at her daughter while the doctor snapped his bag shut and disappeared outside, followed by the men from the divan. In the ensuing commotion, Maryam edged closer to the door in the hope that she, too, could slip away unnoticed.

"Stay where you are," came her mother's sharp voice.

She sat down again, too timid to challenge her while one of the men disappeared round the back of the house. He returned with a brace of cockerels in a reed basket, the kind that villagers used to carry their poultry to market in. With a respectful bow, he held them out to the doctor who pointed to where the mule stood.

"Hitch them to the saddle across from my bag," she heard him say through the open door.

The doctor was clearly used to bartering. Then with a creak of leather, he mounted his mule and clattered off up the hill. As soon as he was out of earshot, Wadee'ah clutched her head in her hands.

"The white plague, the white plague," she began to wail. It was what they called consumption in the villages. The murmurs inside the room rose quickly to a discordant crescendo.

"May God help you, Abdallah!" one of the women cried as she got to her feet and made for the door, followed by the others who filed out after her making the sign of the cross.

Before long only Wadee'ah's immediate family was left in the room. They settled back onto the mats while her daughter poured some water from a pitcher into two chipped cups. Maryam accepted hers with reluctance as her cousin fetched a bowl of dried fruit from a shelf and set it out on the floor in front of them. Dusting off a wrinkled fig with her sleeve, she offered it to Sa'adeh.

"May God give him strength," she replied as she sipped water from the cracked rim of her cup.

An enormous sense of relief washed over Maryam as she followed her mother out into the bright sunshine, pausing only to breathe in the fragrance of wild thyme wafting down from the hills. Down in the valley, the fragile blossoms of the apple and pear trees had already blown way, leaving behind only the fleshy nubs of the fresh fruit. But her reverie was soon interrupted by the shrill sound of her mother's voice.

"They should open the shutters and hang up some dried herbs to cover the smell!"

"They can't, Imme," said Maryam, for once daring to disagree with her. "People with the white plague can't bear sunlight."

"What do you know of such things?" she grumbled, dismissing her daughter's words with a wave of her hand. "You're just a village girl."

With that Sa'adeh strode up the hill, leaving her daughter to trail behind. But Maryam was in no hurry to catch up, ambling along on her own until the crunch of dry branches and the low murmur of male voices brought her back to earth with a jolt. She looked around to see where the sound was coming from and noticed, for the first time, an orchard opposite the bend in the road.

Out of the corner of her eye, she glimpsed two men with white headcloths moving among the fruit trees. The warm air eddied up around them as they worked in their undershirts. The older man sported a large moustache that all but hid his mouth. The younger one's cheeks were still smooth and when he turned his face towards her, Maryam realized that she had seen him once before during the Saint George's Day festivities a year earlier.

Despite the occasional bouts of tension, the Druze and Christians of Ayn el-Louz always celebrated Saint George's Day together. In the course of their merrymaking, the farmers talked openly about the pasturage on the mountain and the condition of their fruit trees. When they were not busy wagering with each other or yelling encouragements at their sons and nephews, they would find themselves deep in conversation about the prospects for the forthcoming harvest.

Her interest piqued, Maryam slowed her pace down to a shuffle as she walked by. From the little she could see, they appeared to be building a *'arzal*[6], a rough shelter where the boys and men slept outside in the fields during the hot summer months to guard their crops against thieves and marauders. Being a girl, she had never been allowed to spend the night outside her home, but she knew that her brothers preferred sleeping out in the fields.

"We can do what we like," they used to tease her. Sometimes as it grew dark, they would creep up behind her and yelp like foxes.

Both men had now moved to the edge of the orchard where it touched the pathway. The younger man's muscles bunched and rippled beneath his undershirt as he cut lengths of wood from amongst the tangled undergrowth, handing them to the older man who was weaving a hurdle. From the ease with which they were working together, Maryam assumed that they were father and son.

When the son stopped to wipe his forehead, a bead of perspiration hung for an instant on the edge of his chin before dropping into a fold where his pantaloons were cinched at the waist. Without realizing it, she found herself staring at his delicate cheekbones which were more like those of a girl than a boy. The soft black down on his upper lip suggested he was no more than a year or two older than she.

As he reached down into the pile of sticks, his eyes caught hers and before she knew it, her face turned a bright shade of pink. Was he smiling at her or had she just imagined it? A breathless moment passed between them when suddenly she heard her mother's voice shouting at her from some distance.

"*Yalla, ya binet*[7]. Whatever are you staring at?"

"I'm coming!"

She gathered up her skirts and set off after Sa'adeh. Stumbling in her haste, she skinned her knee but barely felt it in her excitement.

"I don't know how they live there." She was still complaining about the filthy state of her sister's house when she caught up with her mother. "If your Khalo Abdallah dies, I don't know what they'll do."

"Won't we help them?" Maryam felt she ought to contribute to her mother's monologue. Fortunately for her, the dash up the hill had warmed her cheeks, disguising her earlier flush.

"If we help them all, we'll have nothing left ourselves," her mother grumbled.

But by the time they arrived home, Sa'adeh had forgotten about the misfortunes of her sister's family.

"*El-'amah*[8]!" she said, looking up at the sun. "We've wasted half the day already."

Her youngest children, a boy and a girl, were feeding the chickens from a pile of peelings while their grandmother squatted on a flat stone in front of the house, plucking the outer leaves from a pile of artichokes. Her alert eyes darted constantly from the children to the vegetables and back. Every now and then, she would glance up to see if anyone was coming up the track.

Each of Imm George's cheeks bore a geometrical blue tattoo, clearly visible against mottled skin that was as wrinkled as the bark of a scrub oak. Gathered up in a knot, her grey hair was partly covered by a piece of blue cloth that she habitually wound round her head. Several untidy tassels hung down from it like martens' tails. Around her neck she wore an old copper coin on a leather thong stamped with a woman's face on one side and an anchor on the other. Although it was clear that she knew very little, if anything, about its origin, the old lady often swore that it was this amulet that had kept the house safe from the evil eye.

"All well, Imme?" Sa'adeh called out cheerfully from the road.

"Fine," Imm George replied with a chuckle. "And I'll outlive you both."

Maryam watched her mother smile. It was obvious from her remark that Imm George had already heard about Abdallah's illness. Their household enjoyed a sense of domestic harmony, a rarity in that village. In some of the other families, mothers bickered constantly with their sons' wives. By contrast, Maryam knew that her mother actively enjoyed the old lady's company.

Together, both women held sway in the house during the day. But when her father returned at dusk, their light-hearted banter would cease. It was then that Sa'adeh would give her husband her full attention and Imm George would find other things to do. Ignored by their mother, the younger children would glance up shyly at their father hoping that he would reach down and play with them, which he occasionally did because George loved his children.

As for Maryam, she adored her father and sensed that he was not the dour man he sometimes appeared to be. He always treated her kindly and would, on occasion, come and sit beside her in the evening if he was not too tired from the day's toil. When the time came, she secretly hoped that she would marry a man like him. The very thought of spending the rest of her life with someone like her slothful cousin, Faris, made her shudder.

Abandoning the chickens outside, the two children began tugging at their mother's skirts while Maryam set to work sweeping the floor with long strokes of the broom, taking care to clean behind the food chest. By the time Sa'adeh came back with a bunch of coriander to season the stew, Maryam had almost finished dusting the shutters and was moving the furniture back into place. She was about to steal away to one of her hiding places when her grandmother spotted her.

"Come and help me finish peeling these beets. The rinds are too tough for my old hands!"

Taking the knife from her, Maryam sat down beside her grandmother and began to peel the last of them while Imm George stroked her hair. Maryam doted on the old lady and enjoyed her company. In the evenings, she would go and fetch a cup of thyme tea for her, sweetening it with honey or a spoonful of carob *dibs*⁹. That would bring back fond memories of the old days, especially of the time when she was just a new bride.

I was married to my cousin when I was your age, Maryam. At first we lived with his mother and father, but after a few years, we managed to build our own house with the help of our neighbours. But it wasn't like any of the other villagers' houses. The stonemason we hired from the town built us solid walls with blocks that fitted together perfectly. As you know, the saying goes, "Spend well now and save later."

Back then, we used to till the same plots of land that ibni¹⁰ *George does now. Whenever the bailiff came round to collect the landlord's share, we always paid our dues and we never haggled over the amount. I was the one who always insisted on putting aside part of the harvest each year so that we would always have food on the table and there would be enough left over to pay the* miri¹¹.

When your grandfather died of pneumonia after one particularly hard winter, may God rest his soul, he wasn't even forty years old! I wore black and spent forty days in mourning. The whole village called on me to offer their condolences and I even made a modest donation to the church in his memory.

But she would never tell her grandchildren the whole truth. Imm George had only admitted to Sa'adeh the relief she had felt at her husband's passing. As she let slip to her daughter-in-law once in an unguarded moment, he had contributed less and less to the family over the years while relying on her more and more. After his death, she lost little time in rearranging her affairs.

Ignoring the wishes of her two married daughters, she had invited

21

George and his family to move back into the family house. From the start, she was careful not to interfere in matters that did not concern her. Instead, she spent her days tending silkworms and looking after their supplies of food, personally seeing to their storage during the cold winter months. She spent the rest of her time pickling vegetables and making conserves and spirits from plums and mulberries.

As a little girl, Maryam remembered watching her grandmother examine the apples and pears on the shelves. She turned each fruit over slowly in her hands, feeling for blemishes and bruises. When she was satisfied there were none she placed them carefully back, separating them from one another so that they did not touch.

"We don't want to lose everything to one bad apple," she would tell her granddaughter whenever she came to help.

During the bleak evenings in winter when the frigid wind blew hard from the north and the rain and sleet beat against the shutters, she would sit with her brothers at her grandmother's feet in front of the brazier to hear her stories about the great palace of Beiteddine, the House of Faith.

"Have you ever been there, Teta[12]?" Maryam had once asked, her eyes aglitter at the thought.

No, Imm George admitted, she had never been to the town of Deir el-Qamar nor had she seen the great palace, not even from a distance. It was zealously guarded by the Hamada sheikhs, she explained somewhat mysteriously, the same tribe of people who had once ruled the mountains before the time of Emir Fakhreddine. But the old lady had certainly heard of its wonders. Amongst them was a luxurious bathhouse where the women of the court bathed themselves in pools of hot water. People said that shafts of light shone through the stained glass windows high up in the walls, illuminating the *hammam*[13] in a kaleidoscope of colour.

Maryam loved her teta's stories, especially her fanciful descriptions of the palace with its lush fountains and courtyards. She herself knew of nothing but the village where the only pools were those made by icy mountain torrents and where there was no glass in the windows, only wooden shutters to keep out the sun and rain. The stories gave her a glimpse into another world, one in which anything could happen, while she lay awake at night listening to the snuffles and snores of her family. It was at times like these that she wished she was not the shy girl she believed herself to be, destined to spend her days in the village, never daring to venture into the world outside.

CHAPTER TWO

"I hear that a Frankish lady is coming to Ayn el-Louz. They say she'll live here."

Although Sa'adeh tried to conceal her curiosity, Maryam managed to detect a hint of excitement in her mother's voice. It was also rumoured that Frankish engineers were working on the Beirut – Damascus highway[14] nearby, but nobody in the village had ever seen one, let alone met one. Although it was no more than a two-hour walk from Ayn el-Louz, they rarely had cause to go there.

Imm George sat stirring the cooking pot while Maryam squatted outside the door, baking unleavened bread on an open oven. Baboush, her pet goat, stood nearby, watching her with his big brown eyes. She was making the thin, crisp loaves of the mountains, not the thicker ones of the plains. Her skirts were bunched up at the knees and she had knotted a simple scarf over her head to keep her hair from falling in her eyes.

Her grandmother had taught her how to make bread when she was only a little girl, but in those days she had been more interested in playing with the dough than baking it. Spinning the floppy disk round with her right-hand fingers, she teased its edges outwards until the flatbread had stretched to several times its original size. Then she spread it on the hot dome where it hissed and blistered. Dark spots began to appear from the air bubbles trapped in the mix. When it turned a crisp shade of golden brown on one side, Maryam eased the flatbread off the hot plate and flipped it over, smoothing out the wrinkles. But baking did not hamper her from eavesdropping on the conversation taking place inside between her mother and grandmother, and what she had just heard intrigued her.

"Why is she coming here?" she called out through the open door.

"To open a school," Sa'adeh said. Imm George looked up from the pot of vegetables she was stirring.

"Don't make things up."

"I'm not making it up," Maryam heard her mother's indignant reply. "Abouna[15] told me."

"I don't believe a word of it," retorted the old lady. "Why should she come here when she could just as well go to Hammana?"

That Imm George doubted the truth of Sa'adeh's words was not surprising. Maryam knew that her grandmother had little time for the village priest. She thought him too greedy when it came to collecting donations for the church and disliked his constant meddling in matters that did not concern him. That was why Imm George was disinclined to believe any rumour he bred.

"Anyway, schools teach things which are of no use to us."

Sitting outside with streaks of flour on her face, Maryam wondered why her grandmother should object to the opening of a school. After all, such places were known to flourish in the great cities of Damascus and Beirut and even in bustling entrepôts like Zahleh where there was a need for trained bookkeepers to keep record of the commerce that thrived there. She did not have to wait long before her grandmother made her true feelings known.

"What is the use of learning in a village?" she said as though she were stating the obvious.

Everyone in Ayn el-Louz knew that villagers, including the more prosperous ones like Imm George's family, relied on their sons to till the fields and look after their animals when they went out to graze on the hillsides. Girls, on the other hand, were required to fetch water from the spring and help their mothers take care of the house from an early age.

"But that's what he said," Sa'adeh insisted. "A Frankish lady is coming to open a school in Ayn el-Louz."

"What else did he have to say?" Imm George appeared to have

ceded the point.

"That the school would accept boys and girls. But that it's against church law for them to sit together."

Maryam pulled the last flatbread from the hot plate and carried the pile into the house, stacking them neatly on the table. She picked up the top one and tore it into three pieces, giving the largest to her grandmother. Then she reached for a small clay pot from one of the shelves and removed the lid, pouring a dash of olive oil over the creamy white curds which lay beneath.

All three women sat around the brazier while the stew simmered, eating their late breakfast with relish. Outside, there were squawks and fluttering feathers as the two younger children chased the chickens. This was the time of day that they all looked forward to. George and the two older boys would not be back until dusk and that gave them a rare opportunity to gossip amongst themselves. Maryam chewed her bread in silence. If what her mother had said was true, she wondered whether she would be allowed to attend the new school. *Maybe I'm already too old*, she thought. *Or worse, they might be expecting me to be married by then.*

"God help me if it's to Faris," she muttered to herself under her breath.

Neither her mother nor her father could read or write, nor could anyone one else in the village, as far as she knew, save the priest. But then he also claimed he could speak French, something he said he had learned during his short stay with the fathers.

"Where does she come from, Imme?" Maryam enquired. She glanced up at her mother who had finished her piece of bread and was about to get to her feet. Sa'adeh never sat idle for long.

"He doesn't know," she answered. "He says that she's not one of the sisters from the convent and she can't speak French properly like him."

Maryam drifted to the back of the room, still turning the matter over in her mind. She opened one of the wicker baskets and took out a mulberry twig. A mass of cream-coloured caterpillars were busy devouring the fresh green leaves while all around them the fragile remains of their old skins hung in translucent tatters. They had only hatched a fortnight before and had already grown to several times their original size. Maryam picked up one of the grubs and peeled the remains of the dead skin off its plump body, uncovering several crescent-shaped marks.

"They've almost finished their third moult, Teta."

Imm George grunted with satisfaction as she wiped the dirt off the faces of her two youngest grandchildren.

What Maryam was talking about were not just any insects but *Bombyx Mori*, domesticated silkworms whose fluffy white cocoons generated whatever surplus income the family enjoyed. It was the repeated success of this crop, and this crop alone, which made them more prosperous than their neighbours, not the surplus fruit from their orchards or the small amount of tobacco they grew.

While other families in the village also kept silkworms, none did so with the skill of Maryam's grandmother. In a good year when the mulberry leaves were plentiful and the worms free of disease, they might produce as much as a couple of *rotolas*[16] of cocoons.

Every season Imm George deliberately spared some adult moths long enough for them to breed. But even for those lucky few, death followed shortly after their soft grey bodies had been exhausted by the rigours of egg-laying. All the same, it was a kinder fate than that suffered by their fellows who would have already been boiled alive inside their cocoons. Imm George needed to kill the emergent moths before they ruptured the three hundred yards of silk filament with which they had so miraculously enshrouded themselves in preparation for their final metamorphosis.

It fell to Maryam to go out every morning and afternoon to the terraces where the mulberry trees grew and gather armfuls of fresh leaves to feed the silkworms. Sometimes her brothers would come along and climb up high into the trees to fetch the most delicate leaves. But the boys were impatient and loudly dismissed leaf gathering as women's work. They would soon wander off, leaving Maryam to navigate the steep path by herself as she led the donkey down from terraces festooned with bundles of mulberry leaves. She did not complain because she had long ago accepted that boys enjoyed privileges that girls could only dream about, and her brothers were no different. What mattered to her most was that they were kind to her.

Imm George's excitement really began to mount after the final moult. She watched intently as the silkworms started to weave their cocoons with delicacy and precision, tracing figures of eight around the bare twigs with their spinnerets.

"Don't let them ruin their own handiwork," the old lady would say as she seized handful after handful, merrily tossing them into the large black bowl of boiling water that bubbled on the brazier.

In the old days, a travelling silk spinner with dark twinkling eyes and a ragged turban on his head used to arrive each year to buy all the cocoons the village could offer, turning the raw silk into thread right there in the village with his *roue* Arabe. Teasing out the filaments from seven or eight cocoons with a comb, he would combine them into a single gossamer thread using the creaking wheel he turned with a wooden foot pedal. When he rode into the village on his donkey with his wheel strapped to its rump, the women would rush out to greet him as he went by. The men, on the other hand, would scowl at him, knowing that their wives would pay them scant attention during his stay. They all knew Abou Hilal would cost them dearly in food for his belly and tobacco for his long reed pipe.

But as the years went by, the old spinner came by less frequently and the villagers began to sell their cocoons to the merchants from Deir el-Qamar instead, who sent their agents to the villages in the mountains every June. Although they paid the villagers less, they rarely stayed in Ayn el-Louz for more than a few hours and did not ask for food and tobacco as Abou Hilal once had.

"I still prefer the ways of the old spinner," came Imm George's verdict. "At least he had some good stories. These new men talk of nothing but money."

The key to the silk harvest was where the eggs came from and Maryam had heard from her mother that this year would be a good one. They were using eggs laid by their own moths.

"They're free of disease. They won't shrivel and die."

"How much money will we get for the cocoons?" Maryam asked, sensing her mother's growing interest.

"Let's see," Sa'adeh said as she counted on her fingers. "We should get about three *rotolas*. That's more than a hundred-and-fifty piasters."

Earlier that day, Maryam had seen her father and elder brother, Joseph, set out for the other side of the valley to check on the mulberry trees which they had pruned the previous winter. Her younger brother, As'ad, had not gone with them. As usual, he had taken the flock up into the mountains above the village to graze. In addition to their goats, there were a couple of sheep that George had bought from the wandering herdsmen who arrived in the mountains at the beginning of each summer in search of new pastures. They were for slaughtering on feast days.

Imm George would skin the carcasses and tan their hides, scouring them with lime and rubbing them with a mixture made from their own brains. But first she would cut away the fat and preserve it in jars that she placed in the coolest parts of the house. That's what gave her stews their body and flavour.

"Come over here and try this."

Maryam joined her grandmother by the cooking pot as she spooned out the stew, pouring it over the cracked wheat that she had heaped on two plates. Every day, she cooked a pot of *yakhneh*[17] which she would serve to whomever was in the house including the neighbours who came by to visit them.

"Why are you so quiet today, *ya binti*[18]? Normally you're full of stories!"

"I'm thinking about the school, Teta."

"Ah, the school," she said. "Do you want to learn to read and write or just flirt with the boys?"

"I want to learn how to read and write." Maryam's tone was more serious than she had intended.

For once Imm George kept herself from making one of her usual wisecracks. Outside, Maryam could hear chickens clucking and the occasional donkey braying in the distance. The embers in the brazier glowed and crackled under the stew pot. The old lady put down her ladle.

"If the priest's story is true," she said, "then I'm glad that she's coming to our village."

"You've changed your mind?" The thought that her grandmother might now approve of the scheme made Maryam glad.

"Perhaps it would be good for all you youngsters to learn from books," Imm George went on, brushing aside her granddaughter's question. "But I still can't see what good it'll do you here."

Maryam searched her face for tell-tale signs of her grandmother's real feelings. Sometimes Imm George made contentious remarks just for the sake of it.

"Why do you say that, Teta?"

"Because our men are ignorant and they won't marry a girl who has learned to read and write. It would make them feel like *hameer*[19]!"

Maryam looked down at the floor to hide her own disappointment. She might have expected a comment like that from her father and quite probably her mother too, but she had always hoped that Imm George would be more sympathetic towards her own modest aspirations. But her thoughts were interrupted by the sound of approaching footsteps.

Suddenly, her little sister burst into the room, shouting at the top of her voice that two visitors had arrived. Maryam could hear them talking to her mother outside through the door ajar. Even Imm George looked up from her pot of stew.

"Abdallah's cough is much worse. He may die before nightfall," one of them was saying. There was a pause as they looked expectantly at Sa'adeh.

"We've come about his family," came the same man's voice again. "They won't be able to pay the *miri* this year."

"God will provide for them." Her mother's words sounded cold, almost dismissive. Out of the corner of her eye, Maryam noticed her grandmother following the conversation keenly. At the mention of taxes, the old lady rose to her feet with only the slightest hint of stiffness and adjusted the tasselled turban on her head. Then she strode through the door to join her daughter-in-law outside. The men nodded politely in her direction.

"They should have set something aside already," Imm George burst out without bothering to return their greeting. "Every year the sheikh's man takes a third of our crops and half of our silk and olive oil."

"That's true, Imm George," said the taller of the two men. "But then they won't have anything to live on through the winter months."

"Wise people make provisions before the harvest is gathered, not after they've eaten it," Maryam heard her grandmother say, smiling to herself at the sharpness of the old woman's wit. "Besides, they ask us for help every year and they have almost as many *dunums*[20] as we do."

The two men looked at each other. They had come to the house to ask for help from George on Wadee'ah's behalf, not from his mother who was well-known in the village for her sharp tongue.

"Have you no compassion, *ya Sitt*[21]?" whimpered the taller of two.

He had decided to try a different tack in an effort to get Imm George to relent. Maryam saw her grandmother stoop down and pull up a stem of wild barley that was growing by her feet. With an air of defiance, she began to suck on it noisily. Her mother stepped between them just as Maryam's enjoyment of Imm George's verbal sallies began to give way to rising panic. She hated real confrontations.

What would her father say if he were to come home and find that his own mother had sent her aunt's relatives away empty-handed? The poorer families in the village always expected some assistance from their richer relatives and Wadee'ah's family was no exception. In the years when the sheikh's man came twice to collect the *miri*, starvation became a real threat, especially if the grain harvest had been poor and the vegetables ruined by blight.

The question of taxes was a vexatious one in the mountains, pitting the feudal landlords against their peasant farmers. In order to maintain the right to govern themselves, the inhabitants had to pay dues to their own leaders who were held responsible for their collection by the Ottoman authorities. But this system often led to abuse, and news had recently reached Ayn el-Louz from the north that a popular uprising had broken out against the largest family of Christian landowners and their tax collectors.

Further south where the Druze and Christians lived side by side, there was less appetite for outright revolt. And around Ayn el-Louz, the Druze villagers had been counselled by their elders not to join in any uprisings against their landlords, who were of the same faith. Without their support, the Christians had little option but to pay up.

"Fetch some water for our guests," her mother called out to Maryam as the two men continued to linger in the shade of the fig tree, reluctant to give up on their mission. The sun was hot and the atmosphere outside the house had grown tense. Maryam poured cool water from a pitcher into two cups and carried them out to the men who eyed her with sullen resignation as though they held her responsible, too.

"Come back tomorrow when I have spoken to my husband," her mother said. But as they turned to go, Maryam saw the glowering figure of Imm George dart forward with no warning.

"We have lived in peace with the Druze for many years and, God-willing, we'll do so for many more," the old lady yelled at the backs of the departing men. "Don't make trouble between us over the *miri*."

With her rebuke still ringing in their ears, they stalked off swiftly down the track, muttering angrily to each other as they went. Sa'adeh took her mother-in-law by the hand and tried to lead her back towards the house, but she refused to go.

"*Yuh, yuh*," Maryam heard her splutter in disgust. "A couple of troublemakers."

"Calm down, Imme," said Sa'adeh. Maryam brought over a chair that the old lady sat down on, still quivering with rage. Standing behind her, she began stroking her hair to calm her down.

"Wadee'ah's husband didn't work hard even before he got sick," said Imm George. "And her sons are not much help, either; especially that eldest one, whatever he's called." Maryam looked away, not wishing to remind her grandmother of the one person in the world who disgusted her the most.

"Faris." Sa'adeh prompted her.

"Yes, Faris," the old lady spat out his name. "An idle good-for-nothing who sits around all day boasting with his friends from sunrise to sunset. He doesn't go out to work in the fields like your two." The thought of her grandsons brought a fleeting smile to her wrinkled face. "Now they're good boys."

"Don't be so harsh. Faris is not so bad," said Sa'adeh in an attempt to mollify her mother-in-law.

But Imm George had already calmed down and now sat glumly in her chair, looking out over the valley. It was well into the afternoon and the sun was beginning to sink towards the western horizon. The tall grass waved lazily in the gentle breeze as the evening *ghtaita*[22] drifted slowly up from the sea, covering the valley with a blanket of mist. From time to time, they could hear the bleats of goats grazing up in the surrounding hills. Already some of the men were beginning to return to the village from their fields and orchards.

Relieved that calm had returned once again, Maryam sat down on the ground beside her grandmother and watched a couple of men following a heavily-laden donkey as it picked its way down the hillside opposite them. She idly wondered if one of them might be the Druze boy she had encountered earlier that day, and as she did so, a secret smile stole across her lips.

CHAPTER THREE

For Joseph, the day began as any other. He watched as his father propped himself up on one elbow and swung his legs off the mattress he shared with his wife as the first patch of light crept through the cracks in the shutters over the barred window. Then he set to work preparing lentils and *burghoul*[23] for breakfast, the remains of their meal from the evening before. Taking down a thin muslin bag of yoghurt that had been left hanging from a beam overnight, he spooned some of its creamy contents into two clay dishes, pausing only to admire its smooth consistency and fresh smell.

His father was a thickset man with a deeply tanned face. His shoulders were broad from constant work in the fields and heavy scars crisscrossed the backs of his gnarled hands. His palms were calloused from the plough and his fingers stained a dull orange from years of toil in the red topsoil. The stern look in his eyes, peering out from beneath bushy eyebrows, coupled with the heavy line of his jaw gave him a rather severe aspect. Those people who did not know him well often mistook him for a curmudgeon and avoided him. But there were others who thought him kind and fair. Nearly everyone in the village agreed on one thing, however: George was a man of his word.

"Come and eat, Abee[24]," said Joseph as he spread out a mat on the ground for their breakfast. "We have a lot to do today."

George grunted as he picked up his black headcloth, shaking off the dust from the previous day. Instead of wrapping it around his felt cap, he draped it over his shoulder instead.

"Clearing those new terraces will be hard work," he muttered. "The rocks are huge."

His father wiped the side of his nose with the back of his hand. It still dribbled on occasion from when it had been broken in a heated argument over water rights a few years earlier. He had been called to mediate in a dispute by one of his Druze neighbours who had discovered that Christians from a nearby village were trying to divert a mountain stream towards their land.

At first George had tried to reason with them, explaining that the water had flowed along the same course for as long as anyone could remember. But the strangers had been spoiling for a fight and were in no mood to be persuaded by mere words. Before long, one of them became so enraged at his quiet reasoning that he hit George full in the face with a hoe. In the ensuing mêlée they had been driven off by the Druze, leaving the direction of the watercourse unchanged.

Handing his father some of yesterday's bread, they sat down together to eat in the half-light. Joseph was still mopping up the last smears of oil when his father got to his feet and walked away. Its distinctive taste reminded him of how the previous autumn he had taken their glossy olives to one of the nearby villages to be pressed. As he watched the golden liquid tinged with green run down the stone channel into the storage jars, he realized for the first time why his family cherished their stony fields and cultivated them with such care. The thought made his chest swell with pride.

He slipped out as quietly as he could and walked round to the lower room where the goats were penned at night, fumbling in the darkness for the iron billhook that hung from the wall. Then he picked up a heavy mattock and was about to go back into the house when he stopped short, remembering that his father would be saying his prayers. Every morning George sought the blessing of the blue and white Madonna who guarded the door before going out into the fields. Instead, he took out a whetstone and began sharpening the blade of the billhook. When he opened the door a few minutes later, he found his father had already left and his younger brother was still asleep.

"Wake up you lazy good-for-nothing," he whispered in his ear as he grabbed the boy by the shoulder. "It will be noon by the time you're out on the slopes and the animals will be half-starved!"

"Get off me," As'ad said as he fended him off sleepily. "I was soaring like a buzzard until you came."

"Like a buzzard," Joseph scoffed. "You're more like a lizard."

Reaching for his top clothes that lay in an untidy heap on the floor, As'ad pulled them on hurriedly, ripping one of the seams of his shirt in the process.

"You made me do that," he whined.

Rubbing his bleary eyes, he reached over to grab what little food remained on the mat. Then clutching the leftovers in one hand and his pantaloons in the other, he stumbled out through the door. Had his mother not been asleep, the boy would have certainly received a slap for not washing his face.

Lying awake next to her grandmother on the other side of the room, Maryam had tossed and turned for most of the night. All she wanted was to enjoy those first few precious moments of calm before the day's work began. The cramped confines of the house made it difficult for her to find time to be alone with her thoughts.

Although her brothers had woken her, the young man she had seen in the orchard the day before was the one who disturbed her sleep. The fact that she could still remember what he looked like both surprised and perturbed her. More disquieting still, she had found herself imagining how his curly hair would feel were she to run her fingers through it!

Looking around the room for a distraction, her eyes picked out a spider's web in the rafters above her head. Droplets of condensation from her family's damp exhalations now beaded its silken filaments. Following one of the threads from where it was anchored on a beam to the centre of its web, she marvelled at its beautiful symmetry. A slight movement in one of the corners caught her eye, alerting her to the presence of the spider.

How simple my life would be, she thought staring idly upwards, *if I were a house spider with nothing to worry about except Teta's broom.*

Across the room, she could hear her mother snoring lightly. Imm George, on the other hand, made no sound as she lay with her eyes shut, one hand placed loosely against her chest.

"Go away," Maryam whispered as the insistent nudges of Baboush's muzzle put an abrupt end to her early morning musings. One of her brothers must have left the door ajar. She stretched herself, and put her clogs on before disappearing in the direction of the dung heap with Baboush at her heels. The outhouse was concealed at the back of the garden behind the spiky lobes of a giant prickly pear.

Her first chore of the day was to go down to the spring in the lower part of the village to fetch water. It was hard work but Maryam usually enjoyed it because it gave her the chance to meet up with the other girls. As they waited their turn at the stone basin, they exchanged news with one another. Sometimes they would just talk about the latest gossip circulating in the village. But more often than not, they chatted about themselves and in particular their own marriage prospects. These daily gatherings were among the few moments in their closely chaperoned lives when they could share secrets about the village boys safely out of earshot from their mothers and grandmothers.

Picking up a pitcher and a felt pad, Maryam climbed the steps at the front of the house and set off down the track. On the way, she passed several women throwing out scraps of food for their chickens. The occasional crowing of a cock or braying of a donkey protesting the tightening of its girth shattered the early morning stillness. As she drew near the spring, she realized that two other girls were following her.

"Your grandmother was in a good mood yesterday," one of them called out sarcastically as she hurried to catch up.

Although she knew both girls, she decided to ignore them. They were almost at the spring now and the gurgling of the fresh water as it splashed into the basin all but drowned out their voices. But as she took her place in the queue that had formed in the shade of the almond tree, they persisted in their taunts.

"My Teta is like that," said Maryam, unable to ignore them anymore. "What can I do about it?"

"I wouldn't want a teta like that," said the plainer of the two. "She might scare off my cousins and then who would marry me?" The other girls laughed. This was the kind of talk that they enjoyed most.

"That wouldn't bother me," said Maryam. "I hate my cousin. He's stupid and lazy."

"Stupid and lazy!" repeated a girl with a round face and plump cheeks. "That's nothing. Mine's got a hare lip."

"Don't judge him by the way he looks," said a gawky girl standing at the rear. "He might be kinder to you than some of the better-looking boys."

"But he spits like a snake," said the plump girl, pulling a face. "How would you like that for a husband?"

Maryam was too preoccupied with her own thoughts to listen to their prattling. In front of her were two Druze girls whom she knew by sight but had never spoken to before. Their heads were covered with white *mandeels*[25] and on their feet they wore red slippers. They stood quietly conversing with each other, ignoring the girls' excitable chatter. One of them nudged the other when she noticed Maryam looking at them.

They think I'm rude, she said to herself as she looked away.

Maryam waited for them to finish before taking her turn at the basin. Holding her pitcher's mouth below the surface, she gazed down at her reflection as she waited for it to fill. Something her grandmother once told her came into her mind unbidden.

They're not like us. They keep to themselves.

Several large bubbles rose to the surface and exploded, obliterating her image in a series of eddies and swirls. Feeling the pitcher sink towards the bottom, Maryam grabbed it with both handles and heaved it up onto her head without spilling a single drop. It was a technique she had perfected over the years.

By the time she made her second journey to the spring, the queue had all but disappeared and there was only a couple of girls in front of her. They were too busy gossiping about the Frankish lady to notice her walking up behind them. It seemed that word of the new school had found its way around the village already.

"Can you imagine boys and girls from different families all sitting together?" one of them was saying.

"They'll make us sit at the back," the other replied glumly.

Maryam's growing irritation at their frivolity finally overcame her reluctance to join in. To her mind, the establishment of the school was a serious business.

"Don't you two want to learn to read and write?" she interrupted them. "Or do you just want to fetch and carry water all your lives like donkeys?"

Taken aback by her unexpected outburst, both girls covered their mouths with their hands to hide their smirks as Maryam scowled at them.

"I'd like to go to school," one of them said after a moment or two. "But I don't know if my father will let me."

"I don't know if mine will either, but I'm going to ask him," said her friend.

"Good," said Maryam who had surprised even herself.

Taking care not to trip over any loose stones dislodged by the hooves of the farm animals that morning, she began to make her way back up the track, carrying the full pitcher on her head. Before she had gone very far, Maryam thought she heard the sound of footsteps behind her. Someone or something was following her. She walked on a short way to be sure and then stopped in her tracks, twisting her body slowly so as not to spill any water.

There, to her astonishment, stood a young man only a few yards behind her. He was standing in the middle of the road with his arms by his side, making no attempt to move to one side or the other in order to pass her. Instinctively, her free hand shot up to hide her face from the strange man. But her initial alarm quickly gave way to a rosy hue that blossomed on her cheeks in the split-second it took for her to recognize that he was the boy from the other day.

"May peace be upon you," he said politely.

"And upon you too," she breathed.

There was a long pause while they both looked at each other. Those few moments seemed like an eternity to Maryam who was caught completely off-guard by his sudden appearance. Her panic at being seen with him alone was only just outweighed by a secret thrill at the fact that he was there at all. But he was a stranger and a *Dirzi*[26] at that.

"Can I help you?" he said at last, smiling awkwardly.

Maryam nodded. She looked around to see if there was anyone watching, but they were standing at a bend where the track doubled back on itself as it climbed upwards. Only empty fields and orchards lay on either side of the road. Gently lifting the pitcher off her head, he placed it on the ground by the roadside and propped it upright with a handful of stones placed carefully around the base.

Rising to his feet, he brushed the dust off his hands. Maryam could not help noticing the precision of his movements, so different to those of her clumsy brothers. The smooth skin over his jaw tightened as a look of resolve settled on his handsome features.

"Can I show you the shelter I'm building?" he said. "It's over there."

Maryam touched the tip of her tongue to the roof of her mouth. She was about to say *la*[27], but the word died on her lips.

CHAPTER FOUR

An obedient and doting girl by nature, she normally made every effort to please her mother, and more particularly, her father. Despite the affection she knew he had for her, the high regard she held for him bordered on fear. And now, by talking to a strange boy, she knew that she might have already jeopardized her reputation.

Village customs dictated that girls should not encourage the attentions of young men to whom they had not been officially introduced. With none of her relatives present to act as chaperone, she knew that she should decline his invitation, however innocently it had been made, and walk away. To make matters worse still, the boy in question was Druze.

Everyone in Ayn el-Louz was aware of the rundown house at the very bottom of the village where several ragged children were often seen playing outside by themselves. Maryam sometimes passed it on her way to pick mulberry leaves in spring or when she was out gathering fruit in autumn. One time, a haggard woman wearing dirty clothes called out to her from inside, but instead of stopping to speak to her, she had hurried on past.

The shame of her cowardice still lingered with her although her mother had told her when she was only a little girl that the family who lived there were outcasts. The woman had married a Druze man, she had said, and now neither her family nor his would have anything to do with them or their children.

"Isn't that unfair?" Maryam had asked.

"No," Sa'adeh had said with unusual firmness. "When you marry outside your faith, you leave your people."

Yet in spite of the severe scolding she would surely receive from her parents should word get back to them, Maryam was irresistibly drawn to say yes to the boy. Whether it was because she had been dreaming about him the night before or just the faint scent of male sweat that clung to his clothes, she did not know. But she was sure of one thing. If she did not follow him now, she knew she would spend the rest of the day wishing she had.

She looked around carefully to see if anyone was coming in either direction. But there was nobody in sight, and all she could hear was the soft buzz of insects as they sipped nectar from the warm summer flowers that coloured the fringes of the roadway. She looked up at the smiling face of the young man standing in front of her and, with her heart pounding in her chest, gave a simple nod.

He led the way through the fruit grove to where the shelter stood. Maryam had to hitch up her skirts to avoid them getting entangled in the thistles that grew everywhere. When they reached the low stonewall which surrounded the orchard on two sides, he helped her clamber over it. Although the tips of his fingers were hard and calloused like those of her brothers, his touch was gentle.

On the other side, Maryam sat down in the shade of a carob tree and tried to disentangle the head of a star-shaped thistle from her skirts. Painstakingly, she pulled out the brittle spikes one at a time. Without warning, he leaned across and stretched the hem of her skirt taught, brushing his hand against her cheek in the process. Her skin tingled from the accidental touch of his fingers even before she realized what had happened.

When she had successfully freed the last of the spikes, he reached over and took the thistle from her, stripping off its outside skin with quick and deft movements of his hand. She shook her head when he offered her the peeled stalk, so he popped it into his own mouth instead and began to chew with relish.

"It's good for your liver." There was a serious expression on his handsome face.

Maryam had never seen anyone eat a thistle before, not even her grandmother. In the silence that followed, she swatted at a fly that had settled on her cheek.

"My name is Mohanad," he said as he threw away the tip. "The name of the golden sword the Arabs brought back with them from *al-Hind*[28]."

Maryam's eyes widened, impressed by the sound of his unusual name and its grand associations. A golden sword from a place she had never heard of sounded very exciting to her untutored mind. *Al-Hind* was clearly some distant land, far away from her own world.

"What's your name?"

"It's Maryam," she said. "The name of..."

"The mother of the Prophet Jesus," Mohanad finished her sentence for her as he broke a pod off the carob tree and hefted it in his palm. Maryam's eyes rested on his long, slender fingers.

"I saw you with your mother yesterday," he said after a moment or two's reflection. "Were you visiting your relatives?" The quiet and respectful way he spoke appealed to her. It was so different to the way her brothers and cousins usually addressed her.

"Yes," she replied. "My sick uncle. The doctor says he has the white plague."

Mohanad frowned and his mouth twitched at the corner. Maryam thought that it might be a sign of his kind nature although she couldn't be sure, having had little experience with men outside her own family.

"*Allah yihfazo*," he said gravely. "May God preserve him."

Their eyes met and hers lingered on his face for what seemed like an endless moment. When she realized she was staring she quickly looked away, thankful that they were hidden by the wall from the curious gaze of passers-by. But in spite of her guilt-ridden feelings, the intimacy she was experiencing for the first time was already beginning to thrill her. He dropped the shell and reached down to help her to her feet. As she stood up, she brushed her hands down her skirt causing unexpected pins and needles in her hips and legs. Just as it was beginning to fade, she felt his fingers touch the sleeve of her blouse. Instinctively, she shook her arm free from his grasp. She glared at him, but he just chuckled in amusement. Pointing to a small orange beetle, he carefully picked it up and tossed it over the wall.

"This way," he said.

Although they were now standing in front of the entrance to the shelter, Maryam hung back, reluctant to go in. Her fragile confidence, which had built up as they sat talking under the carob tree now suddenly deserted her, replaced once again by the creeping fear of discovery. Stooping down, Mohanad pushed his way in front of her, gently pulling her after him. She stood blinking in the fractured light, gazing at columns of dust suspended in the sunbeams. Several wooden poles stood in the ground at intervals to form uprights around which branches and twigs were tightly entwined. Above her head, a makeshift canopy of leaves and fronds perched on top of crooked beams. Patches of light dappled the ground at their feet where the sun shone through the dried grass stuffed into the gaps.

Maryam took a step forward but faltered when Mohanad picked up a rush mat from one corner of the hut and dusted it off. He unrolled it in one fluid motion. Taking both of Maryam's hands in his own, he lowered her onto it. He stepped backwards and pulled up the end of his shirt to wipe away the sheen of sweat from his face, revealing at the same time an expanse of tawny skin stretched tightly over his lean stomach. His chest rose and fell with each breath as he stood just inside the entrance, the outline of his body silhouetted by the sunlight behind him.

Maryam's palms had become moist. She shifted her position as Mohanad took off his sandals and squatted down on strong knees beside her on the mat. With a reassuring smile, he took out a leather pouch and placed it on the ground. Untying the leather string that held it sealed, he produced some bread and olives together with a few small oval-shaped fruits. Then he reached over to where a small jug of water stood partly covered with a thin piece of cloth.

"Would you like some?" he said. "It should be cool."

Although she was not thirsty, Maryam reached out for the jug and in doing so, splashed some water onto his arm.

"Did I knock into you?" he asked her.

"No, no," said Maryam hastily, "I'm just clumsy."

She raised the jug and let the cool water flow into her mouth, spilling some down the front of her blouse. Then she handed it back to Mohanad who nestled it in the crook of his arm and took a long draught without spilling a single drop. Maryam watched his prominent Adam's apple bob up and down in his throat as he swallowed.

Rinsing his fingers, he put the jug back against the wall before tearing off a piece of bread. He folded two olives inside the flap and handed it to Maryam. She felt him gazing down at her, his dark eyes flecked with gold like obsidian. Easing himself back on one elbow, Mohanad helped himself to the bread and olives while Maryam sat there, paralyzed, her food clutched in her hand. In her house, the men and boys always ate before the women. He did not appear to notice at first, but when he paused to brush away some crumbs from the corners of his mouth, he saw she had not taken a single bite.

"Aren't you hungry?" he said in his soft voice.

"Yes," she replied. "I am."

"Then eat, Maryam." She began nibbling at the bread. The fear she had felt standing at the entrance was almost gone now, leaving behind only excitement.

"These olives come from the trees here," he was saying. "And the bread was made by my sister Fatmeh this morning. Do you know her?"

"I see her at the spring sometimes."

She wondered absently why he had asked her. The girls generally only knew each other by sight, rarely by name. Perhaps he was expecting her to compliment his sister's baking. "It's very crisp," she stuttered.

He beamed at her, as if acknowledging the compliment on his sister's behalf. Then he leaned forward and picked up one of the fruits, turning it over in his hand so that she could see it. She was struck by the dull orange colour of its blemished skin as well as by the way one end opened out like a pair of lips puckered in a kiss.

"They only taste good when they're almost rotten," Mohanad said in a serious tone.

She giggled without knowing why. For some reason, she found the way he said it amusing. Taking a knife from his belt, he began to peel the fruit methodically, dropping the rind onto the mat in even strips. When he had finished, he cut it open and carefully picked out the large dark seeds. Then he sliced the flesh into several pieces, offering them to Maryam. When she did nothing, he jiggled them up and down in his palm as though he were trying to tempt a child. Finally she reached out and took one.

"What does it taste like?" she asked.

"Hmmm… Like an apple only sweeter."

"Does it have a name?"

"*Akkidinya*[29]," he said. "Haven't you seen one before?"

She shook her head as she examined the medlar with suspicion.

"My uncle found them in the market when he was in Zahleh a few days ago," he explained. "A trader must have brought them from the south."

She put some into her mouth and began to suck it as delicately as she could, trying not to make any sound as the sweet and sour juice ran down the back of her throat. Then she chewed the remains slowly, squeezing the pulp against the roof of her mouth with her tongue. To her surprise, it tasted sweet and not in the least bit overripe.

"We must go now," he said. "Or your family will start to wonder where you are."

His words brought Maryam back to her senses with a jolt. All at once she remembered that she was sitting alone with a boy she scarcely knew, and the guilt that she felt when they had first met flooded back. Her eyes wide, she stared straight at Mohanad, searching his face for some sign or acknowledgment of what had passed between them. But he merely smiled and, taking her hands in his, helped her up.

"We should leave separately," he said as they stood together by the entrance. "It'll be better that way."

With the palm of his hand, he gently nudged Maryam forward. As she stepped out into the bright morning light, her forehead creased into a worried frown and her eyes blinked anxiously. On the wall opposite, a lizard lay motionless, warming itself in the sun. Startled by her sudden appearance, it raised itself on its bandy legs and scuttled off into the tall grass.

Maryam clambered over the wall and made her way through the brambles towards the road. Remembering her pitcher at the last moment, she looked around frantically only to find it still standing upright where Mohanad had left it. She swung it up onto her head and set out to cover the short distance home as fast as she could, hoping that no one had noticed her absence.

CHAPTER FIVE

Later that day, Maryam stood outside the house watching her father as he made his way back from the higher terraced fields where he had been helping Joseph mend the walls left damaged by last winter's rains. The light was fading and dark clouds, blown in from the west, were gathering over the mountaintops. Poised above the next ridge, the sun was giving up the last of its light in a magnificent burst of red fire.

She watched him as he paused for a moment to look up at the sky. Although the rains had given way to the drier summer months some weeks before, Maryam could tell from her father's expression that something was wrong. Maybe there was a storm brewing.

One of the things she admired most about him was his uncanny ability to predict even the slightest change in weather. He would stand with his face to the wind, feeling its force on his cheeks. Whether it was a summer squall or the onset of rain or snow in winter, he always seemed able to detect it before anyone else.

He continued his climb down the steep bluff towards the village, picking his way through the bushes and roots with his wooden staff. Sliding down the last few yards of the hillside where the vegetation had worn away, George found the main road leading back to the village. He unwound the black headcloth from around his cap and shook his head from side to side.

He's tired, Maryam said to herself as she kneaded the dough.

By the time he arrived home, her father was hardly able to loosen the twine that held the flaps of his leather boots together. He lowered his heavy frame onto a wooden chair Imm George had placed for him by the door and stretched out his legs. A few moments later, Sa'adeh appeared with a glass of cool water from the pitcher.

"Do you think there will be a storm tonight?" she asked.

"Maybe. I've already sent Joseph to help his brother. Have they come down yet?"

She shook her head before adding, "Stop worrying, George. Only God can control the weather!"

He drained the last drops of water from the cup and handed it back to his wife who glanced at the back of his hands.

"Show me," she said as she prodded them gently with her finger. "They're as cracked as the mountains!"

He looked down at where the jagged limestone had torn into his flesh as if noticing the cuts for the first time.

"I'll find something to clean them with," Sa'adeh said as she disappeared inside, leaving Maryam alone with her father.

"Is there really a storm coming, Abee?"

He nodded absently as if he had only just noticed her presence beside him. Normally, she would have accepted this lack of attention without a second thought because she was a girl, but the day had been anything but normal. She yearned for some sign of his approval.

It was the unplanned tryst earlier with the Druze boy that made her feel the pressing need for some token of affection from him, a smile, or even a few words. She could not deny the exhilaration she had experienced in the 'arzal with Mohanad, but the last thing she wanted was to be cast adrift by her own family like the woman at the end of the village. She glanced up at him again but the moment had already passed. His thoughts were elsewhere.

Only the crackle of the fire interrupted the silence while Sa'adeh washed the abrasions on her husband's hands and rubbed some homemade ointment on them. Inside, Maryam could just hear the dull *chkok-kok-kok* of a knife on wood as her grandmother chopped up carrots and potatoes to add to the pot that sat simmering on the metal brazier.

Somewhere in the distance came the tinkling of bells as the

flocks returned from the upper pastures; and further down the hill, donkeys brayed as they were unharnessed. When darkness fell, the sun's golden orange glow gave way to the flickering light of cooking fires that spread out across the valley. Strange shapes began to appear on the dark walls in the soft glow of oil lamps.

The sound of shuffling hooves and cacophonous bleating outside the house announced the arrival of Joseph and As'ad with their herd of sheep and goats. Abandoning the animals to his brother's care, the younger brother marched over to where his father was sitting, his face flushed.

"Why did you send Joseph to help me?" he asked indignantly. "I was bringing them down by myself."

"I know, my boy," George said as he reached forward to ruffle his son's hair. "But what would you have done if one had gone lame on you?"

"I'd have carried it," he rolled his eyes. George leaned back and smiled at his younger son in a way that he rarely, if ever, did at Maryam. She saw him wink at Joseph over the boy's shoulder, amused by his younger son's outburst.

"You're too puny to carry a kid, let alone a goat." Joseph cuffed his brother playfully over the head and when As'ad pushed him away, a scuffle ensued. But their horseplay was soon interrupted by Imm George who appeared in the doorway, hands on her hips.

"Enough of that tomfoolery," she said. "It's time you men were fed."

With that, Maryam knelt down and left a stack of freshly baked loaves beside them while Sa'adeh brought over the pot and began ladling lentils over the heap of cracked wheat in their bowls. Then she followed her mother to the back of the room as she always did, allowing the boys to eat alone with their father.

"This *yakhneh* is too hot, Imme," As'ad moaned as he blew on his stew.

The moment the steam had stopped rising from their bowls they both began slurping it down, pausing only to suck their fingers. George, meanwhile, stirred the contents of his bowl, contenting himself with picking out bits of vegetable as the mixture cooled. Suddenly, he turned to Joseph just as he was scooping up the last of his food with a scrap of bread.

"Go and find Faris and his uncles."

"What do you want with him?" blurted out As'ad. "He's an idiot."

This time George glared at the boy while Maryam stifled a giggle.

"Tell them it's important," he added without raising his voice.

"Important? Why, Abee?"

George ignored his question, so Joseph got to his feet and set off towards the village to fetch them while As'ad slipped on his sandals and went off to feed the vegetable peels to the animals. The smell of rain hung in the air. Suddenly the clouds over the mountains to the north were lit up by a brilliant flash of lightning, followed seconds later by the rolling crash of thunder. Out of the corner of her eye, Maryam saw her father shift uneasily as he waited for Joseph to return.

It was not long before the scuff of boots and the murmur of men, muffled by the roiling wind, announced their arrival. George greeted his guests affably enough.

"*Tfaddalou*[30]," he said, pointing to where Maryam and her mother had arranged the mattresses and pillows they slept on at night into a divan. The three men settled themselves while Sa'adeh went to bring them some refreshments.

"Prepare the *argileh*[31]," she murmured to Joseph in passing.

He took down a jar from one of the shelves and chose a few dried leaves from amongst the mass of tobacco stored in it. Shredding them with a knife, he took a generous pinch and tamped it down into the clay head. Without being asked, Maryam picked up some hot coals from the brazier with tongs and laid them carefully on top. The water in the glass bowl gurgled and the coals glowed red as her brother breathed in a long draught through the hollow reed mouthpiece.

Before long, the air in the room was redolent with the acrid smell of village tobacco, softened by the sweetness of dried apple skin. The men puffed contentedly, passing along the pipe from one to the other in turn. So intent were they on their smoking that they barely noticed George standing beside his mother in the shadows at the back of the room. It was clear that the old lady was sulking.

"We have guests," George was pleading with her. "Bring them a glass of your *tout*[32]."

"Give them our tobacco and sherbets?" she replied. "They're like ticks on a dog."

"Don't be so harsh, Imme."

She got to her feet and, with unabashed reluctance, shuffled off to prepare the mulberry cordial. Seated between his two uncles with a fatuous grin on his face, Faris appeared delighted by the invitation, particularly as it had come from his wealthiest relatives. The fact that his father lay dying less than half-a-mile away did not seem to have dampened his spirits. When Sa'adeh brought over the cups, he rose to his feet in a brazen attempt to ingratiate himself with his aunt.

"*Ahlain*[33], *ya* Khalte[34]," he said.

Sa'adeh gave only a cursory nod and handed him a cup while Maryam stayed as far back as she could. She found his presence in her father's house almost unbearable. Worse still, she saw him look around and then walk over to where George was sitting.

"May I ask a favour of you, 'Ammo?" he said in a voice that crept under her skin.

"Of course," said George. "Do you need some money to pay the doctor?"

"It's something else entirely," he murmured as if he was drawing George into some kind of conspiracy. "Permission to court your daughter."

At first Maryam could not believe what he had just said but as it sunk in, she shuddered. Her worst nightmare was coming true.

Just as she was beginning to despair, Imm George swooped in like a vengeful spirit.

"Running after a girl when your father's on his deathbed," she shouted at him before George could prevent her. "*Ya 'aybishoum*[35]!"

Taken by surprise, Faris sat down, deflated. Maryam heaved a sigh of relief while her uncles pretended they had not heard the exchange. They continued to sip their mulberry cordial and puff on the water pipe, trying to conceal their relief that Imm George's ire had fallen on their nephew instead of them.

"Delicious," they said in unison. "*Bijannin*[36]."

Imm George's expression softened for a moment before settling back into a stage scowl. Flashes of lightning flickered through the shutters, followed by the low growl of thunder. The conversation died down as they listened to the raindrops pattering on the ground and the gusts of wind swirling around the house. It was some time before the intervals between the flashes and claps of thunder began to lengthen. Only after the main part of the storm had moved north did the taut lines on George's face begin to smoothen.

"Four Druze were killed yesterday," he began as he turned his attention back to his guests. "On the Damascus Road."

The three men nodded. They had heard rumours earlier that day of a confrontation on the Medairij Pass. Only Joseph and As'ad, who were sitting beside their father, seemed surprised by the news.

"But have you heard this, Bou Joseph?" asked one of the uncles, addressing George by the name of his eldest son as a mark of respect. "Three of our men were killed just south of here a few days ago. At Jisr el-Qadi."

George nodded. The story had become common knowledge after some muleteers had passed through the village the day before on their way to Damascus. Even Maryam had heard about it from the other girls at the well.

"So we're even," said Faris.

In his excitement at being invited to attend the council, he had forgotten to show proper respect by speaking out of turn. His uncles said nothing, unwilling to reprimand him in public while George ignored him altogether. Joseph and As'ad looked up at their father expectantly as Maryam edged nearer to the men.

"These things must not happen here," he said after a long pause. "Whatever is going on elsewhere is none of our business. Here these people are our neighbours, and we should keep it that way."

"But what if they turn against us and try to seize our property?" objected one of the uncles, the same one who had accused Imm George of having no compassion the day before. "Right now we have only pruning forks and billhooks to defend ourselves with. Let's get firearms from the bishop's men in Beirut."

"If we don't give them reason to, they won't attack us."

"But Abouna says they're conspiring against us in secret," he persisted.

George cleared his throat and Maryam noticed that her father's right leg had begun to twitch. She looked round at Faris and his uncles and saw only excitement in their eyes. Even her brothers' faces had lit up. To her surprise, her mother and grandmother were both silent. Sa'adeh was busying herself heating a pan of water while Imm George had chosen not to speak out although she of all people had the most reason to. She had lived with the Druze all her life.

Only Maryam nodded her head at her father's words and in return received a warm smile. It was the sign of affection that she had been waiting for from the moment he had arrived home. He turned back to the others, his jaw set firm. She had seen that resolute look on his face before.

"I don't care what the priest said. Or what is happening elsewhere." His voice sank to a low murmur. "If we don't provoke our neighbours, they won't attack us."

The heated discussion was interrupted by the tea's arrival. As

Sa'adeh served the men, her eyes fell on As'ad who was sitting idly on the floor, his mouth agape.

"Strip the leaves from those twigs your sister spent all afternoon collecting," she snapped at him, pulling the boy roughly to his feet. "And you, Maryam. Offer our guests some honey."

Hot steam scented with the spice of thyme floated up from the cups. Steeling herself, Maryam took down a little jar of last summer's honey and began to offer it around. As the uncles were spooning the sticky liquid into their cups, there was a sudden commotion outside. Someone was banging loudly on the door.

"Faris! *Ya* Faris, come quickly." It was a boy's voice calling out in panic. "Baba has passed away."

CHAPTER SIX

～～～

At first Faris continued stirring his tea, oblivious to the cries of his younger brother. His uncles, on the other hand, turned pale as they looked around the room to see who would make the first move, leaving it to George to put his arm around Faris's shoulders. Pulling him gently to his feet, George led him outside and together they set off down the track.

"Come on, Maryam," Sa'adeh said, seizing her shawl. "Let's go."

The bravado Faris had displayed earlier in the evening seemed to have all but deserted him and a look of dull resignation was now in its place. The men were almost outside her aunt's house by the time Maryam and her mother caught up with them. As the sound of keening came towards them on the swirling wind, Faris began dragging his feet until he came to a complete halt outside the door of his father's house. He stood there, shaking his head.

"Be a man," George whispered, pushing him forward.

The door swung open on its rickety hinges to reveal the priest in his dusty cassock beside the dead man's body, reciting a prayer from memory. In one hand he held an unopened prayer book and with the other he was fending off Wadee'ah as she clutched at the hem of his frock.

"*Ya dillee 'alayyee*[37]," her aunt was screaming as Maryam followed her mother inside. "I'm all alone in the world."

The stifling air in the room was burdened by the wails of women who had converged on the house to mourn Abdallah's passing. Maryam was immediately struck by the change from her last visit. The morbid curiosity created by the doctor's "cupping" had been replaced by near hysteria. Some of the mourners rocked backwards and forwards while others rubbed dust in their hair. Two oil lamps guttered in the draught from the open door, bathing the crowded interior in a flickering yellow light.

"Do your duty as the eldest son," she heard her father say as he pushed Faris forward.

Rousing himself from his torpor, Faris knelt down and kissed his dead father on both cheeks, lifting him up by his thin shoulders. Behind him, the priest hurried through the remainder of the prayers, making the sign of the cross when he had finished. Abdallah's eyes were already closed, so George took out two silver coins and placed them over the dead man's sockets.

"Prepare him for burial," the priest said.

He picked up his cap and, pausing only to inspect the hem of his robe, made his way as quickly as he could towards the door. As if on cue, the mourners ceased their wailing and filed out after him. In the eerie silence that followed, Wadee'ah began to strip the soiled clothes from her dead husband's body. Aided by Maryam and her mother, she washed him with water from a jug, draping a simple cloth over his stomach and legs to conceal his private parts. As the grime sloughed off, it revealed pale skin tinged with grey.

"Help me," Wadee'ah said to Faris as she struggled to pull a clean pair of pantaloons over one of Abdallah's legs.

His limbs were already stiffening and the women were finding it difficult to dress him. To Maryam's disgust, Faris remained where he was as if he had not heard her. George stepped forward instead to straighten the dead man's arms and legs so the women could dress him.

When they had finished, he stood back to allow Wadee'ah to cross her husband's hands over his chest in the habit of prayer and wind a simple rosary around them. Just as she was bending down to kiss it, there came a knock at the door.

"May God make good your loss."

More neighbours arrived soon afterwards, carrying with them an assortment of dishes. Unlike the mourners, they had come prepared for the night's vigil. Maryam could see the strain in her aunt's face as she welcomed them and invited them to sit with her beside her husband's corpse. The visitors laid food out on the mat while she assumed her position by his head, flanked by Sa'adeh. Giving Faris a wide berth, Maryam knelt beside her mother.

At dawn the next day, Abdallah's body was placed in an open casket and carried through the village on a bier by Faris and his uncles. Maryam walked behind her aunt, now a gaunt figure wearing a black shawl over her hair. Many of the Christian villagers joined in the procession as it wound its way past the spring and on to the little church on the knoll as the bell tolled rhythmically, creaking on its wooden beam.

Following at a distance were several of Wadee'ah's Druze neighbours who had come to pay their last respects. But the procession came to a sudden halt in front of the entrance to the church when the pallbearers realized that the bier was too wide to pass through. After a brief altercation, Faris and his uncles set the bier down in the shade of a cypress tree while the priest, who had been waiting for them in the nave, came out to meet them.

"I will conduct the service here," he said after assessing the situation.

Squinting at the coffin in the bright sun, he stumbled over the Syriac words of the funeral rite. Although it was the formal language of his faith, he had never mastered it. Distracted by the buzzing of a fly, he waved his hand repeatedly in front of his face, adding to his awkwardness. When he finally reached the committal, the pallbearers picked up the bier once again and carried it to the graveyard where the newly dug grave was marked by a pile of red earth and stones were heaped high on one side.

Bang... Bang...

Just as the priest was embarking on the most solemn act of all, several shots from a firearm rang out somewhere in the distance; the explosions echoed round the mountaintops, bouncing off the faces of the rocks. With the exception of an ashen Wadee'ah, the other mourners looked anxiously at one another. Were these gunshots from a party of men hunting quail and partridge, or were they the harbinger of something more sinister?

The rumours of the last few days had them all on edge. The priest paused before resuming his prayers, mumbling the words in haste. There was an unnatural silence as the coffin was lowered into the ground until it bumped on the loose stones at the bottom of the grave. Without warning Wadee'ah lunged forward, shrieking loudly.

"*Bihyat wladee*[38]," she wailed, swearing on her children's lives. "I have nothing left."

"You have your children," said Faris in a half-hearted attempt to comfort his mother.

Maryam held her breath as her aunt forced her way towards the grave. She was sure Wadee'ah would have thrown herself in had her mother not intervened at the last moment. Sa'adeh wrestled her away from the edge before leading her towards a toppled gravestone where it took several minutes for her fit of grief to subside. In the confusion, one of the Druze families slipped quietly away and hurried off towards the heart of the village. George handed the priest a few coins, which he slipped into the pocket of his cassock without counting. His attention was focused on the mountains.

"Do you see that?" he said, pointing to a spot on the slopes above them.

Following the line of his arm, Maryam could just make out a ragged man scrambling down the mountainside. He was moving with such haste that his feet dislodged a quantity of rubble and rocks which clattered down towards them. Disappearing momentarily behind some thick brush, he re-emerged bareheaded and with one of his sleeves almost ripped off. Then he resumed his descent, finally tripping over an exposed tree root and tumbling into the graveyard.

"We're at war with the Druze," he stammered as soon as he had caught his breath. "They've just attacked us." George and the priest exchanged glances.

"May the Lord and Saint Maroun defend us," the priest said as he rubbed his hand against his stubby nose.

George stooped down and helped the man to his feet, leading him to the same gravestone that Wadee'ah had been occupying a few moments earlier. Beckoning Joseph over, he told him to bring some water and strips of cloth.

"Let me go too, Abee," said Maryam. "I know where the ointment is."

Together she and her brother ran the short distance to the house and by the time they arrived back, the stranger had almost recovered himself.

"My friend," their father was saying as he squatted down beside the man. "Tell us exactly what's happened to you."

Taking a cloth, he wiped away a trickle of blood from a gash in his forehead. Maryam knelt down beside them and handed George the little pot of ointment made from the resinous leaves of pink rockroses. It was a well-known village remedy for open wounds.

"Have you heard the Druze have been storing up weapons in the mountains for some weeks?" the man said. Both George and the priest nodded.

"Yesterday there was fighting on the plains of Beirut," he went on. "Many villages were torched." George frowned, thinking the man was exaggerating. The priest, on the other hand, appeared to harbour no such doubts.

"That's the very thing that Bishop Tobias has been warning us about." The stranger nodded.

"Yesterday, two hundred Druze gathered on the Medairij Ridge and set off towards Zahleh. Some had muskets, others just fowling pieces." He paused to allow George to finish cleaning the gash. "But we beat them back."

"*Alhamdullilah*[39]," said the priest, his face lighting up in zealous glee as he seized the blood-smeared man by the shoulders and hugged him.

"Did anyone come to your aid?" asked George.

"Some men from Zahleh," the man admitted reluctantly. "They helped us chase them back over the pass."

"How many were killed?" From her father's persistent questions, Maryam could tell that he doubted the truth of the man's tale. "And who took care of the wounded?"

"Only a few on either side. We took our own dead and wounded back to the village."

George took the little jar from Maryam and began to rub ointment into the edges of the torn flesh with his large fingers. Then he turned his attention to his other cuts and scratches.

"They say that one of their leaders was badly injured," the man went on. "That's why I've come here to warn you."

"But we're on good terms with our neighbours."

"In case they fall on you in your sleep to avenge their leader's death," he replied sardonically. The priest leaned forward, eager to hear more; it had the makings of a fine Sunday sermon. But George seemed to have heard more than enough already.

"Stay with us tonight." From her father's tone, Maryam could tell that this was more than just an invitation. She knew her father would insist if need be.

"It's not safe to return to your village. We'll send someone with you tomorrow."

Tearing a strip off his own turban, he wrapped it around the man's head. Then he helped him to his feet and led him up the track towards the house. Maryam followed behind with Joseph.

"I wish I could join them," her brother said when he was sure that he was out of his father's earshot. "But I'm sure that Abee won't let me."

Maryam did not reply.

"He doesn't understand that they're threatening us."

The gunshots followed by the frantic man's sudden appearance during the burial had only increased his excitement from the night before. His sister, by contrast, walked on staring glumly ahead.

"What's the matter?" he said after a while, perplexed by her silence.

"You men always think you can solve things by fighting," Maryam found herself shouting at him. "What about the Druze people in this village? We've lived next door to them all our lives!"

"You're just a girl," said Joseph, giving Maryam a playful nudge. "You don't understand these things."

That evening as they sat eating their supper, George ordered his sons to build a shelter on the terraces where the fruit trees grew.

"We must take precautions," he said. "If you see armed men, spread the alarm. Don't try to tackle them alone." Maryam saw her brother pull a face, his disappointment evident.

"If it's only one or two, Abee, we can drive them off ourselves."

"No," said his father sternly. "These are uncertain times, and we don't know who will try to take advantage of them. Maybe the Druze or even Christians from other parts. It's happened before."

The injured man sat in silence under the impassive gaze of Imm George, barely able to eat his helping of stew. When they had finished their meal, Joseph and As'ad moved away to a corner of the room. Maryam could only just make out what they were saying because they were whispering to each other. But they need not have bothered because their father had stolen himself away and was sitting outside, staring into the darkness.

"It will be like the old days Teta told us about," Joseph was saying to As'ad, "when the Zahleh men won a great victory and chased the Druze back to Hawran."

"Were they like the people who live here?" asked his younger brother doubtfully. "We chase lizards together."

"No," Joseph said with hesitation, seeming unsure of his facts.

"They were different."

"Let's ask him," said As'ad, pointing to the stranger.

But the overwrought man was already half-asleep, his head nodding with fatigue. Some time later, George came in to check on his dressings while Sa'adeh went off in search of some spare bedding. Maryam helped her spread it out beside her brothers' mattresses. Before showing him where to sleep for the night, Sa'adeh took Joseph and As'ad to one side.

"Don't ask him any more questions," she told them, wagging her finger.

"Why not?" they whined.

"Because it will upset your father," she said. "Do you want to add to his worries?"

CHAPTER SEVEN

Mohanad had also heard about the confrontation between his own people and the Christians as well as the wounding of Ali Emad, son of Sheikh Khater. His father often spoke of the sheikh who was well-known among the local Druze in their village and the surrounding districts. A tall man with an angular face, they sometimes saw him when they gathered at the prayer halls on Thursday, or glimpsed him afterwards in deep conversation with the elders when they sat together in private.

When news reached the village that his son had been hit by a rifle shot fired by one of the Zahleh men and that he was close to death, there was widespread dismay amongst them. Boys carried the message to farmers as they worked in their fields and orchards and even up onto the steep mountainsides. Their women spoke of nothing else when they passed in the street or paid visits to one another's houses. Old men muttered about it as they sat outside their doors, recalling confrontations from years past.

That evening, when his family were all gathered in the house, Mohanad asked his father, Mahmoud, if they should join the other fighters whom, he had heard, were preparing to assemble in large numbers near the Damascus Road east of Sofar. It was said they wanted to avenge their defeat at the hands of the Christians the day before.

"People in Ayn el-Louz have talked about nothing else all day, Abee," he said with the same excitement that Joseph had shown the previous evening when he had learned of the incident at Jisr el-Qadi.

At first Mahmoud was reluctant to involve himself. When pressed by his son, he said he was unwilling to undermine the cordial relationship they enjoyed with their neighbours and the mutual trust that had been built up over the years. But when word arrived after dark that Ali Emad had died of his wounds and that Sheikh Khater had sworn revenge, his mood darkened and he changed his mind.

"We'll leave the village at dawn and join our brothers," he said to Mohanad whose pulse quickened at the prospect of joining in the war. His mother looked across the room at him with soulful eyes, but he ignored her.

"Although we have no quarrel with our neighbours here," his father duly explained, "there are times when a man must support his brothers."

The following day, while the morning dew was still clinging to the ground, father and son set out at first light to join the Druze force gathering where the road from Ayn el-Louz crossed the Beirut – Damascus highway. According to the latest rumours, they were planning to march on the hamlet of Dahr el-Baidar to open the road to Zahleh, one of the Bekaa Valley's central towns.

By the time they rounded the bend at the top of the village, the early mist had begun to lift. The villagers had yet to stir from their beds and wipe away the sleep from their eyes. Just as they were about to leave behind the last of the houses unobserved, Mohanad stopped in his tracks. His attention was drawn to a sturdy house with an ancient fig tree standing prominently to one side and a well-tended grapevine trailing over a wooden trellis.

He realized with a start that it was where the pretty Christian girl lived, the one whom he had talked to the day before. A smile teased the corners of his lips as he pictured her in the shelter, recalling her glossy hair and large, almond-shaped eyes. Try as he might, he still could not explain to himself why she had reacted in such a strange way to the medlar fruit they had shared together. Hadn't she enjoyed the taste?

His decision not to accompany her back to her family's house had been for both their sakes. Their meeting had happened by chance and his invitation to her was something he thought of on the spur of the moment. He was well aware that her parents would not welcome him and he did not want to get her into trouble for no purpose. Nevertheless, he made a mental note of where she had disappeared from view as she hurried home with the pitcher on her head.

Mohanad walked swiftly to catch up with his father who was striding on ahead of him, staff in hand. With no muskets or fowling pieces, they had armed themselves only with the billhooks they used every day in the fields.

"How will we defend ourselves?" he had asked his father before they set out.

"With these." Mahmoud had brandished a billhook above his head and stuck it in his waistband. As for provisions, they were carrying some coarse flour for bread as well as olives and dried fruit sufficient for only a couple of days since they had no idea how long they would be gone for. They had also brought their felt cloaks with them to guard against the night chill.

After two hours of brisk walking, father and son had skirted the wooded slopes of Jabal el-Barouk and reached the pass beyond. The highway stretched out ahead and on the other side, an area of open ground was dotted here and there with spiny clumps of broom adorned with clusters of bright yellow flowers. To the north, ancient tree-covered slopes led down to the steep valley of the Metn River and in the far distance, they could just make out the village of Bayt Meri where scuffles had broken out a few days earlier.

"We're here," said Mohanad, pointing across the road.

In front of them, scores of men were milling about in spite of the early hour. As they came closer, Mohanad's eyes alighted on a tall horseman swathed in a black cloak trimmed with gold thread. A sword hung from a colourful sash across his shoulder, its hilt glinting in the sunlight as he rode to and fro. Men swarmed around his white horse and clung to the saddle.

Most were dressed in *shirwals*, deep-seated pantaloons cinched below their knees. A few wore goatskin boots, but for the main part they were shod only in sandals, leaving their lower legs bare. Mohanad could see the horseman was giving orders to his lieutenants who, in turn, passed them on to their men. Little by little, the disparate mass began to coalesce into blocks.

"That's Sheikh Khater," his father shouted to him over the noise. Mohanad nodded. It was difficult for him to tear his eyes away from such a striking figure.

"I recognize him."

Men continued to pour onto the open ground from every side. Some carried only billhooks while others had come better armed. They wore swords over their shoulders and carried firearms of varying antiquity and manufacture in their hands. There were fowling pieces for hunting rabbits and partridge, brassbound muskets and matchlocks, family heirlooms passed down over generations. Very few, however, carried the new rifled musket. The Minie was considered to be especially deadly, being both powerful and accurate up to six hundred yards.

The oldest among them were grizzled veterans of earlier wars waged against a variety of enemies. They had fought the soldiers of Ibrahim Pasha amongst the abandoned villages and deserted monasteries of the Ledja, the volcanic wasteland to the east of Lake Houleh. They had dwelled in caves and hollows and ventured out at night like wolves, falling upon the Egyptian invaders as they slept in their camps. These men had experienced real hardship, forced to drink water from underground cisterns because the region ran dry of rivers and streams. As for food, they had eaten whatever they could catch, for the most part snakes and lizards. Only on rare occasions would a rabbit be added to the pot.

But wherever they had come from, uppermost in their minds that day was a desire for revenge against the swaggering arrogance of the Zahlawis. They had answered the call to arms because they felt in their hearts that the very Christians whom they had once welcomed into their villages were now threatening their way of life by challenging them for supremacy in their own mountain homes.

As for Mohanad, he was already feeling caught up in the excitement around him without knowing why. One of Sheikh Khater's lieutenants was giving orders to new arrivals astride a mule on the other side of the road, so they crossed it to present themselves.

"We've come to join our brothers." Mahmoud stood squarely in front of the man. The lieutenant looked down at them and asked them whether they had any previous military experience.

"None," said Mahmoud, shaking his head. He pointed to a motley group of men nearby.

"Join them," he said. "You can make up their numbers."

As they walked over to join the other recruits, Mohanad began to fidget with his bag of provisions. His father, on the other hand, stroked his moustache impassively.

"Where are you both from?" A fellow with sunken cheeks called out as they approached. The man carried an old flintlock in one hand. Hanging from a sash at his waist was a powder horn together with a leather pouch for musket balls and wadding.

"From Ayn el-Louz," Mahmoud answered in brief.

"I hear you grow fine apples there," he chortled. "Almonds, too?"

Mohanad looked round at his father's face and smiled to himself. He could see from his unchanged expression that he was unimpressed by the man's familiarity.

"Well, this evening we'll be taking our supper in Zahleh, if God favours us," the man went on, unperturbed. "Who knows what delicacies we'll find there?"

With little to do but to await further orders while the Druze forces assembled into some kind of marching order, Mohanad and his father sat down on a smooth rock and began to eat some of the food they had brought with them. Mahmoud took out a handful of dried apricots and divided them between himself and his son, but Mohanad was too excited to join in. Perhaps it was the pride that swelled in his chest at the sight of so many of his own people gathered in one place, a feeling that grew as the Druze emblem with its five-pointed star was unfurled. The light breeze made it flutter gracefully from side to side, obscuring the single point at the centre where the double triangles of green, red, yellow, blue, and white all came together.

"Green is the colour of peace," his father grunted. "I doubt we'll have much of that today."

The sun had now risen well into the sky and the day was becoming warmer. With the exception of a few stragglers, the men had already been divided into eight divisions of fifty or so, each one under the command of a lieutenant. Sheikh Khater rode along the front ranks, pausing to address old comrades. His review complete, he signalled to the whole force to march two abreast towards the town of Hammana, lying at the headwaters of the Metn River.

A murmur of surprise swept through the ranks at the order. Most of the men had been expecting to march east along the highway in order to engage the Christians directly, not away to the north. But a deafening drumroll drowned out the dissenters and the narrow column set off with its banners lowered and furled for the journey. Father and son marched side by side, falling into step with their comrades as they began the steep climb onto the opposite ridge.

As he glanced around him from the top, it became clear to Mohanad why the wily old sheikh had ordered this detour. It enabled all eight divisions to form up above the village unobserved by their enemies below. The stratagem had clearly been planned to avoid the mistake made by his son, Ali. Three days previous, he had attacked the hamlet from the road in full view of its defenders and failed.

Mohanad lay crouched in the brush beside his father, his heart beating wildly in his chest. In his hand he clutched the worn handle of the billhook. A few moments later, they were signalled to advance and the banners, which until then had been kept out of sight, were unfurled and held aloft. As the drums began to beat, Mohanad, whose earlier bravado had waned somewhat during the march, glanced anxiously at his father. But Mahmoud was already thinking of the fight to come and waited patiently beside his son humming the words of the old Druze war song under his breath:

We are the sons of Ma'rouf,
To whom honour and tributes are due.
We find sanctuary in our rocks,
And our secrets are known to few.
But when our blood is aroused,
And our spears have grown rusty,
And our swords are unsheathed,
But our scabbards smell musty,
We will burnish their blades,
Make our spear points glisten,
Until our anger fades,
And our enemies listen.

Their war cry swelled to a mighty roar as the voices of five hundred men joined together as one. Already cracks of sporadic musket fire could be heard from the village. As the noise around them grew louder, Mohanad's apprehension lessened and then disappeared altogether. He no longer cared what he was doing or even why. Below them, defenders ran from one side to the other, firing wildly without pausing to take proper aim.

At a command from their leader, the Druze divisions rose to their feet and began to advance steadily down the slope, trampling over the rocks and bushes that had hitherto hidden their presence. His heart racing, Mohanad quickened his step to keep pace with his father who held his wooden staff out in front of him like a lance.

As they neared the outlying houses, white puffs of smoke began to appear and the deafening crack of firearms became louder and more frequent. Mohanad could see clearly that the road at the western end of the village had been barricaded and that the villagers were only just beginning to take up new positions along the northern perimeter.

Some of them fired in ragged order at the advancing men. Others, keen to take the fight to their attackers, broke ranks and charged up the hill towards them while shots from their comrades below whistled over their heads. Holding the line, Mohanad was marching steadily forwards when he heard a loud crack. Almost instantly, he felt a dull impact against his right shoulder that spun him around, knocking him to the ground where he lay motionless while his comrades streamed past him down the hill.

When he came to his senses a few moments later, he staggered to his feet trying to retrieve his billhook but collapsed again, overcome by giddiness. The sounds of battle around him grew fainter and fainter until the last thing he remembered seeing was his father's face looking down at him, a dark form blotting out the open sky. He winced as he felt the pressure of his rough hands on his shoulder. Realizing that he could no longer hear the heavy footfalls of his comrades, he tried to look around but could not. In the distance, there was a crackle of musketry as the Druze charged forward.

In spite of Mahmoud's repeated attempts to stem the bleeding, blood continued to trickle from the hole in his son's shoulder where a musket ball was lodged. The minutes passed, and the initial numbness gave way to a deep, throbbing ache. Mohanad caught his father's eye as he knelt down beside him.

"Leave me, Abee. Join the other men."

"No." Mahmoud's forehead creased into a frown. "They will take the village without me. My place is with you."

Mohanad smiled back weakly. He lacked the strength to brush away the flies that clustered around his open wound. Shutting his eyes, he breathed in the smell of trampled earth. There was something else that he recognized, something he associated with his grandmother. His smile was little more than a pained grimace when it finally came to him that it was the smell of the crushed valerian roots she sometimes used in her concoctions.

The pressure of his father's hand on his shoulder eased momentarily and then he almost fainted as a fistful of dock leaves was packed against the wound and bound into place with a coarse piece of cloth. Far away, there were loud cheers as their comrades broke through the last defences and swept into the village. Their success, however, passed unnoticed by Mohanad who had already drifted back into unconsciousness.

When he awoke some time later, he became acutely aware of being jolted along on a makeshift stretcher. It felt rough against his back, and worse still he could not keep himself from rolling from side to side. The ache in his shoulder had become almost unbearable. Gritting his teeth against the pain, he reached out and grabbed hold of the forearm of one of the stretcher-bearers, thinking it was his father's…

Mohanad had begun to shiver, and by the time the party turned off the Damascus Road towards Ayn el-Louz, he was shaking uncontrollably. When they arrived back in the village, it was late afternoon and the sun had already started its descent. Some of the villagers came out of their houses to see what was happening as the small party made its way down the street. But upon seeing their sombre faces they retreated, hesitating to enquire openly about what had happened. Alerted by one of their neighbours, Mohanad's mother rushed up the road with his grandmother and his sister close on her heels. At the sight of his motionless body, they began shrieking but the stretcher-bearers ignored them and walked on in silence until they had reached the house. There, they set him down gently on the ground.

In the confusion that followed, Mahmoud tried to explain to his now hysterical wife that her son was not dying but had been wounded in the shoulder. He took her hand and pressed it to the boy's forehead, hoping that the warmth of his skin would reassure her. But she continued sobbing until he was finally forced to rebuke her.

"Take care of him," he said at last in exasperation. "Don't leave him here to lie with a ball in his shoulder."

Mohanad's eyes flickered open as she bent over him. He saw her push her white *mandeel* off her head and onto her shoulders. When she grasped his hand, he flinched with pain so she released it and began to mop his forehead instead, wiping away the film of dust and sweat. As he slipped back into oblivion, he heard her ordering the men to pick up the stretcher and carry it into the house.

His sister had already been despatched to her uncle's house to ask him to ride for the doctor, leaving his grandmother to set a pan of water on the brazier in preparation for the wound cleansing. They moved him onto a paillasse and covered him loosely with a blanket while his body continued to convulse. His dark eyes shone bright with the onset of fever.

Outside, neighbours were gathering at the door to learn first-hand what had happened. Unable to send them away, Mahmoud ushered them in one by one, explaining in the privacy of his own home what had taken place that day. News of the Christians' defeat had already reached Ayn el-Louz, but there was no public rejoicing amongst the Druze villagers who saw little reason to provoke their neighbours. Elsewhere in the Chouf, however, it was a claimed victory and volleys of shots were fired into the air in celebration.

But their triumph had come at a price; twenty of their own men had been killed in combat and many more wounded. The Christians, on the other hand, had suffered only half that number of casualties in spite of their defeat. There was one thing, however, that both sides could agree upon; namely that it was the superior leadership and guile of Sheikh Khater combined with the Druze army's discipline that had carried the day.

At dusk, the same doctor who had tended to the dying Abdallah only days earlier arrived on his mule to treat Mohanad. He examined the wound and immediately ordered the brazier to be stoked. As soon as the flames had subsided, he placed a cauterizing iron among the glowing coals. Pulling his surgical pincers from his leather bag, he set to work on Mohanad's shoulder while two men held the boy down.

Mohanad writhed in pain as the doctor poked around for broken bones. Failing to find any, he grunted and wiped his brow on his sleeve. Then he inserted his pincers into the hole and extracted the lead ball, dropping it with a clatter into a clay dish. Noting with satisfaction the dull red glow of the iron spoke in the fire, he ordered Mohanad's mother to stuff a wad of leather between the boy's teeth. Then he placed the rod against the tattered edges of the wound and rolled it delicately within his hand.

Sssssssssss, came the sound of hot iron on flesh.

Immediately the smell of burnt skin pervaded the room. The boy's body jerked violently before slumping back on the mattress. The wad of leather slipped out of his mouth and his arms fell limply by his sides.

Ignoring his mother's cries, the doctor continued to apply the hot iron until the wound had been thoroughly cauterized. Only then did he douse it in water and wipe his hands with a cloth. Sensing Mohanad's grandmother hovering behind him, he instructed the old lady to apply a poultice to draw out any infection which might have set in.

"It will help heal the flesh," he said to her as she nodded vigorously in agreement.

With the operation finished, Mohanad's mother regained her composure and quickly cleaned the doctor's instruments while Mahmoud pressed some coins into his hand. Following him outside, he handed him his bag and held the mule by the bridle as the doctor prepared to mount.

"We are in your debt, *Hakeem*[40]," he said, his voice heavy with gratitude.

"Doctors are required to heal the sick," he replied. "It's only a flesh wound, but it could become infected. Tell the old lady to give him something to sedate him."

"What should she give him, *Hakeem*?" Mahmoud asked. "She knows only village medicine."

"I'm sure she has a remedy to put him to sleep," he called out as he rode away.

Despite her son's scepticism, the boy's grandmother had understood at once what the doctor had meant and immediately produced a pot of dried tubers which, though wizened with age, still retained a pungent odour. She picked out two roots.

"What's that?" Mahmoud asked her.

"Indian spikenard," she replied. "It will send him to sleep."

With the shock of cauterization beginning to wear off, Mohanad was now awake and groaning with pain.

"Calm down, child," she said to him as she boiled some water over the fire and placed them in a small sachet. "I have something to take your pain away."

She soaked it long enough for the roots to infuse the hot water with their oil and then lifted the bowl to her grandson's slack lips while his mother raised him up.

"*Ughhh*." Mohanad took a sip of the liquid and nodded his head from side to side, but his grandmother insisted that he should take another and then another. With much effort, he managed to drain the bowl of all but the last dregs before falling back onto the pillow.

Then after a moment or two, his eyelashes began to flutter and the contorted muscles of his face relaxed. Under the watchful eyes of both women, he fell into a deep sleep.

No one in the village knew it at the time, but the skirmish that had taken place on the pass that day marked the beginning of a conflict that would rage on unchecked until the arrival of two foreign armies at the docks of Beirut. Within three months, what had begun as a series of domestic disputes among the villages of Mount Lebanon would spread from Beirut to Damascus and as far south as the villages and towns of Palestine.

CHAPTER EIGHT

Maryam had been outside sweeping the roof when she saw the small procession pass by her house late in the afternoon. Looking up in alarm, she noticed a group of men with white headcloths carrying a stretcher among them with a body strapped to it. It was a moment or two before she recognized the bushy moustache of Mohanad's father. He was walking beside them, his tunic ripped in several places and blood spattered on his sleeves. Maryam let her straw broom clatter to the floor.

"What's happened, Baboush?" Kneeling down, she held her pet goat's bony head in her hands. She blinked rapidly, betraying her anxiety.

Although Maryam had still been asleep when Mohanad and his father passed by at dawn, a dark sense of foreboding descended over her later that morning. The sight of the body-laden stretcher had only confirmed her worst fears as had the dishevelled appearance of Mohanad's father. She could already guess what must have happened. The boy she had shared those intimate moments with the day before had been badly injured or, worse, killed.

It was shortly after midday that she had heard a vague report about a confrontation between the local Druze and Christians from Zahleh near the Damascus Road. Although the news had unsettled her, she was not convinced that it was true. And it had never occurred to her that any of the combatants could have come from Ayn el-Louz.

But later in the day, rumours began spreading like wildfire amongst the villagers, disseminated in large part by strangers from both sides. Messengers had made their way south along the valley of the Barouk River in order to alert their brothers in faith to what was happening further north.

A stranger did indeed arrive in Ayn el-Louz later that afternoon in search of her father. He walked up to the house and asked for George by name. Sa'adeh invited him to sit down outside in the shade of the fig tree. She returned with a cup of water, the contents of which he gulped down in seconds.

He spoke of how they had barricaded the western entrance to their village in anticipation of an attack from that direction, but had been taken completely by surprise when the Druze charged down on them from the north. They had been defeated by trickery, not by force of arms, he fumed. Sa'adeh listened politely but Maryam was growing more and more nervous.

"Were many people killed?" she asked when he had finished.

"More of them than of us," the man boasted. "We fired at them as they ran down the hill. Some of us had the new Frankish rifled muskets."

"And injured?"

Sa'adeh looked sharply at her daughter, surprised at her unexpected curiosity.

"I don't know," he said, put off by her insistence. "I came straight here to alert you."

Her mother did not appear to be overly concerned. There had been confrontations between villages in the past and this might just be another one of those. But the stranger's remarks about Druze trickery seemed ominous, and Sa'adeh found it difficult to believe that their neighbours were capable of such things. But her opinion was not shared by her informant.

"You should take precautions," he warned as he drained the last of the water from his cup.

After accepting some bread and olives, he bade them farewell and set out into the fields to find George. Not long after he had left, Imm George arrived home. She listened intently to her granddaughter whose words confirmed some of the rumours she herself had heard during her visit to the neighbours. Her eyes narrowed as she adjusted a stray lock of grey hair that peeped out from under the tassels of her black turban as she waited for Maryam to finish.

"The Zahlawis are not the *qabadayet*[41] they once were," the old woman said with a dry laugh.

"Why do you say that, Teta?"

"Driven back by a few hundred men with muskets and billhooks in spite of those new-fangled Frankish guns?"

"Do you know if anyone from the village was involved?" Maryam asked, hoping that her grandmother might put her mind at ease. "Did any of them join the Druze army?"

"No. They should have more sense than to join in this madness."

Sa'adeh overheard her mother-in-law's remarks from the back of the room where she was spooning out grape molasses for the younger children. Dipping their fingers into the sticky syrup was one of their special treats.

"We're stronger than them," she called out. "We can raise twenty-thousand men to their ten."

"Maybe," replied Imm George. "But will they all fight on the same side? Just look at what that ruffian Taniyus is doing in Keserwan, attacking his own people and stealing their property."

"But the Alkhazens are rich and we're poor."

Maryam smiled despite her anxiety. She was witnessing one of the rare disagreements between her mother and grandmother.

"They have many things we don't, things we pay for with our taxes," Sa'adeh went on. "Rice and coffee while we make do with *burghoul* and *za'tar*[42] tea."

"That's the way it is," Imm George chided her daughter-in-law. "If things change, it won't necessarily be for the better."

At dusk, her father and brothers returned from the upper pastures. To Maryam's surprise, George made no mention of the stranger whom Sa'adeh had sent looking for him. Even when he sat down to take his boots off, he remained silent.

Together with her mother, Maryam served the men their food before retiring to the back of the room to let them eat alone. The smell of sweat from their bodies mingled with the rich aroma of the broth. Outside the only noise came from the rustling of chickens and the occasional barking of a dog. Suddenly, her brother broke the uneasy silence with a simple request.

"Let me join the army, Abee," Joseph asked his father without any warning. "I promise I'll be back in time to help gather in the harvest."

George carried on picking his teeth with a twig. After a moment or two, he stood up and put his arm around his eldest son.

"All young men want to do these things," he said. "But your place is here with us."

Maryam glanced round from where she was feeding the leftovers to the chickens. Her mother and grandmother were also paying close attention to what her father was saying.

"All the other boys are talking about it," Joseph protested. "I don't want to be left here all by myself."

"Have any of them already done it?" George replied, a note of firmness sobering his voice. "Besides, I've already discussed the situation with some of the other families." He fell silent and Maryam could tell from the look on his face that he was trying to find some way to convince her brother not to go. She knew that he preferred reason to restriction.

"It will antagonize our neighbours," he said finally in an effort to persuade his son to see the sense in what he was saying. "They're not threatening us and we shouldn't threaten them."

"But they already have," blurted out Joseph, the colour rising in his cheeks. "One of the boys has already joined with his father. It was him they were carrying back on a stretcher this afternoon."

"How do you know that?" George said, clearly surprised by the news.

"The boys told me when we were bringing the goats down from the mountains."

From the back of the room, Maryam let out an involuntary gasp. She instantly buried her face in the folds of her skirt, hoping that her family would think she was just sneezing. Her father and brothers looked round briefly while her mother, who was busy putting the mattresses out for the younger children, scarcely seemed to notice. Only Imm George, alert as ever, spotted it. She knew at once that her grandmother had not been fooled by her clumsy pretence.

The following day, Maryam got up as usual after her father and brothers had gone out. She had lain awake through most of the night, unable to prevent the vivid memory of yesterday's solemn procession from preying on her mind. Worse still, she felt unable to discuss the cause of her distress with anyone, not even her own grandmother. The way things were going, she feared that even Imm George would have little sympathy for her if she were to tell her the truth. She set off down the road with her empty pitcher and as she approached the spring, she became aware, for the first time, that something was seriously amiss in Ayn el-Louz.

To her surprise, the Christian girls were lined up on one side of the big stone basin with the Druze on the other as they waited their turns. But there was something else that struck her as odd. Instead of chattering and gossiping, the girls were talking amongst themselves in muffled whispers. Before long, Fatmeh appeared on the opposite side of the basin. Guessing how long it would take her to reach the spout, Maryam let two girls go ahead of her.

She had misjudged and by the time her turn arrived, Fatmeh had almost finished filling her jug. Nevertheless, she managed to catch her eye over the gurgling waterspout just as she was turning away.

"It was your brother they bought back yesterday," Maryam said quietly, barely able to hold back her tears. "What's happened to him?"

Instead of replying, Fatmeh merely nodded. She lifted the pitcher onto her head and began to walk slowly back up the trail towards her house. Maryam hastily filled her own jug and set off in pursuit. In a few moments she had caught up with Fatmeh, who ignored her and kept on walking with her eyes fixed firmly on the ground ahead. In desperation, Maryam tugged at her sleeve.

"Tell me. How is he?"

"Asleep."

"Is he badly hurt?"

"A musket ball hit him in the shoulder," replied Fatmeh in a neutral voice, neither friendly nor hostile. "He's weak."

"Oh my God," gasped Maryam. "May the Lord give him strength…"

"The doctor came yesterday evening to take the ball out," she continued in a monotone. "He sterilized the wound with fire and then my teta gave him some medicine."

A huge wave of relief swept over Maryam at the news that Mohanad was still alive. She smiled shyly at Fatmeh but as they walked on side by side, Maryam found to her shame that her initial relief had given way to a nagging feeling of frustration caused by the realization that she would never be able to find a reason to visit him in person, at least not while the conflict lasted. There was only one way to make contact, a way that would require the goodwill and cooperation of his sister.

Their encounter in the ʿarzal had excited her in a way she had yet to fully understand. It was the first time that she had been alone with a boy she found so attractive, and her girlish desires were intensified still further by her visceral dislike of Faris. She yearned for a way to communicate with him without a messenger, even if his sister were to agree to act as one. If only they could both read and write, they would be able to exchange letters. She knew in her heart what hers would say but wondered how he would respond once he had recovered enough to write back. Would he even wish to see her again? The sound of footsteps trailing behind them interrupted her thoughts, causing both Maryam and Fatmeh to stop in their tracks. It was one of the Druze girls from the spring.

"Why are you talking to her?" she spat at Fatmeh. The girl said nothing and continued walking.

"Shame on you!" the girl continued, no longer bothering to keep her voice down. "They've killed one of our leaders and wounded your own brother. We're at war."

Lifting the pitcher slowly off her head, Mohanad's sister turned to face her accuser while Maryam stood by meekly, hoping she would not be drawn into the confrontation.

"Elsewhere maybe," hissed Fatmeh. "But here we're not at war and if I want to talk to one of them, I will."

Taken aback by the vehemence of her response, the other girl just stood in the road, her mouth agape.

"Stay away from me," Fatmeh warned her. With that, she picked up her jug and set off again towards her house while the other girl glared back, seething with indignation. In the confusion, Maryam quietly slipped away.

Later that day when she was lighting the fire for the *tannour*[43], Maryam saw her father coming down the track well before dusk.

"Where's Joseph?" he called out, while he was still some way off. "He went out to the terraces this morning," he said with urgency, pointing to the northern slopes. "And I haven't set eyes on him since."

When neither Maryam nor her mother replied, he looked round at Imm George who was skinning a rabbit beside a stack of pruning, the sleeves of her blouse rolled up to the elbow and a sharp knife in her right hand.

"I haven't, either," she said as she picked up a hatchet to chop the head off the carcass. "And I've been here all afternoon."

George frowned. Lines of worry furrowed his brow. He sat down beside his mother and rested his head in his hands. Out of the corner of his eye, he glanced across at Maryam.

"Did you speak to him this morning?" he asked her gently.

She was about to say no but hesitated, remembering something unusual that had occurred. She wondered whether she should mention it to her father. As much as she hated the idea of her brother joining the fight, she also did not want to get him into trouble. It wasn't something either of them would easily forgive.

"He came back for his felt cloak this morning," she said finally. "When I asked him why, he just laughed."

Without another word, George threw down his mattock and bounded up the steps two at a time. The moment he reached the top, he set off in the direction of the Damascus Road.

CHAPTER NINE

Joseph had been thinking of joining the militia ever since he had first heard that one of the boys from the village, along with his father, had been part of the Druze army that had attacked Dahr el-Baidar a few days earlier. He had been bitterly disappointed by his father's refusal, so that night as he lay awake next to his younger brother, he vowed to strike out on his own even though it meant disobeying him.

"I could be doing what Teta used to tell us about," he muttered to himself as he tossed and turned.

The next day, before As'ad set out for the high pastures with the flock, Joseph took his younger brother aside while his father was off fetching his mattock and told him of his plan. As'ad was about to insist that he, too, should go when George returned. Unable to continue his protest in front of his father and surrounded by bleating goats, the boy just stood glowering at his brother in envy.

Joseph followed George into the fields that morning and waited patiently for his chance to abscond. When his father told him to go over to the northern terraces and finish mending the walls there, he could hardly believe his luck. Leaving George wandering among the mulberry trees, he set off in that direction before doubling back to the house to retrieve his cloak. Moments later, Joseph was heading for the Damascus Road with nothing but his billhook and his cloak bundled up under his arm. As for food, he carried only the meagre provisions that he usually took for his midday meal. Without an elaborate plan to go on, he only knew he should turn east when he reached the highway and look for the army at Dahr el-Baidar.

After an hour's brisk walk, he sat down on the side of the road near the remains of an abandoned village to drink a mouthful of water from his flask. With his back against a tree trunk, Joseph listened to the chirps of the small birds flitting through the branches above his head. His spirits were only dampened by the thought of what his father would do when he discovered that he had run off. The best he could hope for was a sound thrashing. It was not that George was cruel towards his children, but at times he could be strict and Joseph knew that he would not take kindly to being deliberately disobeyed over such an important matter. One trait he shared with his father, though, was determination. And now that he was resolved to join the fight, nothing could dissuade him from doing so. Setting off again, he skirted around the weathered limestone spur that lay east of the village.

It was not long before he caught his first glimpse of the highway and the sight of so many people bustling along the carriage way stopped him in his tracks. It was the first time Joseph had travelled any real distance from Ayn el-Louz, and there he was standing on the main route along which travellers and tradesmen journeyed back and forth from the coast to the interior.

Although the paved surface was only wide enough for one wagon to pass at a time, to Joseph it seemed as broad as anything he could imagine. Within moments, an oncoming cart forced him to jump aside to let it hurtle by. Before he had time to recover his wits, another came barrelling towards him from the opposite direction. He watched open-mouthed as both carts clattered towards each other in a cloud of dust.

At the very last second, one of them lurched to one side, avoiding a collision by no more than a whisker. Grumbling angrily, the driver who had given way pulled his horse back onto the road and narrowly avoided scraping his wheel on a pile of paving stones left at the roadside by the Frankish engineers. They had been engaged by the authorities in Beirut to widen the carriageway, but as soon as they had caught wind of the clashes in the mountains, they abandoned their work and decamped unceremoniously for the coast.

As he made his way up the steep incline towards the pass, Joseph came across a steady stream of people travelling in both directions. Some rode on the backs of mules and horses, but most tramped by on foot. His ears were assaulted by a cacophony of different accents, greetings, and curses shouted by the travellers to one another as they went by.

"May God lighten your footsteps, *ya hajjeh*[44]," one man called out to an old woman as she shuffled by with a basket over her head.

"And may He bless your hands," she cackled back.

"Why are you in such a hurry, Abou Steif?" called out another. "Are the bailiffs at your heels?" The man in question hurried on, ignoring the remark.

"Move out of my way, you old donkey," yelled the driver of a smartly upholstered carriage.

Taken aback by the man's rudeness, Joseph wondered whether he was trying to impress his master by cursing the elderly peasant who had just stepped in front of him. Unperturbed, the old man turned his weather-beaten face towards the driver and gave him a malevolent stare before retreating just far enough to avoid being hit by the wheel hub.

As shocked as he was by some of the exchanges, Joseph was nevertheless thrilled by the sheer variety of the people he saw all around him. When a party of rich townsfolk rode by on well-groomed horses, he tried to stop himself from gawking at their retinue of servants and pack animals loaded high with baggage. Never before had he seen such a sight.

Jostling for space with the other travellers were men and women in simple mountain dress making their way to the local markets. Some carried large baskets of fruits and vegetables strapped to their backs, held in place by bands of coarse sacking stretched taut across their foreheads. Others toted wicker cages full of squawking poultry or dragged behind them a single bleating goat.

Joseph strode on through the tumult towards the top. It took some time to reach it, but when he got there he found himself looking down on a huge valley stretched out like a patchwork quilt, bounded by a second chain of mountains in the hazy distance. To the southeast, a tracery of ditches and rivers snaked lazily through a lush wetland and beyond them, the snowy cap of a huge mountain surged majestically into the sky. To the north, the plain broadened and stretched off into the distance. Some of the higher peaks on its western edge were still streaked with ice and snow despite the early summer sun.

Throwing his cloak over his shoulder, Joseph set off again and as he rounded the next bend, he came across a villager armed with a musket standing by the remains of an overturned barricade. On his head was a black turban.

"Is this Dahr el-Baidar?" he asked him politely.

"It was," the sentry said gruffly, pointing behind him at the remains of a building. "Where have you come from?"

"From Ayn el-Louz, *ya 'ammee.*" The man scowled at him from beneath the folds of his turban.

"If you've come to fight the Druze, you're too late," he said with ill-tempered sarcasm. He gestured at a house not fifty yards away that was still smouldering, its roof caved in and the front door lying in pieces on the ground where it had been ripped off its hinges.

"I'm here to join my brothers," said Joseph.

"They've gone to Kfar Selwan," the sentry retorted. "Maybe they'll do a better job for them than they did for us."

Joseph looked down glumly at his boots. He had never heard of the place and had no idea where it was. It was already midday, the time when he would normally have found a shady tree to rest under. But this was no ordinary day, and although he had left home only that morning, he already felt that his old life was now far behind him. Determined to fulfil the vow that he had made the night before, he stood his ground.

"Show me where this Kfar Selwan is."

The man set down his musket and stared at Joseph. Sensing that the boy was serious, he pointed northwest.

"It's on the other side of that mountain," he said. "But the climb is too steep and the ravines too deep for you to walk there as the crow flies. Go back down the road and take the track which passes by the waterfall above Falougha." Joseph nodded to show that he had understood.

"Don't go into the village because you won't be welcome there," he continued. "Skirt around it and follow the curve of the mountain."

"Is it far?" Joseph felt somewhat daunted by the prospect of setting out into the unknown all alone.

"If you leave now, you should arrive before sunset."

Shouldering his musket, the man began walking back towards the smoky ruins of his village while Joseph hitched up his pantaloons and retraced his earlier steps. He found the road with little difficulty, turned north over the side of a mountain, and then down into a large, grassy depression strewn with shale. As the shadows began to lengthen, Joseph quickened his pace, fearing that he would not reach his destination before dark. The distant bark of a jackal echoed against the sides of a ravine somewhere ahead, making him shiver at the prospect of spending the night alone in the mountains. Hunching his shoulders, he pressed on through the wild and desolate countryside.

It was sometime later that several flickering lights appeared in the gloom of the early evening. Thinking that he had at last reached the village, he hurried towards them until the sound of babbling water made him stop short. There was a rustle from a thicket of poplars near the bank. At first he thought it was a heron but after a few moments, a sentry emerged from behind the trees holding a musket with its hammer raked back.

"Who are you?" he said, peering down the barrel at Joseph.

"Joseph from Ayn el-Louz," he replied with one eye on the musket levelled at him. "I have come to join the militia."

"Follow me," the man said after a long pause.

There was a soft click as he released the hammer. He led Joseph through the trees to a clearing where a number of men were sitting around a fire, fishing for pieces of broiled meat in a pot. One of them delved into the greasy stew with his wooden skewer and brought out a rabbit's leg impaled on the tip.

He held it out to Joseph who took it in his fingers, muttering his thanks. His long trek through the mountains had left him tired and starved. As he began to pull the meat off the bone with his fingers, the sentry bent down and whispered something into the man's ear. The others peered at Joseph with a mixture of curiosity and suspicion.

"We're here to protect the villages," the man said in a voice that had a ring of authority. "Can you help us?" Joseph nodded, his mouth too full to speak.

"I cannot spare any of my men," he continued. "But you can go and find Taniyus of Reifun."

Joseph paused while he tried to remember who this Taniyus was. He had heard his grandmother mention the name but, for the life of him, he could not remember when or why.

"Who is he?" he said finally, overcoming his reluctance to show his ignorance in public.

"The leader of the *'ammiyyeh*[45]," the man explained patiently. "They say that he can call on ten-thousand armed men in Keserwan alone."

"What do you want me to do?" Joseph was puzzled. He could not understand why a newcomer like him should be asked to carry out such an important task.

"Ask him to join us."

"Why me? Why not one of your own men?" There was an uncomfortable silence as the other men looked at him.

"He may be a simple blacksmith, but he's as cunning as a fox," their leader said at last. "We've sent word to him before but he's still in

Keserwan with his men." The men gathered around the fire nodded their heads in agreement.

"Perhaps a lad like you will have better luck by appealing to his sense of pride."

At this, the men started to laugh amongst themselves. But Joseph could still feel their eyes upon him in the darkness. He wondered briefly if he was capable of carrying out the task before realizing that this was why he had come all the way to Kfar Selwan in the first place. After a moment's thought, he nodded in acceptance.

"Tonight you stay with us," said their leader, seizing him around the shoulders. "Taniyus and his men are camped outside Bikfaya, a day's travel to the northwest. Set out at daybreak and I'll give you an official letter of request before you go."

The suspicious looks were now replaced by friendly smiles and words of encouragement as the men gathered around him, welcoming him into their camp. Wrapped in his felt cloak and seated at the fire's edge, Joseph listened to their stories of the defeat the day before. The heat from the fire made him feel drowsy and after a while he began to look around for a quiet place to sleep in spite of the camaraderie of his new friends. Noticing the boy's weariness, the leader gave him the letter that had been drafted earlier in the evening by the only literate man in the camp.

"Make sure you give it to no one else," he said, handing over a sealed pouch.

Joseph awoke before the others had begun to stir, just as dawn was breaking. Filling his flask from the nearby stream, he set out north in the direction that he had been shown the night before. Ancient pine forests lined either side of the trail, broken here and there by terraces of mulberry trees. After five miles or so along a narrow ridge, he rounded a spur and immediately found his path disappeared into a deep ravine with a torrent flowing swiftly along its bottom. Although he did not know it, he was standing above Wadi el-Jameijim, the valley of skulls.

Forced to decide between crossing and making a wide detour, he gazed down into the sunless depths with dismay. But as his eyes grew accustomed to the dim light, he found the faint trace of a path that had been carved into the face of the cliff. Lowering himself over the edge, he began to clamber along it, clinging onto the tangled roots above to steady himself.

It was sometime before he reached the far side. Each time a piece of rock broke away in his hand, it skittered down the wall before landing at the bottom with a single, reverberating thud. Levering himself over the topmost ledge, he finally collapsed on the ground where he lay panting. By the time he looked up again, the sun had already passed its zenith.

He got to his feet and trudged off down the track past the bulky silhouette of a *serai*[46] on a hilltop. A group of surly-faced muleteers were driving their heavy-laden animals towards him. They ignored him and continued on their way, shouting gruffly to one another as they switched the rumps of their mules with their long canes.

In spite of the sharp pangs of hunger, Joseph pressed on, determined to meet with Taniyus and his men as soon as he could. To keep his spirits up, he took to humming a song that the old ladies of his village used to sing on wedding days.

Aweeha[47], *what a lucky bridegroom!*
Aweeha, how beautiful a bride!

It was late afternoon by the time he came across Taniyus's men camped in an orchard above Bikfaya. No sentry challenged him nor was there anyone on watch. Instead, all he heard was the sound of men's raucous voices from below. When he looked down, he saw a large encampment spread out haphazardly among the trees.

Some men were sitting beside bivouacs made from jute sacking while others lay sprawled under awnings tied between the tree trunks. Uncertain of his welcome, Joseph decided to keep out of sight until dusk. He found a spot to hide in and settled down to wait, observing the comings and goings below.

The Keserwanis went about their daily chores as the shadows grew longer, unaware of his presence above them. Some gathered quince and apple sticks for their cooking fires while others mended their clothes or sharpened their knives and swords. A few tended the mules and horses that were picketed in a line along the camp's perimeter.

When darkness fell, he started walking down the hill towards them. The closer he came, the more he felt there was something strange about their camp. Even to his untrained eye, he could see that it was oversupplied with provisions. Strewn around on the ground or stacked carelessly in heaps under the awnings were sacks of grain and large clay jars, the sort used to store olive oil and wine. He paused by the picket lines to count the horses. *Where could they have all come from?* That was when he remembered what his grandmother, Imm George, used to say.

"They're an undisciplined rabble!" The old lady had been complaining with her usual bluntness about their reported habit of carrying away what plunder they could and burning the rest. That kind of wanton destruction affronted her sense of husbandry. She was just as critical about their uprising against their landlords.

"Why are Christians fighting each other, Teta?" Joseph had asked her once.

"Because they're donkeys who can't pay the miri *even in the good years," Imm George had said with undisguised disdain. "And what's worse is they've chosen some ruffian blacksmith as their chief."*

With a start, Joseph now realized that the blacksmith in question was the very man whose help he had been sent to enlist. No wonder the men at Kfar Selwan had been so delighted when he had accepted the commission the previous evening. Too late to change his mind, he looked around and out of the corner of his eye saw a man tending to his horse on the picket line. The fellow ignored him and continued loosening the horse's girth.

"Where is Taniyus of Reifun?"

"So you want to speak to the great *za'eem*[48]," he said at last, chuckling to himself in amusement. Joseph touched his shirt where the precious letter was concealed.

"I have an important message for him." The horseman laughed and carried on unsaddling. When he had finished, he gestured in the direction of the camp.

"Over there."

Following his arm, Joseph saw that he was pointing to a group of men gathered round a lanky fellow sprawled on some cushions. A newly lit fire blazed nearby, throwing shadows onto the canvas stretched above his head. In one hand he held the mouthpiece of a water pipe and in the other a small cup of steaming liquid from which he took the occasional sip. Around his shoulders was a finely woven goat-hair *'abaya*[49], trimmed with gold. By contrast, his companions were dressed only in simple felt cloaks.

In front of him, a man lay pinioned on the ground by two guards. At his order, they relaxed their grip and allowed the prisoner to rise to his knees. He began to babble and then dodged between them, seizing the hem of the man's cloak in his hand. To the crowd's amusement, he began covering it with kisses. There were loud jeers as the guards dragged him away and drove him into a nearby thicket with a barrage of well-aimed kicks. Seizing the opportunity, Joseph stepped out of the shadows.

"*As-Salaamu 'alaykoum*[50], Excellence," he began awkwardly. The crowd laughed, amused by his deference.

"I have a personal message for Taniyus of Reifun," he began in a nervous monotone. "From the defenders of Dahr el-Baidar."

The man in the *'abaya* took a long pull on his pipe and stared back at him. Then he let out a hoot of laughter and, as if on cue, all the men around him joined in. But their merriment ceased abruptly when he turned to Joseph with a scowl, shaking his unkempt hair and scratching his beard.

"I'm Taniyus. What do you want with me?"

Joseph drew the letter out of his shirt very slowly to avoid alarming the guards and handed it to him. Breaking the seal with his clumsy fingers, Taniyus passed it at once to a man standing behind him who pored over it for a minute or two and then leaned forward to explain its contents to his chief.

"I came with my men from Reifun when I heard the so-called *qabadayet* of Zahleh had been beaten by the Druze," Taniyus said after a brief pause. He chortled to himself at some hidden irony while his companions smirked.

"Now they're asking me to protect the Christians and the Shehab princes who cower like dogs in their palaces at Baabda."

It was clear to Joseph that this speech was aimed at his followers, not him. Nonetheless, he was a courageous boy and held Taniyus's gaze, refusing to be browbeaten by the man's bluster.

"Why do they turn to me now?" he said with a coarse laugh. "Is it because I'm the man who curbed the greed of the Alkhazens and sent them packing to Beirut?"

Joseph continued to stand his ground.

"Your people used to treat me like a blacksmith," he continued. "But at least the priests showed me some respect. The Turks, too."

"He's right," the men around him muttered, nodding their heads in agreement. Joseph shifted uneasily from one foot to the other while Taniyus reached over to take a sip from his cup.

"You can tell whoever sent you we have enough to do here," he said with a flourish, concluding his little homily. "They say the Druze will take us on. Let them. As for the Chouf, that's the Zahlawis' problem."

With that, he picked up the letter and threw it in the fire before turning his back on Joseph. The interview had come to a sudden end. Realizing that he had failed to secure the man's support and not knowing what else to do, Joseph trudged wearily back to the horse lines. Then just as he was wondering where he would find a meal, the horseman whom he had spoken to on his arrival called out to him.

"Are you hungry, *ya walad*[51]?"

"Yes," Joseph replied.

He made his way over to the fire where he sat down silently as the horseman rummaged through his bags before preparing a simple meal of *hummous*[52] and wild greens. When they had both eaten, Joseph wrapped himself in his cloak and lay down at the fire's edge, listening to the rustling and snorting of the horses and mules as they cropped the damp grass in the darkness.

At first he felt shamed by his lack of success. But after a while he realized that his mission had been doomed from the start. It was clear that the Keserwanis had no intention of leaving their plundering grounds to risk their lives against the Druze. Disappointed but still determined to play his part, Joseph resolved to leave the camp at first light and travel the road to Zahleh.

"Perhaps I will meet with better luck there," he murmured to himself as he closed his weary eyes.

PART II

Take us the foxes, the little foxes that spoil the vines: for our vines
have tender grapes.
My beloved is mine, and I am his; he feedeth among the lilies.
Until the day break, and the shadows flee away, turn, my beloved,
And be thou like a roe or a young hart on the mountains of Bether.

~ Song of Solomon 2:15-17 ~

CHAPTER TEN

Hasbaya
Late May, 1860

Nadeem Rayyes, the confidential secretary of the Emir Sa'deddine, looked out in despair from the roof of the citadel where he and his family lived in comfortable apartments on one of the upper floors. The rambling old castle had belonged to the family of his patron since the Shehab family had won it in battle from the Crusaders in 1170 A.D.

The last rays of the evening sun cast a soft luminescence on the kaleidoscope of mosaics decorating the walls, glinting off the pink, black, and yellow stones quarried in the nearby mountains. He continued to stand there with a creased brow as the sun dipped over the horizon leaving the market town of Hasbaya, perched on the foothills of Mount Hermon, in unfathomable shadow.

All afternoon, a procession of peasants and farmers from the surrounding countryside had been heading for the safety of the citadel and protection of their Emir. He watched as they made their way through the olive groves beside the Hasbani River and across the stone bridge that spanned it just southwest of the town.

A large number of families had arrived earlier that day and were already camped out noisily in the castle's main courtyard as well as the forecourt of the little mosque that stood opposite. Nadeem glanced at the two stone lions flanking either side of the entrance. He could not help but wonder, *do they truly believe that these ancestral beasts will protect them as they do the rabbits to which they are forever bound by these chains carved into stone?*

The advancing Druze had caused the Christians to flee not only from their villages to the south of town, but also from as far away as Banias at the head of the Jordan Valley. Rumours of a confrontation the previous day at the village of Deir Mimas had made them fearful of the large Druze force that had marched northwards from Hawran. Its presence had undermined the trust and tolerance that had hitherto existed between the two communities.

The fact that the Christians had so far succeeded in fending off their attackers had neither reassured them nor delayed their hurried exodus from the countryside. And so headlong had their flight been that most of those seeking refuge in Hasbaya were barely able to load their most valuable possessions onto the backs of mules and donkeys.

Rickety oxcarts struggled up the hill towards the town beside those on foot who carried just their cooking pots on their heads and their bedding strapped to their backs. They had brought with them what little food they could carry in the hope that it would sustain them until they could return to their houses and farms.

It was late May and the grain harvest had yet to begin. Stalks of wheat and barley stood tall and uncut in the fields, their ripening ears nodding gently in the fresh valley breeze. On the rounded hillsides of Wadi Taym, the silvery leaves of olive trees fluttered on twisted branches as their fruits began to swell with oil. Clusters of unripened grapes hung from the vines on higher slopes under the early summer sun.

Nadeem himself was a cultured man who had come to the market town of Hasbaya from the great city of Damascus where his family, Greek Catholics of the Melkite order, had lived for two generations. His grandparents had arrived there from Ma'loula, a town of monasteries and churches lying in a gorge some distance northeast of Damascus.

He had taken service with the Ottomans and found employment in the governor's office, first as a clerk and then as a secretary overseeing matters of trade and commerce. Around that time his mother had found him a suitable bride, a girl from another Melkite family, as was customary in those days. Shortly after they were introduced to each other, the couple became engaged and were married.

To Nadeem's relief, he soon discovered that his new wife had attended classes at a convent in the city and, like him, had learned to speak French. His marriage to Layal proved to be a success from the start. Although it had been arranged entirely by his mother, Nadeem had submitted willingly to her plans and had approved of her choice for him. He found his new spouse had everything that he could wish for and more.

His quiet efficiency and good judgement in matters of business together with his fluent knowledge of French soon brought him to the attention of none other than the Emir Sa'deddine el-Shehab, the traditional ruler of Hasbaya and its surrounding towns and villages, who had taken up temporary residence in the city after fleeing from his more rebellious subjects.

During the several discussions he had held with Nadeem, the Emir had tried to convince the young Ottoman functionary to give up his post and accompany him back to Hasbaya. On one occasion when they were taking coffee and dates together in his private rooms, they began discussing the chinaware on which the refreshments were served. It bore the mark of an English manufacturer.

"The Franks prosper from their science and industry," the Emir had said, "while we – the descendants of the noble Arab tribes – continue to dwell in our dens among rocks in spite of our glorious past."

"With all due respect, Your Highness," Nadeem had replied, "we live in a great and cosmopolitan empire under the enlightened rule of the Sultan."

"That may be so," the Emir responded with a sigh as he set down his cup. "But it is you who must help me learn the secrets of the Franks."

Despite the promise of advancement and the prospect of considerable wealth, Nadeem had been reluctant to leave the Ottomans at first. It was only when he had been offered full responsibility for the conduct *of the Emir's affairs as his confidential private secretary that he had finally accepted.*

He and his wife bid their families farewell and followed the Emir and his retinue back to the provincial backwater of Hasbaya. Not surprisingly, it had taken time for them to settle into their new surroundings although they had been given some of the best-appointed apartments in the castle.

Little by little, they had both come to enjoy the bucolic simplicity of this quiet market town. But there were some aspects of Damascene life that Nadeem sorely missed, among which were the long afternoons he used to spend in the luxury of the city's bathhouses. He longed to feel the rasp of the loofa on his back and the tingle of cold water on his skin after the clammy heat of the hot rooms.

Little else compared to the Noureddine Hammam, an oasis of tranquillity and a hotbed of gossip located in the sprawling Hamidiyyeh market. There he could sit with his friends over a cup of tea by the fountain or relax in the hot rooms as the mousawabee[53] *kneaded his shoulder muscles while telling him of the latest rumours circulating in the city.*

It had not taken Nadeem long to realize that the Emir's coffers were already sadly depleted. Like elsewhere in Syria, its traditional clothing industry was fast disappearing, a decline hastened by the London Convention which the Ottoman Sultan had signed twenty years earlier in order to curry favour with the European powers. As a result, more and more Ottoman citizens were wearing clothing made from cotton spun and dyed in the factories of France and Britain instead of the hand-woven jubbahs[54] and kaftans for which the Syrian towns had once been famous.

"Since our Sultan signed that treaty with the Franks, the number of looms here has fallen from two hundred to less than fourteen," Nadeem had reported to the Emir during one of their daily audiences.

"I know," the old man sighed. "That's why we must discover their

secrets before it is too late."

The decline had forced Nadeem to think of other ways to make up for the lost revenue; which was why his thoughts had turned to the fertile hillsides of Wadi Taym with their rich olive groves and vineyards. They produced a steady income along with the fields of wheat and barley that chequered the valley floor. A ready market for these crops already existed in Zahleh and Damascus, unaffected by the terms of the new treaty.

He had initially climbed the worn stone staircase to count the number of men and women now clogging the narrow streets of the town. But the sheer size of the influx made it impossible to tally. The best he could do was make a rough estimate of the crowd below.

The Emir, too, had heard reports of the large numbers arriving from the surrounding countryside and had already ordered his kitchens to provide them with as much food as they could spare. But in spite of his generosity, such was the scarcity of bread that a bundle of loaves, which usually cost no more than a few coins, was now selling for a whole purse of piasters.

Some of the poorest families had neither food nor money and had already been reduced to eating whatever they could scavenge from the houses of wealthier townsfolk. Many could be found scouring the gardens and public places in town for unripe mulberries which they chewed for what little nourishment they could glean from them.

Earlier that afternoon, Nadeem had been summoned to the apartment of the Emir to take down a formal letter addressed to the Ottoman Governor of Damascus, which the old man had dictated to him in a voice wavering between indignation and despair. It contained an official complaint against the new garrison commander, Osman Bey.

Though couched in the obligatory courtesies, the letter made it very plain that he was failing what the Emir considered was in his primary duty, namely that of providing protection for the Shehab family. An undertaking, the Emir sought to remind the governor, that he himself had given before the Emir had left Damascus to return to his castle.

The discord below reminded Nadeem of something that had happened a few days earlier which still weighed on his mind. It was Osman Bey's insistence that the Christians, and not the Druze, should surrender their arms in order to defuse the growing tension in the town. At a meeting the previous day that he had attended, the garrison commander had assured the Emir the intentions of the Druze were peaceful.

What appeared to be warlike posturing, he had said, were actions aimed only at protecting their own people. To this effect, he had also informed the Emir of a recent meeting he had held with the Druze elders just to the south of town at the sacred prayer halls of el-Bayada. There seated on the circular stone bench in the shade of an oak grove, the elders had given him their solemn oath that their people would not attack the Christians.

"Why should the Christians not give up their arms?" the garrison commander had argued. "If it ensures peace…"

Nadeem had counselled the Emir against advising his subjects to accept the plan. He was worried by the presence of so many local Druze camped on the outskirts of town and by rumours that reinforcements were on their way from Hawran. But in the end, the old man was too fearful to turn down Osman Bey's request.

"We will complain to the governor," he told Nadeem later in a voice filled with quiet desperation. "He'll order the Turks to protect us. If we don't agree now, I fear they'll attack the town."

Nadeem had not insisted, and a few days later a large number of the Christian inhabitants had deposited their muskets in the courtyard of the citadel. Osman Bey was there to witness the spectacle. When they had finished, he ordered a small detachment of Ottoman soldiers to load them onto mules and take them away. Striding up and down the courtyard trailing the tip of his sword in the dust, he had assured the now defenceless Christians that he and his men would come to their aid if they were attacked.

But the mule train had no sooner left the town than rumours began to circulate that the Druze had seized the weapons under the very eyes of the Ottoman escort who, it was said, had stood aside and let them do so. When these stories got back to the townspeople, they began cursing Osman Bey, muttering to each other that they should have never trusted the Turks in the first place.

Nadeem had tried to verify these rumours so that he could lodge an official complaint with the Ottoman authorities in Damascus, but he could find no eye-witnesses. No one would come forward and testify that they had seen the weapons seized.

As soon as Nadeem was finished writing the letter and the Emir had placed his crimson seal on the soft wax, he had sent down to the stables for a horseman with instructions to ride straight to Damascus.

"Seek immediate admittance to the governor's presence," he had told him. "If you are questioned, say you have a message from the Emir Sa'deddine el-Shehab."

CHAPTER ELEVEN

Descending the stairs, Nadeem made his way along the stone corridor to his own apartments where he knew his wife would be waiting for him. Outside, he could hear the blind *mu'ezzin* singing the evening call to prayer from the top of the hexagonal minaret as the silver-faced moon climbed into the night sky. Stopping by one of the windows, he saw the Emir shuffling stiffly across the courtyard towards the little mosque, saluting the families camped there with a limp wave of his hand. Several of his sons and grandsons accompanied him, the gold thread of their *'abayas* glinting in the moonlight.

Layal was there to greet him at the door and pour rosewater from a delicate brass bowl over his hands. Drying them gently, she led him over to a divan on one side of the main reception room.

"Bring a pipe and some coffee," she called out to the servants.

Nadeem sank into the cushions, trying to put the worries that had plagued him all day out of his mind. His shoulders slackened as Layal's fingers kneaded the muscles of his back with the expertise of a *mousawabee* although her touch was lighter and much more soothing. Closing his eyes, he abandoned himself to the movement of the servants around him and the rich aroma of freshly ground coffee. His wife's lips grazed the shell of his ear.

"*Ya habeeb qalbee*[55]," she murmured softly. "I've been to see what I can do for the poor people in the courtyard below." Nadeem said nothing, waiting for her to continue. He knew that Layal would not be denied her say in the matter of the refugees.

"They're complaining that Osman Bey has tricked them," she began. "They fear they'll soon be at the mercy of the Druze if they attack the town." Nadeem nodded, easing his body forward so that Layal could apply the gentle pressure of her hands to his lower back.

"Did you know the women are making a collection of their jewellery?" she purred. "They're planning to give it to Osman Bey as a bribe in the hope that he'll protect them."

Nadeem shook his head as she continued. "But the garrison commander has already taken money from *Sitt* Nayfeh[56], so he'll do only as she tells him."

Nadeem remained silent as he listened to his wife's stories of collusion and intrigue. One of the servants came in with the water pipe. Taking a pinch of finely cut tobacco from a box, Layal crumbled it into the clay bowl and placed some coals on top. Then she picked up the mouthpiece and inhaled deeply, causing the coals to glow red and the water in the bejewelled bowl to gurgle softly. The fragrance of honey and tobacco suffused the still air in the room, tickling his nostrils. When Nadeem opened his eyes, Layal was holding the mouthpiece out to him and breathing smoke through her nostrils like the legendary dragon of Saint George. Between them the tube lay coiled in its velvet sheath.

"But *Sitt* Nayfeh says she bears the Christians no ill will," Nadeem observed evenly as he took a puff. "She's even offered to take in those who ask for her protection."

Layal grimaced. "Don't believe it!" she retorted. "The woman's a witch. She'll have us all killed."

Nadeem smiled at his wife, unwilling to be drawn into an argument over *Sitt* Nayfeh's intentions that, even to him, appeared opaque and difficult to fathom. He knew Layal would prove a formidable advocate for those who harboured suspicions against the new leader of the Druze. And after spending most of the afternoon counselling the Emir on what action to take, he had little desire to carry on the discussion.

"Those Christians who still have their guns won't give them up now," he said, hoping to bring it to an end. Layal rearranged the green silk shawl she wore around her shoulders and flipped her long silky hair backwards, making her hooped earrings jingle. She reached over to where the brass coffee pot stood on the brazier and lifted it up carefully, pouring out two cups. The distinctive smell of cardamom mingled with the tobacco smoke. She gave one to her husband and placed the other on the top of a wooden table decorated with mother-of-pearl inlay. Nadeem could not help but notice the graceful movements of her long legs beneath the folds of the silk kaftan.

During the years they had been married, he had grown to appreciate her unique beauty. She had neither the moon-shaped face of a Herati miniature with its seductive eyes nor the rounded curves of women in European paintings. These he had seen when he was a boy in a book of Italian frescoes in the library of the Franciscan Mission.

Instead, her *chevalin* face resembled that of the Madonna in the triptych of Saint James's Church in Damascus. But unlike the icon's somewhat expressionless face, Layal's reflected her feelings very readily. When she smiled, her lips turned up at the corners and her eyes lit up with the glow of a hundred oil lamps. Most of all, Nadeem liked the way she tucked her legs under her when she sat down.

"Why don't you squat on your heels like an Arab?" he would say just to tease her.

"Because I wasn't born in the desert," she would pout. "I'm a Damascene, not a bedouin."

His evening relaxation was suddenly interrupted when the doors flew open and a small boy of four or five burst into the room, calling out for his father. It was Wael, their only child, named after his grandfather. He ran over to where his parents were sitting and, barely avoiding the water pipe, threw himself at his father with a shriek of delight.

"Baba! Baba! Have you seen all these people down in the courtyard? What are they all doing there?" Hugging his son, Nadeem glanced across at Layal but she only pursed her lips, moving her head almost imperceptibly from side to side.

"I don't know," his father replied. "Perhaps they're here for a saint's day."

"Can I go down with you and see them, Baba?" Wael insisted.

"Not tonight." Then he noticed the look of disappointment on his son's face.

"Tomorrow, I promise."

Early the following day, those who had not surrendered their weapons gathered into an armed band and marched out of the town to confront the Druze in the orange groves beyond the furthest houses. After a brief skirmish in which only a handful of fighters on either side were killed or wounded, they found themselves driven back by the superior numbers of their opponents.

But as they were falling back towards the main square, some of the men went rogue. Driven by anger and frustration at their unexpected reverse, they began to set fire to the houses of peaceful Druze families. These petty acts of savagery angered Nadeem, prompting him to call on the garrison commander for an emergency meeting.

There was little time for etiquette and protocol; he did not stop to consult the Emir first. In his heart he was hoping that if he could persuade Osman Bey to act quickly, a massacre would be avoided. But before Nadeem could gain entrance to the building, a beefy sergeant sitting outside on a rush chair rebuffed him.

"He's busy," the guard growled, showering him with the husks of the pumpkin seeds he was cracking open with his teeth. "Osman Bey has no time to see anyone."

"Tell him that the Emir's confidential secretary is here," Nadeem persisted. "It's urgent."

"No," the sergeant replied mulishly.

With his way blocked, Nadeem had no choice but to return to the castle. Although not a superstitious man by nature, he had a deep foreboding feeling that the next day would usher in events more terrible than he could imagine. Close to despair, he stopped to light a candle in one of the alcoves of the Melkite Church. While the priest continued to say vespers at the altar, he bowed his head for a moment or two in silent prayer.

That night was long and sleepless. He kept imagining there was a commotion outside, but Layal prevented him from getting up from the bed they shared. Every time he swung his legs off the mattress and struggled to his feet she gently pulled him back, wrapping her long legs around his midriff in order to restrain him.

CHAPTER TWELVE

As dawn broke and the call to prayer sounded from the little mosque, Layal gazed sleepily at her husband as he rose and opened the shutters, peering out into the half-light. The flames of houses burning on the outskirts of town illuminated the bedroom wall with an orange glow while the cries of an angry mob marching towards them carried through the window. She blinked her eyes open as he shook her fully awake.

"Light of my life," she heard him say, "we must leave now. The Druze will attack this place because it's the castle of the Shehabs[57]. They'll drive them out."

Layal protested at first, unwilling to contemplate leaving the security of her home. But the urgency with which her husband had spoken made her realize that they must now be in grave danger. She gathered up a few items together with a small bag of food while Nadeem rounded up the servants.

"Take these," he said, as he handed them some coins. "Leave immediately and don't come back here."

When they had gone, he opened the strongbox he kept hidden in one of the smaller rooms and took out a bankers' draft drawn on a well-known counting house in Damascus. Layal watched as he stuffed it together with some precious jewels into leather bags and concealed them in his pockets.

"If anything happens to me," he said, "Take these."

With the clamour outside growing ever louder, they hurried down the stone stairwell into the courtyard below. Layal clutched Wael tightly by the hand. As they emerged into the open courtyard, they could hear nothing but the desperate pleas of the families encamped there.

"What will happen to us?" one woman called out as she threw herself in front of them, blocking their way.

"I do not know," said Nadeem. "We're all in God's hands now."

But Layal leaned forward and embraced her, pressing a few coins into her palm before her husband pulled her away. As daylight broke over the mountains to the east, they left the citadel behind them and made their way towards the house of Ahmed Bey, a cloth merchant from Damascus who kept a second home in town because of his frequent visits there.

They shoved their way through the narrow streets now congested with the crush of humanity trying to escape the devastation befalling the districts nearby. When they arrived at Ahmed Bey's house, Nadeem knocked vigorously on the door but it remained firmly barred. After what seemed like an eternity, a shutter opened, revealing metal bars. Dark eyes stared back at them with suspicion.

"It's you, Nadeem," the merchant said by way of an apology as soon as he recognized his friend's face. "Be patient; we've had to close the door to strangers."

They stood anxiously outside in the street until the heavily barred door swung open, admitting them into a courtyard bordered by a small gallery with a screen. To their surprise, the merchant did not take them to the *selamlik*[58] but instead conducted them to the women's quarters.

"You'll be safer here," he explained.

They entered a large, airy room furnished with low divans and illuminated by two stained-glass windows. Sunlight fell in coloured patterns on the wall opposite, marking the early hour. At the sight of a strange man, the two women huddled together on one of the divans promptly pulled their veils over their faces. A little girl ran up to the merchant and hugged him around the knees, abandoning the beads she had been playing with on the floor. He picked her up and kissed her while she stroked his beard.

Outside, they could hear people running up and down the street, shouting and pleading for admittance at every house they came across. Now and then, strangers pounded on the door or shutters of Ahmed Bey's house, wishing God's blessings on its inhabitants if only they would take them in. Ignoring the noises outside, Ahmed Bey called for one of the servants to bring tea. The man nodded and disappeared in the direction of the kitchens only to return a few moments later, visibly agitated.

"There is a family outside begging for admittance, *ya Effendi*[59]," he said.

"Tell them to go away."

"I tried, but they won't go."

Excusing himself, the merchant left the room only to return a few minutes later with a stranger accompanied by two women and several children. Their faces, streaked with soot, wore an unmistakable look of terror. Without warning, the man fell to his knees and grasped the merchant's feet. Ahmed Bey brushed him off gently and motioned for the entire family to be seated. The women muttered their thanks while the children hid behind their mothers' skirts. A few awkward moments passed before the man had recovered himself enough to speak.

"Our house has been attacked and set on fire," he gasped. "There's a mob chasing us through the streets." Pausing for a moment, he asked for a glass of water. When he had taken a sip or two, he passed it to one of the women. "We were running up the hill towards the citadel when my wife suggested we should seek shelter in the house of anyone who would let us in."

"Is the garrison commander doing anything to defend those who've been attacked?" Ahmed Bey asked him, not unkindly.

"Nothing! I swear on my children's lives," the man continued. "There are no Turks to be seen in the main square. They're still in their barracks."

As he spoke, his expression changed from one of terror to sullen resentment at the inaction of the Ottomans. But it was only short-lived. Moments later, there came a loud banging on the door, much heavier than before. It was the unmistakable sound of armed men bent on gaining entry, something that caused the newcomers to shrink back in fear. The merchant's face darkened as he got to his feet and crossed the courtyard in order to confront the intruders.

"What do you want?" he yelled through the grill.

"Are there any *rayahs*[60] inside?" a hoarse voice demanded. That was what the Muslims called Ottoman citizens of other faiths, the "protected ones."

"No," lied the merchant. "This is a Muslim house."

"Then let us in so we can see for ourselves," yelled the same voice. "We're after a man and his family. Have you given them shelter?"

Without waiting for his answer, the men outside began battering the door down with their axes and clubs. The bars groaned under the violent assault and finally gave way with a crack of splintered wood. The door burst open and a group of men flooded the courtyard, armed with swords and billhooks.

Their faces were flushed and their coarse clothes smelled of sweat tinged with the metallic tang of blood. The first man to enter spoke with an accent that was not local to the region, possibly from Jabal Hawran. His narrow eyes shone with the fever of excitement above his sallow cheeks.

"Search the rooms," he barked, ignoring the merchant.

They began entering each room and seizing anything that was small enough to fit in the belts or pockets of their pantaloons. When they tried to gain access to the women's quarters, Ahmed Bey planted himself firmly in their way.

"This is the *moharram*[61]. You cannot enter."

The man paid him no attention and shoved him aside, forcing the door open and throwing aside the beaded curtain. He blinked as his eyes adjusted to the dim interior and then smiled cruelly when he saw the terrified faces peering up at him.

"They're the ones we're after," he said, pointing at the family of new arrivals. Raising his sword, he placed its curved blade against the man's neck and was about to press down on it when his victim blurted out, "Stop, you're mistaken! We're Jews, not Christians[62]."

He paused, keeping the blade in place. In the confusion that followed, Layal sensed her husband plant himself in front of herself and Wael as he spread his arms wide in an effort to protect them. His sudden movement caused the intruder to swing his sword in an arc with such force that the blow nearly severed Nadeem's right hand. Blood spurted onto the wall and began to drip slowly down onto the silk cushions below. There was a moment of utterly stunned silence. Then he swung at Nadeem again, this time slicing through his neck and crushing the top of his spine.

Layal screamed and put her hand over her son's eyes while he stood rigid beside her, his limbs stiff with shock. The Jewish family cowered in a corner and the merchant stood back, seemingly powerless to intervene. Ahmed Bey's wives added their own screams to the mêlée and began tearing at their hair while the little girl dropped her beads and hid herself behind the divan.

There were sounds of a scuffle outside in the courtyard as some of the other men tried to push their way into the room through the narrow doorway. Their leader poked Nadeem's lifeless body where it lay slumped on the divan, causing it to topple over onto the floor at Layal's feet.

"Leave them with their women," he grunted, gesturing at Ahmed Bey and the Jewish man with his blood-spattered sword. "Why waste our time here?"

He turned to give the merchant a final scowl. One of his wives pulled some gold bangles off her wrist and held them out, mistaking his gesture for a threat.

"Take these," she begged. "And spare us."

The man seized the bangles and stuffed them into his pockets. Then he strode out followed by his companions, leaving the remains of the splintered door swinging feebly on its hinges. In the streets, there was pandemonium as more and more of the attackers began running in the direction of the citadel, brandishing their swords and knives in the air.

We will burnish their blades,
And make our spear points glisten,
Until our anger fades,
And our enemies listen...

The war song echoed through the streets of Hasbaya as the marauders swarmed up the rise and poured through the old crusader gate under the impassive gaze of the stone lions. The columns shook as the families camped in the courtyard fled to the apartments on the upper floors in a desperate effort to escape the onslaught.

Dust rose in the sunlight as the first of the Druze to reach the foot of the steps halted, peering upwards. Then, emboldened by the press of men at his back, he began to climb the stone stairway. When he had reached the third floor, he found his way blocked by the presence of the Emir Sa'deddine who stood there motionless, flanked by his sons and grandsons.

"You are violating the sanctuary of my house," the Emir said as he turned his rheumy gaze on the man. "Withdraw at once."

For an instant the man stood stock-still, halted by the dignified tone with which he had just been addressed. Behind him, others bounded up the stone steps two at a time in their eagerness to join in the attack. One of them pushed his way to the front and grabbed the Emir by his turban. It came away in his hand, revealing a shiny, bald pate crowned by a few whispery hairs. He threw down the silk cloth in disgust and slashed at him with his sword. Toppled by the force of the blow, the Emir fell to his knees as a pool of blood began to spread out over the marble floor. His assailant raised his blade again and swung down, severing the old man's head from his body in a single blow. Lifting it up in the air for his comrades to see, he tossed it into the courtyard below where it landed with a dull thud, its glassy eyes still open and staring skyward.

That was their cue. Those who had gathered behind him rushed towards the Emir's sons and grandsons, hacking them down before they could flee. Others bringing up the rear spread out to search the rooms and apartments, seizing any men or boys they could find but sparing the women. Some succumbed without a fight while others put up a spirited defence, warding off their attackers with anything they could find until finally subdued by the hail of blows that followed. And it was not only the men who fought back. Enraged by the attacks, some of the more courageous women threw themselves at their aggressors who retaliated by pushing them away, ripping their clothes and slapping their faces. When they persisted, the women lashed out at them and poked them in the eyes with their fingers.

Some families tried to escape by fleeing along the corridors and balconies in the direction of the ruined church, hoping that their pursuers would not follow them there. Others headed for the stables behind the courtyard only to encounter more armed men storming the castle's dungeons. The massacre consumed life and light in the mad heat of the day and lasted into the early evening.

At dusk when it seemed that the killing had come to an end, an uneasy calm settled over the citadel. It was said that almost a thousand inhabitants perished that day as well as seventeen members of the Emir's family. Only a handful of men survived, either by feigning death or hiding themselves beneath the piles of corpses in the courtyard. The stench of stale blood and human decay pervaded the place, banishing the clouds of incense that had smouldered in its many rooms and apartments only the day before.

CHAPTER THIRTEEN

News of the massacre found its way to Layal who, still numbed by her own husband's death, remained in the merchant's house waiting for darkness to fall and for the violence to come to an end. Rejecting the other women's efforts to comfort her, she sat dull-eyed in a corner of these strangers' quarters with her son by her side. Nothing in her life so far had prepared her for the shock that now held her paralyzed and unable to think.

At first she could not bring herself to touch her husband's corpse, neither would she let anyone else go near it. But as the hours wore on, she finally managed to overcome her revulsion and summon the will to prepare for his burial. First, she washed away the blood and then sewed up his body in a shroud with the help of Ahmed's wives. Closing his eyes, she kissed him lightly on his cold forehead while Wael looked on in silence, too traumatized to say a word.

By nightfall, Layal had abandoned all hope of finding a priest. She waited until news reached them that most of the attackers had left town for their encampment down by the river. Then she spoke briefly to Ahmed Bey, and together they left the house in a hastily assembled funeral procession, carrying the shroud on a makeshift bier. The men supported its corners on their shoulders while the women walked behind the cortège.

With only the silvery light of the full moon to guide their path, they picked their way carefully over the bodies that littered the streets. When they reached an olive grove on the western edge of town, the two servants scraped a shallow grave in the ground, taking advantage of a natural declivity. Then they deposited Nadeem's body in it. Holding her dejected son by the hand, Layal said a short prayer while Ahmed Bey stood at a respectful distance beside his wives and the Jewish family.

When she had finished, she threw a handful of earth on top of the shroud and signalled to the servants to cover it. They set to work at once, taking care to cover the body to a sufficient depth in order to prevent wild dogs and hyenas from digging it up and feasting on the remains. As a final act, Layal gathered a few stones and arranged them in the shape of a cross at the head of the grave. As she was putting the last stone in place, she looked up to see the merchant standing beside her.

"Will you still leave town tonight?" he asked with a genuine look of concern. "Return to my house where you will be safe."

Layal stood up, her tall outline silhouetted against the moonlight. A solitary tear ran down her cheek and settled on her lip where it glistened with the lustre of a pearl.

"Thank you," she said, "but we cannot stay here. They may come back tomorrow and then you will all be in danger for sheltering us."

"What will you do?"

Pausing to wipe away the tear, she shivered despite the warmth of the night as she struggled to compose herself. "I'll find a guide and make the journey to the coast."

Ahmed Bey sighed, his eyes revealing his disappointment at her choice, a decision he was obliged to accept despite his misgivings. Had she decided to stay with him, he would have been more than prepared to offer her his protection, perhaps even marriage. She was an attractive woman and he would be following the tradition of the Prophet by marrying a widow. Instead he gently snapped a twig off a nearby olive tree.

"May this little branch bring you good fortune," he said, handing it to her. "Our fates are all in God's hands, whatever religion we are born into."

Layal smiled at him wanly. Still too shocked to think clearly, she nevertheless remained resolved and resourceful.

"I'll find a guide for you, a sure man," he continued. "But it will be a long and dangerous journey." She nodded in silence. "Come with us now. I'll arrange for you to leave at dawn."

With the question of Layal's departure settled, the little party set off back into town, taking care to avoid the few groups of men still lingering in the squares and alleyways. As they walked through the streets, they heard dogs barking and the crackle of smouldering timber as fires burned into the night.

Some women wandered about forlornly, searching amongst the dead for their husbands or sons while others crouched over corpses, scratching their faces and rubbing dirt into their hair in their grief. Everywhere bodies lay unattended, covered only in what remained of their blood-stained clothes. Come daybreak, jackals and crows would already be feasting on their flesh.

In the predawn chill, Layal and her son prepared themselves to leave Hasbaya for good, guided by a local man whom Ahmed Bey had found for them, a muleteer he often hired to carry bales of cloth to the markets of Damascus and Beirut. She had given little thought to her destination or even how she and Wael would reach it. But as the numbness began to subside and her mind began to clear, the desperation of her plight slowly came into sharper focus. What made matters even worse was that the Emir Sa'deddine, under whose patronage they had lived, was now dead if the accounts she had heard the day before were true.

The citadel, once their home, had become a scene of savage butchery. The sight of death in the streets and the wretched state of those left alive had both appalled and terrified her. In the back of her mind, a fuse had already been lit and was quietly smouldering. It would lead to an explosion of grief and sorrow when she least expected it to. Layal had loved Nadeem dearly and grown to rely on him more than she cared to admit during their short married life together.

Her initial thought had been to return to her family in Damascus, but Ahmed Bey counselled her strongly against it and for good reason. The journey north through Wadi Taym and across the myrtle-clad slopes of Jabal Rihan would be dangerous, he said. Not only were there robbers to contend with but also the Druze army which, he had heard, was planning to sweep north towards Rashaya and Zahleh. While the latter were unlikely to bother refugees, he nevertheless advised them to keep their distance.

Layal was disheartened by his warnings so she thought briefly of travelling south to the great city of Jerusalem despite the fact that she knew nobody there. She wondered in desperation whether she, a Christian widow, could expect to find sanctuary among the monks and nuns who maintained the Holy Places there. When she mentioned the idea to the muleteer who had been summoned to meet her at the house, he shook his head.

"It's a long journey south," he answered. "Whichever road we take."

"Is there more than one?" she asked.

"Yes, there are two. Either through the swamps of the Houleh Valley which is swarming with brigands and mosquitoes," the muleteer began, "or by crossing the hills southeast of here which are controlled by the *Metouali* sheikhs. They may not give us their protection and we cannot pass through without it."

Layal nodded distractedly. She was finding it difficult to concentrate and her thoughts wandered, frequently returning to the woman she had embraced in the courtyard before the massacre. Was she also now widowed and in search of a place of refuge too? The thought plagued her all afternoon and on into the night.

Without warning a wave of despair swept over her, forcing her to consider the dismal possibility that, with their pampered existence in Hasbaya no more than a memory, she and her son might have to spend the rest of their lives as little more than beggars, living off the charity of others. She had to think of some other place where they might find safety. It took some time before she remembered that her mother had some distant relatives in a largely Christian town across the mountains to the northwest.

"I have family in Jezzine," she said at last to the muleteer. "If it is on the way to the coast, let's go there." Instead of answering her, he looked down at the ground.

"Will you guide us?" she prodded when he did not reply. The look of determination that appeared on Layal's face forced him to agree.

Two hours later, he returned with a sturdy donkey that he hitched outside to the remains of the doorframe by its halter rope. Ahmed Bey gave them what food he could find in the kitchens and accompanied Layal and her son out into the alleyway to bid them farewell. Apart from a dog barking nearby, the town streets were silent and desolate.

"May the Almighty keep you in His care," he said, touching his right hand to his forehead in a brief salutation.

"And reward you for your good deeds," Layal replied, turning her face away so he would not see her tears.

Without further delay, the muleteer helped her mount the donkey with her son and led them through the main square and down the hill towards the olive groves, glancing from left to right for signs of marauders. They made their way past ruined houses where bodies lay unburied amongst the blackened walls and fallen timbers. Each time there was a sudden movement in the shadows Layal flinched, but neither the donkey nor its master paid her any heed. The muleteer walked with the ease of a man well-used to travelling long distances. Ahmed Bey had assured her that he knew every path and track through the mountains.

"Where do you come from?" Layal asked him as they plodded along in silence.

"Near here," he said. "The village with the temple."

She nodded. Nadeem had once mentioned a ruined temple with Greek inscriptions that he had passed on one of his many journeys into the countryside to see for himself the agricultural practices being used in the Emir's domains. She remembered him saying how its remains stood grandly amongst the trees while the undergrowth had all but engulfed its fallen columns.

When dawn finally broke, they were already descending the western slopes of the hills. As if by magic, the countryside around them had undergone an abrupt change. Gone were the pitted chalk gullies and thorn bushes, replaced by undulating sandstone plains broken here and there by a few rocky outcrops. The summer blooms carpeting the ground in front of them caused a faint glimmer of hope to stir in Layal's heart. Scarlet poppies danced beside the delicate white and yellow heads of wild carrots and radishes in the gentle dawn breeze.

"Perhaps there's a new life for us somewhere here," she said to her son as she gazed at the array of colour on the plain before her.

Sometime later they came upon a wide river.

"Where are we now?" Layal was looking at the stone bridge ahead of them whose three arches spanned the sluggish flow.

"The Litani," the muleteer said, wiping his forehead.

They had reached it at the point where its course veers sharply to the west before emptying its waters into the sea a few miles north of Tyre. It was from this ancient port that King Hiram had once shipped cargoes of cedar logs to his son-in-law Solomon for the construction of the temple in Jerusalem. Layal brightened at the muleteer's mention of the name.

"The River of Lions," she murmured to Wael in the hope that her words would prompt him to speak. "It flows south from a place called Baalbek, the ancient city of the Sun God." The little boy looked at his mother, but to her disappointment, said nothing.

By the time he halted the donkey in the shade of a tall tree, they had already travelled high up into the hills. In the distance, they could hear the muffled roar of the Zahrani as it flowed through the gorge below. Several hours had passed since they had crossed the bridge and they had only stopped twice. The sun was now high in the sky and they could feel its warmth on their backs despite the altitude. In the distance, a flock of storks rose in an elegant spiral from one of the valleys, soaring into the limitless sky with gentle beats of their curved wings. Their long legs trailed behind them like streamers from a flagpole.

"Better than riding a donkey," remarked the muleteer, who had noticed Layal looking at them.

"Yes," she replied wearily.

He grunted as he lifted Wael down before helping Layal dismount. Giddy from lack of sleep, she hobbled over to the tree and waited quietly in its shade while the muleteer unsaddled the donkey and set the sweaty pad to dry against a rock. After clearing a patch of ground, he spread out his cloak and invited mother and son to make themselves comfortable.

Layal lowered herself stiffly to the ground and stretched out her long legs, covering them with the folds of her kaftan as best she could. The dried leaves and needles felt soft under the muleteer's cloak, providing a welcome relief to her aching body. Taking off her ragged cap and veil, she let the gentle breeze ruffle her hair and scratched her aching scalp with her dirty fingernails. Beside them, the donkey stamped its hooves to dislodge the flies under its belly. Fetching out the sack of food the merchant had given them, she laid out some bread and salty cheese together with a few dried apricots. But when she looked around for the muleteer to invite him to share their meal, she found he had disappeared.

"Where did he go?" she said to her son who was pointing to a cleft in the mountainside.

As she struggled to control her mounting panic, it occurred to Layal that she had only Ahmed Bey's word for his trustworthiness. Certainly his service to them so far had been exemplary. But in spite of that and the merchant's recommendation, she was gripped with the fear that he had abandoned them in this wilderness. Cursing herself under her breath, she remembered that in their rush to leave Hasbaya she had even forgotten to ask Ahmed Bey for the man's name.

Perhaps he had crept away and was now hiding somewhere up on the mountain making plans to rob them of the few possessions they still owned. Maybe he had accomplices hidden nearby? She was on the verge of allowing her worst fears to overwhelm her when the muleteer suddenly appeared out of nowhere carrying a goatskin filled with water.

"Drink and let your son drink too," he said, holding out the goatskin. "I'll fill it again with fresh water before we leave."

"Where have you been, *ya mokairee*[63]?" Layal almost shouted at him, her voice shaking with anger as she seized the goatskin from his hand. "You abandoned us."

"The afternoon prayer," he replied apologetically. "I missed the ones at dawn and noonday."

Taken aback by his words, Layal suddenly realized that the man was a Muslim and not the Christian she had mistakenly assumed him to be.

"Please forgive me," she said with a sigh of relief. "I haven't even asked you your name."

"Mohammed," the muleteer said, bowing stiffly. "And whatever you ask, I'm ready to do it." Layal smiled back in gratitude as she held out the goatskin to Wael.

"Come," she said. "Drink some water."

Seeing the boy's reluctance, the muleteer mimed the action and pointed at his mouth as he made a swallowing sound. As if on cue, Wael reached out for the goatskin and held it up as he had been shown. At first he took only a sip but then he gulped down the cool water, spilling some over his face.

"Please share our meal," Layal said.

The muleteer squatted down on his haunches and, reaching into the copious pockets of his pantaloons, took out a large shepherd's knife to divide up the bread. At the sight of the blade, Wael let out a shriek of terror and hid himself behind his mother who began murmuring endearments in his ear to calm him. Realizing that he had been the cause of the boy's fright, the muleteer wiped the blade and put it away.

"I'm sorry," he said. "I've scared the boy."

Layal smiled at him, but the damage had already been done. In the uneasy silence that followed, the muleteer shared out the bread and cheese while she prepared mouthfuls for herself and Wael, who was now cowering behind her, too afraid to come out. They finished quickly and remounted the donkey.

From the time that they had crossed the Litani, they had not seen another person, not even in the distance. The muleteer had purposefully avoided taking the road north to Jezzine, instead leading them along a series of narrow winding paths which clung to the limestone cliffs east of the town. At times the track was barely wide enough for two people to travel along. Layal was forced to put all her trust in him as he forced the donkey as far away from the cliff's edge with his shoulder as he could.

Suddenly he halted and pointed at a tiny speck in the valley below. Layal could just make out a man climbing steadily up the side of the bluff towards the spot where they were standing. Without realizing it, she began to shiver. Noticing her distress, the muleteer helped them down and motioned for them to find somewhere to hide.

Gathering her son in her arms, she ran the short distance to a nearby cave and crouched down behind some boulders in its mouth. From her hiding place she could watch the man's movement. As he neared the top, the muleteer stood up to make himself plainly visible before retiring again to the shade of the trees, waiting for him to arrive. As the moments passed, the palms of Layal's hands became clammy and her temples throbbed. Behind her, Wael sat playing with some pebbles in the dust, recovered from his earlier fright and now seemingly unconcerned.

Finally, the man reached the top of the cliff and sauntered over to the muleteer. Layal moved forward as far as she could without revealing herself as the two men greeted each other, but she was still too far away to hear what they were saying. When the muleteer finally beckoned her over, she stood up and readjusted her cap and veil, brushing the dust off her skirts.

CHAPTER FOURTEEN

"Don't go on to Jezzine," the newcomer said somewhat gravely, catching his breath after the steep climb.

He was dressed in the manner of countrymen, not the townsfolk. On his head, he wore the dark blue turban of the Maronites and on his feet tall goatskin boots. Layal was immediately drawn to his green eyes that peered out from beneath shaggy eyebrows.

"What's your name?" she asked him.

"Isaiah," the man replied. "But people here call me Abou Jameel."

"And why should we not go to Jezzine?" Layal went on. "I have family there and we've been travelling since before dawn."

"Your guide told me that and about the death of your husband. May God make good your loss."

"*Allah ysalmak*[64]," she said, accepting his condolences.

"Jezzine has already been attacked." His tone was bitter.

A blank look crossed Layal's face. Could her situation possibly become any worse than it already has?

"Forgive me," he stammered. "I'm angry because so many villagers here have lost everything and are now fleeing to Sidon. They say there is a Frankish warship there."

Layal glanced at the muleteer for confirmation of this news, but he merely shrugged his shoulders.

"And don't go to Sidon, either," the man continued. "The road is unsafe and there are bands of robbers attacking the people on it."

Exhausted by her arduous journey, Layal tried to steady herself. Feeling more wretched and forlorn than ever, she looked around for support. The muleteer took her gently by the arm and set her on the ground.

With her cap awry and her veil pushed back, she dabbed at her eyes to staunch the flow of tears that welled up so fast she could scarcely wipe them away. The stillness of the mountains was broken only by the sound of her sobs and the sighing of the wind in the trees.

"I'm travelling south towards Jabal Amel through the land of the Metouali65 sheikhs," the stranger continued when Layal's sobs began to abate. "I've heard that the Druze have angered them and that they dare not show themselves in that region."

"How's that?" The muleteer seemed surprised by the news. "In the Bekaa, they have joined with the Metoualis against the Christians."

"It's a strange story," the man replied, wiping his forehead with the end of his turban.

"Then tell us," said Layal who had recovered herself a little.

"Some time ago, a party of Druze killed a Christian who had taken refuge with one of their holy men," the man said. "They ransacked his house and stole some of his possessions. When his wife tried to stop them, they insulted her."

The muleteer swore under his breath, cursing the violence that was now pitting village against village and people of different faiths against each other. It was not that it had never happened in the past, but this time it was on a grander scale.

"Come with me south. You'll be under my protection and I'll arrange safe passage to Jerusalem for you if you wish it."

Layal turned from one man to the other. She was too overwhelmed by what she had just heard to think clearly and needed the advice of the one person she now trusted above all others. It was the muleteer.

"And if we go north towards Beirut?"

Although she could not explain why, she felt something drawing her towards the brash new city on the coast about which she had heard so much. There was a silence while the muleteer sucked his teeth and began to draw a little map in the dust with a stick. Deep furrows appeared on his forehead as though he were trying to solve a riddle.

"It is a long way from here to Beirut and the road to Sidon is too dangerous to travel," he said, shifting his weight uneasily from one leg to the other. "We'll have to pass through the Chouf where the Christians and Druze live side by side."

"Will it be any less safe than travelling south?" asked Layal.

"Perhaps." He paused, glancing up at the long chain of purple mountains stretching north as far as the eye could see.

"I agree with Abou Jameel," he said finally. "You should take the road to the south."

Layal realized that the stark choice she was now faced with would not only affect the rest of her life but her son's too should they both survive this ordeal. If she were to go south, she would have to seek refuge with the *Metouali* sheikhs in Jabal Amel until safe passage could be arranged to Jerusalem.

She could, however, plead with the muleteer to take them north to Beirut, a place she had heard so much about but never visited. As she sat there weighing the two courses of action, she remembered her husband had told her that in Beirut, unlike in Damascus where they were subject to Ottoman rule, European governments openly offered their support to the Christians who lived there. He had added as a joke that if they were to take up residence in the city, they would enjoy the protection not of the Sultan in Istanbul but of the French Consul instead.

Looking down at her son, she tried to imagine what the future held in store for him. Born into this bittersweet land of beauty and suffering, she wondered if his destiny now lay in the east with the Turks as his father's had done or amongst the Franks in Beirut. More importantly, would he find a better life for himself there and prosper? Even in her reduced state, Layal was a decisive woman. The next time she spoke it was clear to both men that she had made up her mind.

"We will go north if you'll guide us," she said to the muleteer. He grunted and tugged at the ends of his moustache. After a moment or two of moody contemplation, he nodded in acceptance.

"I am at your service."

Layal touched his sleeve lightly before turning to Abou Jameel.

"Thank you," she said to him politely, "but our path lies north to Beirut."

"As you wish," he replied, stooping down to pick up his bag and tossing it over his shoulder.

"Make your way towards the tomb of the Prophet Job." He pointed to the north. "It is a holy place but don't go in. There has been fighting nearby."

"Are there any places where we can stay along the way?" asked the muleteer, who had not travelled through this part of the Chouf before. "The boy and his mother will have to sleep out in the open otherwise."

"You'll find the villagers hospitable enough," the man replied. "And if necessary, you can spend the night in the cave where the Emir Fakhreddine hid from the Turks. It's high on the cliff and there's plenty of water there."

With that, he strode off south following the ridge that led to Shqif, the old crusader fortress of Beaufort perched on the crags above the village of Arnoun. Layal and the muleteer waited until he had disappeared before following the narrow path down the side of the gorge to the river. When they reached the bank, the muleteer left them among the rushes so that Layal could wash and attend to her son.

He himself mounted the donkey and rode off in search of a dwelling or cave where they could spend the night. This time Layal did not fret as she watched him disappear behind a stand of shimmering poplars. The man had proved to her beyond the shadow of a doubt that he was as good as his word. She did not see him again until the sun had disappeared behind the hills, leaving the gorge in deep shadow.

131

"I've found a place," he said to Layal some time later as he slid off the donkey's back. He led them a little way up the side of the ravine before striding off down a well-worn path. Layal glanced up at the huge cliffs on either side, searching for signs of human life. All of a sudden, a shack made from two stone walls built squarely into the side of the cliff appeared in front of them as if out of nowhere. The roof was made from a mass of packed earth and dried leaves supported by twisted branches. Colourful mats hung down from the outermost beam, reminding Layal of the tents of desert-dwelling nomads on the Syrian steppe.

Outside stood a woman dressed in a shabby brown skirt and orange bodice with a little baby nestled against her back in a sling. As they came down the path towards her, she waved at them in excitement. It was not until Layal had almost ridden up to her that she saw her hands and wrists were discoloured and covered with large blotches. Alarmed at the thought of spending the night in a leper's home, Layal called to the muleteer to stop but he ignored her and continued up to the door.

The woman greeted them cheerfully and at once invited them in, leaving the muleteer outside to unsaddle the donkey and feed it. The interior was clean and well-kept in contrast to its ramshackle appearance. Layal looked around for signs of her husband or some other member of her family but she found none. Noticing her puzzled expression, the woman smiled.

"He went to Jezzine two days ago and hasn't come back yet."

Realizing at once that she knew nothing of the attack on the town or the outbreak of violence in the surrounding districts, Layal found herself in a quandary for the second time that day. Although Abou Jameel's warning was still very much at the forefront of her mind, she did not want to create unnecessary alarm by telling the woman about it. Perhaps the woman's husband had heard of the attack and had escaped unharmed or was hiding out in the hills, waiting for the opportunity to return to his wife and child.

In the end she decided to say nothing, not wishing to be cursed for being the harbinger of bad news. But there was something else upsetting her too. It was the thought that she and Wael were about to spend the night in the house of a leper. Sitting exhausted amongst piles of cloth strewn everywhere, Layal could not stop herself from thinking about the blotches on the woman's skin. Had they escaped the horrors of Hasbaya only to put themselves at risk of contracting some terrible disease?

"God preserve us," she whispered to herself in a fit of self-pity.

But the moment she uttered those words, she began to feel a deep sense of shame bordering on self-disgust. Strong-minded and at times wilful, Layal was nevertheless a compassionate woman at heart. It had been she who had stopped to give comfort to the widow in the courtyard, not her husband. The earlier mention of Job's tomb had reminded her of the story of the Hebrew prophet who had been afflicted with a plague of boils by God as a test of his faith.

If he had borne his misfortunes so stoically, why should she even consider insulting this poor woman by refusing her hospitality on account of some unfounded suspicion? In an effort to regain control, she pulled aside the mats and went outside to spend the little time left before dusk alone. Lost in the melancholy of her thoughts, she wandered down towards the river.

"Go and play with the stones over there," she said to Wael who had followed her.

The little boy ran off and disappeared behind some bushes while Layal sat on the bank, her head in her hands. There she stayed, lost in her own thoughts, until darkness fell. With a start, she came to her senses and remembered that she had neither seen nor heard her son for the entire time she had been there. She stood up and walked over to the clump of bushes where he had vanished earlier.

Peering over them, she saw him standing by a large stone basin with a wooden ladle in his hand. Scattered around were bundles of roots and leaves as well as a pile of walnut shells. A heavy iron cauldron hung from a blackened tripod over the remains of a fire, its smouldering embers crackling in the fading light.

Clangggg! The cauldron rang with a deep, reverberating sound as he banged the ladle against the metal rim.

"Listen, Mama," he said with a look of delight on his face.

All at once Layal realized that her fears of leprosy had been groundless. The woman and her husband were simple dyers! The blotches on her hands had doubtless come from the yellow and brown dyes extracted from walnut shells and the roots of the bedstraw that she had seen growing wild in the hills nearby. She let out a huge sigh of relief and sat down to watch him play until it was completely dark, not even bothering to scold him when he started poking at the fire with a stick.

They only returned to the house when the woman called them inside for supper. Layal sat down with Wael on a pile of cloths while their host squatted in front of them and offered them some water and dried fruit. Her baby now lay sleeping in a reed basket at the back of the room. A rich aroma of mutton fat rose from a pot cooking on the brazier.

"You must be very hungry," she said as she stirred the pot.

"Yes," Layal said with a weary smile. "We are."

Handing her the spoon, she went outside to bake some flatbreads. While she was gone, the muleteer pulled aside the curtain of mats and came in.

"She doesn't know about the attack on Jezzine," Layal whispered to him as he sat down. "Her husband went there two days ago and hasn't returned since."

"Did you tell her what we heard?"

Before she could say anything, the woman came in carrying in her hands a bundle of crisply baked loaves. She filled three bowls with stew and handed them out in turn, beginning with the muleteer. He took his bowl and, after reciting a short prayer, dipped his bread into the steaming broth and began to eat. Layal blew on the hot food to cool it but Wael pushed his away.

Without a word, the woman knelt down beside him and began coaxing him to eat with little clucks of her tongue. To Layal's amazement he responded at once, first taking a few mouthfuls and then spooning it into his mouth with gusto. By the time they had finished, Layal's eyelids had already begun to droop. Her body ached all over from the long journey and she could barely stay awake. Noticing their fatigue, the woman led them to a corner of the room that was screened off with a large orange cloth. Shyly, she pointed to a worn mattress.

"Thank you," said Layal as she took several coins from an inner pocket and slipped them into the woman's hand.

"No, no," she protested, shaking her head vigorously. "You're always welcome here." But Layal insisted.

"These are harsh times," she said, gently closing the woman's fingers around the coins. "We must all be ready for whatever fate has in store for us."

CHAPTER FIFTEEN

While Layal and her son were making their way north, Druze reinforcements from Hawran, led by a warrior known as "the speckled wolf" had already joined the men who had attacked Hasbaya. Considered a great warrior by his men, Isma'il el-Atrash was the commander who had held the Egyptian army of Ibrahim Pasha at bay for almost a year in the rocky wastes of the Ledja.

The combined force swept through Wadi Taym, attacking and burning its villages as they went. It took them four days to reach the fortified hill town of Rashaya, ruled over by a relative of the Emir Sa'deddine.

They attacked it the day after the commander of the Ottoman garrison had issued a proclamation guaranteeing the safety of all its citizens, setting fire to houses and looting its churches. Almost half of its men were killed and the only Christian survivors were those who sought and were given protection by the local Druze families.

Now numbering more than five thousand men, they pressed on towards the gates of Zahleh, the last remaining Christian stronghold in the Bekaa Valley. Just as the muleteer had predicted, they were joined by *Metouali* farmers from the surrounding districts. This was unusual because, in the past, they had often sided with the Christians in disputes with their neighbours.

Their change in allegiance was in the main part down to the behaviour of the *qabadayet*, the Christian bailiffs of the town. The farmers resented the arrogance with which they and the tax collectors who accompanied them rode out to their villages to collect the rents on behalf of the sheikhs of the Bekaa and the pashas of Damascus. Their mood soured by years of ill treatment, they were now only too eager to join in the attack. Their aim was to redress their long-standing grievances against the *qabadayet* as well as to indulge in a little plunder for their own account.

The sun was going down by the time Joseph finally reached the hills above the town. It had been a long and arduous walk, this time crossing the spine of the mountains to the north of Jabal el-Knisseh. He paused for a moment to look down in awe on the bustling entrepôt that lay halfway between Beirut and the ancient city of Damascus at the edge of the Syrian plains.

Before him a mass of orchards and gardens spread out in all directions, bounded on the far side by a triangle of pine trees. The town itself lay sandwiched in a narrow valley carved out by the Berdaouni River as it flowed down from the snow-streaked heights of Sannine to the northwest.

The sight of so many grand buildings clustered together was something entirely new to him and his pulse quickened as he made his way towards the town's main gates. But it was only when he found the road that led to the southern entrance that the unmistakable signs of the devastation taking place to the south became clearer and clearer. It seemed as though the violence had already reached Zahleh itself.

Just beyond the main gate, Joseph came across a group of men hastily digging a ditch and piling up the earth on the far side to form a rampart. He stopped as one of them picked up a musket which was propped against the newly-constructed wall and pointed its barrel through one of the crenulations. Having verified his field of aim, he lowered the firearm and placed it on the ground beside him. Out of the corner of his eye, he noticed Joseph standing there.

"Have you come to join us?" he called out. "Where are the others, the reinforcements we were promised from Keserwan?"

"Still camped below Dhour Shweir," Joseph replied somewhat

apologetically. "I was sent by your comrades to ask them for help but they refused to come."

"*Yuh*," grunted the man. "Is Karam coming down from the north?" Joseph looked at him nonplussed. It was a name he had never heard of.

"Damn those miserable Keserwanis," a voice from behind suddenly boomed out. Looking round, he saw a large, burly man leaning on a shovel. He had evidently just overheard their conversation.

"Come and help us," he said as he spat in the dust and wiped the sweat off his forehead with the end of his turban.

But Joseph was too tired from his long journey through the mountains to volunteer for the work party. Instead, he walked off in the direction of the gates, impeded by large crowds of refugees who were also trudging wearily towards the city in a desperate attempt to escape the fighting around their villages. He noticed the blank expressions on their faces. Then he noticed an old lady who looked about the same age as his grandmother shuffling along as quickly as she could in the crush. He felt his heart squeeze inside his chest.

What if the violence were to spread to Ayn el-Louz? How could I help defend my home and family if I wasn't there?

He shook his head wearily, unable to find an answer. Prosperous though they might be in normal times, the streets of Zahleh were now thronged with townsfolk who jostled each other in their desperate efforts to buy up whatever stocks of food they could lay their hands on, regardless of the price. The richer people rode to and fro on horseback or sat in their carriages, directing their servants to scour the shops and market stalls while the poorer ones scurried from one store to the next in the hope of finding anything still remaining on the shelves. For them, even a small sack of flour or a bag of lentils was a worthy prize.

Rumours were rife that the town would soon be blockaded and they would be reduced to eating the very rats and mice that pillaged their grain stores in better times. The fact that the Ottoman authorities, under pressure from the European consuls in Beirut, had already despatched a contingent of three hundred men under the command of Colonel Nuri Bey had done little to settle their fears. Some Zahlawis had already begun making plans to flee north should the city fall to the attackers who, they had heard, were assembling in great numbers just beyond its gates.

It was close to sunset by the time Joseph found himself on the right bank of the river which divides the city, searching for any group of armed defenders that would adopt him into their ranks. Pausing to quench his thirst at a water fountain, he realized that he, too, would soon need to find food and shelter for the night. He had scarcely eaten all day and his stomach was rumbling. Besides, his legs were stiff and sore from his solitary march through the mountains.

The sudden clatter of approaching horses interrupted his thoughts and made him look up. People disappeared into doorways or alleys or wherever they could find a place to squeeze into and in a matter of moments, he was alone in the deserted street flanked on either side by high walls. Turning in the direction the noise was coming from, he saw a column of horsemen bearing down on him three abreast. He was forced to flatten his body against the wall behind him to avoid being crushed.

It took several minutes for the entire column to ride by. When the last of the horsemen had disappeared around the corner, Joseph eased himself away from the wall and brushed the dust from his clothes. His eyes strayed up to where the last of the sun's rays glinted off the balcony above. It was surrounded by a lattice screen but one of the shutters was half-open. Peering through it, he saw the face of a young woman looking down at him.

Shading his eyes against the glare of the setting sun, he squinted upwards to take another look, but the shutter closed abruptly with a click. Disappointed, he turned away and was about to walk off when his attention was drawn to an ornate door encased in a heavy stone frame. Compared to the rough, lime-washed planks that hung in the doorways of Ayn el-Louz, he was struck by its beauty and strength. As he ran his fingers over its burnished metal petals and iron studs, he wondered absently what great fortune must be lying securely behind it. By contrast in Ayn el-Louz, doors were rarely, if ever, closed. It was considered un-neighbourly.

The sonorous clanging of a bell nearby interrupted his contemplation. Glancing around, he could see no church, only several fine residences like the one outside which he was standing. Darkness was falling and he still had not found a place to stay for the night. For want of a better plan, he followed the river and had not gone far before he came across a street that led up a rise and on towards a number of white stone buildings bounded by an elegant cloister.

A large church stood at one end, its bell tower capped by a white campanile. Relieved, Joseph strode up the little hill leaving behind the clamour of the crowded streets. A few stately cypress trees grew in the courtyard, their tall shapes silhouetted against the classical lines of the buildings. When he reached the top, a tall man walked up to him clad in the humble black robes of a priest.

"Do you wish to pray?" he said. "Vespers will be beginning soon."

"Not today, Abouna," Joseph replied. Standing there, he felt the power of the man's scrutiny as the priest looked at his stained clothes and unkempt appearance.

"This is the Convent of Our Saviour, the most famous place in all of Zahleh," he replied without a hint of condescension. "Is it your first visit, my son?"

"Yes," he admitted. "Can I find shelter here for one night?"

Rather than reply, the priest took Joseph over to a stone bench in the cloisters and invited him to sit down. Leaving him there he walked off, only to return several minutes later with a clay jug, some bread and a pat of *labneh*[66] wrapped in a piece of white cloth. He poured some water into a cup and gave it to him before handing him the food.

Murmuring his thanks, Joseph devoured his supper and hardly noticed when the vespers bell began to ring again and the priest rose to his feet and strode towards the church. Famished after his long journey, he finished his meal without looking up once. In the background, he could hear the drone of the monks reciting their prayers in a language he did not understand. It bore little resemblance to the stumbling recitals of the village priest in Ayn el-Louz.

Gathering up the remains of the *labneh* with his last scrap of bread, Joseph settled himself comfortably on the bench to await the father's return. Despite the strangeness of his surroundings, his eyes soon began to close. The sounds from the church and the cool press of the stone against his back made him feel drowsy. When he opened them again, he had no idea how long he had been asleep. Standing over him in the crepuscular darkness was the figure of the priest. He held in his large hands a small cup of steaming liquid that gave off a rich and pungent smell.

Joseph took the cup, trying his best not to spill its contents. The blood mounted to his cheeks as he held it while the priest sat down beside him, stroking his silver-streaked beard pensively. His awkwardness caused the father to smile.

"Drink it," he said, not unkindly. "It will wake you up."

Sniffing the contents cautiously, Joseph took a sip and grimaced. It was quite different to anything he had come across in the village where they only drank herb tea or, on special occasions, fruit cordials. More surprising still, it left a bitter aftertaste on his tongue.

"What's this?" he asked.

"A drink made from roasted berries," the father replied. "It will refresh you."

"I hope so," said Joseph ruefully. "If the attack comes tomorrow, I want to join the defenders."

"Don't worry about that now, my son," said the priest, picking up the empty cup. "Let the future take care of itself. For now, just enjoy the scent of jasmine on the cool night air."

Taking some sweetmeats from his pocket, he offered one to Joseph who ate it in one mouthful before licking the syrup from his fingers. To his surprise, he now found himself fully awake.

"You should have been here last week," said the priest. "It was our great Feast of the Korban[67] when the whole town is lit up by torchlight. The people make their way through the streets to give thanks for Zahleh's deliverance from a plague which threatened the town fifty years ago." Joseph continued cleaning off the last of the syrup as he listened to the priest's story.

"The townspeople prayed to God for their deliverance. Christians joined together with Muslims, Melkites with the *Roum*[68]."

"Do you think He'll save the town tomorrow?"

"Only He knows that," the father replied thoughtfully.

They remained side by side in the darkness, priest and peasant. For the first time since he had arrived in the town that afternoon, Joseph felt properly welcome. Even his grandmother might have approved of this man in spite of her habitual distrust of priests. After a while, the coffee's effect began to wear off and Joseph's eyelids drooped.

"You should rest," the priest said. "Follow me."

He led him to an empty stable nearby. With scarcely another word, Joseph knelt down on the clean straw, placing his bag under his head and covering himself with his felt cloak. Even before the priest had closed the creaking door, Joseph shut his eyes, oblivious to his surroundings. He did not even have the time to think about the new world he had stumbled into.

CHAPTER SIXTEEN

As the first rays of dawn peeped through the cracks of the stable door, Joseph awoke to the sound of movement along the road outside. He blinked and stood up stiffly, stretching each leg in turn. Finding some water in a forgotten pail, he splashed it over his face and then shook the loose straw from his cloak.

Squinting into the harsh sunlight, he saw a line of men marching south along the riverbank. One of the marchers towards the rear, a large man with an ancient matchlock slung over his shoulder and a pruning hook stuck in his belt, glanced round and, seeing Joseph, beckoned him over. Delighted by the invitation, Joseph stumbled down the hill just as they were disappearing out of sight.

"Aren't you the fellow I saw yesterday?" the man asked him when he had caught up with them.

"Yes," Joseph replied a little sheepishly, wondering if he would now be berated for not volunteering to help the day before.

"Then join us," he said with a broad grin. "We are off to fight the Druze. Damn me if we don't drive them back to Hawran before the day's out." Before Joseph could reply, he had put a heavy arm around his shoulders pulling him along.

"Do you have something better to do?"

Joseph shook his head, falling into step beside him.

"Good," he said. "I'm Habib. What do they call you?"

"Joseph."

"So you're from the mountains, eh?" Habib chortled at his accent. "A real terrace builder. What are you doing here?"

"I've come to fight," said Joseph somewhat indignantly, bridling at the man's good-humoured jibe.

"But have you brought a weapon with you?" said Habib, looking down at Joseph's empty hands. At this, the men around him burst into guffaws of laughter.

"No," Joseph admitted. But when he turned to look at his new comrades a second time, he found they were grinning, not sniggering at him. How different it was to his reception in Taniyus's camp. From what he could tell, they appeared willing to accept a mountain boy like him into their ranks and were glad to have him, too.

"Take this," said Habib, drawing the billhook from his belt with a flourish. "You should be able to hack a few people to death with it." He chuckled at his own joke, displaying an uneven set of yellow teeth. Taking the hook from him, Joseph ran his thumb down the edge and flinched.

"It's sharp."

"Of course. No use if it isn't."

The makeshift infantry company stopped at the Damascus Road to discuss tactics among themselves before agreeing to turn west towards the mountains. With no one person in command, Joseph wondered what they would do when they came upon their opponents, but rather than broach the matter with Habib, he kept his misgivings to himself. An hour or so later when the sun was well up, those in the vanguard spotted Druze banners rippling in the wind above a village where the road to Beirut began its upward climb over the mountains. Habib tugged at his sleeve.

"What are you staring at?" he growled. "Look ahead. Those are enemy flags ahead."

As they came closer to their positions, the men around him fanned out haphazardly, taking cover in the fields and ditches. Some of those carrying muskets began firing them in the general direction of their opponents, shouting wildly to each other in their excitement.

"Idiots," muttered Habib under his breath. "Out of range and they're giving away our positions."

They soon found themselves crouched in a ditch peering through the tall grass at the Druze. Around them, the sound of sporadic gunshots continued with little apparent effect. Habib bit the base off one of his homemade cartridges and held it between his teeth as he pulled the dog's head back to half-cock.

Joseph's eyes flitted nervously from his new friend to their enemies. They had begun advancing towards them, slowly but deliberately. The sun glinted off their sword blades and as they came nearer, the relentless beating of their drums grew louder and louder. His throat went dry and the muscles in his legs began to twitch. Next to him, Habib had already spat the bullet into the barrel. Taking a ramrod from beneath it, he tamped the ball down three times.

All around, Joseph could hear battle cries as their opponents charged towards them with their swords and knives drawn. At first the Zahlawis fired several wild volleys but as they closed in, Joseph saw men leap up from their hiding places one after the other and run wildly towards the road as though pursued by *jinn*[69]. With little or no support from their comrades, the few who did stand to fight were soon pushed back and forced to flee too.

Ignoring the commotion around him, Habib brought the musket up to his shoulder and took aim at a large man whose face was partly obscured by a fold of white cloth. Lumbering towards them waving his blood-spattered *yatagan*[70], he presented himself as a sitting duck.

There was a loud crack as Habib fired and the man staggered backwards, clutching his chest while his comrades halted in their tracks. Taking advantage of their momentary hesitation, Joseph sprang forward and was almost out in the open before Habib gripped him by the waistband and pulled him back to safety.

"There is nothing to be gained here except an early death. We'll soon be the only two left," he growled.

They scrambled out of their fox-hole and set off as fast as they could towards the road, leaving behind the clamour of battle punctuated now and then by the odd shot. By the time they had caught up with their comrades, the Christian forces were already in full retreat.

"We'll drive them back to their lairs some other time," said Habib smiling at the look of disappointment on his young companion's face.

Together they trudged the few miles back to Zahleh under the hot sun. Although they had been defeated, the Christians' marked reluctance to engage in hand-to-hand combat spared them large casualties, with only a dozen or so killed or injured. Dishevelled and exhausted, the dispirited Zahlawis made their way past the barricades and into the town. Instead of hurrahs, however, the townsfolk greeted them with loud mutterings and accusations of cowardice.

Not knowing what else to do, Joseph followed Habib back towards his house in the sprawling market of Housh al-Zarani on the far bank of the river. The maze of narrow streets was crowded with workshops and little manufactories. A rich smell of worked leather led them to a quarter where rows of shoemakers and saddle-makers sat stitching boots and harnesses in front of their shops.

At the corner of the street, a flyblown leg of mutton hung from a solitary metal hook in a butcher's shop. Habib paused in front it, peering into the dark interior.

"Hand me that leg, Sameer," he called out to the proprietor who was nowhere to be seen. "There may not be many customers tomorrow."

"Give me the money," a voice answered him from inside.

"Be generous," Habib replied with a chuckle. "It might be you on that hook tomorrow." From the rear of the establishment, a thin man peered out at Habib with suspicion.

"With you on our side, maybe," he muttered. "You're brave enough when it comes to collecting rent from people like me, but against the Druze..."

He took down the meat without bothering to weigh it. "Take it and give me a piaster. That's a bargain."

Handing the butcher a coin, Habib picked up the leg and brushed away the flies. He was about to wrap it in a piece of cloth when he noticed a brindle-haired dog looking up at him expectantly. Taking a knife from the counter, he sliced off a sliver and tossed the meat to the mongrel. It growled in appreciation and scurried off with its prize.

Round the next corner, they came upon an old abandoned caravanserai[71]. Inside its crumbling walls, there was a courtyard surmounted by a high-vaulted ceiling, heavily cracked and fissured. Seated on an old cinderblock just inside the entrance was a large woman with a prominent mole on her chin. Habib's wife had clearly been waiting for him for some time.

"Thank God you're still alive," she called out in a loud voice when she caught sight of him. "Is it true they'll attack tomorrow?"

"Don't worry about them, woman," replied Habib jovially. "We have a guest."

She gave Joseph a cursory glance while her husband ambled over to a series of shabby apartments at the rear of the courtyard which might have once been the stables. He pushed the door open with his foot and disappeared inside. Following him in, Joseph found himself in one of several sparsely furnished rooms divided by rough wooden partitions.

"Take this," Habib said, handing the meat to his wife. "Let's make the best use of this gift from the Almighty while we still can."

With surprising agility for such a large man, he squatted down on his heels and pulled off his boots, putting on some worn-out sandals.

"Ask Najla to bring some almonds and dried fruit," he continued, "and some *arrack*[72], too. I'm thirsty and so is our guest." While his wife bustled off to find her daughter, Habib grinned at Joseph.

"No food and precious little water," he shouted at her retreating back. "And we've only killed one man all day."

Joseph removed his own boots and sat down on some cushions that were piled up against the far wall while his host propped up his musket in the corner opposite, carefully placing his pouch of powder and shot on a rickety table beside it. Joining him on the cushions, Habib stretched out his large body and yawned.

A young woman appeared a few moments later carrying a small metal basin and a jug of water drawn from the trough in the courtyard. She set it down in front of Habib and waited while he scooped some of it up in his large palms. When he had finished washing his face, she smiled provocatively at Joseph and motioned for him to do the same. She withdrew reluctantly only to reappear a few moments later carrying a heavy-laden brass tray. Kneeling on the floor, she set down a plate of nuts and raisins together with two short glasses and a flask of clear liquid that gave off a powerful smell of crushed aniseed.

Joseph felt her sneak a look at him as her father leaned over to pour a generous measure into the two glasses. She arched one eyebrow and twisted her body to face him, displaying her ample bosom to its best advantage. Taken aback by what she had just done, Joseph looked away to hide his embarrassment. There was always talk that such things occurred on Saint George's Day in Ayn el-Louz, but he had never encountered such brazen behaviour among the girls of his village.

"Where is the water, *ya* Najla?" Habib bellowed, seemingly oblivious to his daughter's antics. She went out to fetch a jug but before she had the opportunity to linger further, her father dismissed her with a grunt. Habib poured the water into the glasses until their contents turned a milky white. Then he handed one to Joseph and, taking care not to spill a drop, raised his own in a toast.

"Here's to victory tomorrow," he proposed, taking a large gulp. "If not, we're done for."

Imitating his host, Joseph raised his own glass and took a swallow. At once he felt a burning sensation at the back of his throat. His eyes watered and he had to put his hand over his mouth in order to control a violent fit of coughing. Habib, on the other hand, was too busy enjoying his own drink to notice the *arrack*'s effect on his young friend. He raised his glass to Joseph a second time.

"*Kesak*[73]," he said, with a wave of his hand. "To your health." Joseph took a deep breath and touched his glass to Habib's, pretending to drink some more.

"We're the men of Zahleh," said his host with a flourish, "and tomorrow we'll be the victors." He drained his glass to the dregs à second time and wiped his mouth with his sleeve.

"As for those *Metouali* villagers," he continued, his spirits buoyed by the alcohol. "We'll teach them to turn against us."

He chuckled genially and winked at Joseph who said nothing and instead ate a handful of raisins hoping they would take away the cloying taste of the alcohol. For a moment, he wondered what his father might think of the jovial bailiff; it would be hard to find two such different people. Meanwhile, his host began tearing roasted meat off the mutton leg with his teeth, pausing only to compliment his wife.

"Your cooking *bijannineh*[74], my little *bulbul*[75]," he bellowed at her. But she had already retreated to another room taking her daughter with her and leaving the men to wolf down their feast alone. From somewhere within the cavernous apartment came the sounds of children playing together.

"Death to our enemies," said Habib, raising his glass. "May we give them a good thrashing and force them to lick their wounds among the snakes and jackals of Hawran."

Joseph clinked his glass against that of the burly bailiff. But, try as he might, he could not bring himself to drink any more. Habib, on the other hand, emptied his in one swallow and, patting his stomach, belched contentedly.

"It was a fine meal," he said as he reached for the *arrack* again.

CHAPTER SEVENTEEN

Joseph did not sleep well that night, kept wide-awake by the loud snoring of the bailiff who lay beside him fully clothed. His wife had appeared around midnight to clear away the leftovers, helped by her daughter. Under her watchful eye, the girl had been unable to attract Joseph's attention, which left her with a crestfallen pout.

Habib, meanwhile, had continued drinking although Joseph had refused more than a second glass in spite of his host's insistence. He waited until the bailiff had been rendered insensible and then found his way to the courtyard where he swilled his mouth out repeatedly. Even the water from the hand pump had failed to cleanse the sting of aniseed in his throat.

When dawn finally broke and he heard Habib's wife and daughter stirring in the next room, he leaned over and shook him awake. At first, the bailiff's head rolled from side to side but then his bloodshot eyes slowly opened.

"What's happening?" he croaked as he scratched his coarse beard. "Are the Druze here already?"

"No," replied Joseph. "But it's time to join the others."

Habib rubbed his eyes with back of his hand and called out to his wife for water. Seizing the jug by its neck, he splashed some on his face before taking a long draught from the spout. Then he shuffled over to the corner and picked up his musket. Squinting down the barrel, he took a greasy rag from a ledge and wiped it down before scraping the firing pan clean with his thumbnail. Handing Joseph the billhook, he stuffed a flask of water into his large pockets along with leftovers from the night before. Then he bade his wife a cheery farewell and strode out of the caravanserai with Joseph following closely behind.

The streets around the house were eerily silent; the shops and workplaces that had been open for business the day before were now all boarded up. They made their way through the alleys towards the river that bisected the town and then began walking swiftly along the main road beside its banks in the direction of the southern defences. They had already covered some ground when Habib suddenly halted.

Seeing him standing there lost in thought, Joseph began wondering whether the bailiff had changed his mind. Was he now planning to flee with his wife and family through the mountains at the head of the gorge? He became even more agitated when Habib abruptly turned on his heel and began striding back up the river in the direction of the gorge.

"Where are we going?" Joseph shouted after him, fearing that the bailiff was no more than a braggart after all.

"I may be a fool," Habib answered him in a serious tone. "But I have a feeling they'll attack from the north. Let's take up our positions there so that we can warn the others if they come along the road from Dhour Shweir."

"But their camp is to the south," Joseph objected.

"You never know with the Druze," said the bailiff as he wiped his nose with his sleeve. "They're tricky customers."

Crossing the river back to the other bank, they turned north past the street that led to the Church of Our Saviour and the monastery before entering the gorge and climbing up into the hills beyond. Their progress was slow, hampered by overgrown vines and high terrace walls.

A warm breeze rustled the leaves as they looked for a suitable spot from where to observe the northern perimeter of Zahleh without being seen. The bailiff spotted a shallow depression just below the crown of the hill overlooking an area of open ground as far as the springs. To the west, the road to Dhour Shweir Joseph had come down two days earlier twisted up the side of the mountain like a coiled serpent.

Habib sat down heavily and took a swig of water from his flask before handing it to Joseph. Rivulets of sweat poured down his forehead into his thick eyebrows. Laying his musket on the ground in front of him, he began double-checking its firing mechanism.

Joseph could now clearly see why Habib had changed his mind. From this position, they could look out over a stretch of countryside from the road to the springs. The freshness of the early morning had given way to a warm summer's day filled with the rasp of crickets and the hum of bees. To his relief, the lingering smell of the *arrack* had finally disappeared and his head had cleared. Some movement in the far distance caused a ripple of excitement to run through his body. He prodded Habib who was nodding off as he struggled to stay awake.

"Do you see something over there?" Joseph said, pointing at the far ridge. "It looks like a flag." Habib squinted in the general direction of his finger.

"Not a damn thing."

"Look!" Joseph insisted. "It's coming closer."

"God save me from the pleasures of this life," Habib groaned as he strained to focus his eyes on the spot. "I swear I'll become a hermit when this is over."

"Perhaps it's Taniyus," whispered Joseph exultantly. "Maybe he's come at last."

"Damn him," muttered Habib in reply. "He wouldn't help anyone unless there was some plunder in it."

Placing his musket within easy reach, he took cover behind the bushes. There was now no mistaking the large body of men advancing in their direction from the northwest. The sound of drums carried on the breeze towards the spot where they lay motionless in the undergrowth, waiting for them to come into clear view. Before long, Joseph was able to make out the colour of their flags and emblems.

"I think they're the Keserwanis!" he said excitedly. "Aren't those pictures of the Virgin?"

Before Habib could restrain him, he had leaped up and begun running across the open ground towards them. When he saw the flags were adorned with an image of the Virgin Mary, he let out a whoop of joy. But it was not until he was well within range of their muskets that Joseph noticed something strange about the men. Instead of the customary black or blue turbans, they appeared to be wearing white ones. Baffled by this apparent contradiction, he ducked behind a bush.

At their helm, he could see a tall man on a white horse trotting back and forth, halting now and then to give orders. His sharp eyes focused themselves on the man's face and the longer he looked at him, the more certain he became that it was not Taniyus. His manner seemed altogether too dignified and besides, he could not see the blacksmith's mane of lank hair.

The beating of the war drums grew louder and the chanting swelled to a deafening roar. It took only a few moments for Joseph to distinguish the words.

We will burnish their blades,
And make our spear points glisten,
Until our anger fades,
And our enemies listen...

He recognized them at once. It was the war song his grandmother had taught him and his brother when they were younger. Cursing his stupidity, Joseph now realized they were Druze! Habib's instincts had been right all along. They had circled round from the south to attack Zahleh at its weakest point in a strategic move that only a wily and experienced commander could have devised.

His heart racing, Joseph glanced over his shoulder towards the lookout post where he had left Habib and waved at him in warning. Then he turned and bolted back up the hill until the crack of a shot above his head forced him to take cover amongst the brambles. Ignoring the spiky thorns, he broke cover and raced on, twisting and turning from side to side like a hare in headlong flight.

Suddenly, Habib's bulky frame emerged into full view ahead of him, silhouetted against the sun. Pausing only briefly to fire his musket at the oncoming Druze, the bailiff turned and began lumbering down the hillside towards town. By the time Joseph caught up with him, he was already panting heavily.

"They've tricked us," he gasped. Joseph nodded, too breathless to speak.

"It may only be a diversion," Habib stammered. "But we must sound the alarm before they start burning houses."

With the Druze at their heels, Joseph and Habib half ran, half crouched through the grapevines. The terraces that had hindered them on their way up now provided cover as they bolted towards the town.

"They're coming! They're coming!" they cried out at the top of their lungs. When they reached the Convent of Our Saviour, they stood in the courtyard flushed and out of breath while the monks and priests went on about their daily chores as though it were just another day.

"They're coming from the north," Joseph shouted to one of monks who was sweeping the dust off the steps in front of the church.

"You're wrong, my friend," he replied, unperturbed. "They're attacking from the south. Calm down, this is the house of God."

Habib tugged at Joseph's sleeve. "Leave them be," he wheezed. "Let them take their chances like the priests of Rashaya."

But Joseph hesitated, torn between his desire to stay and protect the monastery and the urgent need to alert the defenders at the other end of town to the imminent threat from the north. Beside him, Habib seethed with frustration.

"Damn you," he blurted out, "we must get to the barricades as soon as we can! The northern approaches will be overrun."

"I'll stay behind with the priests," said Joseph, resolutely. "You go on."

"It's people like us who must defend Zahleh," Habib shouted, spitting on the ground, "and not the priests."

The monk looked away in disgust, ignoring the bailiff's blasphemous outburst.

At that moment, a tall figure appeared from the shadows of the cloisters and came towards them, the same priest who had taken care of Joseph two days earlier. Ignoring the bailiff, he smiled at Joseph. When the monk began to explain to him what had happened, he raised his hand.

"Go with your foul-mouthed companion," he said, quietly putting his arm around Joseph's shoulders. "What he says is true; there is nothing for you to do here."

"But you have no one to protect you, Abouna," Joseph replied.

"God will protect us," the priest continued evenly. "The Druze have their own holy men and they will not violate the sanctity of our church or harm us. We'll be safer without you."

Habib strode off with Joseph following him, but not before he had scowled at the monk one last time. Together they hurried on past the row of large houses where Joseph had seen horsemen riding through the streets. Most of them appeared abandoned, their owners having fled after bolting their wooden doors shut.

Groups of townspeople flooded the main road, heading in the direction from which they had just come. Mothers with infants in their arms shepherded their other children in front of them while elderly men and women struggled to keep up with their families.

"Look at them," said Habib in disgust, pointing to a group of wealthy townspeople shoving their way through the crowd while their servants dragged handcarts laden with valuables behind them.

"They're cowards."

As they approached the southern limits, they could hear the defenders shouting to one another as they readied themselves for an assault by the main body of attackers amassed in the gardens beyond the gates. Everywhere around him, Joseph could see traces of skirmishes that had already taken place that morning. Injured men groaned feebly just inside the rampart where they had been dragged by their comrades. In the distance, the air shimmered above the roofs of farmhouses that had been set ablaze.

"Help me," moaned a wounded man as he grabbed at Joseph. A trickle of blood oozed from the corner of his mouth. Joseph put his flask to the man's blackened lips and then gently disengaged his hand so that he could take his place at the barricade beside Habib.

"They're getting ready," the bailiff was muttering.

"Is it too late to spread the alarm?" said Joseph.

"Yes," replied Habib. "Look at them gathering over there. We'll be lucky if we can hold them off here."

As the drums beat louder, Joseph tightened his grip on the handle of the billhook. He could now see the attackers advancing among the fruit trees. Down the length of the barricade, there were cracks and puffs of smoke as the Christians discharged their weapons, ignoring shouts from their leaders to withhold fire until their enemies were within range. Habib poked his loaded musket through a hole in the wall and waited patiently for a target to present itself.

"*Shidd halak*[76], *ya ibni*," the bailiff said when he saw that Joseph's hands were shaking. "Pull yourself together." For once, his gruff voice sounded almost tender.

To Joseph, the next few seconds were a blur. He heard a crack from Habib's musket and saw him stoop to reload. Further down the barricade, the attackers had already broken through and were running towards them, slashing left and right at anyone who dared stand his ground. Joseph nudged Habib to alert him to the danger, but the bailiff was too engrossed in loading his musket to pay him any attention. One of the warriors rushed at them, brandishing his sword in the air. Catching sight of him out of the corner of his eye, Joseph tried to pull Habib out of the way, but it was too late.

The blade came down on the crown of the bailiff's head with a sharp crack, splitting it open like a walnut. Then the man turned to confront Joseph, but before he could tug the blade free, Joseph had swung his billhook at him with all his might, almost severing his head from his shoulders.

The man slumped forward over Habib's corpse, providing an accidental shield for Joseph against the ones following behind him. For a few moments he remained where he was, crouched beneath the two bodies. But as soon as the immediate danger had passed, he crawled out from under them and peered out over the rampart.

Around him, defenders had abandoned their posts and were falling back in disarray as the Druze pressed home their attack. In the commotion, no one noticed Joseph walking by himself along the barricade. By the time he reached the far end, it was all but deserted. Dazed and confused, he curled up on the ground, still clutching the bloodied handle of the billhook in his hand.

It was some time before his heart ceased its furious pounding. The sun was already beginning its descent when he finally got to his feet and dusted himself off. He clambered out of the ditch and walked around the mud barricade across the ground in front of it where, only a few hours earlier, the battle had raged.

Debris lay everywhere.

Branches and twigs ripped from the fruit trees littered the ground.

Rows of vegetables lay trampled underfoot, their skins split open and their flesh smeared over the earth.

Among them lay fallen men, their limbs twisted and their faces blackening under the beating sun. Crows hopped from one body to the next, driven away only by wild dogs that crisscrossed back and forth among the human remains, sniffing at them for easy pickings.

"There is no power and strength save in God," a man repeated in a dull monotone as he raised his arms towards the sky in a gesture of despair.

More by instinct than any sense of purpose, Joseph set off through the orchards in the direction of the road. When he reached it, he turned west towards the mountains and his home, joining a long line of refugees already heading in the same direction. The elderly rode on donkeys or in carts, but most travelled on foot with their dull eyes fixed on the road ahead. Not far from the village of Chtaura, Joseph found himself in the company of an old man with a wooden crutch. Several women and children surrounded him.

"There are caves near here where we can spend the night," he said after they had walked together for a while. "You are welcome to join us if you wish."

Joseph murmured his thanks.

"And perhaps we can beg for some food from the Jesuit fathers." He nodded, too listless to speak.

Not long afterwards, the family broke away from the main column and headed down a little track out onto the plain. Joseph followed suit with scarcely a second thought. They walked for a short distance until they came to a small hill where they began to disappear, one by one, into a gap in the rocks behind a large boulder. Stooping down, Joseph edged his way into the mouth of the cave and immediately found himself in a narrow passageway just wide enough for one person to pass through. He made his way along it, crouching whenever his head brushed against the low jagged ceiling. Then, all of a sudden, the corridor opened out into a large chamber. A single candle burned in the centre, its light barely enough to dispel the gloom of its secret surroundings.

As his eyes became accustomed to the near darkness, he was able to distinguish dim shapes moving about in the shadows. Several families sat against the damp walls and in the little ingresses chiselled into the rocky sides. Beneath the low murmur of their conversation, he could hear plops of water dripping steadily from the roof onto the stone floor.

"What is this place?" Joseph asked the old man who was standing beside him.

"It's a grotto the Jesuit fathers once showed us," he answered. "But today, it is our sanctuary." Joseph nodded wearily. War to him had lost its lustre.

Outside, Zahleh burned. The once radiant bride of the Bekaa had been assaulted and her citizens driven out. Flames lit up the hazy dusk with bursts of orange light. Inside the town armed gangs raided houses, forced open locked gates, and smashed down doors with axes and rams. The majestic ones that Joseph had so admired on his arrival now lay splintered in their frames, and the houses they guarded, ransacked.

The majority of the city's sons and daughters had chosen to escape before it was overrun. Some of the younger and more agile defenders climbed over the rooftops, leaping from house to house and only daring to climb down when they thought themselves safe before fleeing into the hills to seek shelter among tombs and hermits' caves. The attackers took whatever they could find, even forcing the women to hand over their jewellery. Chests and strongboxes were pried open. If they found no coins or silverware to loot, they stuffed their gunny bags with damask curtains and silk robes before torching the houses.

The Arab tribesmen who had joined the attack broke into the stables. They ran their hands along the horses' flanks and down their legs, looking for splints and spavins. When they found a mount they fancied, they saddled it then and there and rode off.

By nightfall, not a soul was left stirring in the town. A few fires continued to burn, but the churches for the most part had escaped the wanton acts of desecration that had taken place in Hasbaya and Rashaya. All but one of Zahleh's priests had been spared. It was rumoured that a courageous father had been killed as he stood on the steps of his church, trying to bar looters from entering it.

A considerable number of Zahleh's inhabitants escaped through the vineyards at the head of the gorge rather than taking the road west towards the coast as Joseph had done. When they reached the Christian heartlands of the Metn and Keserwan, they sought accommodation with their relatives. The ones who had none in those parts pleaded for sanctuary in convents and monasteries.

CHAPTER EIGHTEEN

News that Zahleh had been ransacked spread throughout the mountains like wildfire and reached the hamlet of Ayn el-Louz only fifteen miles away in no time at all. By the next morning, the feeling of mistrust between the two communities, which had been bubbling underneath the surface, intensified to the extent that when the village girls went to fetch water from the spring, they barely even acknowledged one another's presence.

Out in the open fields and on the terraces, the Druze and Christian farmers greeted one another with no more than a cursory nod instead of their usual cheery salutations. Lifetime neighbours, who only a day or two before would have been happy to assist each other in repairing a terrace or clearing a piece of land, now eyed one another with suspicion when they passed in the village.

But despite these unwelcome changes, there was one cause for celebration. Although his mother and sister constantly fussed over him, Mohanad was no longer teetering on the verge of death. His grandmother's homespun remedies had flushed out his fever, and the chills, which had caused him to shake uncontrollably, had all but disappeared. The flesh around his shoulder wound was scarred from where the doctor had cauterized it with the hot iron, but the angry swelling had begun to subside. Although weak and barely able to prop himself up on his pillow to drink the broth his mother spooned into his mouth, he had already started regaining his strength.

From time to time, Maryam would overhear Fatmeh talking about him at the spring with the other girls when she went to fetch water. So far, their muffled conversations had revealed that her brother's condition was improving, but little else besides. Resisting the urge to ask her directly about Mohanad as she had done when he had first been carried back to the village, she bided her time waiting for an opportunity to enquire about him in private.

It was while Maryam was enduring a spell of silent anguish that the village priest had come to their house one morning accompanied by a tall woman whom she had never seen before. She wore a blood-stained kaftan and a silk cap on her head, covering the tattered remains of a muslin veil. A small boy with wide eyes peeped out from behind her skirts.

"Welcome, Abouna," said her mother, looking from the priest to the woman and back.

"Good morning," he replied with his usual air of self-importance. "I hope that your family is well."

Her mother merely nodded, making no mention of the disappearance of her eldest son although Maryam was sure from his lack of curiosity that the priest must have already heard about it. Nothing remained a secret in the village for long. He cleared his throat, a sure sign that he was about to ask for a favour.

"There is something I wish to speak to you about, *Sitt* Sa'adeh." He paused as he nudged the woman and the little boy forward.

"These poor people have fled here from the town of Hasbaya. A muleteer left them at the door of the church this morning. I found them when I went to unlock it."

Leaning forward, she took the woman gently by the arm. After a brief glance, she waved aside the rest of the priest's introduction. Here were two people who needed her help.

"What is your name?" she asked her softly.

"Layal," the woman replied.

"May God recompense you for your kindness," said the priest, eager to have his own contribution recognized. "She is newly widowed."

"You will be safe with us, *ukhtee*[77]," Sa'adeh murmured into the woman's ear as she helped her through the door and into the house.

Delighted to have found the refugees accommodation in one of the most comfortable houses in the village, the priest hurriedly bade them farewell. Despite their ragged appearance, he sensed they came from a wealthy family and might be of use to him in the future.

"Go and fetch some water," said Saʻadeh, turning to her daughter. Maryam knew better than to dawdle when her mother was in one of her purposeful moods.

"They must have travelled a long way," she muttered to herself as she examined Layal and her son more closely. "Look, they're covered in dust and their clothes are all stained."

The forlorn state of their guests caused even Maryam to forget her brooding. Although she could tell from the woman's clothes and manners that they were not villagers, she had no real idea where they had come from. The name Hasbaya meant nothing to her.

But I'm glad they've come to our house, she thought as she picked up an empty pitcher and set off in the direction of the spring. Maryam had good reason to be pleased by their unexpected arrival. The house had been a gloomy place since her brother had vanished. Her mother was always irritable and her father barely spoke. Nobody, not even her grandmother, now dared mention his name in front of them.

She returned to find her mother talking to their guest, who was now seated in her grandmother's chair, her long legs tucked beneath her. Maryam's eyes fell on the necklace she was wearing. She noticed the way the woman absently touched the purple stone with her fingertips from time to time. Her little boy sat silently on the floor, watched by Maryam's own brother and sister who stared back, too timid to go near him.

"Good," said Saʻadeh brusquely. "Now pour some water into the bowl."

Maryam did as she was told and handed her the half-filled bowl although she resented the way her mother ordered her around in front of the strangers. Then she fetched a piece of clean cloth from a shelf and held it out to her.

"*Tsuh, tsuh*, child," clucked her mother, taking the cloth. Sa'adeh soaked it and handed it to Layal who thanked her politely. Murmuring endearments all the while, she began wiping the dirt off the little boy's face. Then she rinsed it and washed her own, removing the layers of caked dust from her pale skin with delicate movements of her slender hands. The tired muscles at the corners of her eyes gradually began to relax.

Without realizing it, Maryam found herself staring at their guest. Never before had she come across a person with so much natural grace and beauty, except perhaps for Mohanad. When her mother got up and walked over to the brazier to prepare something for them to eat, Maryam took the opportunity to edge closer to her. For once the house was almost empty. Her grandmother was out visiting neighbours and the men had not yet returned. Layal wrung out the cloth and hung it on the side of the bowl to dry. She gave Maryam a weary smile and pushed her little boy forward towards her.

"Say hello to the lady."

Maryam smiled back at him nervously although she loved children. She noticed that Layal pronounced her words in a soft, lilting accent which was quite different to the way the villagers spoke. To her ears, her voice sounded like honey.

"I'm Maryam," she finally stuttered. In an effort to overcome her awkwardness, she reached out to take the little boy's hand, but he retreated behind his mother's skirts from where he looked at her with his big, sad eyes.

"He's so beautiful," she said.

An idea came to her as she watched him peering out from his hiding place. Going to the back of the room, she returned with a little purse made from spun silk. It was a present from her grandmother, handcrafted out of the discards from the old spinner. The old lady had stitched them together into a simple patchwork pouch and embroidered it with songbirds. Kneeling down, Maryam folded back the corner of the floor mat and emptied out a handful of black and white pebbles. To her surprise, the little boy began watching her with interest.

"Come and help with the food," her mother called out, interrupting her. "Your father and brother will be back shortly and they'll be hungry." She smiled at Layal shyly to excuse herself.

Imm George returned from her visit to the neighbours while Layal and her son were in the middle of eating their *burghoul* stew. Maryam heard her grandmother coming down the path and saw her hesitate the moment she caught a glimpse of the strangers through the open door. Noticing the old lady gesturing at her, she went outside and explained what had happened that morning.

"They were brought here by the priest, Teta."

"Who are they?" Imm George asked. "Where've they come from?"

"A place called Hasbaya. The priest said there was a massacre there." Baboush pushed his way through her legs and trotted into the house while she was in the middle of her explanation.

"Get that animal out of here before I turn it into a stew," her mother shouted. Leaving her grandmother still standing outside, Maryam rushed after her pet only to find Wael already stroking it. She turned to look back at her mother, awaiting further instruction.

"Never mind," Sa'adeh relented. "Let him stay for now, but be sure to put him out before your father comes in."

In the commotion, Imm George had slipped quietly in and, without hesitating, walked straight up to Layal.

"*Sharraftoona*," she said somewhat formally. "We are honoured." Layal got to her feet stiffly. The sight of her standing beside her grandmother made Maryam realize how tall she was.

"It is you who do us the honour," Layal replied with an elegance of expression that masked her physical and mental exhaustion. Imm George nodded at the compliment and her wizened face creased into a smile of approval.

"Excuse me," she said as she turned away. "I have some work to do."

With that, Imm George retreated to the back of the room and began to inspect the silkworms that had just begun the intricate process of spinning their cocoons. Maryam could hear the creaks of the wicker hinges as her grandmother opened the baskets and took out the shelves one by one to inspect the pupating grubs. Meanwhile without anyone noticing, the little boy had drawn a chequered square on the dirt floor and was busy arranging the pebbles in rows on it.

"What are you doing?" Maryam asked him.

"I'm setting them out." He barely paused to look up at her from the board. Even his mother was smiling. These were the first words he had spoken since they had arrived.

"He's playing *Dama*[78]," she said softly. "It's a game his father taught him." Maryam looked down at the floor embarrassed and afraid that the memory of her husband would cause the widow to begin weeping. Instead, Layal touched her lightly on the shoulder.

"He'd be delighted to play checkers with you when you have time."

Outside, they could hear the bleating of the goats returning from the mountain pastures followed by the voices of As'ad and George as they drove the animals round to the back of the house. Maryam waited until she heard the hurdle being dragged across the entrance before slipping out of the room to alert her father. She wanted to be the first to tell him the news. George listened carefully to what she had to say before asking for some water and a bowl so that he and As'ad could wash themselves. Then he walked solemnly over to where Layal was sitting without a word to either his wife or mother.

"*Ahlan wa sahlan*," he greeted her. "You are most welcome in our home." Layal rose to her feet, pulling what remained of her veil over her face, but George gestured for her to stay where she was.

"Make yourself comfortable," he said. "My son and I will eat over there."

To Maryam's surprise, her father went to the back of the room where the women usually sat, something she had never seen him do before. After exchanging a brief word with Imm George, he took his place on the mat and indicated to As'ad to do the same. While Sa'adeh served their supper from the pot, Maryam brought them a cup of water each, but he dismissed her with a wave of his hand.

"Go and talk to our guests," he said. "Make them feel at home."

As darkness fell outside, Imm George took down several jars of herbs and dried flowers that she kept stored high up on the shelves and set some water to boil on the brazier. Then she sent Maryam outside to pick some fresh thyme. Taking a pinch from this jar and a few leaves from that, she set about preparing a special tea.

"This will make you feel better," she said when she had finished. Layal took the proffered cup from her and even Wael stopped his game long enough to look up at the old lady.

"Thank you," said Layal, taking a sip. "It tastes good."

"*Wala yhimkon*[79]," Imm George replied.

While they were drinking their tea, Maryam laid out a mattress for them on one side of the room and hung the largest piece of cloth she could find from the beams so that their visitors could enjoy a little privacy.

CHAPTER NINETEEN

The next day as she was walking down to fetch water from the spring, Maryam overheard the other girls gossiping about Layal and her son while she was still some distance away. As soon as they spotted her coming towards them, one of them walked up to her and began bombarding her with questions.

"Where did those strangers come from, the tall lady and the little boy? We saw them arrive with the muleteers yesterday."

"*Wattee sawtik*[80]," Maryam hissed, but the girl took no notice of her.

"Why did she have bloodstains on her clothes?" the girl went on as the others crowded around them. "Tell us the whole story, Maryam."

At first Maryam refused to tell them anything, not even what the priest had said when he had first brought them to their door. She felt it would be a betrayal of confidence. But the longer she held out, the more they pestered her.

"They come from a town near Damascus," Maryam said eventually, repeating what her mother had told her the evening before. "That's all I know."

"*Yalla*, Maryam. You know more than that." The crowd closed in as they tried to wheedle more information out of her.

"There was a massacre and they fled," she said finally in exasperation. "Now leave me alone."

But they would not. Clustering around her like flies, the girls continued to ask questions and make wild guesses about them. They had never seen anyone quite like Layal and her son before and they could not contain their curiosity. How had they got there? Could they really have journeyed all that way through the mountains with just a muleteer to guide them? Were they really city dwellers?

Even the Druze girls kept shooting her curious glances as they spoke in hushed whispers to one another. Eager to get away, Maryam filled her pitcher as quickly as she could and began to walk back to the house. But she hadn't gone very far when she heard footsteps trailing behind her. In mounting anger she spun round, thinking it was one of the Christian girls. But to her surprise, it turned out to be Mohanad's sister.

"How's your brother?" she asked, after they had greeted each other.

"Better."

"Has his shoulder healed?" A note of concern crept into her voice.

"Not yet."

They walked for a short distance side by side until she unexpectedly turned to face her with a serious look.

"You were talking about the woman and the little boy who came to the village yesterday with the mule driver," she said softly. "My friends have asked me to find out who they are."

Maryam began by repeating what she had told the others, and before she could stop herself, she was describing how ragged and exhausted they had looked when the priest first brought them to the door. Fatmeh nodded as she listened intently.

"How they must have suffered…," she said, more to herself than to Maryam. "The little boy is as thin as a stick."

Leaving her to retrace her steps, Maryam continued on up the track. When she reached the house, she found her mother deep in conversation with Layal. Wael was sitting cross-legged on the floor, playing with the pebbles while her little brother and sister watched, still too shy to speak.

"Why did you head for the coast instead of Damascus?" Sa'adeh was asking her as Maryam opened the door.

"After my husband was killed," said Layal, "we had to choose between returning to the city and heading west towards Beirut."

She wiped away a solitary tear and sighed. It had taken several days for the full weight of her grief to manifest itself and when it did, she was forced to ask the muleteer to halt. She had been shaking so much that she could no longer go on. Leaving Wael with him, she stole away to a secluded spot and there she wept until she had no more tears left to shed. Layal had not wanted her son to see her so anguished.

"Then I remembered my mother had some relatives in Jezzine," she sighed, "so we set out in that direction. But before we reached the town, we were told by a traveller it had been attacked too."

"*Ya dillee 'alayyee*," Maryam heard her grandmother muttering from the back of the room.

"The hardest part was from Jezzine to your village. We had to travel high in the mountains. We slept in caves and drank water from mountain springs, but we didn't dare go near the villages." It seemed that the muleteer had taken them as far as Ayn el-Louz because of its proximity to the main road to Beirut.

"What did you eat?" Sa'adeh asked, concerned as usual with the practicalities of life.

"Very little," replied Layal. "If we came across a secluded house, Mohammed would ask the people there for food."

"You trusted a Turk to guide you?" said Imm George, looking up from the silkworm boxes in astonishment. To her, all Muslims were Turks.

"Why not?" said Layal. "We had many Muslim friends. Most of the Emir's family were Muslims and they were killed trying to save us."

A morose silence settled over the room as her mother and grandmother went back to their chores, careful not to make Layal's grief any worse with their probing questions. Seizing the opportunity, Maryam placed the pitcher by the door and sat down beside Layal who, in a gesture of spontaneous affection, stretched out her hand and took Maryam's in her own. Wael stopped playing with the pebbles and looked up. For the first time since they had arrived, a genuine smile lit up the corners of his small face.

"Will you play with me now?"

"Sure," Maryam beamed back. "But first you'll have to teach me."

"Don't you use them to play checkers with?" he asked, evidently surprised by her reply.

"No," she said. "I only use them for sewing patterns."

He placed eight pebbles of the same colour on opposite sides of the chequered square he had drawn in the dust on the floor, arranging them systematically into two lines and leaving the last row at either end empty. Then he moved one of the white pebbles forward.

"You can only move them in straight lines." His tone was serious, like a teacher.

Maryam watched him do the same with a black one. She was already concentrating so hard on the game that she barely noticed when Layal got up from her chair and walked over to the divan. A beam of sunlight from the barred window caught the green silk in the weave of her kaftan, making it shimmer as she moved. Meanwhile, her son shuffled the black and white pebbles in turn until they faced each other across the board.

"Now watch what happens."

With a quick movement of his wrist, he hopped one of the black pebbles over a white one. Picking it up, he placed it on the side. Noticing that Maryam was struggling to keep up, he stopped to explain the move.

"Black ate white," he said simply. He countered the advance of the black pebble with a white one from the row behind.

"It's going to eat this one, too." He made the black pebble hop over a white one. After a few more moves, one of the black stones had reached the other end of the board.

"That's a flyer now," he said to Maryam, his little face lighting up with pleasure. "It can move as much as it wants."

"Why don't you use it to eat the rest of the whites?" asked Maryam.

"You'll see why in a moment," he replied.

Over the next several turns, Maryam was so intent on watching the black pebbles jump over the white ones that she scarcely noticed when one of the whites reached the opposite end of the board.

"Watch closely now," said Wael, warming to his role as her instructor.

His audience had grown. Layal was smiling down at her son from the divan while Maryam's younger brother and sister had edged closer, eager to see what would happen next. Wael pushed one of the black stones forward and then, taking the white flyer in his hand, he moved it from one end of the board to the other, leapfrogging all the black stones in its path. The pile of pebbles at the side grew larger and larger until there was only a single black piece left.

"How did the whites get the upper hand so quickly?" asked Maryam, mystified by the sudden change in fortune. Everything seemed to have turned on its head like the world they now lived in.

"That's my secret," the little boy grinned mischievously. "I'll teach you some other time." Picking up all the pebbles, he put them back in their original places on the board.

"Your turn," he said, pointing at them.

"Move the white; move the white," chorused the children, now thoroughly excited and eager to see their older sister play.

"*Tayyib*[81]," protested Maryam, "but don't dare laugh at me if I do something stupid."

From then on and for every day that their guests remained in the village, Maryam spent an hour or so learning to play *Dama* after she had fetched the water. Layal would sometimes watch them, encouraging Maryam each time she almost gave up in despair at her inability to learn. The daily contest was so absorbing that even the younger children would stop playing with the chickens and come in to watch.

For Maryam, the morning lessons had one particular advantage: Her mother and grandmother did not disturb her. They had both agreed to exempt Maryam from her usual household duties for an hour each morning while Wael instructed her in the intricacies of Turkish draughts.

As the days passed, Maryam gradually came to know something of Layal's past life. At first, she had been too traumatized to speak about herself. So Maryam would sit on the floor playing *Dama* with her son while she lay on the divan listlessly watching them. But as her strength began to return, her morale improved.

"Tell me something about yourself," Maryam had asked her once during a lull in the game, noticing that she was in better spirits.

To her delight, Layal began to tell her stories about her childhood in Damascus and the life that she had once lived as a young woman in the vibrant city. Maryam sat spellbound listening to her description of its vast size and the thousands of people who thronged its streets. When she told her of the luxuries that could be found in its sprawling markets, Maryam only craved more. When she mentioned the palaces of merchants and pashas, she did her best to imagine them, comparing them with the only thing she knew of that could possibly match them, her grandmother's Beiteddine.

Among Maryam's favourites were stories of Layal's excursions outside Damascus with her cousins on feast days. On those occasions, they would leave behind the bustle of the city for the serenity and freshness of the countryside, taking their picnic baskets with them. These family trips meant more to her than Layal's grand visits to the palaces of pashas' wives in the company of her mother and sisters where they would sit and drink coffee in the splendour of their salons.

"It's beautiful to ride in a carriage to the top of Mount Qassioun and look out over the gardens beside the Barada River," Layal would begin as she set the scene for Maryam to imagine it. "From there you can see the entire city spread out below you in a mosaic of life and colour."

"Go on," Maryam would say, closing her eyes as she tried to picture the scene in her head.

"Look down from the Marjeh to the river with the citadel and the old city in the distance."

"What can I see?"

"Mosques and churches. The biggest one has John the Baptist's head buried in it."

"Go on." Maryam was eager to hear more.

"Then there's the Via Recta, the long street which runs from the Christian quarter in the east to the covered market in the west."

"Is that Frankish?" Maryam once asked.

"No, it's Latin," said Layal, laughing in amusement. "The language of a people who conquered Syria long before the Arabs."

"You know so many things." She gazed at Layal with something close to awe.

"That's because I went to school," she replied gently.

"I want to go to school, too," said Maryam, keeping her voice low. "They used to say a Frankish lady was going to open one in Ayn el-Louz, but that was before the troubles began."

The following day while Wael was busy setting out the stones, Layal turned the tables on Maryam by asking her about her own life.

"Tell me what it is like to live in the mountains?"

"It all depends on the time of year," Maryam began. "The men work in the fields, planting and harvesting crops or looking after the animals. Women sometimes work outside when it's a busy time of year, but mostly we take care of the house and the children."

"Go on."

"We visit our relatives all the time and attend mass on Sundays. My favourite time is the feast of Saint George in early summer."

"What about the Druze people who live here?" Layal enquired. "Do you visit them, too?"

"Not these days," she admitted. "And now who knows if we'll ever be invited to their houses again..."

"But they share the village with you," Layal insisted. "You see them all the time."

Maryam shook her head miserably. The sacking of Zahleh had changed everything. Christians and Druze now lived apart in a state of unease, and the many Druze families with whom they had once been friendly avoided them. In spite of her occasional outbursts, it was Imm George who felt the change most keenly because she had known many Druze women well throughout her life. She was deeply saddened that she could no longer visit them as she once did whether to offer congratulations on the birth of a son or condolences on the death of a relative.

Later that day, Maryam decided to divulge her most important and closely-guarded secret to Layal. It was the chance she had been waiting for, to confide in someone she both liked and admired. While they were sitting together eating supper, she whispered something into her ear, causing the widow to wink back mischievously.

"Tomorrow," she whispered in her honeyed voice.

The following day, Layal rose early to join Maryam as she set off at dawn to collect water. She bent down to pick up the other pitcher as they left the house.

"No," said Maryam when she saw what Layal was doing. "I'll come back for that later."

"Show me how," Layal insisted, ignoring her protests. "I want to see what it's like."

"You'll need this then." She handed Layal a felt pad. "The bottom of the pitcher is very hard."

When they reached the spring, they found the Christian and Druze girls lined up on opposite sides of the basin as they had been doing ever since the first confrontation. As Layal and Maryam approached, the sound of their voices died away and both groups of girls began to stare at the outsider. Embarrassed by their rudeness, Maryam took her place in the queue without looking around. A few moments passed before she turned to see where Layal was.

It took her some time to spot her. But when she did, it was obvious that any fears she might have had about her reception were groundless. Layal was standing happily in line, smiling at everyone. The bolder ones returned her smile while the others stared at the ground or tugged their scarves across their faces as if she were a man.

When it was her turn at the spring, Maryam lowered her pitcher into the basin and let it fill. Layal stood on one side observing her and then began to copy what she had just done. But it was a very different matter when it came to hoisting the heavy pitcher up onto her head. Layal made several attempts to do it but without success. She was at the point of giving up when Fatmeh walked over to her.

"Let me help you," she offered, taking the pitcher from her. Standing on tiptoe, she just managed to place the felt mat on top of Layal's head. But when she tried to heave it up with the help of her friend, she could not do it. Instead, Layal took it back and emptied some of the water out.

"Let me kneel down first," she suggested to the two girls. "I don't care if I look like a hobbled camel." Laughter broke out all around them as Layal knelt down and Fatmeh and her friend placed the pitcher on her head, settling it gently on the mat.

"Your pain is our pain," she said to her as she guided Layal's hands up to the handles. "May God grant your husband better fortune in the next life." The other Druze girls all nodded in agreement.

"Thank you," Layal replied. Then they set off back to the house with Layal doing her best to imitate Maryam by swaying her hips from side to side while keeping her shoulders steady.

"That's the way," giggled Maryam, as she stopped to allow Layal to catch up. "You've hardly spilled a drop."

When they were a little further up the track, Maryam finally plucked up the courage to broach the subject of Mohanad and her feelings for him. The time had come for her to unburden herself.

CHAPTER TWENTY

"She's the sister of the Druze boy I told you about yesterday."

"The one who just helped me?"

"I want to tell you about him." Maryam looked around nervously. "Let's find a more private place. People here are such gossips. They even want to know what you're thinking."

They walked back up the track until they found a shady place not far from the spot where Maryam had first seen Mohanad with his father in the orchard. Maryam set her pitcher down and then helped Layal with hers.

"That's better," said Layal, stretching her neck. "The next time I see someone carrying a water jug, I'll know just how difficult it is." Layal sat down at the side of the road with her legs stretched out while Maryam squatted down beside her.

"It was over there where I first saw him," Maryam said, gesturing towards the trees. "He looked so..." She was struggling to find the words to describe the man who had invaded her every thought, "... different to my cousin Faris. The one my father wants me to marry."

"Tell me what happened." Layal's tone was soothing.

"The next day, he came up to me as I was walking home. He asked if I'd like to see inside his shelter."

"Where is it?"

"Just over there by the wall," said Maryam, pointing to where the shelter stood some way back from the road, partially hidden by a low wall.

"What did you do?"

"Not much," said Maryam shyly. "But he made me feel very special, as if he was interested in me."

"Did you hold hands?" Layal asked the question in such a simple and honest way that Maryam felt no judgment.

"No."

"Hmm," said Layal. "Did he touch you at all?"

Maryam made an unconvincing effort to laugh away the mere suggestion of physical contact although she now wished there had been. Although she was tempted, she did not dare tell Layal how Mohanad had really made her feel.

"He was very correct with me," she said in the best matter-of-fact manner she could muster. And then came the most important question of all. Even though she had grown up in a city, Layal was aware that a village girl's reputation could be smeared very easily.

"Did anyone see you together?"

"No one," said Maryam, looking up at her misty-eyed. "The very next day I heard he'd gone off to fight." Layal placed a protective arm around the younger woman.

"When they brought him back on a stretcher, he had a musket ball in his shoulder." She fought back the stubborn tears that threatened to engulf her. "But his sister told me he's much better now."

"That's good news at least," Layal said, keen to encourage her friend.

"But I still can't visit him. There's no one I can even talk to about him."

"I suppose you can't," Layal sighed. "This fighting is bringing disaster on us all."

They sat in silence while a solitary butterfly fluttered by and alighted on a nearby thistle.

"In our village, Druze marry Druze and Christians, Christians," Maryam went on miserably as she pulled the damp strands of hair out of her eyes. "If you change your religion, it brings shame on your family. They throw you out," she sobbed, wringing her hands in frustration.

"There are worse things than a broken heart," said Layal in an effort to comfort the younger woman. "Just look at me."

But Maryam was so mired in her own unhappiness that she had become oblivious to everything else. She was still sniffling when Layal stood up to go. Wiping her face with the hem of her skirt, she lifted the lighter pitcher onto Layal's head before hoisting the other one up onto her own. Together they began the short walk back to the house. It was not until they had arrived at the door that Layal surprised Maryam with a different question altogether.

"Mohanad's sister told me she wished my poor husband better fortune in the next life." It had clearly been puzzling her since they left the spring. "Did she mean heaven?"

"No," said Maryam who had almost recovered herself. "Druze people believe that every time someone dies, their soul is born again in another person until it becomes faultless."

Inside the house, they found the priest deep in conversation with Sa'adeh. As soon as Wael saw Layal and Maryam walk through the door, he jumped up and ran towards his mother, a huge look of relief on his face. Layal knelt down and picked him up.

"Where have you been, Mama?" he asked her over and over again. "What happened to you?"

"Nothing, *habibi*[82]," she said as she ruffled his hair. "I just went with Maryam to collect water. I promised her I would yesterday." Putting him down, she turned to the priest.

"Is all well, Abouna?" The priest looked at her and scratched his beard with his stubby fingers.

"Yes," he muttered. "As well as things can be these days."

"You have some news?" Layal enquired, sensing this was not just a social visit. He nodded.

"I've heard from the priest in the next village that a mule train will be passing through Ayn el-Louz later today on its way to the coast. They could take you as far as Beirut."

The moment she heard the priest's words, Maryam began praying fervently that Layal would not accept the offer. She was well aware that it was the widow's intention to journey on to the coast from the moment she had arrived with her son, tired and exhausted. But she never thought that they would be leaving so soon.

And she had her own selfish reasons for wanting them to stay. During the short time that they had been living there, she had become attached to both of them. The daily game of *Dama* with Wael had become part of her routine and more importantly, Maryam had at last found someone to whom she could entrust even her most secret confidences. It was an unlikely friendship but one she had begun to set great store by.

"Yes, we'll go with them."

Her heart sank as she heard Layal's words. In desperation she hoped that either her mother or grandmother would speak out against the plan. But neither said anything.

"They may ask for some payment," said the priest sceptically.

"I can pay," replied Layal, indignant at the implication that she had already become a beggar.

"*Tayyib*," he replied, pleased that the matter had been settled so swiftly. "I will bring the muleteers here as soon as they arrive." With that, he climbed up the few steps to the track before pausing as if some afterthought had struck him.

"Where will you go when you reach Beirut?"

"I'll find somewhere," came the widow's reply.

"Let me give you a letter of introduction to an orphanage attached to the Lazarite convent. I'm sure that the sisters there will offer you shelter."

He scuffled off to the village, leaving the four women standing together outside the house. Her mother and grandmother remained silent, leaving Maryam no choice but to take matters into her own hands.

"Stay with us," she pleaded with Layal. "At least until it's safe to travel." The widow smiled at her warmly but shook her head nonetheless.

"We cannot stay here forever."

When the time had come for them to leave, Layal took Sa'adeh aside and offered her a handful of piasters from her purse.

"Something for the expense," she said. "Food is hard to find and you've been very generous to us." Sa'adeh clucked her tongue and shook her head. Even Imm George, who was well-known for her fondness for money, refused to accept the payment when Layal offered it to her instead. There was an embarrassed silence as they gathered in a circle, each wondering what to say. Departures of this sort were uncommon in the village because the people who left nearly always came back. It was only broken when Layal pushed back her hair and unclasped the necklace with the purple stone, handing it to Maryam.

"Take this as a gift," she said. "Wear it around your neck as a sign of our friendship."

Too dumbfounded to refuse, Maryam accepted the necklace. Such thoughtfulness on Layal's part made her feel ashamed of her brooding over Mohanad. She began to ask herself why she had ever burdened the widow with her own adolescent problems. To hide her feelings, she scooped up and kissed Wael who offered no resistance this time. Layal walked over to her as she stood there holding him.

"You have a heart of gold," she whispered in her ear. "Never forget that."

When the muleteers arrived at the house, Layal spoke briefly to the captain and then mounted one of the mules. The man picked up Wael and placed him squarely in front of her. Handing Layal a bag with some food in it that her mother had prepared, Maryam reached into her blouse and pulled out a yellow sash of silk with a tasselled fringe. Its borders were dyed a deep indigo blue. "This is my gift," she said humbly, handing it to Layal.

"*Yislamo idayki*[83]," Layal replied as she tucked it safely into her sleeve. The priest's arrival a moment later cut short any further farewells.

"Here is the introduction to the sisters," he said, handing Layal a letter that bore several impressive stamps. "I'm sure they will welcome you both."

With the mules grunting in protest, the small procession shuffled off in the direction of Beirut. The last Maryam saw of them was when Layal disappeared round the bend at the top of the village. Just as they vanished from sight, Wael turned and waved goodbye with a wide childlike grin, leaving her wondering if she would ever see them again.

The day after Layal and Wael left for Beirut with the muleteers, Joseph was crossing over the Medairij Pass in the company of the little group of refugees from Zahleh with whom he had spent the night in the caves. Fearing attacks from gangs of armed men, they had banded together for safety as they slowly climbed the road that wound up into the mountains.

When they reached the spot where the track to Ayn el-Louz veered off from the main highway, Joseph bade farewell to his fellow travellers and trudged off in the direction of his own village. Besides being footsore and dejected, the fear that violence had already reached his home weighed heavily on him. Would he find Ayn el-Louz in flames? Had their Druze neighbours set upon his family while he had been away?

The nearer he came to the village, however, the clearer it became that his fears were groundless. Instead of burning houses and bloated corpses, all he encountered was a village dog which trotted towards him, wagging its tail. Tears of relief began pouring down his grimy cheeks as he squatted down to stroke the mutt's head. He got to his feet again and walked on past the first houses.

His little brother and sister were outside playing by the door when he came to a halt on the road in front of the steps. As soon as they laid eyes on him, they began shrieking with excitement and their shrill cries quickly brought Sa'adeh and Maryam rushing out. Imm George struggled up the steps after them, praising the Holy Virgin for her grandson's safe return. His mother clutched him to her chest, smothering him with kisses.

"*Alhamdillah 'assalameh*[84]," she muttered. "Thank God you've returned to us in one piece." They all clung to one another in a joyful reunion that lasted several minutes, thanking their good fortune.

"I will light a candle before the Virgin," said Imm George. "It's thanks to her you've been kept safe."

She bustled into the house and found a tallow candle that she lit and placed in front of the little statue her son prayed to every morning. Maryam looked at her quizzically, surprised by her grandmother's sudden show of piety.

"What are you gawping at?" said Imm George testily. "You should know there are times when you must be grateful to those who protect you."

When George arrived back from the terraces with As'ad at dusk, an uneasy quiet settled over the house. No one, least of all Maryam, knew how he would react to having Joseph back home. But instead of giving him a thrashing, George walked over to his son without speaking a word, and wrapped his strong arms around him in a crushing bear hug. When he finally managed to free himself, Joseph stooped to kiss his father's hand, touching it to his forehead. Later as they sat down to eat their supper, Joseph made his apologies.

"I disobeyed you, Abee," he said. His father merely grunted and carried on with his meal, scooping up some of the mutton with a piece of bread while As'ad, for once, held his tongue. His jawbone clicked as he chewed his food.

"Have you heard the news about Zahleh?" he asked, hoping his father would speak even if it was to reprimand him.

"Yes," said George when he had finished eating. "But I'm more interested in what happened to you."

Deciding to make a clean breast of it, Joseph gave them a full account of everything that he had seen and done from the moment he had left the village until his return. They crowded around with the two youngest children sitting on either side of him. Well before he had finished, he was interrupted by a torrent of questions.

"Don't ever do anything foolish like that again," his father admonished him when their excitement had begun to subside. "You could've been killed. Then who would have been left to protect the family? Just As'ad and myself."

"You're right," said Joseph, accepting his father's rebuke in good heart.

"Anyway, no harm's been done," said George. "But these are dangerous times, even in our own village."

Imm George and Sa'adeh both nodded their heads in agreement.

"We don't know what will happen now that Zahleh has fallen," George went on. "Your place is here, not running around with a lot of people you don't even know."

PART III

❧❧❧❧

I rose up to open to my beloved; and my hands dropped with myrrh,
And my fingers with sweet-smelling myrrh,
upon the handles of the lock.
I opened to my beloved; but my beloved had withdrawn himself,
and was gone:
My soul failed when he spake: I sought him, but I could not find
him; I called upon him, but he gave no answer.

~ Song of Solomon 5:5-6 ~

CHAPTER TWENTY-ONE

꒰꒱꒰꒱

Beirut Docks
August, 1860

"Look, Mama! See how big it is!"

Wael was jumping up and down in excitement as he watched a large steamer with "La Borysthène" painted in Frankish letters on its belly approaching the port of Beirut at a glacial pace. The huge vessel slowed to a watery halt some distance from the shore and lowered its anchors fore and aft with a clanking of heavy chains.

From where they were standing on the quay, Layal and her son could just make out the silhouettes of the men on deck. Settling into its moorings alongside a dozen or so other vessels, the steamer gave off two sonorous blasts as if to announce its arrival to the entire city. Almost immediately, a fleet of skiffs and barques set out from the harbour in a ragged line towards the ship, their oarsmen shouting hoarsely to one another as they competed to come alongside her first. Despite the early hour, a large crowd had already gathered on the docks to witness the arrival of the French army.

It was the middle of August, two months after the sacking of Zahleh. Since the unrest in the mountains had threatened to beset Beirut itself, the Christians had been eagerly awaiting the arrival of the expeditionary force from Europe. The restoration of law and order that the Sultan's envoy, Fouad Pasha, had succeeded in establishing through executions and deportations had so far failed to reassure them of their safety.

Even as thousands more refugees poured into the city, a steady exodus of the city's own residents continued onwards to Alexandria, Malta, or anywhere safe passage could be secured. It was said that the

Sultan at his court in Istanbul had been most concerned when reports of the fighting had reached him. The Great Powers would have heard a detailed account from their consuls in Beirut and Damascus and, fearing their reaction to the news, he had immediately despatched one of the Empire's most polished public servants to Syria.

Before he left, the Sultan had invested Fouad Pasha with full military and civil powers and instructed him to quell the unrest in the region by dispensing punishment to the aggressors and justice to the aggrieved. But by the time the Pasha's fleet had reached the nearby island of Cyprus where they stopped to take on supplies, the situation had only worsened.

There news reached him that the Christians of Damascus had been attacked and the quarter where they lived razed to the ground. Acting on this information as soon as he could, Fouad Pasha wasted no time, after making port in Beirut, in marching his army across the mountains to Damascus. But when he reached the once luminescent city, which now lay partly in ruins, he was deeply dismayed. The Sultan's fears had been justified. It was the European consuls' reports on this and other violent clashes that had spurred the French Government of Napoleon III into sending an expeditionary force to Syria, once it had obtained the reluctant agreement of the other European Powers.

That was why Layal and her son, along with many of Beirut's citizens, had made their way down to the port that morning to welcome the army's arrival. One of the first barques to return from La Borysthène carried two fair-skinned officers in its stern. It docked at the quay and the two men disembarked, helped out by the boatman.

"Who are they, Mama?"

"French officers," his mother replied. "Can't you hear them? They're asking for the Consul."

"What's that on their heads?"

"Hats for the sun. Their skin burns in the sun."

The heat intensified as the morning wore on. Nevertheless, Layal and Wael remained on the quay watching the disembarkation under the sweltering sun. More boats now began to return, one after the other, full of swarthy soldiers wearing turbans, some with beards. All of them were dressed in colourful uniforms with baggy pantaloons and carried rifles slung across the tops of their knapsacks.

"Who are these soldiers?" Wael's earlier excitement at seeing the European officers had sunk into fear, as he hid behind his mother's skirts at the sight of the swarthy men.

"Don't worry, *habibi*. They are special troops called 'Zouaves,' part of the French army," Layal said, eager to reassure him.

"But they look like Turks, Mama," he insisted.

❧❧❧❧

For the first few weeks after their arrival in Beirut, Layal and her son had found lodging at the Orphanage of the Holy Sisters of Charity. She had offered to pay them with the proceeds of the banker's draft that Nadeem had given her the day he was murdered. But the mother superior had declined any payment, welcoming Layal warmly, and immediately put her to work looking after orphaned children who were flooding into the city every day from the mountains.

Some had seen their parents slaughtered in front of them, while others had been separated from them in the confusion that followed the sacking of Zahleh and the massacre at the old summer capital of Deir el-Qamar. Together with its churches and gardens, Beirut's streets were now crowded with destitute refugees seeking whatever food and shelter they could find and begging for any scraps they could scavenge off the residents.

Layal had been given a nun's room that was furnished with a narrow bed and a second mattress for her son. Although she attended vespers in the evening, her days were spent looking after orphans, providing them with the maternal comfort that they now lacked. Together with the sisters, she woke them in the morning, washed them, fed them, and comforted them late at night when they wept for their families. She played with them when she had the time and taught them simple rhymes under the approving gaze of the mother superior.

Late one morning, a small party arrived at the convent from the Austrian Consulate consisting of the consul, his wife, and their dragoman, a tall, serious-looking man with a close-cropped beard. Although he was dressed in a traditional *jubbah* decorated with silk facings, he conducted himself in the manner of a Frank.

At first, he had occupied himself entirely with matters of protocol, making introductions and hovering behind the consul and his wife as they were being conducted around the convent by the mother superior. But as the morning went by, their visit became less and less formal. Passing rooms full of orphans who watched them with shy and curious eyes, the party made their way from one part of the convent to another. When some of the more timid children cowered into corners, alarmed by the sudden appearance of strangers, the consul's wife intervened.

"Leave them be," she said, herself the granddaughter of a French émigré forced to flee his homeland by the bloody revolution of 1789. "Do not disturb the little ones for our sake."

She turned to speak briefly to Layal, choosing a moment when they found themselves alone together. Complimenting her on her excellent French, the consul's wife asked how it was that she had learned to speak the language so fluently.

"I used to speak it with my late husband."

"Do pardon me," the consul's wife replied. "I had no idea you are newly-widowed … Do you have any interest in French literature?" she asked, quickly changing the subject.

"Certainly," replied Layal. "Particularly Lamartine. He is well-known here because of his visit to Syria and Jerusalem several years ago."

"How interesting," the consul's wife replied. "Are you familiar with his *Meditations*?"

Layal was on the verge of answering when the dragoman, who had overheard the tail-end of their conversation, came over to where they were standing and asked leave to join them.

"Ladies," he said somewhat pompously, "Monsieur Lamartine's poetry is well-known in our region and I believe he is held in high regard wherever French is spoken." He paused somewhat theatrically. "You are no doubt acquainted with his remarks on the fairer sex?" he went on, seemingly unaware of the effect his intrusion was having.

"No," replied the consul's wife, clearly irritated. "I was about to comment on his depiction of nature. Is there something you wish to tell us?"

"'The eyes of Syrian women are soft for they are veiled,'" the dragoman began. "'But in the eyes of Western women there is more intoxication than in the cup from which I drink.'"

"That was a toast to the European ladies at a banquet given in the Beiteddine Palace by the Emir Bashir," said Layal with a smile as both the consul's wife and the dragoman struggled to contain their surprise. "He was trying to impress."

Her remark had not been meant as a gratuitous display of her own erudition. She realized her mistake and was about to apologize when the consul and the mother superior joined them.

"An excellent visit, Reverend Mother," the consul was saying, "but alas, we have already taken up too much of your precious time."

Leaving behind the rooms full of orphans, the party walked the length of the cloister to the entrance.

"Thank you, Reverend Mother," the consul's wife said. "We have all enjoyed our visit here and we greatly admire what you and the sisters do for these poor children."

"It is no more than our duty to God requires," the nun replied, bowing her head.

"Please thank the lady who accompanied us," the consul's wife added. "She is most charming and well-read."

"We are very pleased to have *Sitt* Layal as our guest," said the mother superior. "It is as though God has brought her to us for a purpose."

After the Austrian consul's visit, life in the convent returned swiftly to its normal routines. The number of Christians fleeing the mountains began to decrease, but those deserting Damascus and neighbouring Syrian towns and villages more than made up for it, swelling the overall numbers arriving in Beirut.

It was not that Fouad Pasha had failed to take severe measures against the rioters. In early August, he ordered the arrest of eight hundred people accused of taking part in the disturbances that had shaken Damascus. Later that month, an extraordinary tribunal made up of Ottoman functionaries from Istanbul passed a death sentence on one hundred and sixty-seven of those accused. Fifty-seven were hanged and their corpses placed on public display, suspended from the city's various gates as well as in its souqs[85]. But despite this show of brutal justice, the flood of Christians towards the coast continued. Driven out of their homes or too fearful to remain in them, they made the long and arduous journey on foot or, if they were more fortunate, in carts drawn by mules and camels.

Against this background of darkness and despair, a messenger clad in formal livery arrived at the convent one day and delivered a note that caused the mother superior to summon Layal to her room.

"It's addressed to you," she said, handing over a sealed letter embossed with a double-headed eagle, the coat of arms of the Hapsburgs. "I believe it's from the Austrian Consul's wife."

Layal took it and broke the seals, opening it in front of the mother superior. It was from the dragoman.

Chère Madame,

J'ai eu le grand plaisir de faire votre connaissance lors de notre récente visite au couvent. J'ai appris récemment que vous aviez souffert d'une terrible tragédie qui vous a laissé veuve.

Veuillez m'excuser de l'impertinence de mes propos, mais je vous prie, après une période de deuil appropriée, de bien vouloir considérer ma proposition.

Vous feriez de moi le plus heureux des hommes si vous m'accordiez la permission de vous courtiser.

Veuillez croire, madame, à l'expression de mes respectueux hommages. Selim.

Layal blushed as she read the letter in silence. Noticing her confusion, the mother superior smiled at her.

"It's not from the consul's wife?"

"No, Reverend Mother."

"Then from whom, my child?"

"It's from the dragoman."

"You found him rather pompous as I recall," she said with a smile. "What is his purpose in writing to you?"

Layal looked down at the floor, too embarrassed to reply. "Am I right in thinking that it is something of a personal rather than official nature?" Layal nodded.

"He's proposed marriage to you, has he not?" She nodded again, unable to speak.

"Do you have any thoughts on the matter? I imagine that you are the kind of woman most men find attractive and you are not without your own funds," the mother superior added with a chuckle.

Taken back by the nun's practical assessment of her situation, Layal was, for a moment at least, at a loss for words. She had not expected to find herself with a suitor so soon after her husband's death. Her grief was still raw. But these were difficult times and she had the prospects of her son to think of, too.

"If he pleases you, my advice would be to accept him in spite of his arrogance," said the nun as she waited for Layal to respond. "Of course, we shall all miss you and your little boy, but you have not been called by God to become one of us."

Clutching the note to her chest, she took the mother superior's hand and kissed it. The nun smiled pleasantly as she waited for her to leave, but instead Layal lingered by the door.

"What is it?"

"If I were to accept his proposal, Reverend Mother, I should have one condition." This time it was the nun who said nothing as she waited for her to continue. "It's that he should adopt my son formally and give him his name. My husband is dead and our old life in Hasbaya and Damascus died with him. This would be a new beginning for both of us."

"Very wise," murmured the mother superior. "Happily, that is a matter for the Bishop to consider, not the Ottoman Authorities. As you may be aware, my child, the Holy Law of the Muslims speaks differently on such things. It does not recognize adoption."

"Yes, Reverend Mother."

"Then let me have your reply when you have given this matter sufficient thought, and I will make sure that it is delivered to the person concerned."

A week later, Layal wrote a formal note to the dragoman in which she gave him her conditional answer. She had agonized over his proposal. Although she was content to remain in the convent with the orphans, it was the future of her son that had tipped the proverbial scale. She knew that life with the dragoman offered a more secure future, whatever kind of husband he turned out to be.

The dragoman, on the other hand, showed no such hesitation. His chance meeting with the young widow had clearly aroused some affection, bordering on admiration, in him that he was keen to pursue. He confirmed his acceptance of her condition in a hastily written reply as soon as he had spoken to the Bishop. Shortly afterwards, Layal received a card inviting her to attend a soirée at the Austrian Consulate. He sent his own carriage to convey her and came in person to greet her at the door.

"You have honoured me by coming tonight," he said as he helped her down. She smiled at him and allowed him to escort her inside where she was warmly received by the consul's wife.

"My dear Layal," she said during the course of the evening when they found themselves together. "My heart is full of sadness when I think of what is taking place here. It must have been the same for my grandfather."

"Yes," replied Layal. "But I've grown accustomed to it. I see it every day in the orphans' eyes."

"Fouad Pasha will be forced to take action," she continued. "My husband has told me they are going to execute the Governor of Damascus and several other senior officers. They're holding them responsible for the massacres."

Layal could do no more than sigh wearily at the news. She had witnessed enough death to last her a lifetime.

CHAPTER TWENTY-TWO

❧❧❧❧

The Chouf Mountains
August, 1860

Hundreds of villages lay in ruin, plundered and set ablaze during the violence that had engulfed Mount Lebanon in those three short months since the first confrontations. Livestock was driven off or slaughtered, while ripened crops were left to rot in the abandoned fields. In some villages, granaries and storerooms were ransacked or torched. Everywhere, the stench of unburied corpses mingled with smoke from still smouldering buildings, giving the once fragrant air of the mountains the stench of death.

The hills and valleys of the Chouf were now largely deserted, their inhabitants having fled to the coast or north to Keserwan in search of safety. The bodies of those who had been attacked before they could escape lay forgotten by the side of the road or at the bottom of ravines, their bellies swollen and distended. During the day, vultures and kites feasted on them, and at night jackals and hyenas fought over their remains.

Those who had survived, for the most part women and children, came to know a fate more cruel than death: famine. They ate whatever they could, foraging in the fields and woods before returning to the wreckage of their houses at night. They gathered little bundles of green thyme, chicory, and mint from the hillsides and handfuls of baqleh[86] from damp places near the streams and springs.

Even as the blazing summer turned to autumn and the sun surrendered its fierce heat, the harvest season brought them little respite from hunger. There was no grain to thresh and few figs and olives to gather. When the first light showers began to fall on the cracked and thirsty ground, emaciated figures swarmed over fallen pine cones, splitting them open for their kernels, and scoured the earth beneath the trees for mushrooms and roots to eat.

In some parts, all the mulberry trees had been deliberately cut down by one side or the other, forcing the villagers into debt and depriving them of their livelihoods. Without their precious cocoons, they would be unable to repay the money the merchants had advanced them earlier in the year for their silk.

Further to the east in the foothills of Mount Hermon, many of Hasbaya's public buildings had been turned into rubble and ash with only the Protestant Mission still left standing among the Christian places of worship. The corpses that were strewn about the town had been gathered up and buried in a mass grave near the main gate by the remaining townsfolk in an effort to stave off the outbreak of disease.

In the Bekaa, evidence of the destruction that had taken place lay open for all to see as far north as the once proud city of Zahleh. Stripped of most of its riches, its streets had become the fiefdom of ghosts and *jinn*. In every direction, this land that had once overflowed with milk and honey now echoed only to the cries of jackals and the piteous wailings of the homeless.

Thieves prowled around at will, ambushing destitute travellers without any fear of punishment. Those villagers who tried to harvest what little remained of their crops were attacked in their fields while they worked. Lawlessness prevailed throughout the countryside despite the best efforts of the French army, which marched up into mountains from the cities and towns below for the express purpose of restoring order.

Bands of armed Christians followed in the wake of the troops, attacking Druze villages in revenge or, as the French officers often observed, out of a simple desire for loot and plunder. Worse still, they would often try to frighten their inhabitants into forsaking their homes altogether by telling them that they would be attacked by the

Franks if they remained behind.

But in Ayn el-Louz, the mulberry trees had not been cut down nor had any of the inhabitants abandoned their homes and fields. In spite of the anarchy and mayhem all around them, the villagers had gone back to greeting one another when they passed in the street or when they were at work in their fields and terraces. The breakdown of order elsewhere had given them common cause to forget their differences and band together.

One autumn day, a detachment of Ottoman troops arrived in the village and summoned all the men to gather in the *midan*[87] by the spring. As the Ottoman soldiers sat in the shade of the almond tree with their rifles resting on the ground, their officer stood up in front of the villagers in his tight tunic with its gleaming buttons, his left hand resting on the hilt of his sword. He cleared his throat and adjusted the well-brushed *tarboosh*[88] on his head.

"You," he said, pointing at the Druze farmers, "must hand over two-thirds of the grain from your stores to us as compensation for the *rayahs*."

He pointed to where the Christians were standing. The Druze looked at each other in dismay, scarcely able to believe what they had just been told. But as his words sunk into their heads, they began muttering angrily under their breath while the Christians remained silent. Eventually Mohanad's father, Mahmoud, spoke up.

"The Christians here do not need our food."

"Maybe not here, but in other villages they're going hungry," the officer barked.

"By whose order must we do this?"

"By the *firman*[89] of Fouad Pasha, the envoy of the Sultan," he said with a flourish.

"We cannot do it, Excellence," Mahmoud stuttered, ignoring the furious look on the officer's face. "If we do, our families will starve this winter."

"You'll do as I say," the man bellowed back at him.

Slowly the lines of anger that had creased his face moments before disappeared and a cruel smile curled his lips. He twisted the ends of his moustache as a heavy silence settled among the men. The soldiers, who had hitherto been enjoying what little they had understood of the spectacle as they lounged in the shade, began to fidget with their rifles.

"You're lucky that we're not also taking your land and houses," the officer continued in a cautionary tone. "The Governor has confiscated the estates of Jumblatt *Effendi*, and he is now rotting in a Beirut prison."

"When will you take our grain?" asked Mahmoud, his words barely audible over the angry muttering of the disgruntled Druze farmers.

"We will return here in seven days' time to inspect the stores in every house. Then we'll take what's due. If you try to hide anything, you'll be punished."

With that, the officer ordered his soldiers to form two ranks in front of the villagers in a show of force aimed at impressing his authority on them.

"Right wheel," he barked. They marched out of the village with their rifles on their shoulders and their boots scuffing the ground, leaving behind a thick cloud of dust.

❧❧❧

Later that evening, George called on Mahmoud in his house, the first time that he had been to the house of a Druze since the troubles began. He had spoken to the heads of some of the larger Christian families that afternoon and explained to them an idea that came to him after the soldiers had left. To his relief, they had all agreed to his plan. Accompanied by Joseph, he arrived at the door where Mahmoud greeted them politely, though not warmly. He led them over to the divan, calling out to Mohanad to join them.

"I hope your son is recovering well," said George, pointing towards the sling that hung round Mohanad's neck.

"He's getting better slowly," replied Mahmoud warily. Fatmeh appeared with cups of freshly prepared sherbet. Pulling her white scarf modestly across her face, she handed one each to George and Joseph before serving her father and brother.

"I'm pleased that your own boy has returned home safely," he added after a lengthy pause.

The two older men eyed each other while the embers of a fire crackled in the brazier. From the back of the room came the sounds of cooking pots being cleaned. After a moment or two, George stopped clicking his rosary beads and leaned forward.

"We heard what the Turks said this morning," he began softly. Mahmoud stayed silent as he waited for him to come to the point.

"This winter may be harsh. You may not have enough *burghoul* to put in your stews or wheat to grind for bread." Mahmoud nodded. Even the women sitting at the back of the room stopped their whispering, eager to hear what George was about to propose.

"So why don't you give us some of your grain before the Turks come back and we will keep it safe for you?"

Joseph took a sip from his cup, savouring the sweet taste of the mulberries. Out of the corner of his eye, he saw Mahmoud say something to his son who disappeared into the back of the room. He returned a few moments later with two sticks in his good hand, one of which he gave to George and the other to his father.

"You cannot write and neither can I, so let's both keep a record of the number of bags on each of these," said Mahmoud as he pulled out a small knife and touched the blade to the wood as if he were making a notch. "This way we will both have a record of what you're holding for us." George scratched his chin thoughtfully before nodding.

"Of course, you'll have to hand over something to the Turks but at least you won't starve," he said.

They waited until they had finished their cups and then Joseph and his father got up and bowed stiffly to the Druze at the door. They had only walked a short distance before they heard Mohanad hurrying after them as fast as his shoulder would allow him.

"Wait. Please come back. There's something else my father wants to discuss," he panted. Joseph saw a look of surprise appear on George's face. There must be something serious at stake to make Mahmoud act like that given the lack of trust between them. Perhaps he wanted his father's help in solving some village dispute involving a Christian and a Druze.

"We've heard reports that thieves are stealing livestock and that grain stores are being looted," Mahmoud began as soon as they had sat down again. "It's not safe to travel on the roads, not even in broad daylight."

"Yes," George agreed. "Just yesterday one of my wife's cousins was robbed on the way home from market. They took fifty piasters from her and now she's forced to beg."

"But we can do something to stop these things happening near our village," Mahmoud went on. "We can get some of our young men to patrol the roads so that people can go about their business without fear of being attacked."

"You mean Druze and Christians patrolling together?" Joseph interrupted before his father silenced him with a scowl.

"Your son's right," Mahmoud said. "If we do it together, we will not favour each other if we're at a fault and neither will you, I'm sure." There was a lengthy silence as both men considered the implications of joint patrols. Finally, George nodded in agreement.

"*Tamam*[90]," said Mahmoud. "Then let these boys work out the details tomorrow." Clasping each other's hand firmly to seal their unusual bargain, the two older men rose to their feet.

CHAPTER TWENTY-THREE

❧❦❧❦

Mahmoud's idea was put to the test the very next day when an incident took place that confirmed, beyond the shadow of a doubt, the need for the villagers of Ayn el-Louz to cast their mutual suspicions aside and help each other. It happened when Mohanad's sister, Fatmeh, was carrying a pitcher of fresh water to her father and brother while they were picking the last of the olives in a grove of theirs some distance from the village.

Joseph was up on the mountainside clearing some dead brush from one of their northernmost terraces when he heard a shrill cry followed quickly by another. He walked along the terrace wall to a spot where he had a clear view of the road below and looked down. There, he saw a woman being manhandled by an Ottoman soldier while his comrade swaggered menacingly across the road towards them.

From the white shawl on her head, he could tell that she was a Druze. Suddenly one of the men pushed her forward causing her to fall to her hands and knees on the ground. He pinioned her arms behind her back while the other soldier began to loosen the buttons of his tunic with slow deliberation. Joseph had seen enough. He hopped over the wall and ran down the side of the hill towards them.

"*Elhaqouni*[91]!"

Although the words came out as little more than a screech, he recognized the voice while he was still some way off. Fatmeh was flailing her arms and kicking wildly at the shins of the soldier who was holding her down but he was too strong for her, and it did not take him long to subdue her. Meanwhile, his comrade continued to undo his uniform. He loosened the waistband of his trousers and stooped down to pick up the pitcher she had been carrying, taking a long leisurely swig.

It was at that precise moment that Fatmeh looked round and caught sight of Joseph running towards them. With calculated ferocity, she sank her teeth into the soldier's hand. He yelped in pain and slapped her across the face so hard it made her ears ring before stuffing the end of her scarf into her mouth. As she choked on the cloth, the other one reached down and ripped the flimsy material of her skirts apart with one violent tug, revealing her undergarments.

"*Trukouha*[92]! She's from our village," Joseph called out from behind.

Turning to see a man armed only with a mattock, the soldier holding her just smirked. But the other one reacted instantly and, grabbing his rifle by the barrel, swung the stock at Joseph. It caught him full on the side of his head, knocking him senseless. As he lay on the ground stunned, the man planted his feet on either side of his head and rested the rifle butt on his neck. The acrid smell of sweat and coarse tobacco wafted over Joseph's contorted face. As he leaned forward to take a better look, his comrade momentarily loosened his grip on Fatmeh.

Seizing her chance, she wriggled free and, spitting the end of the scarf out of her mouth, ran off as fast as she could in the direction of the thick olive groves. Behind her, Joseph groaned beneath a hail of blows as the two soldiers vented their frustration and anger at her escape on him.

When she returned some time later with her father and brother, Joseph was still on the ground and the two Ottoman soldiers were nowhere to be seen. His face was bruised and swollen, but his eyes flickered in recognition as he looked up at the three people standing over him. His lips moved in a soundless plea.

"*Mayy*," he uttered finally in a rasping croak. Fatmeh picked up the pitcher and poured a few drops of water between his bloodied lips.

"Where do you hurt?" It was Mahmoud's voice.

"All over."

He felt Mohanad's father run his calloused hands gently over his chest and arms looking for broken bones. Then, he eased Joseph over onto his side and began to check the heavy bruising on his back and legs where the majority of the blows had landed.

"They've taken good care not to kill you," Mahmoud grunted when he had finished.

Helped to his feet, Joseph began to hobble back towards Ayn el-Louz, doing his best to ignore the pangs that shot up and down his body with each step. Mohanad went on ahead so that by the time they arrived, George was already coming down the street towards them, cursing under his breath as he took his son's other arm. Hanging limply between George and Mahmoud, Joseph managed to stagger the short distance home.

❧❀❧❀❧

"Bring a bowl and some water," Sa'adeh called out to Maryam as she bent down to examine Joseph's injuries while Imm George rummaged through her pots and jars.

Maryam poured some water into a bowl. Just as she was putting it down beside her brother, she happened to glance around and caught sight of Mohanad standing by the open door talking to his sister. The sight of him momentarily took her breath away. It was the first time she had seen him since they had sat together in the shelter. His injured shoulder sagged, making him look oddly lopsided and he seemed slimmer than she remembered. But it was the change in his face that most drew her attention. His skin had lost the soft glow of youth and was now drawn tightly across his cheekbones.

This new gauntness made him, if anything, more attractive in her eyes, contrasting starkly with the rude health of her cousin, Faris. For a brief moment, their glances crossed but he was too busy trying to calm his sister down to pay her much attention. Her excitement at such an unexpected encounter was soon tempered by guilt when it dawned on her that she was making eyes at him when his sister had just been assaulted and her own brother severely injured. Nevertheless, she could not resist the temptation.

"Pass me the cloth," her mother called out impatiently. "Can't you see that your brother is badly hurt?"

Her mother was inspecting the cuts and gashes on Joseph's face while Imm George ran her hands over the livid bruises on his body. She looked away from the door with reluctance as she wrung out the cloth. When she turned to steal a second glance, the doorway was empty. Mohanad had slipped away quietly with his sister.

⋇⋇⋇⋇⋇

Through the red mist of pain, Joseph saw his father turn towards Mahmoud.

"My friend," George said. "Tell me exactly what happened."

"They tried to dishonour her," Mahmoud said angrily. "Thank God your son was there to protect her."

From where he was lying, Joseph could just see his father pick up two chairs and place them opposite each other. In a low voice, Mahmoud began telling him how Fatmeh had come running to find him in the olive grove, dishevelled, with her clothes torn and ripped. Before he could finish, Imm George bustled over to the two men.

"Don't crowd the boy," she scolded them. "Move back so I can put these poultices on."

In her hands she held a steaming bowl. Moments later, Joseph felt the gentle pressure of women's hands turning him over onto his stomach followed by the sudden burning of the hot dressings being placed against the raw skin of his back. He ground his teeth to keep from crying out.

"Keep still, *ya habibi*," Imm George murmured to him as he winced with pain. "Don't wriggle."

Ignoring his feeble protests, his grandmother bound the steaming mash of herbs over the bruises with a large strip of cloth that she wound all the way round his chest. Their sour smell suffused the room.

"Easy, easy," his grandmother cooed into his ear. "They'll make you feel better in no time." When she had finished, she beckoned George and Mahmoud over.

"You can come back now but don't tire him out with all your talk," she cautioned them. "The boy needs his rest."

Still deep in conversation, they carried their chairs back and put them down beside Joseph. He could hear Mahmoud telling George how his sudden appearance had taken the soldiers by surprise, giving his daughter the chance to escape. Raising himself up painfully on one elbow, Joseph beckoned to his father to come closer.

"They did more than just attack her," he croaked. "They were going to..."

"*Wattee sawtak*," said George, drawing his finger across his lips. "He knows. But it's better for the girl if that isn't mentioned."

Not long afterwards, Joseph drifted off to sleep. When he woke again, they were still sitting beside him.

"Have you thought of reporting the attack on your daughter to the local garrison commander?" George was saying.

"No," Mahmoud replied. "The Turks won't do anything against their soldiers and I don't want to add to my daughter's disgrace. What's happened is already a *fadiha*[93]."

"Perhaps they won't ignore it," said George. "I've heard that they are going to execute the Governor of Damascus because of the riots there." Only the rasp of Mahmoud's hand on his whiskers interrupted the silence.

"I'm still not going to report it," he said with a note of finality.

"Then I'll say nothing about the attack on my son," Joseph heard his father say. "I was thinking of going to the Frankish commander in Hammana where the foreign troops are stationed."

Both men sat brooding over the incident. Joseph was about to close his eyes again when he heard Mahmoud say, "We cannot trust outsiders, Ottomans or Franks."

His father nodded. He had heard rumours about the indiscipline of the French soldiers too.

"Let's swear to protect the people of Ayn el-Louz against attack by all outsiders," George suggested, "and to settle any disputes ourselves here in the village."

To his amazement, Joseph saw both his father and Mahmoud stretch out their scarred and calloused hands, placing them one on top of the other. Then they repeated the oath before leaning back in their chairs. His father began to chuckle.

"Who would believe us, a Christian and a Druze, swearing to help each other at a time like this?" Clapping George on his back, Mahmoud's solemn face broke into a grin and he began to laugh too.

"Stop making all that noise," Imm George called out from the back. "You'll disturb the boy."

But in spite of the aches and smarting pains that wracked the entire length of his body, Joseph found himself smiling as well. The events of the last few months had made him appreciate his father's wisdom in a way that he had not done before. Although he did not regret running away from the village, he now understood why his father had tried to stop him.

CHAPTER TWENTY-FOUR

❧❧❧❧

The Chouf Mountains
September, 1867

Around her, steam billowed up from the eighty-one basins in which the silk cocoons floated, bobbing like beignets, as the sticky glue that coated them slowly dissolved. Once it had softened, Maryam and the other factory girls would set to work brushing out the coiled strands. Then they would find the end and loop it through several hooks before attaching it to a spindle. Repeating the process with other cocoons, they would unravel the silk from several at a time, twisting the separate strands together to give the thread its proper thickness.

The high-ceiling rectangular room where they worked their shifts was hot and humid. There were only a couple of windows and the steam from the basins hung in clouds beneath the rafters, condensing on the brick walls. Little streamlets ran down their rough surfaces or dripped monotonously from the protruding beams, forming permanent puddles on the earthen floor.

The village priest had made every effort to dissuade Maryam from working in the local silk factory. Disregarding her own wishes, he had told her outright that she should stay at home and help her mother until a suitable husband was found. When Maryam walked over to the nearest town the next day and found a job there as a reeler, he went further still and expressed his disapproval openly to her mother.

"Why do you let your daughter work in such a place?" the priest had asked her sometime later, furious that his advice to Maryam had gone unheeded.

"Why shouldn't she? She's earning good money."

"She'll mix with men you know nothing about," he grumbled.

"Some of the local people call it by a name I can't repeat because of all the unmarried girls who work there."

"You mean the *karkhaanah*," said Sa'adeh with a giggle. "That just means a workplace. Only gossips think otherwise." The priest's face reddened but he said nothing.

"It isn't a brothel," she added in a more serious tone. "It's a factory and it's not the girls' fault they're better at those jobs than men."

"I'll speak to your husband about it. Maybe he'll understand that working there will ruin her prospects of finding a husband," he continued, unwilling to concede the point.

"Oh, don't worry about that," Sa'adeh sighed. "He's already found her one but she won't agree to him."

"Who is he?" the priest asked, his curiosity piqued.

"My sister's eldest."

When Maryam came back from the factory late in the afternoon, she was already tired from her ten-hour shift as well as the long walk home. She pulled a face when her mother told her about her conversation with the priest.

"It's not what he thinks," she argued. "I have a younger friend who's an orphan who works there. Her name is Rose, and she's nothing like what Abouna says."

Refusing to discuss the matter any further, Maryam stalked off. It was not until later when she found herself alone with her grandmother that she was ready to broach the subject.

"What shall I do if Abee tries to make me marry Faris?" she said. "I hate him."

"Why *ya binti*?"

"He's lazy and boastful. You say it too." The old lady clucked, unable to deny her own words.

"Don't worry, child. Now that your father sees you're earning good money, he'll come around," Imm George counselled, patting Maryam's hand to reassure her.

CHAPTER TWENTY-FIVE

❧❧❧❧

Eight years had passed since Rose had witnessed the violent death of her family at Deir el-Qamar. Her father had been murdered on the afternoon of the first assault as they took shelter in the house of the Christian secretary of the Druze *Qa'im-Maqam*[94]. The throat of her younger brother had been slit. Grief-stricken, her mother had flung herself at his attackers only to be thrown to the floor with such violence that she, too, had died from her injuries. Her death had been deemed an accident, because killing a woman deliberately would have been considered dishonourable. The only member of the family left alive, Rose remained beside her mother's corpse until the fighting in the streets and squares of the town had finally ceased.

In spite of what she had witnessed at such an early age, Rose had grown into a self-confident and resilient girl who could more than fend for herself. An Ottoman officer had found her wandering through the streets and had taken pity on her after the cannon shot had been fired from the *serai* signalling the fighting's end. He had hoisted her up onto the pummel of his horse and ridden back with her to the barracks at Beiteddine.

She remained there for several weeks while the commandant did his best to find a home for her. As a military man, he could not allow the presence of a little girl to jeopardize the discipline of his troops. But in spite of his firm demeanour, she quickly became something of a cherished little darling among the officers and men, which was not surprising since she was the only child in the barracks. She could often be seen riding around the main courtyard on their shoulders or playing hide-and-seek with them around the fountain or in the cloisters.

When a place was eventually found for her at an orphanage run by the Carmelite Sisters, she had to be dragged away and bundled unceremoniously into the back of a cart by two nuns who had come expressly to fetch her. So determined was she not to leave her newfound home that she fought back, even biting one of them in her effort to escape.

"I want to stay! I want to stay!" she had screamed as she was being hauled away. In acknowledgment of her valiant struggle, a drill party assembling in the outer courtyard had cheered for her, chanting her name over and over until ordered to desist by the duty officer.

As it turned out, her stay at the orphanage was not a happy one. At first, she had refused to eat. But as time passed, she stopped her sulking and eventually began taking part in the daily activities. She found the nuns' rules and regulations irksome and difficult to accept, and her misdemeanours led to frequent punishments. While her disruptive behaviour did not endear her to the sisters, it did win her the respect of the other orphans. Although she was one of the youngest girls, it only took a few short weeks for her to become their undisputed leader.

Mischief was her sport. One night she tiptoed up to the curtained bed of the sister who slept at the end of the dormitory and, without warning, pulled the drapes apart. It was a daring act, largely because the girls were strictly forbidden from going anywhere near it. Aghast at the impish face grinning down at her, the startled nun had sat bolt upright and pulled the covers up to her neck. When she realized who the Peeping Tom was, she reached out and slapped her, leaving Rose to skulk back to her own bed in tears.

"Did you see her face?" giggled one of the girls as they began to crowd around her.

"She looked as if she'd seen a ghost!"

"You're a little devil, Rose!" an older girl said with more than a hint of admiration.

On another occasion, she was taken before the mother superior for missing evening prayers twice in a row.

"Why do you do these things?" the exasperated nun had asked her as she looked up from her desk, making the peak of her starched wimple creak. Un-cowed, Rose stood her ground with her chin held high.

"I don't like prayer time, Reverend Mother. It's so boring."

"But don't you want to feel closer to God, my dear?"

"No, I want to play."

"Your penance is to say a hundred 'Ave Marias' before each meal for a whole week. Perhaps that will help you change your mind."

The older Rose grew, the more strong-willed and rebellious she became. Slaps, reprimands, and threats had less and less of an effect on her. Finally, the sisters agreed amongst themselves that her presence in the convent had become too disruptive to live with.

"We cannot keep her here any longer, even if she is the orphaned daughter of one of our benefactors," the mother superior declared one morning. It was a decision she had had to weigh carefully because Rose's father used to bestow substantial gifts on the convent like many of the rich silk merchants. All the other sisters nodded in agreement save one.

"She's just high-spirited, Reverend Mother." The dissenter was an elderly nun with a kind face.

"I disagree." The mother superior pursed her thin lips in annoyance. "She's just irredeemably naughty. Her place should be given to a more deserving child."

"Give her a little time. She'll calm down."

"I doubt it. We'll find a family to take her in until a suitable husband can be found for her."

After making a number of enquiries, the mother superior found accommodation for Rose in the house of a grain merchant who was more than happy to oblige her as a modest act of charity towards the mission. He and his wife lived in a mountain town where one of the new silk factories had been established by a French *commerçant* from Lyon. Two of his children had been educated at the convent, something for which he was still profoundly grateful.

At first, the twelve-year-old Rose had been amenable to whatever her new guardians had asked her to do, so delighted was she to have escaped the convent's confines. She helped the merchant's wife during the day and sat with her in the evenings, keeping her company whenever her husband was away on business. But as the days passed, Rose became restless. She considered running away, but quickly dismissed the idea having nowhere else to go. One evening, she made a suggestion to the woman as they sat alone together.

"Let me find work and I'll pay you for my board and lodging."

Much to her surprise, the merchant's wife immediately agreed. The very next day, she took her to the local silk factory in search of the owner with whom she had some dealings in the past, selling him sacks of cocoons which she collected from the surrounding villages. When they arrived at the gate, she asked the gatekeeper to inform the owner that she was there on a matter of business.

"I wish to speak to the Frank," she said when the supervisor, who had been summoned by the guard, appeared instead.

"He's away in Beirut," the man told her. After a moment's hesitation, she decided to press her request.

"Do you have a job here she can do?" she asked bluntly, pointing to Rose.

"I'll ask the owner when he returns," the man replied. "But she's younger than most of the girls here."

Then the gatekeeper swung the gate shut, signalling that the interview had come to an end. To their surprise, when the owner returned a few days later, he agreed to take Rose on. She was tasked with sweeping the factory floor and clearing away debris, all for the handsome sum of one piaster daily. Rose proved to be a quick learner and it was not long before she asked to become a silk reeler.

"I want to do what they do, Abou Hazeen," she pleaded with him. She had nicknamed him "Father of Sadness" because of his drooping eyes, much to the amusement of the other girls.

"If you can do it well you shall, little Rose," he said with a chuckle. "And if you're any good, I'll double your pay."

Her nimble fingers proved very skilful at the work. Within a short space of time, she had learned how to soften the cocoons with a brush and pick out the ends of the silk filaments. She found it easier than most of the older girls, learning quickly how to thread them through the succession of hooks and rings so that they could be twisted into a long and even thread on the spindles.

Better still, Rose rarely allowed knots to form in the thread like some of the girls when they attached one strand to another by "throwing" it clumsily. Her strands invariably aligned without much of an overlap. Signs of poor workmanship used to infuriate Abou Hazeen who would stalk up and down the factory lines, examining the quality of the silk before it was taken away to be twisted into skeins and baled up.

"This is no good," he would say to some unfortunate girl whose thread was full of bumps. "Spun silk. You can't make this stuff into organzine or crepe. God should have given you nimbler fingers."

"I'm doing my best, *ya 'ammee*."

"Do better, or I'll take it out of your wages."

But Abou Hazeen was a kind-hearted man who rarely acted on his threats, and most of the girls knew it. Rose, on the other hand, received nothing but praise. Within a few months, she had become one of the most skilled reelers in the factory. And as a result, Abou Hazeen often asked her to help the new girls when they arrived fresh-faced from the villages, dressed in their best clothes and eager to earn their own money for the first time in their lives.

That was how Rose had come to teach Maryam when she appeared one morning looking for work at the factory gates. At first, she had found the job difficult and despaired of ever learning how to do it, but Rose was a patient teacher and had encouraged her to keep trying.

"I can't do it," Maryam would moan over the monotonous creaking of the wheels and gears.

"It's easy," Rose would say, getting up and walking over to where Maryam was struggling to unravel the cocoons. "Like this." With a deft flick of her wrist, she would attach a new filament to the old one while Maryam looked on in amazement.

Under her guidance, Maryam's thicker fingers gradually developed the dexterity they needed to produce fine silk thread. As her work improved, Abou Hazeen began to scold her less and less until one day he even praised her, making Maryam beam with pleasure. It was almost as good as her father's approval, something bestowed on her only rarely now that she was at odds with him over Faris.

Although she never attained Rose's proficiency, Maryam nonetheless became a reliable and productive worker. As time wore on, both girls discovered that they enjoyed each other's company in spite of the difference in their ages and upbringing, and before long a strong friendship began to blossom between the two of them. They sat together by the gates during the short breaks between their shifts, enjoying their escape from the stifling bustle of the factory floor. At first they just used to gossip about the other girls. It amused Maryam to hear Rose make fun of the way they looked when they first arrived.

"They're all fumble fingers dressed up in their hats and skirts," Rose used to say. "And some of them need a good scrub, too."

"Did you also think that about me?" Maryam had once asked. But Rose had only laughed and tossed her curly hair.

After a while, Maryam's curiosity got the better of her and she began to ask Rose all about herself. There was something about the younger girl that fascinated her. It was not just that she was so unlike the other girls in her own village, it was also her self-confidence. Maryam admired the brash way she stood up for herself despite being the youngest in the factory. Her boldness and quick wit earned her the respect of her workmates. But when it came to their supervisor, she saw that Rose was clever enough not to antagonize him.

As for Rose, she grew fond of Maryam as though she were an older sister. It was not long before she began to reveal the details of her short but colourful life to Maryam who sat spellbound beside her in the way she once had done with Layal. She shared memories of her childhood in Deir el-Qamar where her family had once lived a comfortable life. Pausing only briefly to wipe away a solitary tear, she tried to capture in words the fear that had swept through the town in the summer of 1860 when it had been blockaded. Although she was only a little girl at the time, she could still remember how tense her mother and father had been during those sultry months when conflicting rumours and reports swirled around the town.

But the memories of the attack were too painful for someone even as plucky as Rose to revisit. She brushed over them, pausing only to tell Maryam about the brief but happy interlude she had spent in the Ottoman barracks. When it came to her convent days, Rose told her new friend vivid stories about how she had rebelled. She embellished them too, feeding Maryam's wide-eyed curiosity.

"You did all those things?" she giggled. Rose wrinkled her nose mischievously.

"Nuns are women like us, Maryam, not saints."

"Maybe, but I could never do that," the older girl muttered.

Maryam's self-confessed docility became even more transparent a few days later when a French woman employed at the factory sidled over to them between shifts. She was one of two foreigners who had been engaged to teach the local girls how to spin the high quality thread increasingly demanded by the great weaving houses in France and Italy. After looking carefully around to see if she was being overheard, she began to speak in French, her hushed voice barely audible over the gurgling of the nearby stream.

"They're taking advantage of you," she told them both. Rose, who had learned French as a little girl and had spoken it frequently in the orphanage, translated her words for Maryam.

"Tell her to go away," Maryam hissed, close to panic. "Abou Hazeen will see us."

But Rose took no notice. She had already made up her mind that if they spoke quietly, few, if any, of the other girls would understand what they were saying. And if, by chance, their conversation was reported back to the supervisor, she would tell Abou Hazeen that she was only being friendly towards the Frankish woman. Rose was eager to satisfy her own curiosity about the world beyond Mount Lebanon even if Maryam was not. So instead of telling her to go away, she invited her to come and share their food. As soon as the Frenchwoman had sat down, Rose brought up the question of their working conditions.

"You say we're underpaid and our shifts are too long?"

"*Oui*," the French spinner said. "Where I come from, we stop working if the conditions aren't good. It's called a strike."

"Then where does the money come from to pay your wages?" she pressed on, somewhat mystified by the idea.

Rather than replying, the Frenchwoman dipped a piece of bread into the grape molasses that Maryam had bought with her from the village.

"That's tasty," she said, changing the subject. "What do you call this?"

"*Dibs el 'enab*," Rose replied. "It's made from grapes. Sometimes carob pods and pomegranates, too."

"It works, believe me," she said between mouthfuls of the sticky syrup. "The bosses try to force you back to work but in the end, they nearly always agree to some of your demands."

At that point, they were interrupted by Maryam's frantic whispering. Unable to follow the conversation, she had been looking around nervously for eavesdroppers.

"He's coming," she said, blinking furiously.

Rose and the French spinner carried on eating and when the supervisor walked by a few moments later, he barely noticed them. But his oversight turned out to be a stroke of luck for Rose because not long afterwards, a rumour spread through the factory that one of the two Frankish women had been sacked. No one knew for sure why, but it was said that she had tried to get some of the local girls to join a protest.

"Will we get into trouble?" Maryam asked Rose as soon as she heard the news.

"No," said Rose, laughing it off. "Stop worrying about it."

In spite of the incident, their friendship continued to strengthen until one day Maryam found the confidence to tell Rose about her most important secret of all, the one which was still causing her such unhappiness. And to her surprise, she found in her younger friend an enthusiastic though impatient confidante. One afternoon in the late summer, she began to talk about Mohanad, slowly at first, but then all her bottled up feelings spilled out in a torrent.

"My life is miserable," she began. Taken aback by Maryam's unexpected words, Rose waited patiently for her to explain.

"My father is trying to make me marry my cousin … and I hate him." Instead of defiance, there was a deep-seated hopelessness in her voice, as if the effort of resisting her father's will for so long had finally worn her down.

"You see," Maryam began tentatively, "I've spent the last eight years thinking about someone else." Tears ran down her cheeks in silent rivulets.

"Does he feel the same way about you?" asked Rose, trying her best to sound sympathetic. Maryam sniffled into her sleeve.

"I don't know," she admitted. "Anyway, he's married now."

Rose sat there, listening to Maryam's revelation with growing amazement. Too young to know about love herself, she was nevertheless intrigued.

"You've left it too late," she said at last when the torrent had finally run dry. Regretting her harsh words almost as soon as she had uttered them, Rose put her arms around her friend.

"I never really had the chance to find out how he felt," she said. "He's a Druze."

Rose's body stiffened and it was all she could do to stop herself from saying something hurtful. From somewhere deep within, the memory of her mother lying limply on the flagstones in Deir el-Qamar resurfaced. She realized with a start that the intervening years had only dulled, but not erased the pain of being orphaned. She took a deep breath in order to compose herself.

"It was the summer the troubles began," Maryam said, barely noticing her friend's visceral reaction. "There are many Druze families living in our village, and in those days we mixed with them quite freely. We would visit one another's houses often."

Rose shifted uneasily in her seat as she struggled to remain silent.

"One day, I was walking back from my aunt's house with my mother, and I saw a boy beside the road working with his father." Maryam had closed her eyes as if she were reliving that summer morning. A smile came to her lips.

"They were building a shelter to protect the crops from thieves and animals. He was such a handsome boy."

"Go on," said Rose, now eager to hear the rest of the tale.

"The next day I saw him again on the way back from the spring. He was alone and he asked me into his shelter."

Rose stifled a giggle, covering her mouth with her hand.

"You're laughing at me," said Maryam, smiling despite her friend's girlish reaction. "Nobody saw us, but now I wish they had. His name was Mohanad."

"What a strange name."

"Yes," she agreed. "He was very proud of it." Maryam placed the palm of her hand on her forehead as if trying to remember something else, something too private even for Rose to hear. It was the way she had felt that day. She had never forgotten it.

"Did you see him again?"

"Not until after the troubles began."

The sun was beginning to set in a pool of orange light, slipping behind the hills below. It was time for Maryam to start walking back to Ayn el-Louz. She got to her feet and brushed the back of her skirt with her hands, the way she had done all those years ago in the orchard. In spite of the warm day, her body shivered with déjà-vu.

"Tell me the rest," Rose pleaded with her.

"Tomorrow," Maryam replied. "I have to go home now before it gets completely dark. My mother will be worried about me."

Rose spent the rest of the evening and the next day at work eagerly anticipating the end of her friend's story. When Abou Hazeen rang the bell at the end of their shift, she rushed over to Maryam and led her out to their usual spot. Taking out some *baklawa*[95] from between the folds of her skirt, she offered her a piece.

"Now tell me the rest," she said with a mouth full of the sweet pastry.

"He joined the Druze army with his father," Maryam took up her tale again. "But he was wounded in the first battle and they brought him back to the village on a stretcher."

"Was he badly hurt?" Rose wrinkled her nose, this time out of curiosity.

"Yes," said Maryam. "And the only news I could get about him was from his sister, Fatmeh." She sighed at the frustration she had experienced at the time.

"Then after the violence had ended, Fatmeh was attacked by two Turkish soldiers," she continued after a pause. "My brother Joseph helped her escape. After that, he and Mohanad began organizing village patrols."

"Did they become friends?" Rose asked incredulously.

"Not really." Her voice was tinged with sorrow.

"Have you talked to him since?"

If Rose had been hoping for a dramatic ending, it was not to be. Maryam shook her head and scuffed the earth listlessly with the toe of one of her sandals.

"I've only seen him once since then."

Without thinking, she leaned forward and kissed Maryam on the forehead. Although she had paid little attention at first to the sadness with which Maryam had told her story, she could now see how deeply it still affected her. More poignant still, the matter lay unresolved. Something warm stirred inside her heart for the first time since her family had been killed. She had at last found someone she really cared about again.

❧❦❧❦

"I was so worried that they would send you away," Maryam whispered to Rose several days later as they were waiting to collect their wages at week's end.

"You mean after the Frankish woman was sacked?"

She nodded.

"Oh, don't worry about me," Rose replied with a toss of her head that made her shimmering curls bounce. "I'll always be fine. Anyway, I've something for you." She fumbled in her pocket and pulled out a little packet wrapped in paper that she had torn from one of the silk bales. It still bore the factory stamp.

"What is it?" said Maryam, her hands trembling with excitement. She had only ever received two presents in her life, one from her grandmother and the other from Layal.

"Open it and see."

Maryam untied the piece of string and unwrapped the bundle with care. Inside was a pair of doves made from the spun silk that Rose had collected over the years she had been working in the factory. Their eyes were black beads and their beaks made from smoothened splinters of wood. She had found some pieces of wire on the factory floor and bent them into the shape of feet so that the birds could stand.

"You and me," said Rose excitedly. "A keepsake for you to remember me by." Maryam's look of joy faded almost as quickly as it had appeared.

"You're not leaving me, Rose?"

Rose shook her head and smiled. "No, but I'm not going to spend the rest of my life here, either."

The thought of her friend's fearlessness made Maryam's eyes widen with admiration. For her, defying the priest and resisting her father's wishes had been the most daring acts of her entire life, and yet here was Rose planning a new life in some far-off place.

"Will you go to Beirut or Damascus?"

"No," she said. "I'm thinking of Europe or maybe even *Amreeka*."

"*Amreeka*?" said Maryam doubtfully. "The schoolmistress in our village comes from there."

"But that's all in the future," said Rose, dismissing the subject as airily as she had brought it up. "Come on. I'll walk part of the way home with you."

Arm-in-arm, the two girls set off in the direction of Ayn el-Louz, chatting with one another as if neither had a care in the world.

CHAPTER TWENTY-SIX

❧❧❧❧

Ayn el-Louz
October, 1868

Time had moved on for the rest of Maryam's family since the grim summer of massacres and the widespread famine that followed. The Ottoman authorities exiled those who had been found guilty of taking part in the violence to remote parts of the empire and levied demands for reparations on their Druze and Muslim subjects. Those who were not exiled were conscripted into the Imperial Army to serve alongside country boys from Anatolia and the Balkans with whom they had little, if anything, in common.

Gradually, the tension in the mountains simmered down and as the years went by, some of the Christians and Druze who had abandoned their villages during the fighting began to return to them. In Ayn el-Louz, where the inhabitants had stayed put throughout the conflict, life returned to normal rather swiftly.

One Sunday afternoon in late autumn, Joseph was busy digging the foundations for his new home with the help of his brother. With his soldiering days behind him, he had settled down to help his father with their smallholding. Not long afterwards, the family had reached a milestone that, inevitable as it was, had come as a shock to all of them.

Forty days had passed since their grandmother had finally succumbed to old age, passing away peacefully in the house where she had spent most of her life. The whole family had stayed behind after mass to say prayers for her soul. Despite enjoying robust health for many years, Imm George had caught a fever not long after the first rains had fallen. For once, the fresh westerly breeze from across the seaward hills and the patter of raindrops kicking up little plumes of dust on the dry ground had not been welcoming signs. When she heard George talking to his wife about calling for the doctor, she summoned her remaining strength and interrupted them.

"Don't bother the *hakeem*. I'm old and he can do nothing for me. My time has come."

"Don't talk like that," Sa'adeh tsked, kneeling down beside her mother-in-law. "The doctor will be able to cure you."

"He can't cure old age," croaked Imm George with a feeble wave of her arthritic hand. "Send me your daughter. Her company will do me more good than all the doctor's medicines."

Maryam came in and knelt down beside her grandmother, smoothing back a few stray strands of white hair from her forehead as the old lady beckoned her closer. Bringing her face down to her level, she did her best to hold back her tears. Slowly and with great effort, Imm George took out a copper coin from within her blouse and placed it in the palm of her granddaughter's hand.

"This will keep you safe," she told her.

"It will remind me of you, Teta," said Maryam as she ran her fingers over the tarnished metal which bore the head of a young woman on one side and a dolphin with an anchor on the other. "I'll miss you so much."

"I know," said Imm George, patting her hand.

Despite his mother's wishes, George sent for the doctor but by the time he had arrived, the old lady was already dead. They buried her the next day in a ceremony attended by almost everyone in the village. The air shuddered with women's wails as the coffin was lowered into the freshly dug earth. George stepped up to the graveside and cast a handful of red dirt onto the lid, rattling the thin wood. Then he walked back slowly towards the house at the lead of a long procession, his head hung heavy with the weight of his sadness. It was clear that, despite their occasional differences, he had loved his mother dearly.

The condolences continued throughout the day and by the time the last of the mourners had left, the light had completely faded.

❧❧❧❧

Joseph was now married to one of his cousins. A good-natured girl from his mother's family, Samia had grown up in the mountains not far from Ayn el-Louz. At first they had lived in the family house, but when she became pregnant with their first child Joseph decided it was time to build a home of his own. And that was how the two brothers came to be arguing that day in the warm sunshine over space and columns.

"If you make it any larger, you'll need a pillar to support the roof," As'ad said as he carefully paced out the length of the walls.

The grubby rascal who had once herded goats was gone and in his place now was a fine young man. His shoulders and chest were broader than his brother's and the muscles of his arms rippled beneath the rough fabric of his shirt. Despite his lack of formal schooling, he possessed an innate ability to calculate sums in his head and could even do divisions using only a twig and a patch of bare earth.

Joseph noticed that his younger brother's numerical skill had particularly impressed his father. But rather than being jealous, he admired him for it. He grew used to seeing George ask As'ad for advice on how to get the best income from silkworms, a crop they had now begun to cultivate in earnest. And when it came to planting more mulberry trees to add to the six hundred odd they already owned, George naturally consulted his younger son over the amount of *miri* they would need to pay the sheikh's man on future harvests.

"I want it to be bigger than our old house," said Joseph. "Can we make it longer?"

"Why," his brother asked. "To impress our neighbours?"

Joseph just laughed and walked over to one end of the plot where they had already levelled he ground. He scratched a line in the earth.

"Up to here?"

"If the roof falls in, don't say I didn't warn you," his younger brother said as he counted out each pace with care.

Joseph had been harbouring his own modest ambitions for some time. Not only did he want to build a larger house than the one he had grown up in, he also wanted to improve the stable at the back where the animals spent the winter. That was why he and his brother had already dug a large pit below, pulling out rocks and roots with their bare hands and heaping the soil on one side for later use in the garden they intended to plant. It was important for him to have enough space to store their tools as well as the little donkey-drawn plough that they used to turn over the stony soil on the terraces to prepare the seedbed.

"We'll use them for the walls," grunted Joseph as he struggled to dislodge yet another one. "If we can split them."

As'ad walked over to the edge, still deep in thought. When it came to practical matters like this, he took charge with the tacit agreement of his brother.

"Let's make a door here," he said, pointing to an imaginary spot in mid-air. "You'll be able to walk straight onto the lower room's roof."

"And the grain store over there to keep it away from rats and mice," Joseph added, warming to the idea. "We can put the figs and grapes out to dry here, too."

As'ad scratched his head, not yet convinced by his brother's ideas. Something about the plan was still worrying him. They had already stacked stones from the little quarry below in a heap so that he could mark each one for splitting and facing. Joseph hoped that his brother's skill with a chisel and mallet would save him the considerable expense of bringing a trained mason from town.

But the ambitious dimensions of the new house were a problem still. Large buildings were a rarity in Ayn el-Louz and the brothers only knew of two. One was the church where several pillars in the nave supported the roof. The other was the new schoolhouse which had created a great deal of excitement among the villagers during its construction the previous year, mainly because it had been built by foreign workmen, which was something of a novelty in the village. They had stared curiously at the hirelings whenever they passed by, sometimes stopping to admire the progress of their work but more often than not simply to exchange a few words with them. The priest, on the other hand, spewed out nothing but criticism for the project, fighting it tooth and nail.

"Who can trust the motives of such people?" he would say of the missionaries whenever the opportunity presented itself.

But there was little sympathy for his views among the locals who had been waiting patiently for the school to open. When the troubles swept through the mountains and many villages had been abandoned, some began to think that it would never happen and for a while it seemed as though it would not. But when peace finally returned, a group of American missionaries travelled to Ayn el-Louz from Beirut and requested a meeting with the village leaders.

George and Mahmoud, who had earned the confidence of their neighbours as a result of their efforts to protect the village, agreed to meet with them. But the priest initially refused to do so since they had neither come with the agreement of the bishop nor with the approval of the Maronite patriarch in Bkerke.

"Our children may be tempted to change their faith if they attend such schools," he had argued. "Also, boys and girls sitting together ... that's just against tradition."

"They need to be educated," George had disagreed. "And if the boys can read and write, they will want women who can, too." At this the priest frowned but before he could insist further, Mahmoud interrupted him.

"*Ya Khoury*[96]," he said, "we value our own traditions even more than you do. But we don't fear education. Our elders say that our young people should learn something of the modern world."

Unable to dissuade either of them, the priest gave way with bad grace and begrudgingly agreed to attend the meeting. When the missionaries duly arrived, they were escorted around the village by all three of them in search of a suitable site for the new schoolhouse. But it was not until they were standing beside the church itself that they all agreed they had found what they were looking for.

"This will make an excellent place," their spokesman had said. When the priest began sputtering objections on the grounds that the land was property of the church, George and Mahmoud took him aside and suggested a compromise.

"Write to the bishop by all means, but in the meantime let them build the school."

Within a few months, the schoolhouse had been erected and it was not long after that an American schoolmistress by the name of Mrs. Butler had arrived to take up residence in Ayn el-Louz. At first, the villagers found it difficult to understand her because she spoke only formal Arabic, but as the months went by her knowledge of the local mountain dialect improved. When her vocabulary failed her, she would resort to speaking in her mother tongue. The children attending her lessons quickly adopted her phrases and repeated them wherever and whenever they could, especially in front of their parents.

CHAPTER TWENTY-SEVEN

❧❧❧❧

"What have you learned today?"

That was the first question Sa'adeh asked her two youngest children the moment they arrived back from the schoolhouse. Like any mother, she wanted to know what the schoolmistress had been teaching them. They were now attending her classes every morning, something they did with great enthusiasm in order to avoid the tasks they would otherwise have had to do in the house.

"Arithmetic."

"What's that?" their mother asked, pausing for a moment amid her bustling housework.

"It's counting," they both began in unison. "One, two, three, five, seven…"

"Good. And what else did you learn?"

"Bible stories and facts about *Amreeka*."

"*Amreeka*?"

"That's where Mrs. Butler comes from. It's a big land across the sea."

Maryam knew that her mother had already invited Mrs. Butler to spend the feast of Saint George with the family that May. On the day of the feast, she helped her mother catch two of their chickens after they had returned from the celebratory mass shortly after sunrise. It was a cumbersome task, made even more difficult by the two youngest who did their best to save the birds. But after much fluttering and squawking, they finally managed to corner them against the wall. Sa'adeh had wrung their necks and given them to Joseph to roast on a spit after removing their hearts and livers.

"Make sure you turn them over so they cook all the way through," she had told him. "Add some extra fat so they're tender."

"Yes, Imme," Joseph replied, seizing his mother around the waist and lifting her off her feet in a clumsy bear hug the way he used to do with his grandmother when he was a boy.

Along with the chickens, she had also prepared a special plate of *mjaddara*, a dish normally made from lentils, charred onions and *burghoul*. This time, however, she had used rice instead although George had objected at first to the extra cost. As far as he was concerned, cracked wheat tasted far better. In the end it was Maryam who had settled the matter by buying a small sack of rice on her way home from work from the grain merchant in whose house Rose lodged. He now imported a regular supply from the wholesalers in Beirut to satisfy the rising demand for the new grain that had once been the privilege of the sheikhs alone.

Their few pieces of furniture had already been set out on the roof in anticipation of Mrs. Butler's arrival at noon. From there, they would have a clear view of the competitions taking place throughout the afternoon in the valley below. Saint George's Day was an occasion when the young men of the village vied against one other for the spectators' approval, especially those doe-eyed young women on the lookout for a handsome husband. It had always been that way.

The contests themselves included running races and spear throwing as well as a game they called *nokhra* which involved hitting a round stone along the ground with clubs fashioned from the knotted branches of quince and olive trees. This year's feast was special for George's family because As'ad had put himself up as a challenger in the traditional wrestling competition which was the highlight of the afternoon's festivities.

"You'll never win," Joseph teased his brother. "That boy will beat you for sure."

"He won't."

Leaving them to argue, Maryam spread a clean white cloth over the wooden food chest that had been placed outside to serve as a table.

"Fetch the chairs," she said when she had finished, shooing her brothers back into the house.

Not long afterwards, Mrs. Butler came into view walking up the hill from her lodgings beside the schoolhouse. She was dressed in a long-sleeved blouse and skirt and carried in her hand a small bag with hooped cane handles. Her black bonnet had a wide brim to shield her fair skin from the sun. Maryam welcomed her at the door and helped her climb onto the roof where her father stood waiting to receive her.

"*Ahlan wa sahlan*," he greeted their guest graciously. "*El-bayt baytik*[97]."

She held out her hand towards him in greeting and, after a moment's hesitation, he grasped it in his own. Then he led her over to the least rickety chair.

"You do *me* the honour," Mrs. Butler replied in her formal Arabic, tucking away a coil of grey hair that had escaped from the prim bun at the back of her head. They were interrupted by the two younger children who came rushing out, eager to greet their teacher.

"Hel-lo, Mis-sus But-ler," they chirped in English.

"These are for you, my dears," she said as she bent down and handed them both bound copies of the new Arabic translation of the Bible.

"Thank you," they replied, clutching them eagerly.

Although they had seen books before in the classroom, there were none in their house because no one in their family could read or write. As Maryam hovered in the background, her brothers came out to join their visitor on the terrace. She herself would have liked to sit and talk to her too, but it was a formal occasion and Mrs. Butler was being treated as well as any male guest. Instead, she slipped into the house and returned with a small jar of *arrack*, the same drink that Joseph had first encountered in the bailiff's house in Zahleh. Unlike the bailiff, George only ever produced it on feast days.

"Will you share a cup with us?" George asked the American schoolmistress politely. Mrs. Butler declined with a shake of her head.

"I'm teetotal," she said with a smile. "*La ashrabou khamran*."

George looked somewhat nonplussed at her words which he had difficulty understanding. Nevertheless, he beckoned Maryam over and whispered something in her ear. Moments later, she reappeared with a glass of mulberry sherbet prepared the way her grandmother had once taught her. George, meanwhile, poured a small amount of *arrack* into some cups and carefully added a measure of water. He gave one to each of his sons. Joseph took his readily, having long since overcome his aversion to the aniseed flavoured liquor.

"To Saint George," George said, raising his glass.

As they toasted the saint, the steady throb of a *tambour*[98] and the first few reedy notes of a flute could be heard in the distance. Pausing to take a sip of her sherbet, Mrs. Butler enquired politely about their prospects for the silk harvest. She had already been in Mount Lebanon long enough to know that the farmers and smallholders liked nothing more than to talk about their silkworms.

"The price is very good these days," said George with a grin. "It's almost thirty-five piasters an *oka*[99]."

Maryam smiled as her brothers leaned forward in their eagerness to hear their father talk about the silk crop. That spring they had been working on reviving the *mawwat*, the dead lands scattered around Ayn el-Louz that had lain overgrown and uncultivated for years.

Easing back in his chair, George began telling Mrs. Butler about his visit to the local sheikh whose permission he had needed to clear the ground of rocks and briars in order to bring the plots back into production. He had been taken aback when the old man agreed to his proposal on the spot. Losing no time, the sheikh ordered a contract to be drawn up by his secretary, awarding George and his family the right to cultivate the lands. The main condition had been that they plant the exact number of mulberry trees specified in the contract.

"What happens in seven years when they're mature?" George had asked as the sheikh's secretary was laboriously scratching out the agreement with his quill pen.

"You'll own a quarter and I'll own the rest," the sheikh had replied with a lazy smile. "But it's still your job to cultivate them all."

George had inked his thumb and pressed it to the bottom of the document, cursing his inability to read what was written on the paper. He trusted neither the sheikh nor his secretary not to swindle him.

Mrs. Butler had been listening to the story intently. In spite of her tentative grasp of the local dialect, she had followed the gist.

"That's the power of reading and writing," she pronounced. "Your younger children will have that advantage when they leave my school."

To Maryam's amazement, George went into the house only to reappear moments later with their mother who greeted Mrs. Butler with a curtsy. Then he insisted that the schoolmistress repeat what she had just said and as she did so, Sa'adeh began to nod her head vigorously.

"Thank you, thank you," she stammered, using the only English words she had learned from her children before sheepishly disappearing back into the house. Maryam lingered outside, listening to the conversation. After their initial scepticism, it seemed that her parents had now truly embraced the power of book learning. She smiled to herself in satisfaction.

"I wish I could have had their opportunity when I was a boy," her father was saying as he raised his glass to the schoolmistress another time. Mrs. Butler picked up her glass of sherbet and touched it to his.

"*Kesik*," he said, taking a leisurely sip.

A little later, Sa'adeh came out again carrying a large platter. She heaped rice and lentils onto the schoolmistress's plate and, in spite of her protests, placed pieces of roast chicken on top which she garnished with almonds and sprigs of coriander. Then she handed the spoon to George who set to work dividing up the rest of the food amongst the family.

"Just a little," said As'ad, covering his plate with his hand. "I want to win this afternoon."

"We all want you to win," his father corrected him as they settled down to eat.

After the meal, they drank Turkish coffee instead of thyme tea. It had become popular in the mountains ever since sacks of South American beans had begun arriving at the Beirut docks in growing amounts, undercutting the price of the traditional imports from Yemen. Maryam stirred the dark brown mixture with care, lifting the pot away from the hot coals just as its contents began to boil.

"I should like to go down to the village to see the contests," said Mrs. Butler as she set her cup down on the table to cool. It was more of a statement than a request.

If George was surprised by her interest, he did not show it. When they had finished their coffee, they all made their way down the path to the valley where a large crowd had already gathered. The general hubbub combined with gypsies' flutes and drums drowned out all but the loudest voices.

"Are they about to race each other?" the American schoolmistress shouted in excitement above the din, pointing at a group of young men who had stripped down to their undershirts and pantaloons.

Maryam, who was standing next to her, nodded. Now that they had joined the other villagers, the earlier formalities were dispensed with. As if on cue, the contestants set off towards the crowd, bounding over the loose boulders and stones that littered their path. They passed the mass of spectators in a cloud of dust before reaching the stunted tree that marked the finish line. One of them was led out in front of the crowd as the others knelt on the ground to catch their breath.

"One of Mahmoud's sons," said George. Leaving them, he walked over to congratulate his Druze friend who stood beside his son, his face wreathed in a smile of victory.

"There's still the spear throwing," Maryam heard her father say.

"And the wrestling," replied Mahmoud with a wry smile. "Your boy won't have it all his own way. We have strong men, too!"

Towards dusk when all the other competitions had been fought and won, the crowd's excitement began to mount in anticipation of the main event. It was almost time for the wrestling match to begin, the contest which would decide who was to be that year's village champion. An area of ground had been cleared of stones, and the spectators had already begun to gather in a circle. Flames from two torches placed some distance apart flickered in the fading light.

"How many bouts?" Mrs. Butler asked Maryam. To her surprise, the schoolmistress was showing a keen interest in the proceedings.

"Just one," she replied. "My brother against last year's champion."

Moments later, the crowd parted as As'ad strode into the middle of the circle, his arms and chest glistening with a thick coating of olive oil. Wearing only an old pair of pantaloons cinched at the waist by a large leather belt, he waited patiently for his opponent to appear. At the back of the crowd, a group of village girls giggled among themselves.

"Why is he smeared with oil?" Mrs. Butler asked.

"It's a trick we learned from the Turks." This time it was George who answered. "More difficult for one man to grab the other."

The crowd parted again to allow As'ad's opponent through. Hard-faced and barrel-chested, the newcomer nodded to his opponent and then gazed around at the crowd with a lopsided grin. The referee stepped into the ring and said a few words to them before taking a step back. Both men stared directly into each other's eyes, trying to gain the advantage.

"*Yalla*," he said. "Begin."

The drums, which had fallen silent, began to beat again as As'ad and his opponent circled each other warily, almost touching foreheads as if they were about to embrace. They shuffled sideways, their feet splayed and their backs slightly arched, searching for a hold that would knock the other man off balance or better still, topple him.

"What are they doing?" Mrs. Butler asked, confused by the slow dance-like start.

"Billy goats," George explained to the schoolmistress as he tapped his knuckles together in case she had not understood him. "They're going to butt each other in the head."

Round and round the two men went, making the occasional feint. Then all of a sudden, As'ad's opponent lunged forward and made a grab for his calf, but his hands slipped and he lost his grip. Pulling back quickly, he steadied himself before reassuming his fighting stance. It was almost dark now and the flames from the two torches danced wildly, bathing both their faces in a warm orange glow.

"Knock him down," yelled one of the spectators over the thud of the drums.

The wrestlers closed in and this time it was As'ad who made the first move. He lunged forward forcing his knee between the other man's legs as he tried to lift him off the ground with the momentum of his body. But his opponent saw him coming and twisted away in the nick of time.

"Go on," the same man yelled, gesturing wildly at As'ad.

It was the signal the crowd had been waiting for. Their voices erupted in a thunderous roar over the sound of the drums and flutes. Fearing that Mrs. Butler would be jostled, Maryam tried to escort her to the rear, but the schoolmistress would have none of it and held her ground at the front of the crowd.

"I'm enjoying it," she said as Maryam tried to take her arm. Mrs. Butler, it seemed, was not the kind of missionary who flinched at such things.

As the minutes dragged on, the champion's experience began to show itself and on a couple of occasions, he came close to knocking As'ad off his feet. Fearing that his son was about to lose the bout, George took matters into his own hands and signalled to him with a slight movement of his index finger. Without taking his eyes off his opponent, As'ad manoeuvred himself round until he was in front of George who leaned forward and whispered something in his ear. His opponent spotted it and relaxed his guard, thinking that As'ad was about to concede.

Instead he shoved himself against the man's upper body with all his might, hooking his right leg around his calf at the same time and jerking it backwards. Taken by surprise, the champion stumbled, and before he could regain his balance, As'ad leaped on top of him and pinned him to the ground.

"Do you yield?" the referee asked the pinioned man.

"Yes," he groaned.

Maryam and Mrs. Butler cheered with delight as George helped his son to his feet. With one hand, he dusted him down while with the other, he held As'ad's arm aloft in the air for the whole crowd to see.

"Here's our new village champion!"

Without call or cue, the wrestling crowd started dancing in merriment and celebration. The gypsies played on until late in the evening as the villagers formed line after line in the torchlight for the *dabkeh*, the traditional dance of the mountains. Side by side, they held hands, stamped their feet to the rhythm before lifting one leg on the third beat. Men crouched and jumped with age-old skill and grace to the sinuous melodies of the flutes.

Disagreements and disputes were cast aside, men whooped and women trilled. Fluttering their hands in the air, the dancers gestured at those on the sidelines to join in. Elderly men and women took their grandchildren by the hand and danced a few half-forgotten steps on their creaking limbs as they relived exuberant moments of their youth. Behind their parents' backs, unmarried girls and boys flirted, taking advantage of the festive occasion. It was one of the rare times when they could mingle freely together while their elders turned a blind eye and indulged in their own revelry.

CHAPTER TWENTY-EIGHT

❧❧❧❧

Later, long after Maryam and her mother had accompanied Mrs. Butler back to the schoolhouse, Joseph found himself walking home beside his father under the starry sky.

"What did you say to As'ad during the fight, Abee?"

"Why do you want to know?"

"Because that's what made him win."

George looked at both his sons with the indulgent smile of a proud father.

"I told him to use his brain."

"Then I flipped him like a flatbread," said As'ad, still elated by his victory.

The following day, Joseph set out with his brother over the mountains on a journey to Zahleh. This time around, he was not only leaving the village with his father's approval, but also with instructions to inspect the quality of fresh produce in the city's markets. The size of their farm had grown substantially after the addition of the dead lands, so George was already beginning to plan ahead. He wanted to know whether, in the future, he would be able to sell some of their surplus fruit in Zahleh's bustling markets.

Joseph had not been there since the city had been sacked in the summer of 1860. Over the years, his mind had often drifted back to the kindly priest at the Convent of Our Saviour and the night he spent in the stable there when he had first arrived from Bikfaya, tired and dispirited. These thoughts afflicted him as they crossed over the pass and made their way down to the plain below.

As the outskirts of the city came into sight, he gripped his brother's arm to slow him down so that they could admire the view together. There were no traces left of the half-burnt buildings and trampled gardens he so vividly recalled walking away from as the city lay ravaged eleven years earlier. Instead, a mass of fresh farms and houses stretched out before him. Some had been rebuilt but most were newly constructed, a testament to Zahleh's restored fortunes. The signs of devastation had all but disappeared, replaced with new life and abundance as far as the eye could see.

"Just look at all this," he said to his brother as he gestured towards several newly built villas with tiled roofs occupying an area where there had once been only orchards and fields.

"*Mish ma'oul*[100]," replied As'ad with his mouth hanging open.

The excitement of the trip had already invigorated his brother who had never been on a journey like this before. The strains and bruises from the fight seemed a thing of the past as he bounded down the hillside towards the city, unable to restrain his enthusiasm.

"Let's go to the *souq*," he said. "I want to see what I can buy with these." From his pocket, As'ad produced a handful of piasters his mother had given him. It was his reward for becoming village champion.

"That can wait," said Joseph. "We have something more important to do first."

They walked into the heart of town beside the river, climbing up the little rise to where the convent stood surrounded by its cloisters. Looking up, Joseph saw the solitary bell hanging in its campanile above the church, just as he remembered it.

"This is where I spent my first night when I came to Zahleh during the troubles," he told his younger brother. "I want to thank the man who took me in."

As'ad nodded. He knew how much this meant to Joseph, so they sat down on a bench and waited for a priest or monk to come by. The sun had begun to dip behind the mountains, casting long shadows across the courtyard. After a while, a young priest appeared.

"Welcome," he said, smoothing his black robe. "Can I help you?"

Both Joseph and As'ad scrambled to their feet and saluted him.

"We've come looking for a priest, someone who lived here before the troubles," Joseph began while his brother shuffled his feet.

"What did he look like?" the priest asked.

"Tall with a grey beard."

"That was Father Beshara."

"Is he here now?" asked Joseph eagerly. The young priest shook his head with genuine sadness.

"He was killed trying to prevent some thieves from stealing the silver chalice from the church. They stabbed him to death over there," he said, pointing to the stone steps.

Taken aback by the news, Joseph recalled the last time he had seen his friend and benefactor. It was when he had been arguing with the bailiff outside the church over whether they should remain behind to protect the monks and priests.

"Is there anything else?" asked the young priest.

"No," said Joseph shaking his head, suddenly deeply disheartened.

"Then may God hold you in His care."

They made their way down to one of the many bridges that spanned the river. Sensing his brother's sadness, As'ad remained silent out of respect. When they reached the other bank, they set off in the direction of the Housh and were soon surrounded by its vaulted khans and market stalls. Here luxury goods from Arabia and Asia Minor changed hands alongside local produce from the Bekaa Valley and a growing number of European imports brought in by camel and mule trains from the coast.

Straightaway, Joseph noticed that many of the merchants had moved their places of business into the courtyards and apartments of the old khans, displaying their goods and stacking them beneath decorated facades and carved ceilings. Saddlers and shoemakers jostled for space with cotton and silk merchants. Beyond them lay a jumble of narrow alleys that Joseph recognized from when he had walked through the same market with Habib the day before the city fell.

The old workshops where the weavers and leatherworkers had formerly plied their trade now hissed with the sound of hot iron being quenched in water troughs and the rhythmic beating of metal on anvils. Their cramped floors were piled high with newly minted ploughs and harrows, winnows and threshing boards. As'ad stopped to examine some millstones propped up against a wall.

"We need one of these," he said, running his hand over the hard surface of the basalt. "And look at those new flails."

Joseph nodded. There was no doubt that they could make good use of something of the sort when it came to threshing the bundles of wheat and barley they brought in during the harvest each year. His new roof would be an ideal place for sorting the grain and drying it.

"What's this?" As'ad asked one of the stallholders, picking up a jar and pulling out the wooden plug to sniff its contents.

"That's wine made from the best grapes you can find. But you mountain lads wouldn't know the difference." The stallholder chuckled to himself as he poured some wine into a cracked clay cup, handing it to Joseph who took a sip before passing it to his younger brother. Taking the cup in his large hand, As'ad downed the contents in one gulp.

"*Walla*[101], it's really good," he said, licking his lips.

"Buy a jug," said the stallholder. "It's only fifty *qroush*[102]."

Without a second thought, As'ad fished some coins from his pocket and gave them to the stallholder who all-too-happily handed him the jug before turning to the next customer without another word.

"Let me haggle next time," said Joseph. "This isn't the village."

They walked on through the narrow streets until they came upon a row of fruit stalls where Joseph bent to pick out some of the apples and pears laid out in wicker trays. He inspected the quality of each fruit before putting it back, taking care not to bruise its flesh.

"Here, taste some," offered the storekeeper, slicing the apple with the blade of his knife. Joseph took a piece and chewed it, savouring its taste.

"Hey, aren't you going to buy some?" the storekeeper called out after him in annoyance as he started to walk away. He was a coarse-looking youth with a pockmarked face.

"No," said Joseph. "The fruit's better in our village and it's famous for its apples."

"Where would that be?" he sneered back.

"In the mountains."

"Terrace builders."

Ignoring the insult, Joseph waited for him to finish with his next customer. "Would you be interested in buying some apples to sell here?" he said when the storekeeper finally turned his attention back to them. "We'd bring them to Zahleh ourselves and charge you a fair price."

"Bring me a few the next time you're here. I'll tell you then."

"Do you want some honey, too?" Joseph continued.

"We can always sell that," the storekeeper said, showing a sudden interest. "Our customers say the mountain flowers give it a real taste." He turned away again but Joseph remained where he was.

"What are we waiting for?" blurted out As'ad. "He said he was interested and I want to see the town before it gets dark."

"Have you ever heard of a bailiff called Habib who used to live near the butcher's shop in one of the alleys around here?" Joseph asked the storekeeper, ignoring As'ad's impatience. "He was killed when the city was attacked."

"Yes," he replied, eying him suspiciously. "He was my father. Why are you asking about him?"

"I'll tell you next time," said Joseph as he turned on his heel, leaving the pockmarked youth gawping after him.

Surprised, As'ad turned to follow his brother. "Why didn't you tell him how you met his father?" he said when he had caught him up. "It's a great story."

"To make him keener to do business with us when we come back," said Joseph, cuffing him playfully. "Don't you remember how he treated us at first?"

PART IV

∞∞∞

Come with me from Lebanon, my spouse,
With me from Lebanon:
Look from the top of Amana, from the top of Shenir and Hermon,
From the lions' dens, from the mountains of the leopards.

~ Song of Solomon 4:8 ~

CHAPTER TWENTY-NINE

∿∿∿

The Chouf Mountains
May, 1874

Rose's friendship with Maryam deepened over the years they spent together at the silk factory. Almost imperceptibly, Rose went from being a skittish girl to a mature young woman who responded to her friend's needs and frailties in a more considerate way. Her wit remained as keen as ever, but she took care only to express her thoughts in a way that did not sound harsh or unkind. As a result, Maryam started to share all her secrets with Rose including the enduring pain of unrequited love which still gnawed at her when she least expected it to.

It was a comfortable, if uneventful, time marred only by her father's continuing insistence that she should marry her cousin, Faris. Although he never mentioned the matter to her directly, she could feel it there between them, forcing them apart and poisoning their relationship. She was thwarting her father's will by her steadfast refusal and she knew it.

"Your brother Joseph is married and has children," her mother would say from time to time.

"I know, Imme."

"You should marry, Maryam. He's not the best match but you aren't getting any younger."

The truth was that while the image of Mohanad remained so vivid in her mind, she could not bring herself to accept Faris or anyone else for that matter until one day, everything changed.

"You seem nervous, *ukhtee*," Rose said as they were talking together by the factory gate. "Has something bad happened?"

Maryam was chewing a stem of grass like her grandmother used to do, her eyes fixed firmly on the ground.

"I came across Fatmeh in the village yesterday," she said at last. "She told me that Mohanad's wife has given birth to a son and she asked me to visit her next week to see the baby."

"Are you going to go?" asked Rose. She nodded.

"I've decided to make a gift for the child with the spun silk I've saved."

The clanging of the bell for the next shift interrupted their conversation.

"I'll give you what I've got left over too," said Rose as they stood up to go back onto the factory floor with its steaming pots and clattering machinery. The rattling of the gears and clanking of the drive shafts seemed particularly oppressive to Maryam that afternoon. Before she left for the day, Rose thrust some spun silk into her hand.

"I hope he wears whatever you're making on feast days only," she said with a wink. "They do have feast days, don't they?"

"Of course they do." It took Maryam a moment or two to realize that her friend was making a joke. The visit meant so much to her and she wanted her present to be perfect.

Over the next few days, she tucked and sewed the little garment whenever she had a moment to herself. Her brothers and sister barely noticed but her mother had a sharper eye. When she asked her what she was doing, Maryam tried to dodge the question.

"Just making a blouse," she murmured.

"Then it must be for a midget," said Sa'adeh.

On the morning of the visit, Maryam sewed the last of the stitches into the little shirt and held it up when no one was looking to assess her work. Deeming it satisfactory, she wrapped it up in a piece of cloth and set off through the village wearing the new bonnet that Rose had given her. The old track that had once meandered between the houses was no longer rutted and uneven. It had been widened and levelled, the first of several improvements the people of Ayn el-Louz had made since the troubles had ended.

As eager as Maryam was to see the new child, what she was really hoping for was an encounter with his father. The thought of it still excited her more than she cared to admit. She knew the best she could hope for was a chance to speak to Mohanad alone, even if it was just for a few moments. The door was ajar when she arrived and just as she was about to knock, it creaked open on its hinges, revealing Fatmeh.

"We're honoured by your visit," she giggled and kissed Maryam on the cheek before leading her inside.

Maryam looked around the room and noticed immediately how neat and well-kept it was, just as Joseph had once described it to her. In the corner, there was a crib with a young woman bending over it. Without waiting for Fatmeh, she walked over to her.

"What a beautiful child," Maryam said to her, making a sign with her hand to ward off the evil eye. "Can I hold him?"

The young woman smiled shyly and lifted the baby out of the crib. He was swaddled tightly in a single piece of cloth with only his head showing. It was crowned by tufts of tawny hair that spilled out of the top. Without hesitating, Maryam put her arms out and took him, rocking him gently from side to side as she cooed to him. To her amazement, the little boy gurgled contentedly.

"Can I see his hands?" she asked.

His mother pulled back the cloth to reveal them. At once he began to wave them about in the air, curling his fingers like stalks of wild barley nodding in the breeze. Delighted by the baby's reaction to her, Maryam began murmuring endearments.

"You don't have children yourself?" the child's mother asked her.

"No."

Maryam was still playing with the baby when Fatmeh appeared at the door followed by her brother. She had been so engrossed that she had not even noticed her slip out of the house.

"He asked me to fetch him when you came," she said by way of explanation as Mohanad took his sandals off outside.

Maryam had only seen Mohanad once since he had shown her the shelter all those years ago, and even then it had only been in passing. It was the day his sister had been assaulted by the Ottoman soldiers and they had brought Joseph back to their house, battered and bruised. Now that he was standing so close to her, she could see how little he had changed over the years. His injured shoulder made him droop to one side but his voice was still as soft as summer rain.

Smiling at Maryam, he asked his wife to take the baby from her in his quiet voice. It now carried a note of authority that had not been there before. He brought over a rush-seated chair for her and she sat down, smoothing an imaginary wrinkle from her skirt.

"How is your brother?" he began.

"He's well," Maryam stammered, struggling to find her words.

"He did us a great service when Fatmeh was attacked," Mohanad observed rather stiffly. Out of the corner of her eye, Maryam saw Fatmeh shiver at her brother's mention of the incident. The assault on her by the two soldiers had brought shame on her family and worse, people still gossiped about it in the village.

"It was his duty," Maryam replied.

"And the wrestling champ?"

"Too puffed up for his own good," she said, chuckling nervously.

He smiled at her spontaneous wit.

With the formalities over, they sat in silence. Fatmeh was busy preparing some refreshments while Mohanad's wife remained at the rear of the room with the child. To her surprise, Maryam could not help feeling a little uncomfortable although she had dreamt about this moment for so many years. As she sat wondering what he would say to her next or what she might say to him, an unexpected thought sneaked into her mind and lodged there.

At first she was barely aware of it, but very quickly she realized that she could neither ignore nor dismiss it as unwelcome as it might be. For the first time since their chance meeting, she was able to see with startling clarity that the image of him she had carried around with her for so long was only as solid as smoke from a fire.

The moment when they had shared the medlar fruit together had been just a pleasant dream on a summer's day, nothing more, nothing less. She could no longer even remember what they had said as they sat side by side in the dappled sunlight of the 'arzal. But perhaps the biggest surprise of all was that the awkwardness she now felt in his company did not make her feel bad. It was almost as if a weight had been lifted from her shoulders.

"You are blessed," she said, finally breaking the silence, "with a beautiful son." Mohanad's face beamed with pride at the mention of the little boy.

"Indeed we are," he replied, glancing fondly across to where his wife was tending to the baby.

Moments later Fatmeh brought over four small glass bowls and set them down on the table. As Maryam looked down at the white whorl of sugar and rice decorated with almonds, Mohanad took one and gave it to her before handing another to his sister.

"Let's celebrate," he said looking at Maryam with his prune-coloured eyes. "I hope that we'll do the same when you have your own children."

"But Maryam isn't married yet," Fatmeh whispered, anxious to avoid an embarrassing misunderstanding. "She's working in the silk factory."

Maryam noticed a look of surprise flicker momentarily in Mohanad's eyes. *He disapproves of me*, she thought.

Setting down her bowl of *mughlee*, she took out the little packet that she had brought with her and handed it to him.

"I made this for your son. I hope you and your wife will accept it as a gift from me."

Maryam watched the meticulous way his fingers unwrapped the bundle. It reminded her of the way he had peeled the piece of fruit for her all those years ago.

"It's wonderful," Mohanad said. A soft smile turned the corners of his mouth up as he pulled out the little shirt and shook it, making the silk shimmer. "Look what Maryam has brought us."

His wife put their son back in the crib and walked over to where they were sitting. Maryam sensed a slight hostility in her manner as she picked up the nightshirt and ran her fingers over the stitching.

"It's well made," she said as she rubbed the silk between her thumb and forefinger. "A little big, but he'll soon grow into it."

"What's his name?" asked Maryam, hoping to overcome the other woman's apparent antipathy now that she had relinquished her claim over Mohanad.

"Mahmoud." Her voice masked a smug tone behind her friendliness. "He's named after his grandfather."

CHAPTER THIRTY

✑✑✑

By the time she arrived back home, Maryam had already made up her mind. She decided that she would end her campaign of resistance then and there and agree to marry Faris. If her mother was surprised by her sudden change of attitude, she did not comment on it. But her father was another matter, and Maryam waited until he came back at dusk in order to speak to him in private. They went around to the side of the house by the fig tree and it was there, in her special place, that she calmly told him of her decision.

"Good," he said, not unkindly. "I thought you'd never come around to it."

The following day during her shift, Rose began pulling faces at her from across the bench. Maryam ignored her until the shift bell rang.

"So what happened?" Rose asked as they took their places in their customary spot outside. As usual, her impatience got the better of her.

"It was fine," Maryam replied. "I saw the little boy – *shou mahdoum*[103]– and gave them the silk shirt I'd made for him."

"Did you get the chance to speak to your sweetheart?" Rose was eager to know all the details.

"Yes," said Maryam, nodding her head. "He seems very happy with his wife and baby."

"And?"

Maryam fell silent and turned away. It was the question she knew Rose would ask her although she had been trying to avoid it all morning.

"I've decided to marry Faris," she said finally.

"*Kizzebeh*[104]," Rose said to her friend, for once almost at a loss for words. "You can't be serious."

"It's the truth," Maryam replied.

Now that she had done the hard part and broken the news to Rose, Maryam began to tell her all about her visit to Mohanad's house. Even so, she still found herself unable to explain how she had come to realize that her obsession was no more than a girlish fantasy she had built up in her mind over the years.

"But I still don't understand," Rose said after she had finished. "Even if that's the case, why did you agree to marry him?"

"I don't know," said Maryam. "Perhaps it was seeing Mohanad with his wife and child, how happy they are. It made me want a family of my own."

"*Yuh, yuh,*" Rose tutted her disapproval.

"She gave me this strange look when Mohanad showed her the silk shirt. I can't really describe it," confessed Maryam. "And then when we were eating *mughlee*, he told me he hoped to celebrate the birth of my own children."

Sensing her sadness, Rose put an arm around Maryam's shoulders as she stared glumly ahead.

"Then his sister told him I was still not married and working here," she sniffled. "He didn't say anything, but I'm sure he pitied me in his heart."

"But that's not a reason to marry someone you don't like," protested Rose.

"It's my fate," said Maryam despondently. "I don't want to end up pickled in vinegar like a spinster."

In no time at all, the word spread around the village that Maryam and Faris were planning to marry in autumn. It was considered an important alliance in Ayn el-Louz. Rumours about Maryam's sudden change of heart also began to circulate, leading to wild speculation. It had been common knowledge among the girls that she disliked him. They gossiped about it at the spring. As for the men, they discussed the merits of the marriage as they inspected the fruit in their orchards and prepared for the harvest.

Maryam was surprised one day to come home and discover one of Faris's uncles talking to her father outside the house. He was one of the two who had come to plead for her family's help on behalf of her aunt when she had been widowed before the troubles. She realized almost instantly that he had come to propose the match formally. Now that her betrothal was official, her heart sank even further and the depression, which she had only felt from time to time until then, suddenly became very real.

When Faris came to their house the following Sunday with his entire family to celebrate their engagement, the last of the wheat and barley had already been gathered from the fields. Maryam sat with the women and watched as Faris ate and drank, making the most of his moment in the sun. To mark the occasion, George had slaughtered a baby goat and Maryam had spent the previous day helping her mother prepare the carcass. They had pounded the best portions and then mixed them with *burghoul* to make *kibbeh*, roasting what was left on an open fire. To accompany it, Sa'adeh had prepared baked eggplant with beans.

The feasting continued until the shadows grew long. The men toasted one another with the *arrack* and wine George had bought at considerable expense in Zahleh. The uncles ate like gluttons, having long since forgotten their undignified treatment at the hands of Imm George. When the last of the plates had been scraped clean, Faris got to his feet and swaggered over to where Maryam was sitting.

"*Sitt* Maryam," he said with comical formality as he gazed around at his family. "Do me the honour of taking a stroll with me."

Despite her revulsion at his suggestion, Maryam had no option but to agree. Together they set off down the road to the village with their uncles and aunts, nephews and nieces all following behind at a short distance. As they were about to turn the first corner, Faris reached for her hand but Maryam was too quick for him and snatched it away.

"Come on now," he chided her. "No one will see us."

"I don't care," she said woodenly. "It's not correct."

"We're almost married," he said with a leer.

᠅᠅᠅

As the summer turned to autumn, Maryam noticed that her mother had begun to collect items for her trousseau. In addition to putting out clothes scented with fresh lavender, she had added pots, jugs, and cups.

"What are these for, Imme?" Maryam enquired as she was examining the collection.

"You won't ask that when you are living at my sister's," she replied as if she had been foolish to bring up the subject. "You'll have nothing decent to eat off or drink from until Faris builds you a new place and that could be a very long time."

But in spite of her general gloominess, Maryam at least found comfort in one thing. Faris had not insisted that she should stop working at the silk factory after their betrothal was made public. But instead of giving him credit for his open-mindedness, she chalked his leniency up to the fact that he hoped to reap some future benefit from her earnings although she swore to herself she would never let him take one *qirsh* from her.

Making the most of her liberty while she still could, Maryam continued to go to work every day. The only difference now was that the hot and humid atmosphere of the factory no longer bothered her, nor did the rattling of the machinery. What had seemed like drudgery only weeks earlier was now her only solace. The routine had become a temporary respite from the constant reminders of her impending nuptials. As the prospect of leaving the factory approached, the time she spent with Rose also became more and more precious. To make the most of it, Maryam would often stay behind after the end of her shift so that they could stroll around the streets together until the light began to fade.

"Please come to my wedding, Rose," Maryam begged her friend.

"I won't know anyone there but you," Rose had replied.

"The American schoolmistress will be there," she said, hoping that the presence of a foreigner would encourage her.

These stolen moments passed all too quickly. On her last day at the factory, the other girls came up to Maryam one by one and presented her with their parting gifts. There were home-sewn sashes and scarves, combs for her hair, brooches, curios, and keepsakes.

"You're so lucky to have found a husband," one of the older girls whispered in her ear, scarcely able to hide her envy.

"And you're leaving the factory, too. I wish it were me," said another. Even Abou Hazeen smiled at her when she came to collect the last of her wages.

"We'll miss you, Maryam," the supervisor said. "You've become a first-rate worker."

"Thank you," she replied, attempting a shy smile to disguise her sadness.

"I wish we had more reelers like you, not these clumsy village girls who come looking for work nowadays," he said, adding a handful of extra piasters.

She looked down at the coins in her hand. "That's too much," she protested.

"No," Abou Hazeen said with a smile. "Consider it a wedding gift."

Later that evening, her relatives and friends called at the house to celebrate her last evening as an unmarried woman. As they arrived, Maryam presented each one with a little packet of almonds lightly dusted with sugar that she had brought with her from town for the occasion. While the men sat and smoked with her father and brothers in the cool night air, the women gathered inside the house to admire the contents of her trousseau.

Spurred on by their curiosity, they picked up the clothes and ran their fingers along the hems of the skirts and blouses. Maryam looked on, appalled as they examined her few pieces of jewellery, weighing them in their hands. Some of them even began to look over the household articles that Sa'adeh had set aside for her as if they were in the local *souq*.

Maryam stood to one side while her mother chatted cheerfully with their guests, occasionally scolding one or the other for being too nosy. Despite the commotion, she felt detached, even resigned to what was happening around her. Later that night, her younger sister mixed some *henna*[105] powder in a pot with a few drops of water and drew simple designs on the palms of her hands with a sharpened stick.

"Don't look so serious," said Sa'adeh when she bent down to inspect them as the mixture was drying. "Tomorrow's your wedding day. You should be happy."

"I know," said Maryam.

The following morning, she rode down to the church sitting sideways on the back of a mule led by her brother, Joseph. The animal was festooned with ribbons and its back was covered with a large colourful cloth, embroidered along the edges. Maryam herself was wearing her grandmother's bridal dress, which Sa'adeh had unpicked and re-sewn so that it would fit her daughter's larger hips and bust.

Her brothers walked on either side while her mother and father followed behind with her younger sister. As they made their way through the village, their neighbours and friends came out to join them. The same gypsy musicians who had beaten their drums and played their flutes on Saint George's Day brought up the rear.

In the distance, the sound of the bridegroom's procession could be heard making its way towards the church from the other end of the village. The clamour grew louder and louder until suddenly the crack of a musket echoed across the hills, followed by a loud cheer. The mule jerked its head up in alarm but Joseph held firmly onto the halter. Maryam shuddered. To her relief, the first face she saw when she looked up again was that of Rose who was walking beside the

American schoolmistress. She waved at them and Rose responded by touching the tips of her fingers to her lips and blowing her a kiss.

When Maryam finally rode up to the church, Faris was already standing there by the door, surrounded by his family and supporters. She tried to avoid his eyes but he kept grinning at her and when she came near him, he grabbed her hand. No longer able to refuse him, she let him take it and lead her into the dimly lit nave where the priest stood waiting for them.

Inside, their relatives jostled one another amid clouds of incense to witness the exchange of their marriage vows. When the priest began to deliver a lengthy homily, the congregation grew restless forcing him to cut it short. So he concluded with an exhortation to the bride to devote herself diligently to her conjugal duties, but his last words were drowned out as the sexton began ringing the bell with vigour.

A cacophony of sound greeted them when they finally emerged from the church. The throbbing of the *tambours* and the wailing of the flutes deafened Maryam as she stood meekly beside her husband, blinking in the bright sunlight. She barely noticed the handfuls of grain or the bouquets of autumnal blooms they tossed high into the air above her head.

Aweeha, what a lucky bridegroom!

Aweeha, what a beautiful bride!

The shrill cries of the women and girls pierced through the din. For some moments, they stood where they were while those around them sang the traditional marriage songs. Small children ran to and fro, dodging in and out of the crowd in their excitement. Then the wedding party formed itself into a *zaffeh*[106] with Maryam and Faris at its head. The procession wound its way through the village and followed the path down into the valley where the Saint George's Day celebrations were held.

There it broke up as relatives, neighbours, and friends gathered around in a circle, preparing themselves to dance the *dabkeh*. Rose caught Maryam by the hand and led her into the centre where she circled around her in a series of neat pirouettes, waving her hands above her head in time to the music.

"Let's show these men how we women dance," she shouted into Maryam's ear over the hubbub.

Within moments, the women and girls had formed themselves into a line beside them, stamping their feet and swaying their hips in time to the drums. It billowed back and forth, engulfing Rose and Maryam and winding itself around them in a protective circle until Faris suddenly pushed his way through into the centre. Urged on by his friends, he dropped to one knee and stretched out his arms towards her in a grand gesture of chivalry. But Rose was too quick for him and whirled Maryam away, leaving him kneeling on the ground like a clown.

"He can wait," she giggled as they skipped to the other end of the line.

When dusk fell, Faris dragged himself away from the company of his friends and prepared himself to carry Maryam through the front door of his mother's house. The dancing and carousing, which had continued nonstop from the time that the procession had reached the valley floor, had finally come to an end and the last of the food platters had been wiped clean.

Outside, members of the two families lined up at the door to witness the entrance of the bride into her new home. In her hand, Maryam carried a lump of dough, the kind used for baking bread on the *tannour*. As she crossed the threshold in her husband's arms, she reached up and pressed it firmly into a hollow behind the rough wooden lintel. Then she felt herself being carried over to the marriage bed that his mother and sister had prepared earlier in the day for them. It was the first time in their lives that she and Faris had been alone together.

"This will be the best night of your life," he said with a smirk.

"Don't disappoint them, they will want to know that I am a man and you are a..."

"Yes, I know."

Maryam felt her body go rigid at the sound of his crude words. Throughout the day, she had tried but failed to reconcile herself to his clammy touch and stale breath. Now the thought of intimacy with him revolted her. As she lay on the bed in her wedding dress with her eyes fixed on the piece of dough stuck to the ceiling, she wondered what she had done to deserve such a fate. He walked over to the door and shoved it shut with his shoulder. The doorframe shuddered and the lump of dough, loosened by the vibrations, flopped to the ground. A cockroach scuttled across the floor and disappeared behind the food chest.

"So much for old wives' tales," he said as he picked it up and threw it onto the chest in the corner.

"It's bad luck," said Maryam sitting bolt upright on the bed. "Our marriage is cursed."

Taking no notice of her words, he pushed her back and began to loosen the stays of her dress with his clumsy hands. When she tried to push him away he persisted, groping and tearing at her undergarments until he had managed to pull them off. Pinioned beneath him, Maryam ceased struggling. She realized with bitterness that there was nothing to do but submit.

"I will accept you as my husband," she hissed, "but our life together will never be more than that."

"Then accept me now," replied Faris with a callous laugh as he fumbled with the buttons on his pantaloons. "Let's not keep them waiting outside for too long."

CHAPTER THIRTY-ONE

❧

April, 1881

Rose would not see Maryam again for another six years. Although she often thought of her friend, she found herself too preoccupied with the daily demands of her own life to make the short trip to Ayn el-Louz. She spent her days at the silk factory where she witnessed the arrival of a constant stream of village girls who presented themselves at the gate looking for work, very much like Maryam had once done. Most left after a few years before their marriage prospects became tarnished by age.

As for Rose herself, she had already decided that she had no wish for a husband. With no one to provide for her, she needed the money she earned to support herself. The factory supervisor had come to rely on her more and more to instruct the new girls in the intricacies of reeling silk thread. When she pointed out to Abou Hazeen that she had now become his chief instructress, he increased her wages without protest.

One day in spring, she was pleasantly surprised to find Maryam's youngest brother waiting for her outside the factory gates at the end of her shift.

"My sister sent me," he said shyly as he walked up to her. Rose looked at him for a moment and smiled.

"I recognize you from the wedding. You're Maryam's little brother." He nodded.

"How is she? I often think of her."

"Fine," he said, clearly uncertain how to go on. Rose smiled at him encouragingly.

"She hopes that you will come to celebrate Easter Day with her and her family in their new house," he said finally.

Rose barely gave the matter a second thought before accepting. It was the Holy Week and she had already seen children from the town out collecting olive and mulberry branches, bringing them to the church to be blessed by the priest. She knew, too, that the factory would be closed for two days, as it was every year, so that the girls who worked there could spend Easter Day with their families in the villages. With no relatives of her own to visit, she was delighted at the idea of spending the holiday with Maryam's family.

"I'll walk over to the village by myself. There's no need for you to come and fetch me," she told the young man.

When Easter Day came, Rose set out early in the morning for Ayn el-Louz. By the time she reached it, the mass had already begun so she took her place at the back of the little church behind the congregation. It was not until after the service had ended and she was standing outside surrounded by villagers greeting one another that she caught sight of her friend.

She scarcely recognized the woman wearing the bonnet she had once given her. Maryam's hourglass figure had lost its shape and her olive skin now sagged beneath sad eyes. Her hair, which once hung down her back in a luxurious plait, was streaked with grey and bunched up sloppily under her hat. Two small children trailed at her heels. But the moment she saw Rose, her face broke into a big smile and she hurried towards her.

"How pretty you look!" Before she could say anything, Rose was smothered in a bone-crushing hug. Maryam's body trembled against hers, racked by a succession of sobs.

"It's so good to see you again, Rose! You don't know how much I've missed you these past years," Maryam stammered with tears coursing down her face.

"I've missed you too, *habibtee*." It took her a moment or two to extricate herself from Maryam's damp embrace. She stood back and glanced down at the two little faces looking up at her with curious eyes. Taking a package from her basket, she handed each one a sticky pastry.

"Say thank you to your auntie," said Maryam.

"She's not one of our aunts," said the little girl. Rose chuckled. She recognized a kindred spirit.

"You're right. But I am your mother's friend."

They stood together while the children ate the pastries. As they were licking their sugary fingers, Rose noticed the priest approaching them out of the corner of her eye.

"*Al-Maseeh Qam*," he said. It was the traditional Easter greeting.

"He has risen indeed," Maryam responded. Rose felt his eyes on her, filled with ill-concealed curiosity.

"I'm Rose," she said, introducing herself without waiting for him to enquire who she was. "Maryam's friend from the silk factory."

"That place." The priest's voice harboured the same hostility it did as when he had first heard that Maryam was planning to work there. Nevertheless, in spite of his evident disapproval he continued to stare at Rose until, distracted by one of his parishioners, he turned and stalked off without another word.

"Do you know what some people think of the factory in the villages around here?" Maryam whispered to her as soon as he had walked away. Rose looked at her friend and saw, once again, the same timidity she had shown during her first days at the factory. She had clearly been cowed by the priest's reaction.

"Yes," said Rose as they began to walk in the direction of the house. "That's why I did it." Maryam gave Rose a look of astonishment and then they both giggled. Relaxed in each other's company once again, they walked side by side while the children ran on ahead.

"Shouldn't we wait for your husband?" Rose asked after they had covered some distance.

"No," said Maryam. "He'll come when he's finished with his friends."

Rose found herself pleasantly surprised at the sight of the new house. During her journey to the village that morning, she had no idea what to expect. She already knew about Faris's slothful reputation. But instead of a hovel, they had come upon a substantial dwelling with two rooms, one built on a higher level than the other in the new style. A rush mat with some cushions and two chairs had already been set out on the roof overlooking the valley. Bathed in the warm spring sunshine, it seemed an ideal place to eat their Easter meal.

"How grand," she said. "Has it been built long?" Instead of the look of pride she had expected, a flash of barely concealed anger contorted Maryam's placid features.

"Since my brothers finished it," she spat out. "Before that, I spent two long years living in my aunt's filthy hovel."

By the time Faris came back home, they had almost finished their meal. Rose could smell the pungent stench of *arrack* on his breath.

"Where have you been?" said Maryam testily. "We have a guest."

He plumped himself heavily on one of the chairs without bothering to reply and glanced at Rose.

"Your friend from the silk factory?"

Rose stood up to greet him, but before she could say anything he brushed her aside with a careless wave of his hand.

"Fetch me some food," he bellowed at his wife. "I'm hungry."

Maryam returned with a dish piled high with pieces of roast meat that she handed to him as he slumped in his chair. At the sight of food, his mood brightened and he immediately began tearing the meat off the bones with his fingers. Using a piece of bread, he dunked them one after the other in the chickpea sauce. After he had stripped the bones bare, he picked them up and greedily began to suck out the marrow.

"Where did you get the meat from?" he asked, looking up from the pile of bones on his plate. "It tastes good."

"It came from my family," Maryam replied. "They always slaughter a goat at Easter."

But her irony was lost on him. Belching loudly, he wiped his greasy fingers on his pantaloons while Maryam looked on sourly. Then he got to his feet and yawned, disappearing inside the house without another word. Once he was gone the two women went to work clearing away the plates and storing the leftovers in earthenware jars. As Rose was passing Maryam a bowl, the children came up to her and asked her for some scraps for the chickens.

"What's your name?" she asked the little boy as she handed him some.

"George," he answered proudly. "After my *Jiddo*[107]."

"*Shou tayyib*[108]," Rose replied, pinching his cheek lightly between her thumb and index finger.

"And what's yours?" she said as she turned to his sister.

"Rose." She picked up her little namesake and gave her a big kiss. Setting her down again she turned to Maryam, her own face wreathed in a smile.

"You've made me part of your family."

"You'll always be part of our lives," Maryam replied, "whatever happens to us and wherever you go."

Leaving Faris behind in the house snoring loudly, they set off together to pay a traditional Easter call on Maryam's family. The children stopped what they were doing and ran after them.

"You poor girl," Rose said with barely concealed fury as soon as they were safely out of earshot. "Now I understand why you refused to marry him for so long."

Maryam just shrugged her shoulders.

"God save me from a husband like that."

"At least my father treated me kindly again."

The village street was packed with relatives visiting one another as they always did on feast days. Every now and then, someone would stop Maryam to exchange pleasantries and enquire after her family. Her brothers had become famous in the village for their smallholding's success and in particular, their expert production of cocoons. Bored with the constant delays, young George and Rose ran on ahead, allowing the two old friends to talk freely.

"And you, Rose," asked Maryam wistfully. "What will you do?"

"I don't know," she replied, glancing at her sideways as they sauntered along together.

The weathered slopes of the mountains had turned a warm shade of russet in the soft afternoon sunlight. Dark streaks marked the gullies and crevices that notched the hillsides. Rose wrinkled her nose in that familiar gesture which Maryam had come to know so well at the factory.

"I'll go to *Amreeka*," the younger woman said simply.

This was no sudden flight of fancy on her part. Ever since a girl at the silk factory had told her about a group of men from her village who had boarded a packet steamer to Marseilles from the Beirut docks, the seeds of wanderlust had been planted in Rose's mind. The men had taken the same packet that often transported bales of raw silk from the silk factory to Marseilles en route for the French city of Lyon. The finely worked fabrics produced in the factories of the Midi were now in high demand among the fashionable ladies of Europe.

But rather than remain in the French port or travel inland from the coast, they had decided instead to embark on a larger ship bound for America. Several months later, the girl had mentioned to Rose that these same men were now living in a huge city, much bigger than either Damascus or Beirut, where a person could find work even if he or she could barely understand the language spoken there. It was from then on that Rose had begun dreaming of leaving Mount Lebanon to make a life for herself in that magical land of opportunity.

"You mean you'll leave the mountains forever?"

"Yes," Rose nodded, shaking her curls free from the confines of her bonnet. "I'm an orphan, and you're my only family."

Maryam fell silent as they walked on together up the hill. Upset as she was by her friend's decision, she nevertheless admired her bold spirit. Once upon a time she might have dredged up enough courage to go with her, but as a married woman with two children, that was now all but impossible. Instead, she pivoted lightly on her toes, dragging Rose around with her. Without any explanation, they set off arm-in-arm in the opposite direction.

"Where are you taking me now?" said Rose. "I thought we were going to visit your family."

"We're going to see the schoolmistress first," replied Maryam with a smile. "It's her country, so maybe she can help you."

In spite of the celebrations going on elsewhere, Mrs. Butler was sitting by herself in the school room reading from a leather-bound book. She looked up when she saw them at the door and greeted them in her formal Arabic.

"*Kollo eidin wa antom bikhayr*[109]." Maryam smiled at her and returned the greeting.

"Who is this young lady?" she asked, peering at Rose over her eyeglasses. "I think I recognize her from your wedding day."

"This is Rose, my friend from the silk factory."

She reached out and shook Rose's hand firmly. As she did so, an enamel locket with gold engraving appeared from beneath the ruffles of her blouse, surprising Rose who had expected her to be wearing a cross. But Mrs. Butler was a practical woman who had confined her activities to education since her arrival in the village and had never trained "biblewomen" to evangelize in the neighbouring villages for fear of making an enemy of the priest.

"I'm always pleased to make the acquaintance of any of Maryam's friends or indeed those of her family," Mrs. Butler said. "Her father helped us establish this school and her children attend classes here."

She arranged a couple of chairs in a semicircle and motioned for them to make themselves comfortable while she went into the next room. From there, they could hear the sound of water being heated on an oil-fired stove. Some minutes later, she reappeared carrying a china teapot of foreign manufacture decorated with blue dragons and birds. It was quite unlike anything Rose had ever seen before.

Mrs. Butler poured the steaming tea into cups that bore the same blue marks, gracefully lifting the spout to prevent the last drops from falling into the saucers. When she had finished, she settled back into her chair and smiled at her visitors. There was a silence while all three women sipped their tea.

"Mrs. Butler," Maryam began at last. "My friend Rose is preparing to travel to your country. She wants to go to *Amreeka.*"

"Am-er-eek-ah, my dear," Mrs. Butler corrected her, enunciating each syllable of the word. Rose waited for the American lady to launch into a lengthy soliloquy in the way that mountain people often did when asked for an opinion, but instead she continued to drink her tea as if Maryam had not spoken. Finally, she set her cup down.

"It's a very large country, Rose. Where will you go after you arrive there?"

"I'll try to find where the other people from Mount Lebanon have gone," Rose ventured.

"Then you'll take a ship to New York, I imagine." Mrs. Butler paused before looking directly at her. "What you will do when you get there, young lady?"

"I've heard you can find work there easily. I'll look for a job as a dressmaker or work in a factory like I do here."

Rose answered with as much confidence as she could muster. She was already beginning to find the direct manner of the American lady's interrogation quite unnerving.

"I see," said Mrs. Butler. "Then I will give you a letter of introduction addressed to the Mission. But it will not help you in New York, I'm afraid. I come from the South, you see, and New York is a different place altogether."

Sitting down at her desk, she picked up a pen and dipped it into a small enamel inkwell. When she began to write, the metal nib made a scratching sound on the vellum. Without looking up, she asked Rose for her full name.

"You mean my father's name?"

"Yes," said Mrs. Butler. "Nobody will know who you are over there."

"Hanna el-Shawish." Mrs. Butler wrote down "Rose Shawish."

She finished the short letter and signed it "Elizabeth Butler." Sealing it in an envelope with a dab of wax, the schoolmistress handed it to Rose together with a printed pamphlet that bore the Mission's address at the bottom.

"Take this too. It may be of some use to you on your travels."

Rose thanked Mrs. Butler and was about to get up to leave when Maryam suddenly put out her hand, holding her back. But instead of saying anything, she stared awkwardly at the floor as though she were at a loss for words.

"Well, Maryam," said the schoolmistress. "Did you wish to add something?"

"Mrs. Butler, can I ask you to write a letter for me to my friend who lives in Beirut? Her name is Layal," she said, finding her courage at last.

"Certainly, my dear, I would be glad to. Is this the Damascene widow with the little boy you told me about? The one who came here from Hasbaya during the troubles?"

"Yes," said Maryam, nodding vigorously.

"Do you know where to address it to?"

Much to Rose's surprise, she did.

"The consulate of el-Nemsa," she said. When Mrs. Butler looked at her blankly, Maryam turned and whispered something to Rose.

"She means L'Autriche, Mrs. Butler." Rose had learned the French names of the European countries during her days in the convent.

"Austria."

"The priest told me that her husband is an important man there, the dragoman," Maryam explained.

So Mrs. Butler wrote a second letter of introduction on behalf of Rose at Maryam's behest, this time requesting that Layal should receive Rose were she to call on her in Beirut.

"And to help her in finding a ship so she can go to *Amreeka*," Maryam added. Just as Mrs. Butler was about to finish the letter, she spoke up again.

"Can you also tell her that I wear the purple stone on special days to remember her by?" she said, pointing to the necklace at her throat.

"Of course," smiled Mrs. Butler as she added the post-scriptum.

It was late in the afternoon by the time they finally arrived at the family house. George had died several winters earlier from a fever but Sa'adeh still lived there with her two youngest children. Both of Maryam's older brothers were there with their families although they had moved out a long time ago and now lived in their own houses. A little stiff with age but still cheerful, Sa'adeh welcomed them at the door. She had spent most of the day helping her grandchildren paint eggshells with *henna* for the egg hunt.

"This is my friend Rose from the silk factory, Imme."

"Yes, I remember her from your wedding day," her mother replied warmly. "Welcome, Rose."

They spent the rest of the afternoon surrounded by Maryam's family. Joseph paid his sister particular attention, noticing Faris's absence at once. Although he had never aired his views about his brother-in-law, it was clear to everyone that he did not like him, and with his father dead, he felt a special responsibility towards his sister and her children.

"Where is he?" he asked her later that afternoon.

"He didn't feel well," Maryam replied somewhat lamely.

A look of anger flashed across his face but before he could question his sister further, Rose distracted him by asking to see his new plough. It was growing dark by the time the festivities had come to an end and they were saying their final goodbyes.

"It's too late for you to walk home now, Rose," said Maryam. "Stay with us tonight."

Left with no alternative and eager to spend more time with her friend, Rose accepted the invitation. Faris had just woken up from his afternoon nap when they arrived back at the house.

"Bring me some water," he called out gruffly to Maryam as she opened the door.

Rose watched as Maryam obediently fetched the basin and poured some water into it. Splashing it over his face, he squinted across in her direction and from his baleful stare Rose could see that his eyes were bloodshot. He wiped his face and went outside. Through the half-open door, Rose could see him staring moodily out into the gathering darkness. She pushed it to and went over to help Maryam who was putting her children to bed at the back of the room.

"Will you be staying with us tomorrow and the next day, too?" little Rose asked her.

"No, *habibtee*, I have to go back to my own house," she said, giving her a kiss on the forehead.

"But we want you to stay," said her brother. They were interrupted by shouts from Faris outside.

"Bring me my pipe and some tobacco. And don't forget to change the water in the bowl. Last time it was as stale as goat's piss."

Maryam stopped what she was doing and immediately went to look for the *argileh*. When she found it, she picked it up and eased the pipe stem out of the jar, pouring the contents of the bowl away. She refilled it with fresh water from the jug. Then she took down the tobacco pouch from the shelf and disappeared outside, closing the door behind her as she went.

Rose heard the muffled sounds of an argument and moments later Maryam reappeared, flustered and upset. She walked straight over to the brazier and picked out some burning coals with a pair of bent tongs, accidently dropping some embers onto her arm.

"*Akhh! Ya imme!*"

She winced but did not drop the tongs. Grimacing with pain, she carried the coals outside to where her husband was sitting, casually tamping the shredded tobacco into the bowl. When she came back in again, Rose took her arm and gently examined the marks. Three powdery wheals had appeared where the coals had burnt her skin.

"Do you have something for the burn?" she asked her. Maryam pointed silently to a jar of salve on a shelf. Rose took it down and gently began to rub the ointment into the charred skin. Under the soothing pressure of her fingers, the muscles in Maryam's hunched shoulders began to relax and the angry flush faded from her cheeks.

"Promise me that you will follow me to *Amreeka*," said Rose. "This is no life for you here with this … man."

But Maryam did not reply. Instead, she took out an iron key that was hanging almost hidden in a crevice on the wall and walked over to an old wooden chest in the corner of the room. She unlocked it and, lifting the heavy lid on its creaking hinges, began to rummage through its contents. Every now and then, she would pull out a blouse or a skirt and show it to Rose before folding it carefully and replacing it.

"Your trousseau?" said Rose. It was more of an observation than a question.

"Yes," said Maryam. "I sometimes open it when he," she paused long enough to gesture indignantly towards the door, "is not here. These are the only things that remind me of my old life."

After a while she stopped searching and took out a small cloth bag tied with a drawstring and some kind of amulet on a leather necklace. It seemed that she had found what she was looking for.

"I want you to have these," Maryam said as she handed both items to Rose. "But make sure you hide them before my husband comes back in."

"What are they?" said Rose, turning over the amulet in her hand.

"This is an old copper coin my Teta gave me before she died. She said it was a good luck charm. Maybe it will bring you luck."

"And the little bag?"

"My savings. Not much, about half a purse of piasters." For once Rose found herself on the verge of tears. Whether it was the sight of Maryam standing forlornly beside the chest or her spontaneous act of generosity, she did not know.

"I can't accept these things," she stammered.

"Take them," whispered Maryam, putting her hand to her lips and pointing to the door. "They're yours now."

"On my life, I swear I'll repay you one day," said Rose, hugging her friend fiercely. "You deserve better than this."

CHAPTER THIRTY-TWO

While she was walking back to the silk factory early the next day, Rose thought back to the rest of the girl's story about the men who had set out for America from her village.

She told Rose that one of their relatives who could read and write had received a letter especially delivered by mule from Beirut. Besides containing a money order drawn on a local silk merchant, it revealed that the men had reached the Americas safely and that they had the good fortune to arrive in New York. There they had found themselves in a city that came alive at night, with busy streets lit by gas lamps and impressively tall buildings under construction on every street corner.

They had taken up lodging across the river in the city of Brooklyn using the money they had brought with them. Before long, some of them were taken on as porters and handymen and started earning a living despite the fact that they could barely understand more than a few words of English. But the one thing that stayed with Rose as the girl was telling her about the letter was the mention of a kind of work the letter writer had described as "peddling."

"What's that?" Rose asked.

"I don't know," replied the girl. "But that's where most of the money they sent to their relatives comes from."

Rose made a mental note of the word. Maybe she should try that kind of work when she reached America if it was honest and gave a good living. But first she had to obtain a *tezkara*, a travel permit from the Ottoman authorities, so that she could board a ship leaving the port of Beirut. Curbing her natural impulsiveness, she waited until the local tax inspector came to the factory for one of his periodic inspections. He was a small, punctilious man who dressed in the

European fashion. In spite of his diminutive size, he gave off an air of self-importance.

Rose sidled up to him while he was inspecting the ledger where each bale of silk sent down from the factory to the warehouses in Beirut was recorded. She had always made a point of being helpful to him in the past whenever he had a technical question about the finished silk that required more than just a simple explanation. Apart from the supervisor, Abou Hazeen, Rose knew more about the factory operations than anyone else, including the French owner.

"Good morning, Mademoiselle Rose," he greeted her pleasantly, turning his attention to her from a page of the ledger which he held flat with one hand while adjusting the *tarboosh* on his head.

"Hello, Mr. Haddad," replied Rose cheerfully. "I hope you and your family are well."

"Yes, quite well, thank you. How can I be of service to you today?" Unlike some of the other officials who came to the factory from time to time, there was never a hint of condescension in his voice when he addressed her. He was always correct, if a little fastidious in his tone. Rose gave him one of her winning smiles.

"I have a small favour to ask," she said sweetly. "It's something only you can help me with." The tax inspector looked at her in surprise with a gleam of curiosity in his eyes.

"Would you be able to obtain a *tezkara* for me?"

"A *tezkara*?" The inspector was more than a little taken aback by her request. "What do you want with a *tezkara*?"

"I need it to travel to *Amreeka*, Mr. Haddad."

"That's no place for a young woman like you," he said disapprovingly. Although a man of the times in many ways, the inspector seemed to find the reason for Rose's request difficult to understand. There was an interminable pause while he considered it.

"You should settle down and find yourself a husband here."

"But there is nothing for me here, and I don't want to marry."

He said nothing and turned his attention back to the ledger, leaving Rose wondering whether he had taken her request seriously or not. Determined, she continued to stand beside him instead of returning to the workbenches while he went back to examining the ledger entries. Turning over several pages in quick succession, he began looking at a column that listed the prices of bales sold to various merchants in Beirut.

When Rose sneaked a second look, she noticed with some surprise that he had moved on to the names of the packet boats which loaded cargo at the port of Beirut and carried it to Marseilles and Genoa. His index finger traced a meticulous line over the entries beside the Dorian, the Ismailia, and the Tyrian, steamers that regularly plied the Mediterranean trade routes.

"So you're determined to go?" he said.

"Yes, Mr. Haddad."

"Then I will see what I can do," he said, giving her a half-smile. "But I'm not promising you anything."

Rose's frown disappeared at once and she beamed back at him.

"You're very kind, Mr. Haddad. But I beg you to keep it a secret between us for now."

With that she slipped away, hoping that Abou Hazeen had not noticed how long she had spent talking to him. Rose had no wish to involve herself in awkward explanations before she had made her plans. During the next few weeks, she began to give away the few possessions she had accumulated during her time in the mountains to the factory girls. She sold several gold bangles once destined for her own trousseau and the few items of furniture she had acquired in an effort to make her sparse lodgings more comfortable.

To disguise the true nature of her intentions, she told everyone that she had a debt to repay, an explanation that the other girls accepted without any questions. With Maryam gone, Rose had become somewhat aloof from her workmates. When the inspector came to pay his next visit, he took Rose aside and told her that he had some news for her.

"I can obtain the documents, but I shall need some personal details from you first."

"Of course," Rose replied, delighted that he had acted on her request so quickly.

"Let's see now," he said as he readied himself to take them down. "Your father's name?"

Rose was unable to mask the sadness she felt at the mention of her family. In front of Mrs. Butler she had kept it well-hidden, but the inspector had caught her unawares.

"What's the matter, Rose?" he asked, alarmed by her sudden change of mood.

"My father was a silk merchant from Deir el-Qamar," she said, struggling to recover her composure. "My whole family was killed there."

"My sympathies," the inspector mumbled as he wiped his eyeglasses on a crisply folded handkerchief.

He, too, had heard about the massacre. It had lasted two days up until the moment when the Druze leader had called on his men to sheathe their weapons. A proclamation issued earlier by the Ottoman Governor of Sidon calling for an end to the violence had been widely ignored in spite of his threat that any convicted offenders would be taken in chains to Acre and hung from the gallows there.

"That's why I live in the lodgings here by myself."

He paused before resuming in a gentler tone.

"But I still need his name in order to obtain the *tezkara*."

"Hanna el-Shawish."

"When were you born?"

"I was four at the time of the attack on Deir el-Qamar," she said counting the years on her fingers. "I'm now twenty-five years old."

"I have made enquiries," said the inspector. "I can obtain the *tezkara* at a cost of forty-five piasters. That includes the customary gift to the official who puts his seal on it. If you wish, I can ask them to issue it, and I'll bring it with me on my next visit."

Rose took out a little bag of money from the sash at her waist. Making sure her back was turned to the other girls, she quickly counted out the exact sum and handed over the coins to him. The following day, she awoke with a growing feeling of elation at the thought of leaving behind her old life in the mountains. The sorrow she had felt at the mention of her father had all but vanished, and she greeted Abou Hazeen at the factory with a smile on her face and a spring in her step.

When the other girls asked her for assistance, she was only too pleased to oblige them. She made encouraging remarks about their work and occasionally shared in their gossiping, something she had not done since Rose had left. Even the steam from the basins and rattle of the machinery were a welcome distraction as she eagerly awaited the muleteers' next visit. When they finally came, she approached the captain and asked him in the strictest confidence if he would take her with them to Beirut once she had received her papers.

"I will, Miss, and at no cost," he said, grinning widely and revealing a perfect set of crooked teeth.

And so when the inspector finally brought her the *tezkara* complete with the official stamps and seal, she had already made arrangements to go with the next shipment of bales. A day or so later, she took Abou Hazeen aside and informed him of her decision.

"I hope you know what you're doing," the supervisor said apprehensively once he had recovered from the shock of learning that his favourite employee was giving him notice.

"I do," she replied.

"Why don't you go to Lyon?" he suggested. "You know about silk and you may be able to find a good job there in one of the weaving houses where they make taffeta and organzine."

"I've made up my mind to go to *Amreeka*," Rose replied shaking her head. "They say it's a land of great opportunity and they need people like me to work there." She paused, softening her tone. "Thank you for all the kindness you've shown me over the ten years I've worked here, *ya 'ammee*."

"You were only a little girl when you came to us," he said with a chuckle. "But I still remember you telling me even then that you preferred the factory to the sisters."

He was momentarily distracted by one of the girls who held out a broken spindle for him to inspect. When he had finished with her, he turned back to Rose.

"Let me know when you're leaving and I will make sure you're paid in full. And maybe a little something extra if I can persuade the owner to dig deeper in his pockets."

CHAPTER THIRTY-THREE

∽∾∽

It was in the May of 1881 when Rose finally embarked on her journey to America. She had been too excited to sleep the night before her departure and so she spent most of it sewing little pockets into her skirts and bodice as a precaution against being robbed. If a thief were to try and make off with her coins, she figured that the least she could do was make it difficult for him to discover where she had hidden her treasure. Gathering her few belongings together, she stuffed them into a carpetbag and, in the chilly darkness before dawn, walked down to the factory where bales of silk were being strapped to the mules. As she drew nearer, she heard the captain discussing with the supervisor where the merchandize should be delivered.

"Take it to the khans down by the docks," said Abou Hazeen. "We still need to fulfil our contracts with the buyers in Lyon and Milan for this year."

"Why not sell the stuff at auction and save on the storage fees?" argued the captain.

"That would be more profitable," he replied. "But we can't disappoint our European customers."

The beasts snorted gruffly and stamped their hooves as their girths were tightened, their nostrils exhaling steamy breaths into the pools of light cast by the lanterns.

"Keep still," yelled a muleteer as one of the animals shuddered violently and began to walk off while he was still tightening the straps.

Rose announced herself to the captain and then waited quietly while the last two bales were lowered by rope from the store room above and loaded onto the back of the mule, one on either side for balance. By the time the muleteers had finished strapping them firmly into place, the captain was already inspecting the loads. Even before he had run his hand over the last buckle, the men had begun cajoling the heavy-laden beasts into line.

"*Yalla*," he called out as he began to lead the little procession of mules and men down the narrow cobbled street from the factory towards the edge of town.

The even surface of the street abruptly gave way to a rutted, unpaved track well before they had left behind the last of the houses. Rose swung her skirts merrily with each step as she walked along at the train's rear, delighted to be on her way at last. When dawn finally broke, a thick mist revealed itself, lying like a blanket across the surrounding hills. Rose could barely see further than the lead mule as it plodded steadily along, snorting occasionally.

For the most part the muleteers walked in silence, occasionally grunting at their animals or switching their rumps with the reeds and sticks they carried in their hands. They passed terraces of mulberry trees, shrouded in the morning haze, their new buds springing up like ghostly fingers from the stumps of pollarded branches. Beneath them, pale pink cyclamen grew in profusion and scarlet anemones peeped out from among the rocks of the terraced walls. As they rounded a bend, the smell of wild garlic suddenly filled Rose's nostrils, making her feel a twinge of unexpected nostalgia for the homeland she was about to leave behind. For the first time, it occurred to her that she might never see these mountains again.

For two hours, the mule train followed the rugged track down to the point where it joined the main highway to Beirut. As they crossed over at the head of the valley, the mist suddenly lifted to reveal a steep hill on one side and the edge of an escarpment on the other. The captain called a halt and at the sound of his voice, the mules immediately ceased their shuffling walk. While the muleteers readjusted their loads, Rose made her way over to the roadside and sat down beneath a stand of pine trees. She took her shoes off and let her legs dangle over the cliff, wriggling her toes in the void.

A river ran along the belly of the valley beneath her, its waters fed by the melting snows from the peaks they had just left behind. Swirling and tumbling in the early morning sunshine, it disappeared behind a spur of rock that jutted out further downstream. Breathing in the fragrant air, she found herself so captivated by her surroundings that she did not hear the mule captain walk up behind her.

"Let's go, Miss," he said, his stern expression softened only by the hint of a smile. "We must reach Ras el-Nabeh today."

Rose got to her feet and brushed away the pine needles that clung to her skirts. The mules shuffled off down the highway, walking in single file past the carts and horsemen that clattered by one after the other. It took them two hours to reach the prosperous hill town of Bhamdoun, and there they broke off their journey, making their way through the streets towards the main square. A large building surmounted by a dome dominated all the others.

"That's the *Roum* church, Miss," said one of the muleteers who had noticed Rose staring at it. "And over there," he said pointing to an unremarkable stone building in one of the side streets, "is where the Jews pray."

"Who are they?" she asked, mystified but eager to learn new things. "I've never heard of them."

"Mostly traders and silk merchants," the man replied.

When they reached the square, the men watered the mules at a trough and tethered them in the shade of a long wall with their loads still on their backs. The animals began to doze off at once, shaking their heads and swishing their tails to flick away the flies that settled in swarms on their sweaty backs. The muleteers themselves sat down on a stone bench underneath a large plane tree and began to eat their *mouneh*[110]. Leaving them to chat amongst themselves, Rose walked over to the captain who was sitting a little distance away from his men. In spite of his gruff tone and domineering presence, she admired his skill and leadership.

"How far is it to the coast?"

"We'll arrive at Ras el-Nabeh before dusk, *inshallah*[111]."

"I haven't seen Beirut since I was a little girl," said Rose, twisting a curl that hung down beneath her headscarf around her fingers.

"Then you'll find it greatly changed, Miss. It's a city of commerce now, richer than either Sidon or Tripoli. Its warehouses and wharves are piled high with foreign goods and its port is filled with their ships."

After an hour or so of resting in the square, they set off again and by the middle of the afternoon, they had reached Aley. That was the last mountain town before the road to Beirut dipped down towards the plain, twisting back and forth between the pine trees. Sensing that they would soon be free of their loads, the mules quickened their pace. When they finally emerged into the open, Rose saw an expanse of fields and farms stretching out before her as far as the shoreline. To the north, the same river they had come across earlier in the day snaked its way lazily across the plain while in the distance lay the city of Beirut, flanked on two sides by the sea whose gentle swells sparkled in the sunlight.

They were now travelling down a paved road bordered by palm trees that rattled their ragged fronds in the gentle seaward breeze. On either side, men and women hoed their crops and tended their vines beside sturdy houses built of well-dressed stone. When Rose called out to them in greeting as they passed, they barely looked up from their work.

Further on, the highway veered towards the marshy river bank. On one side, they could see a group of men seated under the arches of a decrepit stone building and as they came nearer, Rose could hear the buzz of conversation as they smoked their pipes and drank their tea seated on low wooden stools. The smell of simmering beans drifted towards them from a large kettle hanging from a tripod.

"Please halt here," Rose shouted to the captain.

"Why?" he called back, clearly anxious to avoid unnecessary delay.

Hurrying over to him, she murmured something in his ear.

"Then be quick," he said. "We still have some way to go."

Braving the leers of strangers, Rose walked up to one of the boys who was serving them and asked him to show her the way to the outhouse.

"Over there," the youth replied nonchalantly, pointing to a dilapidated shack made of palm fronds and pieces of scrap wood. He continued what he was doing, making no move to help her.

"Do you speak to your mother or sister like that?" Rose snapped back at him. The expression on his face changed at once.

"No, Miss," he mumbled bashfully. Setting down his tray, he escorted her over to the shack. From inside came the overpowering odour of human waste.

"Stay there and wait for me," she ordered him.

Rose pushed open the door and plunged inside, her breath held tight. In the darkness, she hitched up her skirts high enough to accomplish her task before emerging again into the evening light, coughing and choking. Pausing briefly to thank the boy, she hurried back to where the mules were standing.

"I hope the caravanserai isn't as filthy as this," she said to the captain.

"Don't worry, Miss," he replied, doing his best to hide his amusement at the way she had stood up for herself. "It's a respectable place."

They followed the road as it branched away from the river and skirted the sandy expanse of the *horsh*, the huge pine forest where the French troops had once camped. The light was now fading fast and Rose was beginning to feel tired and footsore from the day's march. Nevertheless, she gritted her teeth and walked on in silence. When they finally reached the inn on the outskirts of Beirut, she had barely enough strength left to wash her face in the water fountain. Noticing her exhaustion, the captain walked over to join her in the centre of the courtyard.

"Here are your belongings," he said, holding up her carpetbag. "Come and eat with us."

Rose waited beside the fountain for the muleteers to unload their animals and take them to the stables to be fed. Then she hobbled over to the table and took a seat beside the captain. A few minutes later, a boy arrived from the kitchens carrying a large pot of stew which he set down in front of them.

At the sight of food, the muleteers' mood brightened. They began to eat heartily, famished by the long day's work. Rose, on the other hand, was too tired to manage more than a few mouthfuls. She set her spoon down and slipped away as soon as she could, leaving the men to enjoy their meal by themselves.

Clutching her bag, she climbed up the stairs to the gallery in search of a quiet place out of sight of the other travellers who were still flooding into the courtyard below in a continuous stream. To her relief, she quickly found a secluded spot and squatted down, setting her carpetbag on the flagstones beside her. She looked around and, seeing no one, began to check the pockets of her skirts and bodice to make sure that none of the coins had fallen out during the journey. Satisfied, she lay down fully clothed with her head propped against her bag and fell into a dreamless sleep, oblivious to the comings and goings beneath her.

CHAPTER THIRTY-FOUR

Rose was awakened at first light by the reedy voice of the *mu'ezzin* calling the faithful to the dawn prayer. For a moment she wondered where she was, but the commotion from bustling travellers below preparing for their journeys soon brought her back to earth with a jolt. Hooves clattered and stable boys whistled as horses, mules, and donkeys were led out of their stalls and into the courtyard to be saddled or loaded up. Adding to the din were three grunting camels kneeling down by one of the troughs, their calloused knees and long skeletal legs folded neatly on the ground beneath their large bodies.

Rose yawned and stretched before examining her feet for blisters. Relieved to find only a few, she slipped her shoes back on as gently as she could and descended the stone stairs, pushing her way towards the basin of the water fountain in the courtyard. Pulling her scarf back, she began washing her face under one of the spouts, ignoring the sidelong glances of the men who pressed in on her from all sides. Feeling refreshed and cleaner, she looked around for the now familiar faces of the muleteers among the jostling crowd.

It took her some time before she caught sight of them loading up their mules in the far corner as they prepared to take their cargo down to the great khans by the port. Seeking out the captain, she held out a few coins in her palm as payment for the night's food and lodging, but he refused to take them.

"You have a long journey ahead of you," he said with a curt shake of his head. "Keep your money and may God be with you."

"Thank you, *ya 'ammee*, for bringing me this far," she replied, putting the money away. Leaving the muleteers to their mules, she picked up her carpetbag and walked out through the gates onto the Damascus Road. Skirting the higher ground to the east, she set off in the direction of the citadel, keeping her eyes fixed on the remains of the old watchtower. At first she found her way without trouble but the deeper into the city she went, the more difficult it became. Building upon building crowded in on her on both sides of the road, blocking her line of vision.

Increasingly disoriented, she began looking for a landmark that would tell her where she was. Almost at once, her eyes alighted on the back of a large building flanked by two sloping wings in a side street off the main thoroughfare. From its appearance, it seemed to be still under construction. The walls were made from a warm, dun-coloured stone and its turreted roof was covered with red and green tiles.

She walked around to the front and came face-to-face with a majestic facade several stories high, surmounted by a small stone cross. The morning sun glinted off rows of tall windows, each in its own stone casement. A sweeping double staircase led up to an open door through which she could see a high-vaulted ceiling supported by lines of yellow stone columns.

"It's beautiful is it not, my child?" The voice came from a young, clean-shaven priest scarcely older than herself who had walked up behind her while she stood motionless at the hallowed entrance. His appearance and manners were quite unlike any other priest she had ever met.

"I'm looking for the Austrian consulate," Rose said, trying to hide her relief at the encounter.

"Then continue down the main street," he said indicating the Damascus Road. "When you reach the end, ask for directions to Bab Idriss. That's the quarter of the European consuls."

"And where are we now, Abouna?"

"Bashoura. Some people call it the Jesuit quarter because of our new church. Our old place was outside the walls down by the port."

"It's very beautiful."

He nodded in agreement as she set off in the direction he had indicated. Before long, she found herself in an even more populous area where every available space was occupied by large residences, some two stories high or more. Trailing vines adorned the gardens, and jasmine climbed their lime-washed walls. The cries of street vendors echoed off the walls as they walked up and down the cobblestoned streets and alleys that sprawled in every direction.

"Taste my sherbets and visit paradise!"

It came from a man dressed in a ragged *jubbah* with a large brass urn strapped to his back. In his hand he carried a couple of empty glasses that he jingled together.

"Forget molasses, rice or *foul*[112], these cakes will make even a pasha drool!" cried another, pushing a handcart loaded high with sesame cakes.

From out of a side-street an old woman with a wizened face came up to Rose, peering out at her from under a striped shawl. Draped across her forehead, she wore a string of silver coins and in her gnarled hands she carried three struggling chickens by their pinioned feet.

"Buy one of these and your husband will grant you any wish," she said in a raspy voice.

"I've no husband, *hajjeh*, and I don't want one either," retorted Rose.

Without replying, the old woman just grinned and hobbled off towards the cemetery gates in pursuit of more gullible customers. When Rose came to the top of a small rise a few minutes later, she suddenly found herself looking out over the heart of the city for the very first time. In the foreground were the citadel's ruined walls and beyond them the port. Determined to make the most of her first day in Beirut, she stopped in the shade of a large banyan tree growing by the side of the road and leaned her cheek against its cool bark.

From the shade of its waxy leaves, she could spot on the top of a low hill to her left a huge rectangular building whose sheer bulk dwarfed anything she had come across before including the new church. Its solid symmetrical lines and imposing structure gave it an unmistakable air of authority. A flight of stone steps led up to a grand portico decorated with three arches. Dusting off her clothes, Rose began walking towards it. But the nearer she drew, the clearer it became that its sharp outlines which had so impressed her from a distance were, in fact, only illusory.

Wooden scaffolds and platforms clung to its walls and large numbers of workmen swarmed around it. The air rang with the clang of their mallets as they chiselled away at huge limestone blocks and heaved them into position with the help of long levers and creaking pulleys. Curious by nature, Rose walked up to one of the workmen who had just set down two pails of mortar and was adjusting the yoke on his shoulders.

"What's this?" she asked him as he wiped the sweat from his brow with the end of his headcloth.

"The *Kishlah*," he replied. Rose was baffled. She did not recognize the Turkish word by which the Grand *Serai* was generally known in the city. The workman just shrugged and then noticing Rose's carpetbag, he pointed to the rear.

"If it's the new hospital you're after, it's over there," he said.

"It's not the hospital I'm looking for," she bristled as he hooked the pails to the yoke and began to walk off. "It's Bab Idriss."

Without bothering to stop, he pointed towards the sea before disappearing behind a pile of cinder blocks. Tutting to herself at the man's rudeness, Rose made her way past the *Kishlah* and on until she found herself in a maze of narrow streets full of shop fronts displaying bolts of cloth in a kaleidoscope of colours. The tell-tale clanking of looms and the click of shuttles confirmed her suspicions that she was now in the middle of a cloth market. Ignoring the urge to stop and investigate, she wandered through it until she came across a large church near a gateway that was surrounded by crumbling masonry. Beside it sat an old woman with her back to the remains of the wall, holding out an upturned palm.

"Give alms to this poor widow for the sake of Allah and His Prophet," the old crone intoned, peering up from beneath her veil furtively. A passerby wearing long robes stopped to drop a coin into her hand. When she caught sight of Rose, she changed the form of her supplication with barely a pause.

"Have mercy on this poor widow for the sake of Jesus and His mother Mary." Rose reached into one of her many pockets and took out a piaster, handing it to her.

"Wish me luck, *ya hajjeh*. I am travelling to a faraway land."

The old woman reached out and took Rose's hand in her bony fingers. She muttered something and then blew on her palm three times.

"Luck will follow you wherever you go, my child."

The twisting alleys of the cloth market gave way abruptly to an open neighbourhood of villas and houses that stretched down towards the seashore. The sound of noonday prayers from a nearby mosque reminded Rose that she had been walking through the city streets all morning and was still no closer to finding the Austrian consulate. Noticing a group of porters standing on a corner with their large wicker baskets looped over their shoulders, she went up to them and greeted them cheerily. Their pantaloons marked them as young men recently arrived from the villages in search of work.

"*Ahlan, ya sitt*," they chorused back.

"Is the house of the Austrian Consul near here?" Rose asked, hoping that at the very least they would be familiar with the place where they now pursued their trade.

The men looked at one another and then, without warning, an argument broke out. Every time one of them insisted that he knew of the place, his companions contradicted him. Within minutes, their yells and gesticulations reached a climax at which point one of them turned to Rose. He pushed his battered *tarboosh* back, revealing a patch of pale skin above a sunburnt forehead.

"It's over there." He pointed to several large houses. "That's where the Franks live."

Unconvinced but with little choice other than to let him try, Rose drew two small coins from one of her pockets. If there was one thing she knew how to avoid, it was being cheated.

"I'll give you these if you find the place for me."

The porter's face brightened at once. Leaving his basket behind, he set off in search of the consulate with Rose trailing close behind. After a couple of false starts, they headed towards a group of large villas that stood inside their own walled gardens. Without the slightest hesitation, he began pounding on every door while Rose waited in the street. But their search did not begin well; each time he knocked, he was turned away.

"No luck?" moaned Rose.

"Not yet," the porter replied. "But we'll find it soon, *inshallah*."

They continued their search until they came to a large villa with a uniformed guard standing outside its gate. Above the entrance, Rose noticed a brass plaque with a double-headed eagle emblazoned on it. Below, there was some writing in Roman script that she could not make out. Before the porter had time to knock on the door, she walked up to the guard herself.

"Is this the house of the Austrian Consul?" she asked with an engaging smile. The man nodded but made no effort to admit her. Surprised, she wondered why he had rebuffed her and it was not until she looked down at her clothes that she realized the likely reason. It was her unkempt appearance. She stepped back to readjust her bodice and skirts, before raking her hair back with her fingertips.

"I've a letter for the dragoman," she said pulling the precious document from her bag and holding it out to the guard. He eyed it with suspicion before gesturing in the direction of the porter who was standing behind her.

"Who is this man?" he said curtly.

In her eagerness to gain access, Rose had quite forgotten the porter. Before he could come any nearer, the guard moved to block the gate.

"Just a porter," she said. Taking two coins from her pocket, she handed them to the youth who beamed before stuffing them into his pocket and hurrying off to rejoin his companions.

"Come in," said the guard, opening the gate at last.

Once inside, Rose found herself in a neat and well-kept courtyard with a table and some rush-seated chairs set out in the shade of a tall lilac tree. Leaving her there, the guard went into the house with her letter in his hand. She shifted her weight uneasily from one foot to the other while she waited for him to return, stretching her back in an effort to soothe the aches from the previous day's journey. Finally the guard reappeared, followed by a servant who brought Rose some water before inviting her to have a seat.

"The dragoman will see you shortly," he said, before withdrawing into the house.

But it was some time before the door opened again, and when it did it revealed a tall man who strode purposefully towards her. Without thinking, Rose got to her feet.

"Be seated, Mademoiselle," the man said as he took a seat opposite her. "Allow me to introduce myself. I'm Layal's husband." He was dressed in a *jubbah* with wide sleeves and wore shoes of foreign manufacture. On his head was a well-brushed *tarboosh*. From his expression, the dragoman appeared to be expecting a reply or at least some form of acknowledgment, but Rose was too taken aback by his appearance to utter a word. For the first time in her life, she felt intimidated.

"I have read the letter you gave to the guard," he continued in the courteous manner of a diplomat. She wrinkled her nose but remained quiet.

"Forgive me," he said, as if he had offended her. "I know it was addressed to my wife, but I felt obliged to read it before seeing you."

She nodded.

"Would you prefer to speak in one of the European languages instead?" he went on politely.

"No, Your Excellency." She cursed herself for being so tongue-tied.

"Allow me to finish my affairs here and then perhaps you will come with me to my house. In the meantime, this gentleman," he paused as he gestured towards the servant standing by the door, "will take care of you."

With that, the dragoman got to his feet and disappeared back inside the villa. Tired and travel-worn, Rose settled down to wait in the drowsy warmth of the afternoon with nothing to distract her but the comings and goings of the consulate's few visitors.

It dragged on interminably. Then without warning, the dragoman suddenly re-emerged carrying a finely tooled leather writing case in one hand.

"Let us go," he said to Rose. "I have already sent word to my wife to expect you."

The guard opened the door and saluted as Rose followed him out into the street. Within a moment or two she heard the clatter of hooves, and a carriage appeared from nowhere, coming to a smooth halt in front of them. The dragoman helped Rose up onto the seat and then climbed in after her, giving the driver only brief instructions.

Within a few moments, they were clip-clopping towards the shoreline and Rose felt, for the first time, the salty freshness of the sea breeze on her face. It tasted like hope and freedom. When they reached the coastal road, her heart jumped with excitement at the sight of the waves crashing against the rocks. She had only ever seen the sea from a distance before.

"Look over there at the Hotel Belle Vue," said the dragoman, pointing ahead to an elegant building standing prominently above the tea houses and cafés which leaned out over the water on wooden stilts. "It's one of the finest new buildings in all Beirut."

Rose followed the direction of his hand. Her gaze settled not on the building itself but on one of its ornate balconies overlooking the shore. Brocade curtains hung elegantly on either side of the pillar-framed windows. Beneath them, a foreign lady stood beside a pile of leather trunks holding a parasol in her hand. Rose's interest had not escaped the dragoman who prided himself on his keen observations.

"Frankish travellers come to our shores in ever-increasing numbers nowadays," he said wryly, "in search of their heritage. They call it the Grand Tour."

To Rose this remark meant little, but the sight of the lady standing with her luggage lodged itself in her mind. She settled into her plush seat as they drove further along the shoreline, trying to picture what kind of life she might lead which could afford her such elegant leisure. It was so different to what Rose herself was used to that she found it hard to imagine.

In the lea of a hill surmounted by an ancient olive grove, the carriage turned inland and shortly afterwards came to a halt outside a pleasant but modest villa. The dragoman got down and waited patiently by the step while Rose clambered out after him, encumbered by her carpetbag. A servant appeared from inside the house and opened the door, relieving his employer of his leather case. When he tried to take Rose's bag too, she clutched it to herself in panic.

"No, no," she insisted. "I'll carry it myself." Suppressing a smile, the dragoman reached over and gently disengaged Rose's hands from the handle.

"You have my word, Mademoiselle Rose," he said. "It will be placed in your room. Now, come in."

He ushered her into a large reception room whose interior was illuminated at one end by soft beams of evening light streaming through a pair of arched windows. Against one of the walls stood a sofa upholstered in silk brocade.

"Please make yourself comfortable," he said motioning towards the sofa, "while I tell my wife that you're here."

Rose sat down carefully on it, trying to avoid soiling the expensive-looking cushions with her travel-stained clothes. The luxury of her surroundings made her feel quite ill at ease.

"Some refreshments. Tea or coffee?" he asked her courteously as he withdrew.

"Tea please," she murmured.

CHAPTER THIRTY-FIVE

~~~~

Beirut
May, 1881

Once alone in the room, Rose began to gaze at her surroundings. Several finely-woven carpets covered the tiled floor and various *objets d'art* adorned the tables and shelves. In one corner, there was a highly polished wooden box standing on slender legs. Just as she was wondering to herself what it was, she was startled by the appearance of a tall woman who had entered, unnoticed, through a side door.

"It's a pianola," she said, "a musical instrument. I'll show you how it works if you like." When Rose gave her a bewildered look, she added in a lilting voice. "I'm Layal, Maryam's friend. My husband has just told me you're here."

Dispensing with any formality, she walked straight up to Rose and kissed her three times before taking a step back. She looked her guest up and down, still holding Maryam's letter of introduction in her hand.

"So, you're Rose." She nodded once in silence.

"Maryam's family showed us great kindness that terrible summer when my late husband was killed and we fled Hasbaya for the coast."

The same servant who had tried to take her carpetbag earlier appeared with a teapot and cups of similar design to the ones Mrs. Butler had produced when Rose and Maryam had visited her on Easter Day. Layal took the tray from him and set it down on a table. Rose was struck at once by the grace with which she moved. It was exactly as Maryam had described.

"Take one," Layal said as she sat down on a ladder-backed chair opposite her, tucking her long legs to one side. "It's only dried fruit."

Rose hesitated and then picked out a candied apricot stuffed with an almond.

"It's delicious," she blurted out.

As she relaxed little by little against the stiff upholstery, she noticed that Layal was smiling at her. Her mouth puckered at the corners giving her long face an unusual beauty. Whether it was her lack of formality or simply the warmth of her welcome, the nervousness that Rose felt earlier when she had first met the dragoman all but disappeared. Her hostess seemed part of a different world, like the lady with the parasol.

"Tell me why you've come to Beirut," she said softly. With her mouth still full of candied apricot, Rose was unable to speak. She held her hand up in front of her face as she all but swallowed the sticky fruit.

"To board a ship to *Amreeka*," she stammered finally. She took a hurried sip of tea in an effort to wash it down, burning her tongue in the process.

"Yes, that's what it says in the letter," said Layal, peering at Rose with her large, expressive eyes. "That you're intending to go to America." Her next question caught Rose off guard. Although she had been asked before, it had never been with Layal's evident concern.

"Why do you want to go to such a faraway place?"

With the exception of the confidences she had shared with Maryam, Rose had always kept her most private thoughts to herself. With no mother to talk to or siblings to share her secrets with, she had long ago learned to keep her own counsel. But the woman seated opposite her seemed very different to the other people she had met before. She was Maryam's friend, of course. But there was also something else about her that Rose found difficult to pinpoint. And then she realized what it was; Layal had the look of someone who had suffered great misfortune during her life. There was a curious hint of sadness in her eyes.

She now found herself in a quandary.

Should I tell her how I've wanted to go to America since hearing about the villagers who had taken a ship to New York? Or should I just be honest about the doubts that keep me awake at night?

She turned over both explanations in her mind for a moment until she came to a decision to tell Layal part, but not all, of the truth.

"Because I've heard it's a land full of opportunities for men," she said, "and women, too."

"But there must be other reasons why you're abandoning your life here for a country where you don't know anyone," Layal replied, not unkindly. "It's not as if you're being exiled."

Rose could sense that she did not believe her. From what Maryam had told her, Layal had been lucky enough to find a new life for herself in Beirut. The idea that a girl from the mountains was prepared to go much further to seek her fortune might be difficult for her to understand. Maybe she thought that there was something in Rose's past that she did not wish to reveal, like an abusive husband whom she was fleeing.

"I'm an orphan," she admitted finally. "My parents and brothers were killed in the massacre at Deir el-Qamar when I was a little girl and I have no one to keep me here."

"Go on," Layal said, seemingly intrigued by Rose's tale. The lines at the corners of her eyes deepened, revealing something more profound, perhaps sympathy mingled with her own past pain.

"I was saved by a Turkish officer who found me in the streets. He took me to the barracks at Beiteddine and I stayed there until the commandant sent me away to an orphanage run by French nuns."

"Weren't the sisters kind to you? They were to us when we first came to Beirut." Rose hid a grimace at the thought of her own memories of convent life.

"The reverend mother arranged a place for me with a family in the mountains," Rose went on without answering the question. "Since then, I've been working in a silk factory with village girls but, unlike them, I don't sigh for a husband at night."

"So you want to find a new life for yourself, Rose?"

"Yes, I do."

Layal picked up a little bell from the table in front of her and rang it. When the servant appeared, she asked him to prepare some coffee.

"Would you like me to tell you your fortune?" she whispered as she leaned forward. "It will be a secret between just the two of us. My husband doesn't approve of such things."

"You can do that?" Rose had not expected a woman like Layal to be interested in such things, living as she did amid the splendour and sophistication of Beirut. To her, fortune-telling was the livelihood of old ladies in villages and towns with nothing better to do.

"Yes," Layal said. "But first let me introduce you to my son. He'll take you to the docks tomorrow. From what I hear, they're all thieves down there."

Layal got to her feet and left the room only to reappear a few moments later accompanied by a young man. He stood behind her, waiting patiently for his mother to present him. Rose was immediately struck by the resemblance between the two of them. He had his mother's long face and handsome features. She got to her feet, a little flustered.

"This is the young lady I was telling you about," said Layal. "Help her buy a ticket for the next packet to Marseilles and be sure that none of the officials at the port cheat her. She's going to America."

"Of course, Mama." His voice resembled his mother's too. When he glanced in her direction with a shy smile on his lips, Rose felt her knees go weak. It was the first time a man had ever looked at her that way.

"Mademoiselle Rose," he said, bowing his head as he turned to leave them.

"Take Rose to the docks early," his mother called out after him.

"She has a very important day ahead of her tomorrow."

Rose sensed Layal's eyes resting on her as the door closed behind him, and she wondered if she had noticed the way she had returned Wael's glance. She feared her warm welcome might turn to disapproval if she showed any interest in her son. But if she had noticed anything, Layal gave no sign of it.

"He has already witnessed such sadness in his life," she said when they were alone again. "Just like you."

A few minutes later, the servant brought in a tray with a small brass pot and two little cups on saucers. Layal bent down to inhale the rich aroma of the coffee before filling them both and handing one to Rose. A swirl of bubbles covered the dark surface.

"Drink from one side and be sure to leave some at the bottom when you finish. Otherwise I won't be able to read it."

As they sipped their coffee, Layal asked her about Maryam. So Rose began by describing how they had first met in the factory before telling her how Maryam had finally stopped resisting her father's wishes and married Faris. It was her account of the Easter Day she had spent with them and his boorish behaviour that produced the strongest reaction from Layal.

"I feared that might happen," she said with a deep sigh. "The poor girl feels she cannot escape her destiny."

"But I swore I'd help her, and I'll keep my promise." Rose's tone was bitter yet determined.

How convinced Layal was by her remark, Rose could not tell because she was still struggling to understand the woman sitting opposite her. One thing she was certain about, however, was that she cared deeply for Maryam and was distressed, but apparently not surprised, to hear of her unhappy marriage to her cousin.

"Do what I do three times," Layal said when she noticed that Rose had drunk all but the last dregs of her coffee. Rose watched as she clapped the saucer over her own cup and swirled the contents around.

"When you've finished, flip it over. That's the most important part."

She did as she was told, keeping her thumbs planted firmly against the bottom of the saucer. After checking that none of the liquid had escaped, she sat back waiting for further instructions.

"Good," said Layal, satisfied by what she had done. "Just leave it for a few moments to cool and then we'll see what's in store for you."

"Can I see the music box while we're waiting?" Rose had been admiring it out of the corner of her eye ever since she had arrived at the villa. Layal stood up and led her over to the pianola.

"Open the lid, Rose."

While Layal picked out a simple melody on the keys, Rose let her hand glide over the sound box. It was *Der Tannenbaum*. She opened the lid and watched with fascination as the felt-covered hammers struck the taut metal strings.

"It's beautiful. Where did you get it?"

"Vienna," Layal replied proudly. "It was a wedding gift from my husband."

When she had finished the tune, they took their seats again.

"Pick up the cup." Rose took the cup and saucer and carefully eased them apart. Without warning, a large lump detached itself from the base and flopped into the saucer.

"*Yee 'alayna*," exclaimed Rose, fearing the worst.

"Don't be alarmed," said Layal with a wave of her hand. "That's lucky. Let's see what else it has to tell us." She tilted the cup towards her and carefully examined the shapes left behind on the glazed china. Rose noticed her looking at a large whorl.

"That's the ship taking you across the seas, Rose. And those drops there," she said pointing to some dribbles which had dried before reaching the rim, "are the journeys you'll make in America." Rose continued to look at her expectantly.

"*Dmoureh*[113]," Layal said suddenly. Rose dipped her thumb in the dregs and then pressed its tip against the lip of the saucer. She watched Layal examining the print she had left behind.

"Will I find a good life over there?"

Although Rose found it hard to admit, misgivings were still lurking at the back of her mind about her journey. She knew full well that she was taking a huge risk.

"Yes, I believe you'll find happiness," said Layal with a smile. "But isn't there something else that you wish to know?" Rose knew exactly what she meant. It was what the girls in her village always wanted to know. But she could not bring herself to ask Layal about love and marriage. It was too private a matter. Recognizing her reluctance without being told, Layal did not press the point.

"Don't forget your homeland, whatever sadness it has brought you," she said instead.

CHAPTER THIRTY-SIX

That night Rose slept on a bed with linen sheets for the first time in her life as she revelled in the unfamiliar luxury of the villa. She woke early the next day to find that her outer garments had been brushed and laid out for her while she had been asleep. Packing her few possessions into the carpetbag, she washed her face in a hand basin she found in a corner of the room and went off in search of some breakfast from the kitchen.

She had barely enough time to ask the cook for a *man'ousheh*[114] when she was summoned to the front of the house. There she found Wael already waiting for her with a carriage drawn up by the gate.

"Good morning, Mademoiselle Rose," he said somewhat formally when he saw her come to the door. She noticed at once that he was wearing European clothes instead of the *jubbah* she had seen him in the day before. A stiff collar and cravat showed above the lapels of his frock coat.

"Good morning," she replied a little hesitantly. Not only was she unsure how to address him, but she also wondered whether he had noticed the way she had stared at him the day before. But the awkward moment quickly passed.

"Let's go straight to the port and see if we can find a place for you on today's packet to Marseilles," he said as he helped her up.

He followed her and leaned forward to give some directions to the driver. Then they set off towards the sea, turning along the coastal road in the direction of the port. By the time they had reached the cloth market where Rose had lost her way the day before, the streets were already teeming with people.

"What are those?" she said, pointing at two huge buildings more than four stories high which overlooked the docks. She gazed up at the arches of the narrow gallery that ran along the top floor as they passed in front of the first one. On the other side, some stone steps cut into the sea wall led down to the water.

"They're the khans, warehouses for storing goods." Wael seemed eager to show off his knowledge. "Coffee, sugar, cloth, roof tiles, and of course, silk."

"They're the tallest buildings I've ever seen. Who has the money to build such places?"

"Mr. Antoun and Mr. Fakhry," he replied with a smile. "They're two of the richest merchants in the city."

"You know them?" Rose asked, unable to hide her astonishment at the way their names had just rolled off his tongue.

"No," he said shyly. "But they're both acquaintances of my father's."

In the distance, a number of large ships were anchored off the coastline, riding the gentle swell. Nearer to the shore, a forest of masts all but hid the breakwater. Here ocean-going schooners and square-riggers jostled for position with ketches and lateen-rigged feluccas. These were the boats that plied their way up and down the Levantine coast from Jaffa and Alexandria to as far north as Alexandretta and Smyrna on the coast of Anatolia.

Threading their way between them, skiffs plied back and forth transporting pilots and customs officers around the harbour while lighters bobbed up and down against the sides of larger ships, loaded to the gunwales with goods and passengers. The creaking of the pulleys and hoists was almost drowned out by the shouts and curses of seamen as they went about their work. The carriage finally pulled up outside the offices of a shipping company. Stencilled over the doorway was a sign in Arabic and French: "Agents for Peabody, Wilson & Co."

"Stay here while I make enquiries," said Wael as he jumped down from the carriage.

"Let me come too," begged Rose. "If I'm to go to Am-er-ee-ka," she took care to pronounce the word as Mrs. Butler had done, "I should at least be able to make my own arrangements."

He helped her down from the carriage and together they walked towards the offices. Inside, two clerks sat at a single desk inscribing entries into leather-bound ledgers. Moments later, a man wearing a pair of wire-rimmed spectacles, whom Rose took to be the owner, appeared from a room at the rear.

"Good morning, Monsieur Wael," he said rather obsequiously. "It is a pleasure to see you again. I trust you are in good health?"

"Quite well, thank you."

"And your father?" the agent continued, scarcely pausing to draw breath in his litany of solicitous enquiries.

"He's well, too."

"You have come to see me today on what matter?" He moved on with practised ease to the business of the visit.

"A matter which concerns this lady," said Wael, gesturing towards Rose who was standing beside him. Glancing at her for the first time since they had entered the premises, the agent acknowledged her presence with a perfunctory nod.

"Good morning, Mademoiselle."

"Good morning," Rose replied with a sunny smile, doing her best to hide her irritation at being ignored.

"Please step this way." He ushered them into the same office from which he had just emerged.

"She wishes to book a passage to Marseilles on today's packet and from there, to board a ship to New York," Wael explained.

"Does she now?" the agent replied, peering at Rose over his spectacles.

Thinking that he was about to turn his attention back to Wael and ignore her again, she took a step forward and glared at him from under the peak of her bonnet. As if on cue, the agent cleared his throat and summoned one of his clerks to fetch him a ledger containing the schedule of departures.

"You are in safe hands," he continued as if nothing had happened. "Fortunately we act for a shipping line which operates a regular service between Marseilles and New York. It is well that you have come to me. Other less scrupulous agents might have booked you a passage to the southern part of that great continent, especially if they had empty berths to fill."

"Where to exactly?" asked Rose, confused by what he had just said. She had no idea about the geography of the Americas.

"To Veracruz or perhaps as far south as Santos in Brazil."

When the clerk arrived with the ledger, the agent took it and began to look through the various entries with a practised eye.

"How will you be travelling, Miss?"

"Steerage," said Rose. She had learned the word from a girl in the silk factory.

"Of course." He made a series of rapid calculations with a cedar wood pencil.

"That will be three-hundred-and-fifty piasters. I can accept payment in French francs or American dollars if you prefer. Let me see," he said making a further calculation. "It comes out to twelve dollars."

"I have three hundred piasters here," said Rose, counting out the coins which she had retrieved from their various hiding places the night before and placed together in a small bag.

The agent frowned.

"I cannot accept such a sum, Mademoiselle. We have to pay the shipping line and there are other costs besides." Out of the corner of her eye, Rose saw Wael put his hand into the pocket of his frock coat. She quickly placed her hand on his arm to stop him.

"Take the money, Monsieur," she said to him. "Give me my ticket and may God bless you and your family."

The agent looked from Rose to Wael and back before accepting the bag with a shrug of his shoulders as if he were resigning himself to some distasteful duty. He looked around for the clerk who had brought over the ledger.

"Book a passage on today's packet to Marseilles and another on a sailing in ten days' time from Marseilles to New York."

The agent scooped up the money that Rose had put down. Opening a drawer in his desk with a key attached to a gold chain, he carefully counted the coins out before placing them inside.

"I will be expecting you here this afternoon at four o'clock to collect your tickets," he said, this time addressing Rose directly. "Please be prompt. The sailing is at six." They were about to walk out of the door when Rose stopped.

"How many days will the crossing take?" Her earlier bravado had begun to desert her now that her passage had been confirmed. She realized that there would be no going back.

"You'll not be travelling on one of these," said the agent, pointing to a sketch of a clipper in full sail hanging on the wall. "You will be sailing on a modern ship." Reaching into the drawer again, he produced a daguerreotype of a modern, single-screw vessel.

"The voyage will take about two weeks and your accommodations will be in the bottom of the hull amongst the machinery and cargo. You may find it a little cramped."

"And what if she's seasick?" asked Wael with a look of concern.

"Then I suggest she spends as much time as possible on deck, weather permitting of course," the agent replied, his professional smile tinged with irony. "Good day, Monsieur Wael and good day to you, Mademoiselle."

When they emerged once again into the morning sunlight from the gloom of the agent's office, Rose saw that the carriage was still waiting for them outside.

"I'll stay here," she said to Wael. "I'll wait for the sailing in the port." But he waved her suggestion aside with such a show of gallantry that she began to wonder whether he meant more by it than just the usual courtesy.

"Mademoiselle Rose, I insist on showing you some of the city before you leave. First let me send word to my mother that your passage is booked. She'll want to know that the arrangements have been made."

Wael's invitation to accompany him on a tour of Beirut presented Rose with a delicate problem. Under normal circumstances, she would have been obliged to decline such an offer however much she might wish to do otherwise. Customs at that time did not permit a single woman like her to be seen driving alone in a carriage with a handsome young man to whom she was neither betrothed nor related if she wished to maintain her reputation.

It was not that she knew nothing of men. In the past, she had had admirers who had waited for her outside the factory gate. On the rare occasion when she found someone who pleased her, she would invite him to walk with her to some secluded spot away from prying eyes where they would kiss. And in the case of the handsome young man who worked for the grain merchant, she had gone further still and allowed him touch her intimately, to which she had responded in kind.

But she had always taken great pains to be as discreet as possible and these occasional adventures had never lasted long in any case. But what scandal could attach to her now, she asked herself, in a city where no one knew her and which she was planning to leave that very day? And besides, would she not be surrounded by strangers during the voyage?

Rose watched from the carriage as Wael beckoned to a boy on a donkey and began speaking to him in a fashion that grew more and more animated. The boy finally nodded his head and Wael walked over to one of the many letter writers who thronged the streets around the port, sitting down on a stool beside the battered bureau. The fellow dipped his pen in an inkwell and took down some words, handing the note back to him in exchange for a few coins.

"Where's the money we agreed on?" she heard the boy shout after him as he made his way back to the carriage.

"He'll pay you when you return with a reply from my mother," he said pointing to the letter writer. "Now off with you, you rascal." When he climbed back in, Rose could not suppress a smile.

"What is it?" Wael asked, puzzled by her amusement.

"Nothing," she said with a laugh. "Only the impudent look he gave you the moment your back was turned."

"Do you think I was too harsh?"

"Certainly not!" she replied. "He would have cheated you for certain otherwise."

"Where to now, *Effendi*?" asked the driver, turning his head to look at them.

"To al-Ghabeh, *ya hajj*[115]," said Wael. "Along the cliffs so the lady can have a clear view of the Medawar Point."

The driver tapped the backs of the horses with his long whip. Leaning into their collars, they pulled away from the curb and plodded off down the road. As they drove through the crowded streets behind the port, Wael began describing the various districts of the city to Rose as they passed through them.

"Over here is Saifi," he said, pointing towards a collection of new villas with tiled roofs that extended down the hill towards the bay.

Rose found it difficult to hide her astonishment at the prosperity that surrounded her, riches far exceeding anything she had imagined during her years of work in the silk factory. The grand new public buildings near the citadel and the private residences that clustered along the shoreline were a testament to the bustling commercial centre that Beirut had become.

In the mountains, most of the villages had long since recovered from the devastation and the lot of all but the very poorest had improved. Thanks to the silkworms and their cocoons, money had found its way into the pockets of peasants and farmers, factory girls and owners alike. Indeed, those living outside the towns and villages of the mountains were sometimes heard to complain that even a simple goatherd's hut was now more valuable than a whole farm on the plain. Rather than betray her provincial naivety, Rose kept her thoughts to herself as she gazed at the sights.

"Aren't you enjoying the drive?" Wael enquired solicitously after they had gone some way in silence. "We'll turn back if you wish."

"Of course I am," replied Rose with enthusiasm. "It's wonderful."

"Then let me show you the finest houses in Beirut."

They drove on along the cliffs in the direction of a rocky spit of land that jutted out into the sea. When they came to it, Wael called out to the driver to halt and together they got down from the carriage. Rose had to cling to her bonnet as they clambered over the rocks to keep it from being blown away by gusts of wind that skittered across the water towards them.

On the other side of the promontory, several large villas stood above the rocky foreshore. Rock plants and small bushes clung to the cliff face in a cascade of yellow and green. Two stately cypress trees stood behind them like sentinels while on the shore below, the timbers of a wrecked boat protruded from the water like the upturned ribcage of a whale.

"You must be hungry." Wael called out to her above the whistle of the wind and the sound of the waves gurgling in and out of the gullies.

"Oh yes," said Rose at once.

They continued along the coast to where the river debouched across some muddy flats into the sea. The driver turned inland and drove on until they came across a bridge that spanned the marshy river banks at their narrowest point. Set a little way back was an eating house, very different to the one that Rose had stopped at on her way to the city only two days earlier.

"Stop here," Wael called out to the driver.

Under the arches of the stone building, a bundle of freshly baked loaves lay next to a clay oven. Instead of the stale odour of stewed beans, they were met by the mouth-watering smell of baked fish. Rose settled down at a table looking out over the sea while Wael disappeared into the cookhouse to inspect the morning's catch.

"I think you'll enjoy the food," he said when he returned. A broad grin lit up his delicate features.

∾∾∾

"They're delicious!" Rose squeezed lemon juice over their crisp orange skin, brushing the sprig of coriander aside. Imitating Wael, she split the skin along the line of the backbone and began picking the creamy flesh off the bones.

"What are they called?"

"Sultan Brahim."

"A fish named after a sultan," she giggled.

Outside, the driver sat eating bread and olives while the horses stood motionless in the shade of a tree, swishing their tails. Rose ate with relish, her appetite bolstered by their expedition to the point. When she had picked the fish bones clean, Wael ordered a water pipe to be brought over.

The waiter packed tobacco into the bowl and placed some lit coals from the cooking fire on the top where they smouldered gently. It gave off the sweet smell of dried fruit. He sucked on the reed and let the smoke escape through his nostrils in a long stream.

"Let me try," said Rose impetuously as she seized the stem.

"Have you ever smoked one before?"

"No, but I want to try once before I leave my homeland."

He handed her the mouthpiece and she drew on the reed just as he had. For a moment nothing happened, and then all of a sudden she began to cough violently. Smoke exploded from her nose and mouth, and her eyes began to water.

"Gently, Rose," he chuckled. "It's your first time."

"Bas[116]," she said, handing it back to him. "I've had enough already."

When they had finished the sweet pastries, Wael handed some coins to the owner and complimented him on the freshness of his catch. Then he followed Rose into the carriage and they continued along the river before turning westwards down a paved road in the direction of the city.

"Do you remember Maryam?" she asked him.

"Of course I do," Wael smiled back at her. "She used to play draughts with me when I was a little boy."

"I worry about her," said Rose wistfully as she gazed out of the window at the countryside. "Her life is so miserable and now I'm abandoning her."

"No, you're not," Wael comforted her. "My mother told me about the promise you made her. I'm sure you'll keep it." They drove on in silence, comfortable in each other's company.

"Will we arrive at the port by four o'clock?" she asked him, suddenly remembering her appointment with the agent. Wael pulled out a pocket watch from his coat.

"Don't worry," he said with a reassuring smile. "You'll be there in time although you could still change your mind."

When they reached the port, a large crowd of people was milling around the docks in preparation for the sailing. Layal and the dragoman were already there, waiting for them outside the agency. The last of the cargo had been loaded and the passengers were beginning to board the harbour skiffs for transport to the steamer that lay anchored in deeper waters. On the quayside, women embraced their husbands with tears in their eyes, uncertain when or if they would ever see them again. Their children clung to their skirts or scampered about caught up in the general excitement.

"Wael, where have you been?" Layal scolded her son. "We were worried Rose would miss the sailing." But Rose intervened before she could go any further.

"I've enjoyed myself so much today," she said as she clutched her carpetbag. "Your son has shown me such consideration."

Although she was reluctant to admit it even to herself, Rose had been impressed by more than just his kindness. His shy good looks and the attention he had lavished on her had increased the attraction she had felt when she had first set eyes on him. She wondered again whether she was making the right decision, not for fear of what was to come, but for the first time, out of regret for what she was leaving behind.

Layal seemed to sense her indecision too. Her expression softened as she smiled warmly at the younger woman.

"Come here, *habibtee*. I'll send word to Maryam that you've embarked on your journey as soon as you're safely on board."

Rose stepped forward and hugged Layal as if she had known her all her life. In the short time since they had met, their shared hardships had created a bond between them. Then seeing Wael standing behind her, she threw caution to the winds and reaching up to him, kissed him, too. Overcoming his shyness, he returned her embrace.

"And don't forget to send us word from New York when you reach there," Layal said as she stepped back, a little breathless.

They walked across to where a boatman was embarking the last of the passengers in his flimsy craft. The man held out his hand as Rose prepared to step down into the boat.

"Pay the barge fee first, Miss," he said. "It's five piasters."

"Take this," Rose handed him a few coins. "That's more than enough."

"But it's the official charge," the boatman said. "You're obliged to pay it."

"Next year while you're still rowing your boat, I'll be making my fortune in Am-er-ee-ka," Rose retorted, dropping the coins into his palm.

Helped by the grumbling boatman, she boarded the skiff as Layal bid her farewell from the docks with her husband. Beside them, Wael held his hat high in the air above his head, waving it to and fro. When the packet weighed anchor an hour later, Rose was standing on the crowded deck, gazing out wistfully at the city and the mountains beyond. A village rhyme came to her lips as the shoreline receded and she began to feel the steady swell of the sea beneath her feet.

"*Touteh, touteh, kholset el-haddouteh.*"

"What does that mean, young lady?" asked a tall man in European clothes who happened to be standing beside her at the rail.

"Mulberry tree, mulberry tree, herein ends my story," she murmured.

But in truth it was just the beginning. Clutching Maryam's amulet tightly in her hand, her thoughts had already turned to how she could keep the promise she had once made to a friend.

GLOSSARY

CHAPTER ONE

1 A maternal uncle.

2 A common Arabic expression that means "hurry up," "let's go," or "come on." It is originally derived from *Ya Allah*, which literally means "O God," but its colloquial use has no religious connotation.

3 The Druze or the Mouwahhidoun are an offshoot of Shiite Muslims, who follow the creed of Prophet Mohammad's cousin and son-in-law, Ali Ibn Abi Talib. What originally set the Druze apart from orthodox Islam is that they came to regard one of the Fatimid Caliphs, Al-Hakem Bi-Amr Allah, as divine. After his death, they migrated eastwards from Egypt before establishing themselves throughout the Levant and particularly in the southern part of the Lebanese mountain chain where they became the dominant community. Secretive in their rituals, it was said they had ceased proselytizing by the 11th century in order to avoid unnecessary conflict with their neighbours.

4 Anglicized plural form of a fabric-based wrap that covers the head, worn by both men and women of a certain faith.

5 Literally, "mamma."

6 A shelter made out of wood and other natural materials.

7 Literally, "hurry up, girl!"

8 A common expression that figuratively means "dammit!"

9 Molasses.

10 Literally, "my son."

11 Literally means "belonging to the government" in Turkish. Used here to denote the tax paid in produce to the tax farmers ("the sheikhs") under the feudal (*iqta'i*) system.

12 A colloquial identifier for "grandmother." When capitalized, Teta signifies a direct and respectful address to one's grandmother, equivalent to a proper noun. When used in lowercase, teta signifies any arbitrary grandmother, equivalent to a common noun.

13 From Turkish or Arabic, denotes a bath or bathhouse.

CHAPTER TWO

14 In the 1700s, what was known as Mount Lebanon covered only the mountainous territory north of the road that connected the coast to Damascus, the greatest city of the Syrian hinterland and a once glittering capital of past Arab empires. But as more Christians moved south, the area grew to encompass the entire range from the black peaks in the north to as far south as Jabal el-Druze.

15 An honorific title used to refer to a priest or bishop. It can be used on its own or with the priest's given name.

16 The anglicized plural of the Arabic word *ratl* (pl. *Artal*), which is an Ottoman-period

measurement of weight (3.2 kg in Syria), used at the time for commodities such as silk.

17 A stew that consists mainly of broth and vegetables, but can contain meat or chicken.

18 Literally, "my (grand)daughter," but can be used in a non-filial sense as "my girl," or a religious sense as "my child."

19 Literally, "donkeys;" figuratively, "idiots" (sing. *hmar*).

20 A Turkish word for the measurement of agricultural land during Ottoman times. In the Levant and Turkey, the *dunam* (sing.) is 1,000 square metres (10,764 sq ft), which is 1 decare. It is still used in some ex-Ottoman territories like Cyprus.

21 A title of respect for an older woman.

22 A fog.

CHAPTER THREE

23 Cracked wheat; granulated groats.

24 Literally, "father" or "dad."

25 Anglicized plural form of *mandeel*; a very thin shawl Druze women wrap around their heads in a conservative manner.

26 The colloquial form of referring to a Druze man.

27 Vernacular Arabic for "no."

CHAPTER FOUR

28 India.

29 Also known as "loquat;" an oval-shaped fruit grown on a flowering tree indigenous to China and Japan, but naturalized in the Mediterranean basin and other warm regions.

CHAPTER FIVE

30 An Arabic expression of welcome into one's home, used here in the plural form.

31 An oriental smoking pipe designed with a long tube passing through an urn of water that cools the smoke as it is drawn through; also called "hubble-bubble," "narghile," and "shisha."

32 Mulberries; either the fruit or the cordial.

33 An expression of welcome.

34 Literally, "Auntie" on the maternal side.

35 A colloquial expression that means, "Shame on you!"

36 Literally, "(It/He is) amazing!"

CHAPTER SIX

37 Closest equivalence to "Woe is me!"

38 An expression that means, "On my children's lives."

39 An expression that means, "Thank God" or "Praise be to Allah."

CHAPTER SEVEN

40 A title of respect for a doctor or physician; can also be used to refer to a wise old man.

CHAPTER EIGHT

41 Strongmen.

42 Thyme herb.

43 A traditional inverted cone-shaped kiln placed outdoors and used to bake loaves of bread over a lit fire.

CHAPTER NINE

44 A term of respect for an older woman; not necessarily carrying the religious connotation of one who has been on a pilgrimage to Mecca, otherwise known as the hajj.

45 The people.

46 From caravanserai, meaning inn, or from Turkish and Persian, meaning a palace.

47 A celebratory ululation.

48 A leader (of a gang usually).

49 A traditional long and loose garment, worn like a robe by men and women, with variations in style, colour, and embroidery among different cultures.

50 Literally, "Peace be upon you."

51 Literally, "young man" or "young boy."

52 A thick paste or spread made from ground chickpeas and sesame seeds, olive oil, lemon, and garlic, made originally in the Middle East.

CHAPTER TEN

53 A bathhouse attendant, from the French word "sabon."

54 The Anglicized plural form of a long outer garment with long sleeves (sing. *jubbah*).

CHAPTER ELEVEN

55 Literally, "Love of my heart."

56 *Sitt* Nayfeh Jumblatt (1810-1880) was married to the prominent leader Amin Shams of Hasbaya, but was widowed at age thirty. She is often referred to as the uncrowned queen of Hasbaya and contributed to the expansion of the prestigious Druze spiritual center of learning and meditation, Khalwat el-Bayada. She is blamed by the Shehabs and the Christians for the massacres in Hasbaya. See Samy Swayd's *Historical Dictionary of the Druzes* (2015).

CHAPTER TWELVE

57 Although originally a Muslim family who could trace their origins back to Mecca,

the Shehabs had been acknowledged as the rulers of Wadi Taym ever since they had settled in the district several hundred years earlier. The ruler who had built the great palace of Beiteddine, Emir Bashir, was one of their kinsmen.

58 The portion of a Turkish palace or house reserved for men.

59 Turkish word used as a title of respect to address men of learning or social standing; equivalent to "sir."

60 Anglicized plural form of non-Muslim subjects of the Ottoman Empire, especially Christians.

61 Arabic passive participle of *harrama*, meaning "to forbid;" forbidden.

62 Andalusian Jews fleeing the Spanish Inquisition had arrived on the Levantine coast many years before and several families were now settled in Wadi Taym. Their relations with the Druze, who had granted them asylum there, were often better than with the local Christian families, some of whom resented them.

CHAPTER THIRTEEN

63 Arabic for "muleteer."

CHAPTER FOURTEEN

64 Arabic expression meaning, "God bless you" (masculine inflection).

65 Literally means "follower," a word used to describe the Shiites who had once lived in many different parts of Mount Lebanon. By the 19th century, they were mainly confined to Jabal Amel in the south and parts of the Bekaa Valley.

CHAPTER FIFTEEN

66 Arabic yogurt that has been strained to remove its whey, resulting in a thicker consistency than unstrained yogurt, while preserving its distinctive sour taste.

67 Korban is the Feast of the Sacrifice commemorating Ibrahim's willingness to sacrifice his son Ishmael to show his faithfulness to Allah, something that is common to all Abrahamic faiths. Here, it is used to refer to the Christian Feast of Corpus Christi celebrated by some Eastern, as well as most Latin-rite, churches.

68 Arabic for Romans or Byzantines; used here to describe adherents of the Greek Orthodox Church.

CHAPTER SIXTEEN

69 From Islamic and Arabian mythology. A class of spirits lower than the angels, capable of appearing in human and animal form and influencing humankind for either good or evil.

70 From Turkish "yatağan," a type of Ottoman knife or short sabre used from the mid-16th to late 19th centuries.

71 An inn, usually with a large courtyard, for the overnight accommodation of caravans; also caravansary.

72 A strong, distilled, transparent alcoholic liquor made from fermented grapes.

73 Means, "Cheers," used in the masculine form here. Feminine form is *kesik*.

74 Literally, "Drives me wild."

75 A type of bird.

CHAPTER SEVENTEEN

76 Means, "Brace yourself."

CHAPTER EIGHTEEN

77 My sister; not necessarily of a religious connotation.

78 Turkish draughts or checkers.

79 Means, "Think nothing of it."

CHAPTER NINETEEN

80 Means, "Lower your voice" in the feminine form.

81 Means, "Alright" or "fine."

CHAPTER TWENTY

82 "My love" (*habibi*, masculine); (*habibtee*, feminine).

83 Literally, "Bless your (giving) hands."

84 Literally, "Thank God for your safe arrival."

CHAPTER TWENTY-ONE

85 Traditional marketplace with open stalls and stands (sing. *souq*).

CHAPTER TWENTY-TWO

86 A fleshy-leaved Mediterranean plant that grows in damp habitats.

87 An open space, or esplanade, in or near a town; an open grassy plain; among the Arabs, a race course, or a place for exercizing horses.

88 A word of Persian origin meaning a man's cap, similar to a fez, typically made of red felt with a tassel on top.

89 Turkish word meaning an official order or decree.

90 Means, "Very well."

CHAPTER TWENTY-THREE

91 A panicked cry for help.

92 Literally, "Leave her alone" or "Unhand her."

93 A scandal.

CHAPTER TWENTY-FIVE

94 The title used for the governor of a provincial district during the Ottoman period.

95 Also known as "baklava," a rich, sweet pastry made of layers of filo filled with chopped nuts, sweetened and held together with syrup or honey. It is characteristic of the cuisines of the former Ottoman Empire.

CHAPTER TWENTY-SIX

96 Another Arabic term for "priest."

CHAPTER TWENTY-SEVEN

97 Literally, "Our home is your home." Also means, "Please, make yourself comfortable."

98 A small drum.

99 An Egyptian and former Turkish unit of weight, variable but now usually equal to approximately 1.3 kg (2.75 lb).

CHAPTER TWENTY-EIGHT

100 Literally, "Unbelievable!"

101 An abbreviated expression from *wehyat* or *behyat Allah*, sometimes considered apostasy as it literally means to swear on God's life.

102 Piasters (sing. *qirsh*).

CHAPTER THIRTY

103 A common expression meaning, "how cute" or "how adorable."

104 Literally, "Liar!" An accusation of lying, used here in the feminine form.

105 A reddish-orange dyestuff prepared from the dried and ground leaves of a plant, used especially in south and southwest Asia and North Africa to colour leather and fabrics, to dye hair, and to decorate the skin.

106 A traditional wedding procession.

CHAPTER THIRTY-ONE

107 An affectionate term for "grandfather."

108 A common expression meaning, "how adorable."

109 A formal seasonal greeting which means, "May each year find you well."

CHAPTER THIRTY-THREE

110 Provisions.

111 Means, "God-willing."

CHAPTER THIRTY-FOUR
112 Fava or broad beans.

CHAPTER THIRTY-FIVE
113 Arabic for "Make a wish."

CHAPTER THIRTY-SIX
114 A flatbread daubed with thyme seeds and olive oil.
115 A term of respect for an older man; not necessarily carrying the religious connotation of one who has been on a pilgrimage to Mecca, otherwise known as the hajj.
116 An expression which means, "Enough."